A Dream of Demons

Guy Fawkes: Demon Hunter, Volume 2

Benjamin Langley

Published by Shadow Spark Publishing, 2022.

A DREAM OF DEMONS

First edition. November 5, 2022.

Written by Benjamin Langley.

For the lovers and dreamers.

Prologue

J amie wakes to the chime of bells. The sound in his subconscious clashes with his awakening mind as he stirs. No, the bells of York Minster are not clanging; it's his alarm clock. He jabs the button to stop the cacophonous noise and squirms into a sitting position. A memory of a dream of demons floods his head, his imagination augmenting Sidney's tall tale of Guy Fawkes' young days as a demon hunter.

When Jamie left the hospital, he had every intention of returning to hear more of Sidney's tale. The old man spoke with such vitality, belying his injuries as he sat, propped by pillows in a hospital bed, his burns bandaged.

Still, the burning question ransacking Jamie's thoughts remains: why dive into a bonfire to save an effigy of Guy Fawkes?

Jamie understands why he followed the old man into the flames, why he'd dragged him from the fire. Who could watch another human throw their life away and not act? But to save a straw-filled dummy? If only the nurses hadn't dragged Jamie away, insisting visiting hours were over.

But as the hours passed, the power of the tale had waned. Rationality punched him square in the face before he reached his front door. Jamie's journalistic instinct set alight and another question moved to the forefront of his mind. What evidence does Sidney have? None.

Sleep, however, restored the story's power. Images from his dream flash through Jamie's mind: Master Leonard lashes out and the whip licks at his face. He can almost feel the agony. He touches the spot, and pain flares.

How had he forgotten his own burn injuries? He plays the memory over in his head, watching Sidney stalk across the field, unseen towards the pyre, reaching it the exact second it was set alight. He remembers sprinting to the fire, reaching into the flames to drag the old man out. Pain flares in his burnt hands again.

In an attempt to shift the horror from his mind, Jamie checks his calendar. Perhaps an appointment has slipped his mind. It's blank. He checks his email in case any of the editors he pitched features to have responded. They haven't. But he does have a text from Michael asking how he's feeling.

Jamie responds: *Thanks to you, I'm healing well.* He recalls his meeting with Michael only days earlier, how he'd treated the burns and accompanied him to the hospital. Jamie sends a follow-up text: *That guy, Sidney. Off the record, what's the gossip?*

With the story alive in his mind, Jamie can't help but delve deeper. It's the journalist in him. He googles key names. Yes, Guy Fawkes' father died when he was young. Yes, he had two sisters, Anne and Elizabeth. Other details check out, too. The Wrights attended Saint Peter's School, like Guy. The Council of the North put Margaret Clitherow to death by crushing. The Catholic Church subsequently canonised Margaret Clitherow, albeit not for services to demon hunting. Sandys died shortly after Margaret's death.

Jamie flexes his fingers and winces at the pain in his burnt hands. While anyone could research these details and string a story together, would anyone throw themselves into a bonfire if they didn't believe it? Jamie's heart races as he recalls the heat of the fire, the snapping wood echoing in his ears again. A trickle of sweat runs down his brow. He can't revisit that moment; he needs to focus his mind on something else. What was the name Sidney told him to research? It takes a second to come back to him. He types *Maria Fawkes* into his phone. There are social media profiles and links to pages on ancestry and genealogy sites, but the dates don't correspond. 1798 is around two hundred years too late to be relevant.

He types Maria alongside Guy Fawkes and finds what he's after. A website mentions that Guy Fawkes may have married Maria Pulleyn in around 1590. Jamie skims the page to discover that the church would not have formally recognised or recorded their marriage if Guy and his wife were practising Catholics. With this information, he's ready to return to Sidney.

Jamie's phone buzzes. It's a text from Michael: *You didn't hear it from me, but a colleague told me last year Sidney suffered minor burns trying to snatch a Guy at Rawcliffe Park.*

Jamie sends a response, a shocked emoji, and puts his phone in his pocket.

What does this tell him? Sidney is a serious risk to himself and others. The authorities should publish his photograph around the region every November to ban him from all future fireworks displays, too. But does it not also show he's in earnest and believes this story more than anything?

Jamie wants to know more about Maria Pulleyn, too. After saving York, after finishing what his father started, Guy eventually married if the information he found is accurate. Did he leave demon-hunting behind after his battle with Master Leonard? How'd he go from there to attempting to blow up the Houses of Parliament? And wasn't Pulleyn the surname of Guy's old headmaster?

Jamie realises he's the fish that's taken the bait. The hook is poking through his cheek and Sidney's reeling him in. He sighs and checks the hospital's visiting hours.

• • • •

JAMIE ARRIVES AT THE hospital to find it awash with reporters and staff gathered outside. They've got hold of his story; they're here to steal his scoop. As Jamie closes on the building and sees the volumes of news cameras, he realises it must be something else. Sidney's bonfire exploits wouldn't draw the attention of the nationals.

By the hospital door, a group of nurses boo, but a body of suited gentlemen clap and whoop louder, disguising the sound of disdain. Through the doors, waving both hands and grinning comes the Prime Minister. Alistair Barclay-Fitzwilliam shakes hands with anyone who doesn't withdraw their hand quick enough to avoid his grasp and he clambers into a black limousine. Kristian Byrne walks to the other side of the car. He glances toward Jamie and for a second, their eyes meet.

Jamie can see the cold calculation on the man's face. With the recent news of alleged bribes taken by the Prime Minister, he's on a charm offensive, visiting hospitals to show what a lovely, caring chap he is. Kristian Byrne stands there, his tallow complexion in contrast to the darkness of his deepset eyes. His head twitches, as if he's listening to voices from another plane, and then he slides into the car and slams the door.

As Jamie watches the vehicle speed away toward the next photo opportunity, he recalls more elements of Sidney's story: the corruption of the men in power, Sandys, Hastings and Walsingham. How little has changed in the last four hundred and fifty years.

Perhaps it's the effect of his pain medicine or his body fighting off infections in his burns, but a wave of nausea hits Jamie. He shudders and follows the demoralised staff into the hospital.

When Jamie reaches Sidney's ward, the old man looks up. "Thought you be back."

He's still covered in bandages, the dressing refreshed. His nurse has sat him a little more upright, propped with a couple of extra pillows. There are no cards, no flowers, and no bunch of grapes to suggest he has any family or friends concerned enough to pop in.

Sidney takes a sip of water. "Have you done your homework? Maria Fawkes? Who was she?"

Jamie checks over his shoulder for any hospital staff, as if this is some kind of clandestine conversation. "She was married to Guy Fawkes."

"And?"

"And that's it."

Sidney sighs. "Didn't discover owt else?"

"Should I have done?" Jamie glances at the clock, calculating how long he has in Sidney's company.

Sidney clears his throat and gives a frustrated grumble. "The name John Fawkes didn't come up?"

"No."

"I thought you were a journalist."

Jamie winces. "The distant past isn't my area of expertise."

"You may well need to make it so, lad, after we're done here."

"You'll tell me the rest?" Jamie curses himself for failing to keep the eagerness out of his voice.

"Aye, take a seat, and I will."

Jamie turns the seat to best face Sidney and settles into the uncomfortable rigid plastic.

Chapter 1–In Which Guy Fawkes Suffers the Ill-Effects of a Demon Battle

G uy Fawkes may have saved York from the tyrannical grip of two demon-loving fiends, but who would sing his name in praise? No one,
save his sister, Anne, knew of their heroism. Guy's only song was the laughter
of the skull of Thomas Percy which floated in the corner of his room. What
reward had Guy received for his effort? Physical torture and mental pertur-
bation.

Every bone in Guy's body shook as if each tried to fight its way free from
the pressure of its neighbour. Every morsel of flesh on those bones radiated heat, every muscle spasmed, and every nerve sent pain signals rushing
through his spine and to his brain which refused to do anything but replay
the memory of the foul beast from Hell that had left him in such a state. His
struggle against Master Leonard, the grandmaster of nocturnal revelries, had
taken a toll on his body. Spilt demon blood had burned his flesh, and the
memory of its demonic eyes bored into his soul, ravaging his fragile mind.

When sleep came, it was the sleep of the exhausted; there was no rest, only further punishment. Once shivering had consumed every iota of strength,
and when his muscles achieved perpetual tension, when there was not a drop
of moisture left within him to sweat out or puke up, sleep would take Guy
to a new world of torment. Back he'd be in York Minster, Master Leonard
before him, additional arms bursting out of its side, and they'd rain blow
after blow after blow upon him. Sometimes, he'd wake at this point with a
headache matching the drummed rhythm the demon lord pounded inside
his mind. Sometimes it would be as whips wrapped around his limbs, ever-
tightening, and he'd wake with cramps so powerful it looked like he had
small mammals moving inside his flesh, mammals needing execution with a
solid whack before he could find his tolerable level of suffering once more.
But mostly, when he failed to rouse after all this suffering, he'd wake when
the demon's blood cascaded upon him, with the awful and agonising sensation of being consumed by fire. This dream came so often that the burning
was almost a comfort. So acquainted was Guy with the pain, it was almost

like visiting an old friend—one that wanted him to die in screaming agony, but a friend nonetheless.

Anne, his sister, two years his junior at fourteen, acted as a nurse at his bedside. How he cursed her when she mopped his brow with a flannel or dripped water into his mouth, knowing he'd have to go through such pain to expunge it once more. She brought him the warmth of blankets when he was on the verge of freezing, and cooled him when he became a furnace. Despite going from one condition to the next several times in an hour, she was always there.

On the fifth day, as she anointed his skin with the salve, there was almost relief. It wasn't that Guy's flesh no longer felt aflame, merely that it was roasting at a temperature not as close to the peak of the hottest fires of Hell. He found himself able to speak.

"Anne, what is this?" His voice sounded alien, and his throat was raw, like he'd swallowed a tankard full of sand.

Anne jumped and took a step back, shocked to hear her brother speak after spending the best part of a week mute. "We ran out of the other. I made this myself. Is it all right?"

He wanted to say it was better than all right, that he'd imagined the hands of an angel upon him. Alas, all he managed was, "Aye," but it was enough to bring a smile to Anne's face.

When next Guy slept, Master Leonard materialised, as usual, ready to attack, but utter oblivion was no longer the outcome. Guy dodged the demon's flailing whip. He held his sword, and with it, he fought back, waking only after a lengthy battle in which neither combatant gained the upper hand. Guy woke not with flames of agony, but with utter exhaustion—a clear improvement. Darkness lingered, and the house was quiet, except for the laughter that continued from the skull of Thomas Percy still floating in the corner of his room.

Guy reached for the cup of water Anne had left by his bedside and moistened his lips. He turned to the spectral skull. "Why are you here?"

Thomas Percy stopped laughing and drifted from the corner to hover in front of Guy's face. "For the same reason I've always been here. To talk about your fate."

Guy winced. "I'm done with that."

The floating skull resumed its bout of laughter.

Guy struggled into a sitting position and gasped at the pain. "Hastings is dead. Sandys is dead. I did what I intended."

Thomas Percy swung back in front of Guy. "But there's so much more to do." He laughed once more.

Guy lashed out, but the skull spun out of the way.

Percy's eyes glowed. "Good. That's the fighting spirit we need."

As much as every muscle throbbed, as much as he wanted to still his aching bones, anger stirred Guy to swing his fist, and, again Percy swerved away.

Percy's skull grew brighter. "Yes, you'll need that fury."

Guy slumped back into his bed. "For what?"

"For what comes next."

Guy sighed. "What comes next?"

"First, Durham, followed by a time of change. Now sleep. It's time to rid your mind of demons."

After his exertion, sleep came easy. Guy found himself in the crypt of York Minster with the undead rising all around him. He burst through the flaming door at the top of the steps, the fire spreading to his clothes as he rolled around the nave. As soon as he stood, the last of the flames extinguished, and Master Leonard appeared through a cloud of swirling smoke. This dream differed from his earlier torments. This time, he had the floating skull of Thomas Percy for company.

Master Leonard focused his energy on Percy. The flying skull swerved away from the demon's sword swipes, moving back through the nave toward the entrance to the central tower. Every time Master Leonard flailed its whip, Percy spun away. The demon stomped through the building, its cloven hooves cracking the stone floor with each step.

Guy followed, watching as Master Leonard chased the floating skull, unable to intervene.

"Bone cur! Rancid clod-block!" Saliva dripped from the demon's teeth as it roared its curses. It lashed out with the whip again, but Percy twisted out of its reach.

Master Leonard threw his sword to the floor and clicked his fingers. A long-handled golden war hammer appeared in his grasp. "I'll pulverise your skull!" He swung the weapon, but again, Percy evaded it with ease and it crashed into the ancient walls of York Minster. Percy drifted through the open doorway to the crypt, laughing all the way.

The veins at Master Leonard's temples grew thick and pulsed, signalling his frustration. It roared and set off after the skull. Ashes remained on the stone floor from where Guy had smashed through the crypt door. The hulking frame of Master Leonard was too large to squeeze through. He flung the hammer down the crypt stairs and arched his back. His additional limbs contracted and folded back inside his body, his shoulders closed, and his legs shortened. In his new form, he twisted through the doorway and stomped down the steps.

The ashes on the floor stirred, swirling into a cluster. With a flash, a wooden door appeared, hanging from the ancient hinges in the doorway to the crypt, a lighter wood than what was there before. Guy suspected a skilled carpenter had carved it from an ash tree.

"Close the door!" called Percy.

Guy twisted around, surprised to find the skull behind him. He slammed the door.

Percy rushed to his side. "Now seal it with fire."

Guy jerked back in surprise when he found a flaming torch in his hand, a necessary accessory provided by the dream. While he had destroyed the original door with fire, he suspected this time it would have a different effect. Dream logic told him it was the right thing to do.

The second he touched the torch to the bare wood, it set alight, the heat forcing him to step back. Flame washed over the door like a tidal wave rising to the heavens. The fire extinguished, leaving the door marked with the pattern of an ash tree. The scorched lines of the branches spread beyond the wood of the door into the stone of the wall, creating an unbreakable bond.

From inside he could hear the demon's protest, stone smashing as he took his anger out on the sarcophagi.

Over the hubbub came Percy's voice. "Now rest."

It was the best night's sleep he'd had in a long time.

Chapter 2–In Which Guy Fawkes Set out for Durham

When Guy woke, he was not without aches and pains, but with Master Leonard locked away in a crypt in his mind, sleep's recuperative powers returned. His muscles complained only when stretched, and his flesh no longer threatened to quake from his bones with every movement.

A few days in the open air would do him the power of good. Guy had a promise to keep. He was to ride for Durham to join his friends, Kit and Jack. He was to meet with their uncle and his former mentor, Francis Ingleby, and while they were there, they would bring the life of that demon-loving villain, and Queen Elizabeth's spymaster, Sir Francis Walsingham, to an end. There would be peace. Perhaps, then, the skull of Thomas Percy would leave him alone.

Guy dressed and packed some basic provisions in his knapsack before leaving his room for the first time in days. The stairs proved a challenge; bending his knees flared pain he'd not experienced while lying prostrate or sitting in bed.

"You're up!" Guy's mother, Edith, rose from her seat, not knowing whether she should approach.

Guy held out a hand to still her, settling her mind. "Sit, Mother. I am fine."

Edith sighed. "You don't look fine. Worried sick, we've all been. I've prayed for you."

Guy placed his hand on the wall for support. "And my standing here shows the benefit of your prayers."

"The city is in mourning. Our Archbishop Sandys has passed on. I'm sure you'll know nothing about that." Edith's eyes lingered on her son.

"York will heal." Guy looked about the room. "Where are my sisters?"

Edith glanced at the window. "Elizabeth tends to her plants. I tell her to give nature time to do its part, but she lacks patience."

"And Anne?"

"She has returned to work at the bakery." Edith frowned. "Don't expect her to wait on you hand and foot now you're on your feet again."

"I wouldn't..." Guy eyed the door.

"She's sat by you in vigil, tended to your wounds."

Anne had done more than that. When he struggled against Master Leonard, Anne had attacked the familiar, severing the link between demon and master. "I am forever grateful for the way she looks after me. She is a caring soul."

Edith scowled. "Aye. And a little too much like her brother, I fear."

Guy approached his mother and took hold of one of her hands, ignoring the burning sensation it brought to his skin. "I believe our hardships are behind us now. With our worries set aside, we can prosper. All of York can prosper."

Edith withdrew her hand. "I wish she didn't imitate you in such ways. You put yourself so often in danger."

"That's the risk of doing the right thing, Mother."

"But I don't need to lose both of you down that path. You set off on that road a long time ago. You're too far gone. Anne still has time to make a decent life for herself without all this sneaking about, the secrets and the lies." Edith's face bore a sneer.

"Anne won't be able to follow me this time. Not if I don't let on where I'm going." Guy headed for the door.

Edith swallowed hard and glanced at the door. "You're not leaving?"

"I have to, Mother." Guy shifted his knapsack to relieve the weight from his shoulders.

"But, why? Any fool can see you're barely fit to stand."

"I have a duty to my friends."

"You have a duty to your family. You're supposed to be the man of the house, but Anne and I have brought in more money than you these last few months. It's not right, Guy. The time has come when you must learn where your priorities lie."

Guy opened the door. "I'm sorry, Mother, but I have to go. I will be back, and when this is done, I will be better. You deserve better. For now, don't worry about me."

Guy hurried out the door and closed it behind him, deaf to his mother's inevitable sighs.

"Guy!" Elizabeth leant over the low stone wall from the back garden. "You're up! Are you feeling better?"

"I am."

Elizabeth smiled. "Come into the garden. Let me show you what I've been growing."

Guy glanced at the piles of soil. "I will, Elizabeth. When I return."

"You're going away?" Elizabeth stepped away from the wall.

"I have to."

Elizabeth turned back to her plants. "Mother said you didn't care about us, not deep down."

"Elizabeth, I do, but I have to go." Despite speaking to the back of his sister's head, Guy continued. "When I return, I promise to spend more time with you."

Elizabeth bent to check for fresh shoots, and Guy made for the stables, hoping that at least his horse, Pewter, would be happy to see him and not displeased by the arduous journey he was to force her to undertake.

• • • •

THE STABLES WERE BUSY for mid-morning. The news of the death of the Archbishop of York had brought visitors, some on ecclesiastical business, some mourners, to the city in droves. Guy was glad to escape. He expected that the business of appointing a new archbishop would be underway, but it would be a long time before anyone could take York in their grip in the way the previous incumbent had.

Guy gave Pewter a rub, made sure she took on plenty of water, saddled her up, and began his journey. Climbing into the saddle brought all kinds of pain, and each movement needed controlled breathing to get through. He knew he couldn't ride at full speed. His friends, Kit and Jack, and whoever else they could rouse would have taken only two days to reach Durham. In his condition, Guy expected to take no less than four. This put him further still behind them, but at least he would arrive in better condition, as long as the ride didn't take too much out of him. They would likely have made camp somewhere near Northallerton to arrive in Durham late the next day.

Guy considered several routes, planning many stops along the way, hoping to reach Durham in enough time to locate his friends on the fifth day.

The last week had been dry, and the roads were in good condition, having recovered from the ravages of winter and the heavy footfall of countless troops heading north to protect Queen Elizabeth's interests. Guy was thankful for Pewter taking him away from the scenes of all his greatest hardships. Each yard of distance brought relief, and each breath of fresh air brought a smile to his face. The days were lengthening too, and blossoms decorated many of the trees that lined the more pleasant parts of the road. After a gentle but lengthy ride, excruciating in every way possible, there was still enough light in the sky to reveal Ripon's two-towered cathedral.

Guy considered his previous journeys outside the city, and figured that Ripon must have been as far away from home as he'd ever been, and certainly the farthest north. He bypassed the first inn, given that the stable looked busy, and continued along the road, stopping at a larger place, a newer building whose timber had yet to darken with age. He knew his friends would have made camps along the route, but he needed a proper bed with his body still carrying the agony of his battle with a demon less than a week ago.

As Guy dismounted Pewter, Master Leonard's whips lashed at his limbs once more, tightening around his biceps, his thighs, his calves. He knew riding while still recovering from his battle would be difficult, but this pain was almost as bad as when he had come face-to-face with the demon. The constant shifting of position as he rode had strained those weakened muscles to the point of bursting. He struggled from the stable into the tavern, breathless, sweating and paid for a room for the night. He ordered a meal and enough ale to accompany it and slumped into a chair at the table closest to the bar. Guy was exhausted, but he knew better than to switch off and leave himself vulnerable and kept his eyes and his ears open.

The tavern's patrons spoke of the garrisons that had passed by in recent weeks and whispered rumours of plots against Queen Elizabeth. Some claimed Mary Queen of Scots was likely to be on the move again, and perhaps troops gathered in the north for that reason. While Guy overheard talk of dark deeds, there was not a mention of demonology or witchcraft, and when he retired to his room, Guy drifted off into a dreamless sleep.

Chapter 3–In Which Guy Fawkes Encounters Trouble on the Road

In the morning, a plate full of bacon and eggs mopped dry with a hunk of bread and washed down with a mug of ale invigorated Guy, but in truth, he knew another day's rest would better serve him and allow him to recover. Continuing his journey would only set back his recovery and possibly require a week in bed upon his arrival in Durham. What good would he be to his friends? In the stable, he found Pewter had been well looked after during the night. He tossed the stable boy a coin, asking him to continue to care for Pewter for an additional twenty-four hours. He paid for another night, returned to his room, and let sleep further restore him.

Guy headed off on Pewter the following morning. While still unable to move at a swift pace, an increased speed was possible. Guy considered abandoning his plan to stop in Richmond, instead stopping much closer to Durham, which would enable him to meet with his companions all the sooner and perhaps even join the fray should his friends have planned such antics.

A few miles north of Bedale, where he'd stopped for a rest and a bite to eat and to allow Pewter the same, a felled horse lay on the road immediately before a small wood. It was a little after midday. The sun was high on one of those spring days in which the clouds passed as lone travellers meandering on a breeze.

The awkward position of the collapsed horse, a black stallion, made Guy slow Pewter long before he reached the creature. Questions flooded his head. What had happened to the horse? Where was the rider? He dismounted, tied Pewter to a tree, and approached on foot. The black horse was facing away from him and motionless. Flies buzzed around the head, and as Guy closed, he realised they were drawn to a pool of blood. Guy studied the stallion closer: a severe gash in the neck had felled the beast.

"Mister, thank God, please help..." a young woman ran from the shadow of the trees toward him. He placed his hand on the hilt of his sword, and she slowed. Her ragged brown dress had a tear across the middle, and mud streaked her face. She pointed to the horse. "A madman, mister. He ran from the trees and put his sword to our poor horse's neck. He dragged my brother into the woods."

Guy looked into the trees, but the contrast between the bright sky and the darkness of shadow within the trees made it impossible to see anything.

"Come on! Help him!" Her eyes darted from Guy back to the woods.

One way or another, Guy had to pass through the trees. He took a few cautious steps, the girl close beside him.

She paused before crossing the line of shadow. "They must be in here."

Guy drew his sword and moved into the cover of the trees. Guy had missed the scent of woodland and drew in a deep breath, but in doing so, he set off the pain receptors in his nervous system. The smell coming out of the woods recalled a sensation from his dreams, an unpleasant recollection hidden in the depths of his awareness. Yes, there was a demonic odour within the woods. Whatever had dragged off the poor girl's brother meant ill. From nearby came a scrabbling sound, as if a creature, a wild pig or a badger was digging for something or attempting to burrow deep underground.

Guy brought his sword close to his face and whispered the words to give it power. As the blade grew, the girl gasped from behind him. Few must have seen metal expand in such a way. He took a few more steps, closer to the sound: snuffling now accompanied the digging. From behind an ancient oak, dirt and twigs flew into the air.

"Was it a man that attacked your horse, miss, or was it a beast?"

The girl didn't respond.

"Miss," Guy whispered.

Then came the thudding of her feet on the ground. Guy turned, but too late. She was upon him. Guy had no time to lift his sword, no time to adjust his feet, and when she shoved him, there was nothing he could do to stop himself falling to the ground.

The girl stood on his wrist and kicked his sword away. "Now!" she called as she took cover behind a tree.

Hooves thundered on the ground and the undergrowth rustled. The girl made a high-pitched and manic laugh.

Acting on instinct, Guy rolled to the left as a boar burst through a low shrub close to the oak tree. It threw its head forward, lunging with its tusks at the space Guy recently occupied. It disappeared back through the bush. Guy scanned the ground for his sword, hurried to grab it and muttered the words to enchant it again. He glanced at the girl. How could he have been so foolish? Lured in to help a damsel in distress only to find himself ambushed! It was so obvious now: the tear in her dress ran not with the cut of the cloth, as it would if someone had grabbed her. She, or her companion, had cut the dress to make her a more convincing victim. He could almost see the fingerprints where she'd deliberately smeared dirt on her face. But worse, her eyes were ringed with orange, indicative of demonic possession. The stench of evil cloyed in the back of Guy's throat. She'd have to wait. A greater menace lurked on the other side of the tree.

Guy hurried forward in an arc to come around the side of the oak, keeping the demon girl in his peripheral vision. What he thought was a boar was only half that—a half-man, half-animal hybrid, his teeth twisted into the shape of tusks. In front of the creature, a mutilated body lay, part-consumed by the boar-boy.

Guy held his sword out, stepping back and eying the girl. "I'm guessing this creature before me is your brother, the man on the ground, the owner of the horse, and his poor victim."

When the girl spoke, her voice had become deeper and gruff. "You're a smart one, maggot, but you forgot one part." The girl stepped closer, as the boar-boy raised his head to look at him with diseased eyes.

"What's that?" Guy answered as he scanned the environment.

"Your part as the next victim." She bared her teeth, a row of blackened and broken shards.

It was clear what had become of this pair. Together, they'd attempted to conjure a demon, no doubt to gain wealth or power. That was often the root. They must have tried to turn a wild pig into a familiar creature or use it as a sacrifice. But whatever they'd summoned did not wish to acquiesce with their plan, perhaps considered them too insignificant to bring pandemonium into the world. So instead, the demon had fused the man with the sacrifice, and taken possession of the girl's body. A tale as old as time, but not one often shared in polite company. Maybe it should be.

Boar-boy rubbed one foot into the ground several times and lowered his head while the girl bounced to the rhythm of her lewd laugh.

Boar-boy burst toward Guy. There was no time to raise his sword. If he got a blow away, he'd still be knocked to the ground and pinned under the body, only to be stuck by his demon-possessed sister.

Guy dived, and the creature rushed past. Guy's bones cried out when he hit the ground, the memory of old pain augmenting new. Again, his flesh was aflame, and, still, the sister laughed. Guy shuffled back to a tree and used it to help himself up. The girl's face had shifted, taking on demonic features, the flesh sucked inside, the cheekbones high, the mouth gaping. "Again!" she cried. "Squash the Sapien insect."

Boar-boy followed orders. This time Guy was ready. He pushed himself back onto a low branch at the height of his backside, pushing back, hearing the branch creak, and feeling the force build behind him. He waited until Boar-boy began his charge. Every instinct begged Guy to flee. Instead, Guy waited until his adversary closed. With it only a yard away, Guy twisted aside, releasing the power of the bent branch, which flew forward, thwacking Boar-boy in the face and knocking him onto his side. Guy dashed forward and ran the blade across the creature's neck.

"No!" cried the sister. "Scrabbling beetle! Beetling scab! Die!"

Whatever demon this was, it consisted entirely of rage. There was no strategy. No doubt they had feasted on travellers for some time and faced little in the way of challenge. Guy would use her momentum against her. As she sped toward him, he positioned his sword, ready. When she was but a few feet away, with a simple swing her head and her body were twain.

Despite this separation, the head continued to scream. Guy plunged his sword into her heart, silencing her as he released the demon back to the underworld. His side ached from diving to the ground, and his muscles, which had suffered entropy after only a week out of use, throbbed.

He returned to Pewter, who had feasted upon the grass where Guy had left her. She snorted as he approached. Guy glanced at his filth-encrusted clothes. Pewter whickered unhappily. She wouldn't want him riding her in such a state. Guy knew he couldn't continue on the road in his condition, filthy, and his body aching once more. Instead, he returned to Bedale to make the community aware of the incident, and there, progress for the day ended.

Chapter 4–In Which Guy Fawkes is Reunited with his Friends on the Outskirts of Durham

There's little worse than having to turn back when on a long journey, even temporarily, and Guy resented every moment travelling in the opposite direction to Durham. Perhaps, had he known what awaited him, he wouldn't have experienced such great disappointment.

When Guy reported the events on the road to the patrons of the first inn he reached in Bedale, their lack of surprise perhaps disturbed Guy most. A couple of volunteers offered to recover the corpses and try to identify the bodies. For how long had they known of the danger without a word of warning to travellers? When he had described the girl, all eyes had gone to a sullen man in the corner, but he continued to stare only into his tankard.

While there were rooms available at that inn, a sense of distaste stopped Guy from remaining there any longer. Another inn was only five minutes further along the road–further away from his destination. It was there he spent the night, cursing the delay once more.

The diversion cost Guy not only the rest of that day's travel but further progress too. The battle had set back his recovery, and fresh agony ransacked his body. The next day he only got as far as Richmond (on a thankfully demon-free, but nevertheless uncomfortable horse ride) before he came to a stop once more. When he reached his room, he realised how much the exertion of the last few days had tired him out, how much the continued journey was exhausting him. As he dressed for bed, looking over the slowly healing wounds he understood that it was not only the effect of his current activity that pained him but the ghost of his encounter with Master Leonard, one of the true lords of Hell.

But when he woke after another undisturbed night of sleep, those ravages from the previous days had passed, and the hangover from the earlier encounter had lessened. He climbed back on Pewter, hoping to reach Durham by nightfall. Throughout his journey, he thought warmly of his friends Kit and Jack and the hardships they'd faced, and it brought a smile. Even if he wasn't on top of his game, fighting together, reunited, would make them all better. His reminiscence helped the long hours on the road pass, even as he entered Weardale and the edge of the Pennines. Pewter had little trouble with the incline, and the view of the hills and mountains helped restore some of that zest for life that had been lacking when confined to bed. But the sun was already setting, and he realised his chance of locating Kit, Jack and the rest before nightfall was slim indeed. To the northeast, built on a rise, was Brancepeth Castle. No doubt its present purpose was to garrison troops, but would an approach from that direction give him a better chance of finding his friends?

As he passed a small cluster of ash trees, he heard a call: "Stop!"

It was a cry that came from all around and yet nowhere, and no sooner had he brought Pewter to a halt than he understood why. It was the voice of Thomas Percy.

"Are you not aware that we are close to Brancepeth Castle?"

Guy glanced at the castle's towers. "Aye, what of it?"

"You understand I follow you on every step of your journey?"

"I do."

Thomas Percy swooped down to come skull-to-face with Guy. "And I witness all through your eyes?"

Guy leant back, trying to look past the brightness of Percy's glowing skull. "Is there some kind of point you're trying to make?"

"Yes, Master Fawkes, there is. Why would you be so cruel as to force me to revisit the place of my death?" Percy swooped back, leaving Guy dazzled.

Guy blinked a few times, then gazed at the tall towers of the castle before looking back at the floating skull of Thomas Percy, a constant annoyance to him in his days of bedridden pain. He'd only ever seen him in this form and had not considered him as a complete human being. "If I get your head back on your shoulders, will you leave me alone?"

"Not a chance... but think of my poor mind for a moment. It was here I fell when the Queen stopped our little Rising of the North. Back then, the castle belonged to the Nevilles, but she confiscated it. She took it as her own."

Guy tugged on Pewter's reins to change her direction. "And that's a good enough reason to avoid it?"

"You witnessed yourself the type of people who belonged to the Council of the North, the very body she established to stop any further northern risings."

Guy thought of Hastings, the evil he'd done, and the satisfaction of drawing a blade across his throat. Percy was right. He'd prefer not to walk into a banquet hosted by those kinds of men.

"You know this land?" Guy asked.

"Like the back of my hand."

Guy stared at where Percy's hands should have been if he were more than a floating skull.

"It's an expression."

"And you know a thing or two about rebellions."

"You've got the right man..."

Guy smirked. "Or have I? Yours didn't turn out too well."

"You've regained your sense of humour, Master Fawkes. What is your point?"

"Perhaps you might have an idea where a band of rebels looking to take a stand against Durham might locate themselves?"

"There's a small forest to the east of the city which the River Wear runs through. It's as good a place as any."

"We'll make for the forest. Even if we find no one, we can doubtless make it comfortable to get our heads down."

"Speak for yourself." Percy spun round again.

Guy left the sight of Brancepeth Castle behind him and made for the river. From time to time the cathedral and castle came into view, only to be obscured by trees or another rise. The ever-winding path of the river lengthened the journey, but when he came to the tree line, he knew he'd made the right choice: the telltale orange glow of a campfire indicated the presence of people. He dismounted Pewter and led her through the trees until he was close enough to hear those gathered around the flames. Whether it was the sound of the voices or something about their movements, Guy expected he'd be among friends again soon, but that did not assuage his caution. A second later came the crack of a branch beneath the heavy foot of a sentry.

Guy raised his arms. "Friend, I come in peace."

A figure moved before him, draped and hooded, wielding a drawn bow. "State your name and your business here."

"My name is Guy Fawkes and I seek my allies who fight for Francis Ingleby."

The sentry closed, his breath hot on Guy's face when he spoke. "Guy Fawkes, hey?"

"You know that name?"

"Aye, as I know mud." He spat at the floor. "Follow."

He headed through the trees toward the campfire. Several men gathered close together, holding their hands out, welcoming the warmth.

Guy looked around but recognised none of the faces. The man who had led him to the clearing had departed. Guy tied Pewter with the other horses and approached the fire. "Are the brothers Wright, Kit and Jack, among your number?"

"Aye," said one man.

"Where will I find them?"

"Sentry duty to the north. Follow the river, they'll find you."

"Thank you, friend." Guy rested a hand on the man's shoulder, but the way he turned to him and screwed up his face told him the thanks were not welcome. What had Guy done to offend this stranger? The mood in the camp was far from happy, and their numbers far fewer than Guy expected. Was this only one of many camps?

He looked back to Pewter and, as content as she looked tied close to her kin, he feared this would not be his resting place for the night.

He left the clearing to the sound of grumbles. The trees thickened, requiring a longer route to help Pewter through, emerging from where they were thickest onto the east side of the wood. He stayed close to the tree line and followed it around, and before he made it back to the river, he heard low voices.

"Kit, Jack, is that you?" he called, moving toward the vague outline of figures.

"Who's that?" It was Jack's voice.

"It's me, Guy. Is Kit with you?"

"Aye." Jack's voice dropped.

Jack emerged from the trees. Guy approached, and they embraced.

"So, tell me," Guy said as they broke away, "how goes the campaign at Durham? What news of your uncle?"

"How goes the campaign in Durham?" Kit emerged from the trees leading a black horse. "Good of you to arrive to find out."

Guy remembered Kit's anger in the tavern when they were last together. Guy had declined to accompany them to Durham, choosing instead to remain in York and take on Sandys. "Kit, please forgive my tardiness. After what happened at York Minster, I was off my feet for days."

Kit mounted his horse. "Aye, news of Sandys' demise soon reached Durham."

"And you wonder what took me so long to get here, I imagine?" Guy led Pewter close to Kit.

"The world, you may be surprised to learn, does not revolve around the actions of Guy Fawkes, saviour of York."

Guy stopped. "Kit, if I have offended you, I can only apologise. Now tell me, how goes things with your uncle?"

Jack approached Guy and shook his head.

"You want to see my uncle?" Kit cried. "Follow me." He pulled on his horse's reins and headed for Durham.

Guy leapt back onto Pewter and urged her to follow. By the time Guy caught Kit, Durham's walls were in sight. Every time Guy asked a question, Kit sped ahead once more. They crossed the river at the bridge and approached the southern gate. There, Kit brought his horse to a stop.

Kit allowed Guy to approach. "You wanted to know how Uncle Francis was doing?"

"He's in the city?"

Kit leant in close. "Aye, just about." He pointed.

Guy peered into the darkness. The torch at the gatehouse illuminated a shape hanging from the wall, and as Guy stared, his eyes adjusted. The outline of a figure hung from a rope.

"That's not..." Guy started, but he got no further, Kit's fist knocking him from his horse.

"Uncle Francis was being held at the castle when the news of Sandys' death broke. As a direct response, Walsingham hanged him at the city gate, so all that arrived at Durham would know what happens to enemies of the state."

Guy shifted to a sitting position. He put the back of his hand to his cheek feeling the warmth where Kit had struck him. "Kit, I am so sorry."

Kit dismounted and stood over Guy. "You had to do it your way though, didn't you? You couldn't come with us first to help Uncle Francis, even after all he'd done for you. As always, Guy Fawkes did what Guy Fawkes wanted, and to Hell with the consequences."

Guy stared at Kit's feet. He couldn't meet his eyes. "It wasn't like that."

"This is the last time I'm giving you advice. Don't make your way back to our camp. A lot of men faithful to my uncle don't share our history. They'll not hesitate to put a knife in your back."

Kit mounted his horse.

"Kit..." Guy called, but he didn't so much as look back.

Pewter whinnied and Guy struggled back to his feet. He brushed the dust off his hose and mounted the horse, but he knew not which route to take. In Durham, he could find a bed for the night, but to pass under the body of Francis Ingleby felt like a betrayal. The road home abandoned a friendship that had lasted most of his childhood.

Guy gazed into the darkness across the river, toward the woods where Kit would return. A fresh pain hit him, one he was familiar with from long ago, one he'd never wanted to experience again: loss.

Chapter 5—In Which Guy Fawkes Finds a Friend

As the cold of the night crept into Guy's bones, old pain augmented new pain and his remaining strength faded. A rocky outcrop surrounded by trees a couple of hundred yards away looked the best place to rest. The idea of going any further drained every residual morsel of resilience from him. The thought of the long journey back to York made his body feel heavy. He'd come so far, and for what? He looked back to the silhouette swinging before Durham's gates, before turning Pewter around. Even she seemed reluctant to travel any further. He dismounted at the edge of the trees and led Pewter inside.

But no sooner had he found a comfortable resting place against the rock than the sound of a mass of hooves roused him. He crept toward the road, remaining in the cover of trees. A dozen men on horseback headed for the city.

Pewter huffed, knowing she was going to be called into action again as Guy hurried toward her.

As he rode back toward the city, a horn sounded–the gatekeeper signalling for assistance. After the thud of hooves, came the clash of swords. Guy continued toward the fray, but as soon as those men on horseback had come, they'd turned and retreated.

They were back across the bridge by the time he reached it, leaving only dust swirling in their wake. He gazed toward the city. The guards' lanterns revealed the wounded gatekeeper struggling back to his feet, but what wasn't there was of greater significance: the raiders had retrieved Ingleby's body.

Guy brought Pewter to a standstill and watched the movement beyond the gate. Another horn sounded, and two men on horseback left the city, guards sent in pursuit of their recent assailants. As they approached the bridge, Guy considered intervention. Should he let them follow and chase after his friends? After all, Kit had made it clear they wanted no more to do with him.

Alas, his affection had not waned. And yet, he could not outride the soldiers, not in his condition, not after riding Pewter so hard for so many days.

If he was to get involved, it would be with his sword, or his cunning, the latter of which he had little faith in.

He rode Pewter to the bridge and dismounted, creating a minor obstacle. Maybe making a nuisance of himself would be sufficient.

"Stand aside," called one rider from a distance.

"What's the hurry?" Guy said, not budging.

"Enemies of Her Majesty. Be gone or taste my steel." Orange ringed their eyes.

So, it was true. Those serving Walsingham carried the demon seed. "Taste this," Guy called. He drew his sword and cast it into magnificence, blue flame dancing along its blade. One rider slowed while the other continued at full pace. Guy knew his chances were poor against a mounted opponent. With each closing hoof, Guy's chest tightened. As the rider neared, Guy saw his armour and knew he could not pierce it. He saw the broadsword in the rider's grasp and knew he couldn't block it when swung with the force of a speeding stallion.

No sooner had the horse reached the bridge, than the rider plummeted from the back of it. The stallion dashed between Guy and Pewter, leaving his rider prone on the ground.

Guy sped for the fallen soldier, and as he drew his blade across his throat, he saw what had felled him: a crossbow bolt sticking out of his chest, breaching his armour.

The second soldier had drawn a bow. Guy swished his sword from side to side, inviting the soldier to shoot, daring him to take a shot when he knew he wouldn't get a second off.

But another bolt zipped through the air, bringing that soldier's challenge to an end. Guy scanned the darkness but spotted no sign of his crossbow-wielding saviour.

"Guy!" came a call. It was a voice he recognised, but not one he could place. He calculated the likely hiding place of the shooter and the source of the voice at the same time he emerged from the bushes, but it wasn't until he was much closer that he realised it was Ghost. The pair embraced.

"I knew not you were in Durham." Ever since Guy had first met Ghost, he had relied upon him for wisdom. When hiding at Saint Robert's Cave, Ghost had told so many tales of the first demon hunters, the Templar

Knights and of the ancient artefacts that were hunted down and destroyed to stop evil men wielding power.

Ghost sighed. "I was among the first group that travelled with Ingleby."

Guy gritted his teeth. "I wish I could have been here sooner. Maybe–"

"It would have changed nothing."

"But Kit said–"

Ghost shook his head. "Kit's angry." He stepped over to the nearest soldier and wrenched the bolt from his neck.

Guy gazed at the body. "So, demons occupy Durham, too?"

"Indeed, and everywhere else where Walsingham holds sway."

Guy glanced toward the city gate. "Will you remain here to purge them from the city?"

"It's what the rest of the party wishes, but they won't stick it out. Other than me, Kit and Jack, many of the others have families. They have farms to tend to."

Feeling safe, Guy sheathed his sword. "Is it possible to purge Durham of demons, as we have York?"

"Walsingham has the support of the Dudley family here. The Warthills have also pledged allegiance to him. Purging lord by lord, one city at a time, is a fool's errand."

"Will you return to York?"

Ghost shook his head. "I'm heading south."

"You think it will be free of this curse?"

Ghost smiled at Guy's naivety. "Before they captured him, Ingleby talked of the hope from Spain. How England needed to be shaken from the base of the trunk to bring all the tiers of corruption falling from the tree. He believed it was in the heart of the country, and only wholesale change could save it."

While Guy's father had been dead for a long time, Guy still remembered him speaking of the ills of treason. "But to let his country fall in battle? To pave the way for foreign invaders on our soil?"

"For the greater good. Sometimes sacrifices have to be made. it's better to be controlled by invaders from across the sea than by the denizens of Hell."

"Aye, you've got a point." He pondered for a second before probing Ghost further. "If everywhere is riddled with demons, why go south?"

"When the time comes, I'd like to be closer to the action. And Ingleby spoke of allies there."

"In London?"

"No, Sussex. Cowdray House. And you, back to York, is it?"

Guy thought of his family. "Aye." He remembered what he'd been through to cleanse the city. He'd believed it was the epicentre of infection. If Ghost was right, he'd barely squeezed the pus from a minor wound of a mutilated body. It would only be a matter of time before a new master grasped the mantle. Was it Guy's duty to remain ever vigilant and stop them before they did too much damage? He thought again of his home and his family. Or was his duty truly to them? He needed to secure work once more. They couldn't rely on Anne's wage at James William Wilson's bakery and his mother's needlework to keep food on the table. Perhaps it was time to settle back into the city to live a normal life.

Guy turned to the road. "Are you planning to head south soon?"

Ghost raised his eyebrows. "You looking for a companion?"

"It would be a much less lonely journey if you were beside me, friend."

"I shall make my way back to York with you. Perhaps I'll stay awhile before I head south."

Ghost agreed to head back to his camp, to spend his final night there paying his respects to Francis Ingleby and to meet Guy in the morning to begin their journey. Guy spent the night among the rocks and trees and reunited with Ghost at first light. While the journey back, following the same roads Guy had taken on the way there was uneventful, travelling together at least made it pleasant. Ghost fell back into his habit of story-telling, and Guy once more became a pupil eager to hear more. For all the terrible things that had happened, the journey at least was rewarding up until the moment Guy realised they were close to York.

Chapter 6—In Which Time Passes and Love Falls Upon the Fawkes' Household

There's nothing like returning home in triumph, ready to share tales of glory. The flip side, too, is true, and as soon as the silhouette of York Minster came into view, failure's cold claws tore at Guy's gut. Dark clouds gathered, and moments after he left Ghost at an inn, the sky fell. Heavy rain soaked through his clothes, bringing a chill to his body.

When he walked through his front door, Edith Fawkes gazed at him before returning her eyes to her needlework. Elizabeth, beside her, left her gaze upon her brother.

Guy smiled at his little sister. "I told you I'd be back to take a look at your garden."

Elizabeth glanced out of the window. "I can't show you now. It's raining." She, too, returned her focus to her sewing.

The thudding of footsteps on the stairs, however, indicated his return had pleased someone. Anne threw her arms around Guy, pulling him into her embrace, before releasing him and slapping him on the arm. "How dare you leave in the state you were in?"

Guy rubbed the spot where Anne had struck him. She slapped him on the other arm. "I've been so worried."

Guy took a step back before Anne could assault him again. "It's only thanks to your care I was fit enough to leave when I did."

Anne took a moment to study her brother. "Are you okay? How are your wounds? Are the burns healing well?"

Guy knew he'd have fresh bruises from his encounters and could feel Anne's eyes scrutinising him. "I am well, and I thank you for your care."

"And the business in Durham? Is it done?"

Guy recalled the shape of Ingleby swinging from a rope.

His mother peered over her needlework at him.

"I am done with it, aye."

"What about–"

Guy held up a hand to silence Anne.

Rage burned in her eyes at being told to stop talking.

27

"I shall tell you all, shortly." Guy hurried upstairs and changed out of his wet clothes. A moment later came a knock at the door, and Anne entered. Her ire from downstairs had only bloomed.

"I have to say, Guy, I'm disappointed."

"What's wrong?"

Anne approached Guy again. She stared at the bruise on his face. "After what we did together in York Minster, I can't believe you left me behind."

"It wasn't your fight, Anne."

Anne shoved Guy in the chest, causing him to stumble back. "I can help you, Guy. If you'd only let me."

Guy touched his brow. The vision of Francis swinging from the rope came to him again followed by Kit's angry expression. He screwed his face up in a futile attempt to hold back the tears.

Anne sat on the bed beside him, and he told her everything.

· · · ·

GHOST LEFT YORK A FEW days later, but not before Guy introduced him to Anne. For a time, Guy lived the banal existence he'd longed for. He fell back on the butchery skills taught to him by Margaret Clitherow and took work at another butcher's shop on The Shambles. Anne continued to work at the bakery, and Elizabeth proved she was more than capable in the garden, creating beautiful displays of flowers, and her herbs enriched their every meal. Guy had the idea this was indeed what life was like for most people. This was normal, and he was okay with that.

Not that his life was without bloodshed. He was right to believe that corruption would ease back into the city, but late at night, he'd slip out to ensure it couldn't take root. He was the city's secret weeder, taking out those faithful to Sandys' demon-loving ways. Often, Anne would accompany him, and the times they were alone together, Guy would tell her some of the lore he'd learned from Pulleyn, Ingleby, and Clitherow. He had a duty to share the knowledge they were no longer there to impart.

Perhaps it was the darkness, and perhaps it was the memory of the hardship at the start of the previous year, but Guy felt a deep unease after the winter solstice as 1586 became 1587. Even when the days grew longer, Guy sensed the malevolence lingering. Figures lurked in the shadows and fell back into alcoves to engage in clandestine conversation, but none of his intel pointed at a significant incursion of evil. He saw impossible faces every day: shoppers at Pavement, customers in the butchers on The Shambles, and revellers in the taverns resembled those he'd left behind. He saw his father, his uncle, those that had tutored him at Saint Peter's, the men he'd met at Saint Robert's Cave, each uniquely tormenting him with memories he'd rather forget. Were these the faces of the restless dead, the apparitions he'd trained himself to filter out many years before? Did they have a warning for him? Or was his mind blasting him with faces from the past for another reason? If so, was it a form of mental torture or some kind of warning? As the moonlight shone on one drunkard, for a moment his bald pate had made him look like the ghost of Thomas Percy, but he had no wisdom to offer, no guidance except that found in the bottom of a tankard. Every woman bore the face of Margaret Clitherow and that spring, every laugh became hers as she won the crowd's sympathy and admiration while being crushed by rocks. When he felt low, it was the faces of Sandys and Hastings before him. At those times, it was easy to imagine demons everywhere. Sometimes, the ground beneath him quaked, as if Master Leonard shook on the sealed crypt door deep within that version of York Minster that existed only in his mind. Without a purpose, Guy drifted, but there was always a face there to turn his wandering mind back to misery.

Despair grew stronger when news came that Queen Elizabeth had beheaded Mary, Queen of Scots, at Fotheringhay Castle. Of course, it had been Mary's antics that had allowed the Council of the North and Walsingham to flex their powers and to extend their searches, acts which no doubt led to many of the hangings that took place in Knavesmire. And yet, Guy had always seen Mary Queen of Scots as a symbol of hope. Her links to the continent provided a route out of the darkness, an opportunity in the world outside of the city. Without her, it was as if yet another candle keeping that darkness at bay had been snuffed out.

• • • •

AS EASTER CAME, AND the anniversary of Margaret Clitherow's terrible death passed, some of the ill thoughts dissipated, and Guy sensed a change coming. The raven-haired girl who had been at Pulleyn's hanging and Margaret's pressing returned to his mind. Perhaps it was love that was missing from his life. He was approaching seventeen; it was time he found a wife.

Alas, when Guy looked to the heavens and read the signs of love, he read them wrong; love did not enter his life, but his mother's. It was rare indeed for a widow as young as Guy's mother to remain single for so long. Eight years had passed since the death of Edward Fawkes. Perhaps because they'd left York so soon after that horrible death she was not in the minds of bachelors or widowers looking to remarry. When she ventured back into York, it was only to attend church, and she did so with her brother-in-law, Thomas Fawkes, so once more she would have appeared unavailable. By the time she moved back to York, she was in the guise of Edith Blake, and she kept herself confined to the house, again, except only for church. Those that sought her sewing services came only to the house. Not only that, the darkness gripping the city meant it was not a place of hope, not a place where single people sought meaningful connections. But when light shone on the city once more, old passions stirred. Elizabeth's enthusiasm in the garden brought Edith out into the sun. York became once more that place she had known, and once more, with Guy or Anne or Elizabeth, she would enjoy a pleasant walk in the city on an evening or a Sunday afternoon.

Guy was unaware of when the meeting had taken place, but at some point, his mother had met a widower by the name of Dionis Bainbrigge. He owned land and property to the west of York in the Parish of Farnham. He spoke of a union, promising to take Edith from the city. Bainbrigge had his eyes on a property known as Percy House in the village of Scotton and stated that it would make a perfect family abode.

One Sunday afternoon, after having spent the morning at church, Edith revealed to her children that she had received a marriage proposal. She turned first to her son.

"Guy, there has always been such a weight on your shoulders. The responsibility of being the man of the house for so long put a strain on you, but in the last year, once you recovered from your sickness, you've put your heart and your soul into making sure we have all we need, and I can't thank you enough."

This was more affection than Edith had shown to her son in many long years. He approached his mother, took hold of her hand, and kissed her on the cheek. "Mother, if you believe this man will be kind to you, if you believe this will bring you happiness, I agree this marriage is a fine idea."

Edith hugged her son before urging him to sit.

"All of my joy in recent years has come from seeing my girls grow up. Anne, I'm so proud of the way you've held down your job—"

Anne crossed her arms. "Will I have to give it up?"

"Dionis says if you wish to remain working in the city, he can help you financially with the cost of lodgings."

Anne's brow furrowed. "But I'd have to give you all up. I've not spent so much as a day without your company. No, mother, I can't let you leave me like that."

"You wouldn't need to work in Scotton, but there are jobs available if you want them. There must be a bakery—"

Anne moved over to her mother and hugged her. "If I get to stay with you—if Guy will join us too, what more could I want?"

Edith beckoned her youngest over. "And Elizabeth, you've been at my side for so long. I held you and you've brought me great comfort. I know I won't need words to persuade you, but Dionis has told me one important thing about Percy House."

Elizabeth gazed at her mother with her large, dark eyes. "Yes, Mother."

"It has a fine garden."

Elizabeth embraced her mother. "Can I dig up my plants from outside to take them with us?" Elizabeth did not wait for a reply before rushing to grab her trowel.

So, it was decided. Edith, Guy, Anne and Elizabeth would leave York. Guy would no longer be its protector, and if it went back to ruin, that was its fate. A new chapter in Guy's life was about to begin, one that he hoped would bring him peace.

Rarely do we get what we wish for.

Chapter 7—In Which Guy Fawkes Settles in a New Home and Makes New Acquaintances

Dionis Bainbrigge made arrangements for the wedding and set about renovating Percy House to prepare for the arrival of his new wife and her children. When summer arrived, Guy and his family waved goodbye to York.

In leaving the city, and passing through Bootham Bar, a weight lifted from Guy's shoulders. Aye, York was no longer Guy's responsibility. If the city were to fall back to its old dark ways, he'd be sorry, but the blame would not be his. He had hope, for the memory of Margaret Clitherow and her cruel death had opened the eyes of its bedraggled citizens. A new generation would carry the torch and keep the light shining.

Scotton itself offered little, and this was a blessing. There was a smithy at one end of the village and a couple of public houses. There was a single butcher's shop which was next door to the bakery. Most of the houses were large, with lots of farmland. Grazing sheep and cattle speckled the hillsides. Even the dead were quieter here. Guy had spent much of his life tuning them out, but in Scotton that was rarely necessary. The village didn't even have a church, and that meant no church bells. As the voices of the restless dead were always so much noisier when the bells rang, Guy was thankful no place of worship was nearby.

Dionis purchased sheep, and Guy made their care his responsibility. Shorn of the title of the man of the house, Guy spent increasing amounts of time outside. Not that he wasn't happy for his mother. Her smile transformed her face and took years from her age. When Guy had the responsibility of the man of the house, his mother had taken on the burden of the worry. Without it, she was at ease. Anne did not seek employment at the local bakery but took responsibility in the kitchen, and Elizabeth was alive with pleasure in the garden.

While Guy took some joy in the happiness his family had discovered, he felt it not. Kit's words bounced around his head. When he closed his eyes, Francis Ingleby hung from the gatehouse at Durham. In his dreams, the beast in the crypt at York Minster rattled the doors with increased vigour. Only among the sheep was he content.

Anne, however, refused to let Guy slip entirely away from his old life. She hid swords under rocks in the fields, and when Guy was with his flock, she'd come at him and insist he continued his practice. But over the months, this happened less and less until another winter came and 1588 brought further change.

Scotton was not on the main road, so travellers making their way to towns and cities seldom passed through. The village was often in the dark regarding events elsewhere in England. For Guy, it was a blessing to have a village notice board that wasn't updated regularly. Only twice a year, a representative of the Queen would arrive to post ordinances, but they were rarely of note. The need to continue accepted worship was always stated, but as Scotton had no church, observation was near impossible. Where punishment came to those in York that did not belong to the Church of England, Scotton wasn't worthy of attention. Bainbrigge did not attend Protestant worship and would confess to being a Catholic. When confronted about this, he would pay the related tithes, and the problem disappeared. When his mother converted to Catholicism, Guy did likewise. This was not because of any great spiritual awakening but as an act of petty rebellion. It was a hypocritical society indeed in which Guy lived.

News did, however, reach Scotton in May 1588; a herald arrived proclaiming the news was to be spread far and wide. The forces of the English navy had heroically repelled a Spanish armada. By all accounts, the Queen had ridden to Tilbury, dressed in full battle armour to give a rousing speech to her fleet, and the heroic Sir Francis Drake had orchestrated a battle plan which tore the Spanish forces to shreds.

The herald decreed celebration, with barrels of ale supplied to every tavern in the country. So, alongside the rest of his family and all the residents of Scotton, Guy attended the celebration at The Falconers Arms, keeping his head low, and his ale replenished. While all around him cheered, Guy heard only Francis's words. "Hope lies with the Spanish." What hope now if they had been cast aside? Perhaps hope resided in Queen Elizabeth. After all, was it not her criticism of the death of Margaret Clitherow that had left Sandys vulnerable? If she had the power to repel the invasive force of the Spanish, if someone could persuade her to look inwards, to recognise the evil among her people, she would do something about it.

"Why so glum, friend? Is this not a day of celebration?"

Guy turned toward the voice. The skull of Thomas Percy himself was before him, not floating, but on a well-attired body. The tankard dropped from Guy's hand, and he followed it, collapsing onto the tavern's floor.

• • • •

WITH NOTHING BUT DARKNESS around him, Guy was alone with Thomas Percy, now free of the body.

"Guy, what have you been doing?" the long-dead noble spoke in a low voice.

Guy glanced around the room, trying to find something in the darkness to anchor him to reality, but even with Percy's luminosity, nothing was there. "Tending to my flock."

"You're drifting through life with no purpose." Percy swung from one side to the other as he spoke.

"I have a purpose." Guy grinned. "It's tending to my flock."

Percy swooped in close, glowing brighter than ever. "You have great power. You can hear voices on the spirit plane. That power gives you great strength against the demon scourge."

"You told me before it was a road I couldn't avoid."

"That is true."

Guy stepped back. "I shall tend to my flock until my inevitable calling."

Percy's glow changed to the colour of intensely burning flame. "Others will get hurt if you remain here. Start on the journey now and save yourself that heartache."

Guy shielded himself from the heat and the light with one arm. "People have been hurt regardless of my decisions. I have less power and influence than you suggest."

"Only time will tell Guy. Only time will tell." Percy's light diminished, leaving Guy in the dark of oblivion.

• • • •

WHEN HE CAME TO, GUY was in his bed at Percy House. It took him a while to piece together where he was, and the events of the previous night were confused in his mind. He had attended the tavern to celebrate, somewhat unenthusiastically, the victory over the Spanish, but at some point, his memory became hazy.

He pulled on some clothes. Light ebbed in through the edges of the curtains, so it had to be morning.

Hearing voices, he made his way into the dining room. His mother sat at the table with Dionis. "Sit," she said, standing from the table and pulling a chair out for him.

Guy held up a hand in protest. "No, I…"

"Sit."

Guy sat.

Edith returned to the table. "You've not been eating right. Look at the state of you."

Guy glanced at himself. Aye, his clothes were not as snug as they once had been.

"When that young man helped us get you home last night, I realised what a skinny thing you are. It's not right."

Guy took some bread from the table. "Which young man?"

"The young man you were talking to at the public house."

Dionis wiped his mouth with the back of his hand. "She means the Percy boy. The family used to live here."

The Percy boy? Vague memories of seeing the floating head of Thomas Percy in the pub came to him.

"Thomas Percy?" Guy asked.

"That's the one." Dionis took a sip from his mug.

"But he's… dead." Guy found his appetite waning, the bread heavy in his hand.

"He can't be. You spoke to him last night."

"Where do they live?"

"Follow me." Dionis exited Percy House by the front door. Guy, still gripping the bread, followed. Dionis pointed to a house in the distance. "That's where you'll find them."

Guy decided to call on the Percy household to speak to this young man himself. Why a long-dead revolutionary rode upon his shoulders was one question he wasn't sure how to go about asking.

He returned inside and ate–not by choice. His mother was right; he had lost a considerable amount of his bulk. Some of his strength had waned since he'd given up his demon hunting exploits, and he'd not been eating well. His mother watched as he consumed a larger breakfast than he had done since moving into the house, struggling with every mouthful.

Once Edith was satisfied, Guy headed outside once more and along the road toward the house.

As he strode through the village, many of the residents were in their gardens, either tending to their vegetable plots or taking nourishment from the morning sun to ease aching heads. Each gave him a friendly hello or a wave, which he reciprocated. Once more village life proved more appealing than the coldness of the city.

He arrived at the Percy's home and knocked on the door, but there was no answer.

As he turned away, voices came from the rear of the property.

"Hallo!" Guy called as he walked around to the back of the house. There, he found a middle-aged woman struggling to place a rug on a bench for beating while a young man in a powder-blue doublet and matching hose sat on a low wall perusing a letter.

"Excuse me," called Guy. "Would any of you know where I could find Thomas Percy?"

The young man looked up. "You feel a little more like talking without passing out today?"

The voice brought back memories of the previous night, though he was glad this version of Thomas Percy had flesh on his face.

Guy took a few steps toward him, stopping to help who he assumed was Thomas's mother, Mrs Percy to shift the rug into the position she wanted it.

"Would it be possible for us to take a walk?" Guy asked.

"Aye, please, take him away from me for the morning," said Mrs Percy. "He'll not stop talking and my ears are full of it. Bring him back when he's all out of words."

"I cannot help it, Mother, if I have a lot of opinions and a lot of ideas. It is only right that someone should listen to them, and you are blessed to find yourself so often in my company."

"Be gone with you." Mrs Percy grabbed the rug beater and shook it in Thomas's direction before giving the rug its first whack.

"Come," said Thomas. "Follow me. I shall lead you over hills and into valleys and we can become acquainted."

Guy followed, hoping to give the conversation some purpose before Thomas led him on a merry dance. "Please forgive me last night. I know not what happened."

"You know not what happened? I do! I witnessed it all. You stood in the tavern, looking glum. I recognised you as the young man that tends to the sheep out the back of my old abode, so I thought I'd say hello, and what do you? You fall to the ground, the light in your eyes extinguished. So, I considered it my duty to carry you home. You tried to have a conversation with me, but you spoke only incomprehensible nonsense."

Guy squirmed with the awkwardness of the conversation. He wasn't used to such a frank response. "Thank you for helping me home."

"We never got to the bottom of what made you so morose on a day of national celebration."

Guy looked across the fields, plotting where he could flee to if the next question went wrong. "Before we get to that, can I ask you a question?"

"Ask away, friend."

Guy took a deep breath. Concerns over how best to word his question had troubled him since he stepped on the path to Thomas's house. "Are you the same Thomas Percy..." he paused looking into the distance. "Are you the same Thomas Percy that visits me as a floating head in the night?"

If only a fissure could open up beneath the earth for him to fall into.

"Of all the questions I was expecting from you, Guy—I can call you Guy, I take it? That is not the one I was expecting."

"No, I was mistaken. Please, forget it." Guy stepped away.

Thomas pulled Guy back. "Forget such an intriguing question? You may as well ask me to extinguish the sun. The two are equally impossible."

Guy shaded his face with his hand hiding his embarrassment. "I'm sorry, I was being ridiculous."

"Alas, the words are out there now for me to digest. Where to start? You asked if I visit you at the night. If you have received visits in the night from an attractive young man, it was not me."

"You talk as much as he does." Guy tried to quicken his pace to walk away from Thomas.

Thomas broke into a trot to catch Guy. "But I assure you I am not him, for you state this is a floating head, and as you can see, my head is attached firmly to my neck. Try it." Thomas craned his neck toward Guy.

"No, I–"

Thomas grabbed Guy's hands. He placed them on his neck. "I do insist. Now give it a good tug."

Guy attempted to lift Thomas's head from his shoulders.

"No, give it a real yank."

Guy placed his hands by his side. "I can't."

Thomas grabbed Guy's hands and again placed them on his cheeks. "But you must if we are to set your mind at ease."

Guy pulled again, a little harder this time. "Okay, I'm satisfied your head does not float."

"Good, I can't have you spreading rumours. I have a reputation to protect, don't you know?"

"No, I don't."

"Well, I told you that's the case. Now let us unpick another aspect of your question."

Guy hurried along the path. "Must we?"

Thomas fell into step with Guy. "Oh, believe me, I must. You say the same Thomas Percy, meaning you know another by that name?"

"Oh, I am certain it is another. You have made that more than clear."

"And it comes to you as a floating head?"

Guy sighed. This was greater torture than the birching he'd experienced back at Saint Peter's. "Yes... but I think it's when I'm dreaming."

"But it's not *the* Thomas Percy, is it? The 7th Earl of Northumberland? He that lost his life as part of the Revolt of the Northern Earls?"

Guy looked Thomas in the eye. "You've heard of him?"

"No, never."

Guy's face contorted with confusion.

Thomas chuckled. "Yes. Distant relative, so it happens. And now, finally, you have answered the first question I directed at you."

Guy frantically tried to think back to where their conversation had started. Alas, he'd consigned most of their conversion to a section of his brain never to be unlocked again in fear of causing himself to cringe so hard he'd lose consciousness. "What's that?"

"I asked why you were so glum."

"And I answered it?" Guy hardly dared probe further.

"Well, if you know of Thomas Percy, you're not the sort to be happy about the Spanish armada letting the English put a bunch of holes in their ships."

And for the rest of their walk, Guy spoke almost as much as Thomas did.

Chapter 8—In Which Guy and his New Friend Take a Trip to York

There's nothing like routine to help the days speed by. When one is indistinguishable from the next, some slip away from the memory. Guy continued to tend to his sheep. He spent time conversing with Thomas (though Thomas had become dominant in conversation). Their chats at least suggested opportunity was out there for him in terms of rebellion and civil unrest that didn't involve the same level of trauma as battling demons. Even if Thomas Percy (the fleshless one) was right, that he'd end up back on the demon-hunting road sooner or later, it would be better to ease himself in and learn about the complex political situation.

But when Thomas found him out shepherding one day with a glimmer in his eye, he realised he was likely to be pulled back to the blood-steeped depths much quicker than expected. Maybe Thomas Percy (deceased rebel) was working through Thomas Percy (verbose young man) after all.

"He's returning to York," Thomas said. "Walsingham is resuming meetings of the Council of the North in York, and he intends to gather his allies there next month."

There was no deliberation, no doubt. Guy prepared to return as well, spending time each day with his sword. He ate better, hoping to regain the muscle he'd lost alongside his fitness and sharpness. Needlessly lifting sheep, while disturbing for them, contributed to the development of some additional bulk.

The eve of their departure for York approached. Thomas and Guy came together to discuss their plans. "Things might get a little... weird," Guy warned.

Thomas raised his eyebrows. "Doesn't the fact that I remained speaking to you after you accused me of being the decapitated head that has visited you in your dreams since you were a child suggest I'm in this for the weird stuff? If I didn't want pandemonium, I would have walked away from you long ago."

"Aye." Guy cleared his throat. "We will have to infiltrate the King's Manor to get close."

Thomas dismissed Guy's concerns with a wave of his hand. "Please, I'm already one step ahead. Such events require servants. I have secured us both a position working as servers delivering food to their tables for their banquet."

Guy's forehead furrowed. "But... how?"

"When you have the connections I have, you can get into all sorts of places they don't want common folk in."

Guy smiled. "Perfect. And there was me thinking we'd have to find a way in from the tunnels that lead to the river."

"Do I look the sort to scrabble around in dark and dingy passages half full of water?" Thomas glanced at his doublet and brushed away a piece of fluff.

"No, I don't suppose you do."

• • • •

GUY AND THOMAS SET off for York a day before the banquet. It was half a day's ride, and they wanted to be fresh for the event. The plan was to observe what they could at King's Manor and eavesdrop on any hints of activity, or information which could be useful. Thomas revealed he earned a little coin with information, passing it from one place to the next. While the intention was to watch and learn, Guy brought his sword and made sure that Thomas not only had a weapon but understood how to use it.

They took the ride slowly. Thomas was competent on horseback, but there was no need to wear out either themselves or the horses by racing, and they reached the city walls by early afternoon. Approaching from the west meant a return to the city through Guy's oft-walked route through Bootham Bar. It was impossible not to recall his first encounter with Sandys there, but when he looked up, there was one significant change. While heads still decorated the gate, they were not so fresh. The need to replace them so frequently had passed, and Guy hoped York retained some stability.

A tidal wave of memories crashed upon Guy as they entered the city in the mid-afternoon. The sound of activity took him back to his youngest days and the frequent walks with his father. It was impossible not to think back to afternoons with Kit and Jack following some suspicious-looking gentleman they suspected of engaging in demonic practices. But there were other locations too that brought back unhappy memories—streets through which he'd fled various horrors, places where whisperers gathered, where he'd seen friends fall.

After stabling the horses (using Guy's familiar stable where he knew Pewter would be content) Thomas urged them into a tavern, The Starre. He spoke to the bartender to secure rooms for a couple of nights. They moved to an unoccupied table, sat and had a drink and ordered a bite to eat, and once more talked through their plan.

After a glance to scan the rest of the inn's patrons, Guy leant in close to Thomas. "So, who are we expecting to be in attendance alongside Walsingham?"

Thomas leant back and spoke in his usual loud voice. "Representatives of all the great cities in the north are likely to be there. Earls and Barons and Lords. You know the like."

Guy placed a finger to his lips and spoke in a low whisper. "If they perform any kind of devilry, we may well have to intervene."

Thomas supped his drink and ignored Guy's suggested reserve. "Now Guy, if you think, at a meeting of this magnitude, these gentlemen are going to form a circle to summon a demon, if you think they're going to whip out their dark books and perform black magic, you don't understand politics at all these days!"

A maid delivered their meal of trout and potatoes to the table. Guy nodded in thanks and waited until she disappeared before he spoke. "Nay? The last of these I spied upon was a meeting of the powers of York. Do you know how that ended?"

Thomas smirked. "Given how most of your stories end, I'm going for a demonic giant with a flaming sword cleaving people in two."

Guy stopped with a forkful of fish on the way to his mouth. "It was a giant toad."

"Flame-skinned demon, giant toad. It's all the same to me." Thomas crushed a potato with the back of his fork.

"You still don't believe me, do you?"

"No. Did I ever give you the impression that I did? Guy, and I mean this as a friend, but some of your tales are, frankly, beyond all credibility."

Guy spiked a potato with his fork. "Why bring me here if I'm such a joke?"

"You're a good man, but what you need is a focus. Working as a spy will get you away from all of that fantasy talk of demons and other foul creatures."

Guy smiled and took a sip of his drink.

"I don't like that grin on your face, Guy."

"What?" Guy took another small sip.

"I'm trying to bring you to a position of enlightenment, and you sit there with that grin on your face. I know that grin. Inside, you're saying, 'You'll see,' and you think I'm a fool for not believing in you. Am I right?"

Guy opened his mouth, but Thomas cut across him. "No, don't answer. I know I'm right. In your head, you think the floor's going to open up, the flames of hell will lick us, and Lucifer himself will make his presence known. Perhaps Walsingham and he will do a little dance, nothing fancy, but a dance nonetheless, and that's why you've got me carrying a blade."

"You'll thank me when the time comes." Guy popped the potato into his mouth.

"You'll be the one thanking me when you've a purse full of coins and you can leave your childish fantasies behind."

Guy nodded and continued to chew. Normally, if someone questioned his reason for being, he'd be offended, but it wasn't like that with Thomas. There was something about his relentless enthusiasm for what he did and his unwavering belief. More so, he couldn't wait to see Thomas's face when he found out he was wrong.

Guy drained his ale. "I'll feel better if we take a walk past King's Manor. I want to get my bearings and reacquaint myself with the nearby streets."

"Aye, it'll do us good to take in some air. Lead on."

As the sun started to set, Guy led Thomas on a meandering route back toward Bootham Bar, close to King's Manor. They ventured along the streets that led him to the south to once more follow the river to the Ouse Bridge and the Toll House where Margaret Clitherow had died. Someone had placed flowers on the exact spot where she breathed her last breath which brought a smile to Guy's face. Yes, he was doing the right thing to re-assume his observation of Walsingham. If he intended to make York the centre of operations in the north once more, he needed to be stopped. Walsingham couldn't restore the darkness to the city. In moving to Scotton, Guy had believed he'd left all of this behind, but he couldn't help the way he cared for the city he'd grown up in.

They continued toward King's Manor. Guards paraded outside, no longer bearing the colours of Hastings, but those of their country.

"Looks like several attendees are already here," Thomas said.

Well-dressed gentlemen ambled around on the lawn of the Manor.

Thomas nodded toward a group and listed names: "Baron Morley, Sir Robert Drury, Everard Digby Esquire."

Guy turned to the sound of hooves.

"And here's another," Thomas said.

Flanked by guards came a young man on horseback with a long, narrow face and a healthy head of dark hair.

At the gate, a pair of grooms took hold of the horse while the man dismounted.

Thomas leant in toward Guy and spoke in a whisper, pointing to a man as he exited a carriage. "Ah, here's one I've heard a great deal about: Robert Cecil, the son of Baron Burghley."

"You know him?"

Cecil walked with an awkward gait. His hunched posture made him appear all the shorter, and he rocked from side to side as he waddled along.

"Only by description. His father is Her Majesty's High Lord Treasurer." Thomas rose his eyebrows as if he was delivering impressive information.

"Born into such a position where he's likely to do well for himself, regardless of the character or stature of the man."

"Aye, but I have heard he is a wily one. He won't let his heritage alone dictate his position in society. His cunning has already seen him supplant others in court."

Guy watched Cecil as he made his way along the path to the entrance until movement from the side door caught his eye. He gasped.

"What is it?" Thomas asked.

Guy's eyes remained fixated upon the servant with raven hair. Surely it was her! But then, she was inside once more.

"Did you see her?" Guy asked, turning to Thomas.

"Who?"

Guy pointed to the door through which the young woman had gone through. "The servant–the raven-haired girl?"

"Maria?" Thomas smiled. "Aye, she's quite the beauty."

"You know her?"

Thomas looked over his shoulder. The guards' eyes lingered on them. "We should tarry here no longer."

"But you know the girl?"

Thomas gripped Guy but the arm and took a few steps away from King's Manor. "Aye, that's Maria Pulleyn."

Guy grabbed Thomas's arm. "This is the girl I told you of."

Thomas's eyes widened. "Maria is your angel of death?"

Gur recalled the way she'd run to his headmaster, John Pulleyn, as he swung from a rope, the way she clung to his legs to bring his life more swiftly to an end before a guard had kicked her into the mud. "Tomorrow, is there a chance that you can introduce us?"

Thomas smiled. "Guy Fawkes, you sound smitten. Please, don't let your emotions impede your duty. You won't make it as a spy if the only person you're observing is no more than a servant."

Guy glanced up at the red streaking the twilight sky. "She is so much more than a servant..."

"Yes, yes, Guy."

"You are certain her surname is Pulleyn?"

"Aye."

That would explain why she had been at the execution that day all those years ago. "Is she any relation to John Pulleyn, the former headmaster at Saint Peter's?"

Thomas placed a hand on Guy's shoulder. "Friend, I know not her family history. There are countless Pulleyns in York, Harrogate, and all over the north. She may be a relation. I shall endeavour to introduce you so you may ask her yourself."

For the rest of the night, Guy could not keep his focus on tomorrow's purpose. Why fixate on demons when there was the image of an angel in his mind?

Chapter 9—In Which Guy Fawkes Serves Nobility at a Banquet and Gets into a Spot of Bother

G uy Fawkes did not spend the morning revisiting old haunts. He avoided The Shambles, kept away from the crowds at Pavement, and refused to take a route past where his childhood home once stood on Stonegate. Instead, the duo lay low in the morning and reported for duty at King's Manor at three in the afternoon. Guy had borrowed smart attire from Thomas, and where he'd worked hard to build a little bulk in the preceding weeks, the shirt was tight around the chest. They reported to the chief housekeeper who gave them their first duties: to prepare the banqueting hall for the evening's event. Thomas moved about the room with a confidence that showed this was not the first such event he'd worked at, and Guy followed his lead, placing cutlery in the same positions, polishing candlesticks and making sure that goblets and tankards were clean and in place for every guest.

Once they'd readied the hall, it was over to the staff in the kitchens to get everything prepared. Guy, Thomas, and the rest of the team would not be required again until it was time to bring the food out.

While Guy carried out his work, he remained alert for any sign of movement, hoping to get a glimpse of Maria Pulleyn once more. Now that he had a while before any further duties were required, she was all he could think about.

"Do you think–" Guy started.

Thomas rolled his eyes. "That I can take you to Maria now?"

"I did not say that."

"No, but it is what you intended to say, Guy. I had thought so much better of you! Losing your head over a girl when we have work to do."

Guy glanced wistfully at the ceiling rafters. "If I could spend but a moment with her, I will be able to turn my attention to our duty."

Thomas grabbed Guy's jaw and pulled his head down to lock eyes with him. "Or maybe you will fall in love with her so deeply and so truly that you'll be unable to take your eyes from her, doomed to a life spent captivated by her gaze."

Guy stared into space, lost in his thoughts.

Thomas showed his palms. "Alas, Guy, I do not have the freedom of this building, and I'd not know where to find her, anyway. She is, however, sure to be required during the dinner service. Wait, and she will be before you once more. You have, you tell me, only seen her at a distance?"

"That is correct, but she dazzled me even from afar." Guy's head tilted back once more.

Thomas clicked his fingers, drawing Guy's attention to him. "But what if, Guy Fawkes, what if, when you witness this fine woman in close quarters, you find your raven-haired swan to be no more than a crow?"

Guy crossed his arms and shook his head. "That cannot be, Thomas."

Thomas continued to provoke ill thoughts in Guy until such a time he longer had the power to do so, for when Maria Pulleyn entered the room, laden with cloths meant for the banqueting hall, all other thoughts exited Guy's mind.

"Can I help you with those?" Guy asked as she passed.

Maria glanced at Guy but continued walking. "I'm fine, thank you."

Maria's words filtered through his brain, leaving a lingering sense of comfort and warmth. She was more beautiful than she'd been in his dreams, even with her hair tied in a bun and hidden beneath her bonnet, for that allowed her other features to stand out, her slender neck, the shape of her face.

"Though if you could get the door rather than standing there looking like a poor lost child, that'd be nice."

"Sorry," said Guy, but in moving for the door his wrong foot jerked forward first, and he tripped over himself, falling face-first into the panelled wood. He adjusted his footing and pulled open the door, but couldn't bear to look her in the eye.

"That went well," Thomas called from across the room.

Guy shook his head and grabbed the door handle.

"You're not following her? Please, tell me you've more sense than that?" Thomas rolled his eyes.

Alas, Guy had already entered the banqueting hall. "You must forgive my clumsiness."

"Must I?" Maria said as she returned to her duties.

"It is not like me to trip over myself in such a way, but you–"

"Do you know where they will seat Walsingham?" Maria glanced at Guy before scrutinising the tables once more.

"I'm sorry, I do not." Guy stared at the floor.

"Never mind."

With that, she headed for the exit.

"It was a pleasure to meet you! I'm Guy Fawkes, by the way."

"A pleasure. You try to stay on those feet of yours, Guy Fawkes." She hurried through the door.

As soon as she passed through the door, Guy headed for the nearest pillar and banged his head against it.

"It went well, I take it?" Thomas stood with his arms folded, grinning.

"I wouldn't say that."

Thomas approached Guy and placed an arm around him. "Alas, we have no time to wallow in your pathetic attempts to woo! We have been summoned to the kitchen."

In the kitchen, the master housekeeper explained his instructions–how the plates were to be carried to tables, the order in which they would deliver them, and the speed at which they would exit once the food was served. On the opposite side, Guy spotted Maria among the servants who were being briefed about their duties, including how one should pour wine.

The first duty was to deliver the pottage to the revellers in the banqueting hall. As soon as the maids had returned from ensuring all had a full cup, the procession of soup and bread commenced. The party, sitting at tables arranged into a horseshoe, was notable for the lavishness of their attire, with many a jerkin and doublet decorated with the finest gold threads, and studded with gems. Each tried to outdo his neighbour with their colour choices. Guy swore he'd never seen so much yellow, red and purple fabric in his entire life. But he did not have time to study for long. He had to place the meal on the table and continue around and out of the room, passing close to the tapestries that hung behind every table. It was to Cecil that he supplied the soup, which was met with a groan. He only had the briefest opportunity to look at Walsingham's sneering face on the opposite side of the horseshoe. His cheeks had hollowed and his hair looked to have thinned. Under his eyes was every sign of turmoil: deep and dark bags, no doubt filled with acts of savagery and debauchery.

No sooner had Guy re-entered the kitchen than the housemaster sent the maids to refill drinks. Every goblet had to be kept brimming. But as Maria passed Guy, she gazed at his feet, and Guy stumbled slightly, bumping into Thomas who turned and gave him a scalding look.

"What next?" Guy whispered.

"As long as you don't get taken from service, we'll have to return to collect the empty bowls before we deliver the next course. What did you hear? Anything of interest?"

Guy looked at his friend, puzzled. "What did I hear? Nothing."

"Were you even trying to make out their conversations?"

"Honestly? I was focusing on the soup."

Thomas over-enunciated the words in mimicry. "The soup?"

"Aye, I didn't want to spill any."

"You didn't want to spill any?" Thomas shook his head.

"No."

"Guy, they can train chimps to do this. They do on the continent." Thomas looked Guy directly in the eye. "We're better than chimps, Guy. We can place a plate and use our ears at the same time."

The housemaster signalled the servers to collect the bowls.

Before joining the line, Thomas looked back at Guy. "This time, do better."

Guy followed Thomas, moved around the tables and collected Robert Cecil's bowl, trying to overhear snippets of conversation as he progressed around the room.

Soon enough, they were back in the kitchen. Thomas once more turned to reprimand Guy. "You've got to be more subtle."

"I thought I was being subtle."

The housemaster sent the maids to keep the goblets brimming with wine.

"You walked with your head drooped to one side." Thomas mocked Guy's pose.

Guy leant on Thomas's forearm to shove him upright. "I was trying to listen."

"Go on. Tell me. What did you learn?"

Guy smiled with the pride of a toddler showing his parents what he'd done in a potty for the first time. "The man next to Cecil said it was a pleasant pottage and something about the price of wheat."

Thomas's eyes became large. "What about the price of wheat?"

"I don't know. Something."

Thomas huffed. "Was it rising or falling? That's sellable information."

"I shall keep my ears open."

"Aye, and your head straight."

"If you're such an expert, what have you discovered?"

Thomas took a deep breath. "Baron Willoughby has brought considerable riches with him. I know not for what purpose. Sir Hugh Cholmondeley looks uncomfortable among this company and is making little conversation."

Guy stared at him. "How do you know who these people are?"

"How don't you? You'd told me you went to school?"

"The schools that you and I attended had very different educational purposes." Guy thought once more of Pulleyn as the maids returned.

Maria stopped close to Guy. "How are you enjoying your service so far, Guy Fawkes?"

Surprised at being addressed, Guy's mouth dropped open, but no words came.

"Whatever is the matter with you?" asked Maria. "Tripping over your own feet *and* tongue-tied?"

That was the worst thing Maria could have said while Pulleyn was on his mind, for, all he could picture was what he'd done to his old headmaster, how he'd taken a knife and sliced through his tongue. He babbled some unintelligible noise and Maria returned to the company of the other maids.

Once more, the housemaster indicated it was time for service to resume. The second course was a plate of cold meats: sliced ham, roast beef, and ox tongue. Tongue. Not what he wanted to see on the plate before him. He had to focus on his listening instead. He tried to walk without looking at the plate. If they could train chimps to do it on the continent, he could make it around the table without looking at something which made him feel bilious. He placed Cecil's plate, looked away, and kept his eyes on the ground as he made his way out.

"So, what news?" Thomas asked him.

Guy stared blankly at his friend for a moment. He'd been distracted by the dish of tongue, but he had heard something. "Someone mentioned that Everard Digby had sacked his household staff for losing his son, also named Everard."

Guy expected a reprimand for the inferior information, but Thomas stroked his chin.

"Anything else?" Thomas asked.

"He'd been hiding in some secret alcove... is this important information?"

"All information has the potential to be important if you know how to interpret it."

Guy pondered the seemingly useless information. "What can you tell from that?"

Thomas sighed. "Digby's home clearly has priest holes. He may be hiding Jesuit priests."

Guy's eyes grew large. "You'd not sell him out?"

Thomas looked one way then the other. "No, but if someone is seeking an ally, I know where to find one. Now, onto more profitable topics. I heard Richmond ask Cecil a question about the next appointment of Secretary of State. Did you not listen for the response?"

"Alas, I did not."

Thomas shook his head. "An awful lot is going on in there tonight. Members of the Dudley family are here, so it's clear Durham is still an important part of the Northern strategy. The presence of Warthill suggests Walsingham is expanding his council."

"Anyone else we should be wary of?"

Thomas winced. "There's another face I recognise, but I'm not sure what he's doing here. I believe he's a playwright."

"Where's he sitting?"

"About five to the left of Walsingham—the one with the wandering eyes, but I'd avoid making eye contact if I were you."

They continued the process, taking out food and later collecting empty plates, but it was not until after delivering plates of delicate, golden and flaky pastries that Guy had anything significant to report. "It's not much," he whispered, "but Cecil mentioned a forthcoming meeting with the Earl of Shrews-bury regarding matters of succession."

Thomas grinned. "That's more like it. I knew you had it in you, Guy."

"What more have you learned?"

Thomas tapped his side. "Plenty to put coin in my pocket, Guy. Plenty to put coin in my pocket."

"And you'll not share?"

"With you? I've shared my knowledge on how to gain knowledge. Is that not profit enough?"

"Aye, I suppose I shall have to be satisfied."

"Aye. You will."

They remained silent until it was time to collect the dessert plates. The maids were still in the banqueting hall, the need to refill goblets constant for some of the thirstier guests. With less haste, Guy could take more in. He noted the ripple of the tablecloth. A head poked out, a mammal, perhaps a weasel. So, there was at least one man present with demonic interests, for that was a familiar.

As he approached Cecil to collect his plate, he spied Maria across the room, approaching Walsingham's table with the skin of wine under her arm. Unlike all the other servers who poured into the goblet at the table, Maria lifted Walsingham's cup. Guy watched her delicate fingers, but their twitch gave away an illicit act. She'd dropped something into his goblet. Maria poured the wine and placed the goblet in front of Walsingham

Guy knew he should keep moving, but he ignored the annoyed grumbles and the clearings of the throat by those behind him as Walsingham reached for the goblet.

The tablecloth rippled once more, and the weasel breached the cloth. It raced across the floor, its claws skittering on the stone, leapt onto the table, scattering cutlery to the floor, and knocked the goblet over. Wine splashed across the table and dripped onto the floor.

Maria gasped as Walsingham stood and pointed at her. "This wench tried to poison me." His eyes blazed red and the candles burnt bright.

Guy touched the hilt of his sword. Surely, there were too many people here, all the lords of the north and visitors from the south, for Walsingham to summon something.

Two guards rushed to the middle of the room and drew their swords.

"Take her away. Lock her in one of the rooms downstairs." Malevolence dripped from his every word.

"No!" called Guy.

"So, she has an accomplice. Seize him too."

From across the room, Guy watched Thomas shake his head. Guy released the hilt of his sword. They were being taken for questioning. There was no need for an immediate skirmish, not in front of so many people, not when so many other guards were nearby who would join the fray. In private, opportunities would arise—a chance to escape or a one-on-one situation in which Guy would fancy himself able to overcome any adversary.

The guards took Maria first. She raised her hands in surrender. One guard grabbed her right arm, twisted it behind her back, and led her toward the door.

Guy allowed the second guard to lead him off in a similar way.

Walsingham, he noted, was in conversation with a man in a robe, too healthy-looking to be a familiar. He was some kind of advisor or a personal protector. No doubt Walsingham had tasked him with overseeing the prisoners. He pointed and yelled, and the two guards led Guy and Maria down the stairs into the basement. A few well-placed candles offered a little light for anyone sent to the basement to fetch anything, but the light was insufficient for any other purpose. At the end of the room, a narrow corridor led off to several other small rooms. From the lack of comfortable furniture, it was clear their purpose was incarceration when the residence at York Castle wasn't suitable. So, for whom? Those held that had broken no law, those held without examination, without trial, without sentencing. One guard shoved Maria in first, and Guy followed, but only after being stripped of his weapon. The door slammed shut before Maria could turn and try to shove it open once more, and the sound of a bar dropping against the door signalled their imprisonment.

The basement room had no natural light, and closing the door had shut out the light burning from the lantern outside. As they were hurled in, Guy had observed a trio of low stools, but no other furniture in the room.

"Save your energy," Guy said as Maria continued to try to budge the door.

She gave the door a final kick. "Quite the day you're having, isn't it, Guy Fawkes?"

"How'd you mean?" Guy moved to the wall and felt the stone, searching for weakness and finding none.

"First, you trip over your feet when you try to impress me. Then, you're lost for words when I speak to you. Next, you blurt out a pointless protest and get yourself imprisoned with me."

Guy smiled. "Perhaps I did it on purpose."

"No offence, but from what I've seen of you so far, Guy Fawkes, I don't believe you're quick-witted enough to have done that deliberately."

She had him there. He groped for a stool and sat. "You may as well take a seat until company arrives."

Maria banged on the door once more, sighed, and took a seat. "You must regret taking this job."

Guy shook his head, a gesture that Maria could not see in the darkness. "Can I ask you a question?"

"I can't stop you. If I don't like it, I won't answer."

"Are you a relative of John Pulleyn, former headmaster at Saint Peter's School York?"

Maria chuckled. "Do you always speak in such serious sentences, Guy Fawkes?"

"Do you always use people's full names, Maria Pulleyn?"

The softness left her voice. "Who told you my name?"

"Thomas Percy. He told me you sometimes–"

"Shush! They may be listening outside."

Guy listened for a second. There was no sound of movement, no flicker of light from under the door to indicate a presence. "Could you answer my question?"

"Yes."

"Is that yes you can answer, or yes you are?"

Silence hung between them for either seconds or minutes. Guy couldn't tell.

"Yes, I am."

"And today was about revenge?"

There was a scratch of wood on the stone floor as Maria shifted her stool. She was so close, Guy could feel the warmth radiating from her body.

"Walsingham's wasn't the only name on that warrant, but he's the last one standing."

John Pulleyn's death warrant had been signed by Walsingham and Hastings, with Sandys also present to oversee the salvation of his soul. That was the official line. Guy knew them for the evil men they were. Two had already met their death at his hand.

"What was John Pulleyn to you?"

Maria sighed. "My great uncle. He showed me kindness in times of need. They'd brutalised him before the hanging, and left him to die such a horrible death on the end of a rope."

Guy remembered the day on Knavesmire well. "And you ran to the scaffold and pulled on his legs."

"You were there?"

"Aye. I thought they'd kill you, too."

Marie sniffed. "When I saw him suffering, I ran to help."

"I admired that."

"You know," Maria swallowed back her grief, "they even cut his tongue off in his last days."

Guy took a deep breath. "Aye."

"You knew him, too?"

"I was a pupil at the school."

"There's not too many that say that with fondness. I take it you weren't familiar with the birch?"

Guy chuckled. "First day. It taught me a lesson all right. We got on well after."

"Did you know the others that signed his death warrant?"

"I drew a blade across Hastings' throat."

"You? The man who trips over his own feet?"

Guy was silent for a moment, revelling in the comfort of being in Maria's presence. "When I saw you, I lost control. You've been a part of my memory since that day."

A scraping of wood as someone lifted the bar from the other side of the door cut Guy short. In came two guards, both holding lanterns, which they placed on the wall. Between them was the man who Walsingham had instructed. With a stern look on his face, he brought a cudgel onto one palm with a slap, indicative of his malicious intentions.

Chapter 10—In Which Guy Fawkes Makes an Enemy in Robert Dudley

Perhaps the gentleman before Guy thought he looked intimidating. Guy, however, how been in so many worse scrapes in his life that he did not react to the implied threat of the cudgel. His greatest concern was looking foolish in front of Maria. That would not do. He stared at the man before him, the lanterns illuminating him. While his clothing was not as lavish as that of his master, the orange detailing on his cloak indicated he came from significant money. He was a young man, no older than his mid-twenties, with a prominent forehead, with tight auburn curls framing his face. A thick English moustache, well-groomed, hid the corners of his mouth.

When he spoke, it was in a voice that dripped privilege. "Allow me to introduce myself. I'm Robert Dudley, here tonight as an advisor to Sir Francis Walsingham. I shall advise him on what he should do with you." He grinned showing his sparkling teeth too white, too straight to be real, "But I don't want you to make this easy for me." He ran the fingers of one hand along the length of his cudgel. "If you confess, I don't get to use this." He brought the weapon thudding into his palm.

Guy glanced at the two guards. Both were in standard armour and had swords sheathed. Neither looked formidable and both had bored expressions.

Dudley sat on the remaining small chair.

"You first." He nodded toward Guy. "Why were you here tonight?"

"To serve the soup."

"Excellent," said Dudley. "So, you *do* want to play." He swung the cudgel toward Guy's knee.

Guy knew better than to stop it now. Instead, he dropped the knee slightly, so the weapon clashed with the flesh of his leg instead of the bone of his knee. He cried out, mocking greater pain. Guy glanced up, catching the orange burst in Dudley's eyes. So, he too was in league with demons.

"You came here to spy, did you not?"

Guy saw no harm in answering this one, in mocking weakness. "To spy, yes."

"And your lady here?"

"I'm not his lady." Maria responded so quickly that it needled Guy. Was it so horrific a thought? But... no, why was he getting distracted?

Dudley stood. He stepped close to Maria, placed a finger beneath her chin and indicated she should stand. "Did you, or did you not put poison into Walsingham's cup?"

Maria stepped back, so she was against the wall. "I did not."

"Liar!" Spittle flew from between Dudley's lips. "We spotted you drop something into his goblet."

Maria tilted her head to meet his gaze. "Who's 'we'?"

"Answer," Dudley hissed.

"There was no poison." Maria's voice didn't so much as quaver.

"Enough!" Dudley's voice became deeper and his eyes glowed. He raised the cudgel above his head.

Guy lifted his weight from the stool and grabbed it, swinging it through the air and into Dudley's arm, knocking him off balance and into one of his guards. Guy twisted and thrust the feet of the stool into the other guard, pinning him to the wall.

A knock came from the other side of the door, followed by a voice. "Come quick, Dudley, there's a matter upstairs which requires your urgent attention."

Dudley stood, and the torches flared. His eyes were bright orange now, the skin on his face tight, forcing him into a grimace, elongated canines standing out. He grabbed Guy with one hand and hurled him against the back wall.

"Show no mercy," Dudley said to his guards as his face shifted to its normal form. He opened the door.

From his upside-down position, twisted in a heap by the wall, it took Guy a second to recognise Thomas.

"What's going on?" asked Dudley.

"A revolt!" Thomas cried. "The commoners are surrounding the Manor."

The door slammed shut, leaving Guy and Maria with the two guards. Guy struggled to his feet and moved alongside Maria.

There was a thump against the door, and the room grew hot, and an orange light flashed from beneath the door. The two guards looked at one another, their faces contorting as if their jaws had spontaneously dislocated. They rose off the ground, the space beneath them swirling with dust. Their flesh turned white, and their eyes filled with the deepest black. Their mouths remained open, tongues flopping out like dead fish, and they spoke, the voices radiating from both bodies, but sharing only one voice. "We'll peel your skin! We'll grind your bones to paste. We'll suck on your souls!"

The nails on their hands grew long, like talons, and they flew, arms stretching out toward Guy and Maria.

"Thomas, are you there?" called Guy as he ducked, pulling Maria down with him.

As the possessed soldiers passed over them, Thomas opened the door.

The demons screeched as Guy reached for Maria's hand. She was one step ahead, already barrelling for the open door. He dove after her and together, they bundled into the corridor, barging past Thomas, who stood, staring in dismay at the floating guards. They turned and flew once more toward their targets. Thomas flung the door closed, and as the three of them fled, the wooden door exploded behind them to the sound of more frenzied wails.

"Quick," called Guy, continuing into the main chamber of the basement as the demonic guards followed. Guy scanned the room looking for his sword. The presence of demons made it easier to spot, for his blade had gained a slight glowed when demons were near. It lay on top of a barrel in the corner.

"Stay low," Guy called as the demons entered the main chamber.

They parted, one flying for Maria. She ducked and rolled out of the way.

Guy grabbed his scimitar and slashed at the other, but his blade swept through the air without making contact. He blurted the incantation, gripping his blade tight as it lengthened, and blue flame burned at its edge.

The demons came together once more and spoke again. "Give in to eternal damnation. Your consumption is inevitable."

Guy eyed Thomas. As much as he knew it wasn't an appropriate time to say I told you so, he struggled to resist temptation.

One guard raised an arm, and the shadows in the room grew long. From a candle, a flaming figure rose and marched toward Thomas. He gasped and turned the other way, where another demon awaited.

"Your dagger!" called Guy.

As Thomas pulled the weapon out, Guy chanted the words, and it flashed, causing the demon to whirl away, seeking shelter. Thomas stared at his engorged weapon with huge eyes.

"Don't just look at it," Guy called. "Protect yourself."

Guy ran at the flame figure and slashed his sword. Instead of feeling any contact, the blade passed right through. It had no form. It could not be cut. It could not be wounded.

The flaming figure reached for Guy, only for Maria to grab him by the shoulder and spin him around to safety. "We've got to get out of here," Maria called. She turned to the stairs.

"Not that way," Guy said. "Unless you want to come face-to-face with the worst of the Council of the North."

"But the revolt...?"

"A fabrication, I'm afraid," called Thomas. "I had to get Dudley away from you."

The flaming creature moved to the corner of the room, where barrels were stacked against the wall. As it came into contact with them, they erupted into flame. The demons hissed, poised and ready to attack. One swung for Thomas who awkwardly swiped with his dagger. It was enough to put the demon guard off.

"This way," said Guy, pointing back to where the guards had imprisoned them.

"Are you mad?" Thomas asked.

"While you were studying earls and lords and barons, I was studying the secret passages of York. There's another way out."

In truth, Guy was uncertain. Secret passages had always been Kit's passion, but Guy's father had significant documentation on King's Manor, and that documentation he'd died for. So, when Kit had spoken of subterraneous passages leading from King's Manor, Guy had listened.

Guy spied a low, half door at the end of the corridor. The two demons moved once more, taking opposite paths, one heading to block the corridor, the other covering the stairs. The flaming figure continued to seek combustible materials, starting blazes on wood piles, containers and anything else he could find, causing smoke to billow through the cellar.

"Follow close and cover your heads." Guy took off for the passage. He was familiar with the demon's movements now. He expected when it would swoop and when it would twist away. A yard from the corridor, he took a step to the left and slashed in an arc exactly where the demon swirled to. The blade opened its belly, and the contents slopped onto the ground in a sizzling heap as its body continued, spraying fluid from every orifice. Demonic cries filled the chamber. Guy rushed to the end of the corridor and kicked open the low door. On the other side, a passage led down.

"Get in," called Guy. "I'll grab a lantern."

Maria, her clothes covered in demonic goo, headed in first. Thomas, equally drenched in viscera, followed, scowling at Guy.

Guy ducked back into the room in which Dudley had interrogated him, grabbed the lantern from the wall, and returned to the corridor. The remaining demon careered toward him, spinning with its hands outstretched like some enormous, maniacal skewer.

Guy focused on his blade. With the lantern in one hand, he held his sword out before him in the other. He calculated the length of his arms and the blade together were longer than the demon guard's arms, talons included. All he had to do was hold steady.

The frantic spin of the demon took its fingers first into the blade, and as they struck the flaming sword, they flew in all directions, some clattering with the ceiling, some smashing into the ground. Chucks of arm came next. It was only when Guy's blade came into contact with the skull that his arms tightened. He pushed forward with both legs to hold steady, and, with a crack, the skull gave way and the creature burst. Guy barely had time to shield his face from the liquid explosion of the demon corpse. Visceral slop decorated the corridor: chucks of sinew clung to the brickwork, and blood ran in thick rivulets along the floor.

In the main chamber, the fire demon ran, trying to ignite everything which it came into contact with. It spotted Guy in the corridor and dashed toward him to where the floor in the corridor was flooded with bubbling, demon blood. A sizzle accompanied each step as the fire demon raced forward, oblivious to the extinguishing effect the blood had on its lower parts. Liquid gore covered the slope. Guy used the filth-encrusted walls for stability as he ventured toward the end of the corridor. He looked back, but little more than half of the fiery creature remained. He'd extinguish himself long before he could reach them. What a way to go. Guy closed the door behind them, nonetheless.

"Are we okay?" Guy glanced at Maria and Thomas, both wearing clothes thick with blood and other fluids.

"Those guards were flying," Thomas said, his eyes wide.

"Aye, demons, as I warned you." Guy took a step further down the tunnel, thrusting the lantern forward to illuminate the way.

"Their faces..."

"Again, demonic possession. Let's go."

The path was narrow, and they had to move in single file. Thomas and Maria shuffled on in silence behind Guy. As it continued downwards, it became wetter with the need to wade through water up to their knees at some points.

The water, at least, restored Thomas's ability to speak. "Nearly getting me killed by demons wasn't enough for you, hey, Guy? You were determined to get me in one of these grim tunnels."

"Will you admit I was right about the existence of demons and how they've controlled the politics of the north for generations?" Guy asked.

"I have to say, given the evidence of my own two eyes, tonight, you may not be quite so crammed to the tip of your crown with as much dung as you have led me to believe."

"Do I get an apology?" Guy grunted.

In response, Thomas's voice rose a couple of octaves. "Do I get a thank you for saving you from Dudley?"

"Will you two shut up for a moment? Your babbling is driving me insane!" Maria placed her hands on her head and stamped her foot, causing a splash.

From her tone, Guy detected more than frustration. He wanted to bring her comfort. All he managed was a banal question: "I'm sorry. This must have been quite the unexpected turn of events. How are you feeling?"

"How am I feeling? How am I feeling? I feel like a bloody failure. For so long, I wanted nothing more than revenge on Walsingham, but that rat thing..."

"It was a weasel." Guy gritted his teeth as soon as he said it. There was a time and a place to correct someone, and that wasn't it.

Maria's forehead wrinkled and she spoke through gritted teeth. "That *weasel* sprung from nowhere and ruined everything."

Guy knew he shouldn't speak, but couldn't help himself. "It wasn't *exactly* a weasel."

Maria exhaled, noisily indicating her annoyance. "You said it was."

"It was in the form of a weasel, but it was what we call a familiar, a creature that links Walsingham to the demons he serves."

"So, he's one of them too, like the guards?"

It was a complex situation, one difficult to explain to one not acquainted with demon lore. "Not as such. I suspect Walsingham is in league with demons rather than being possessed like the guards. Did your uncle never tell you about any of this?"

Maria swallowed hard. "He always said there was another world out there and he'd tell me when I was older, but," Maria sniffed, "that day never came."

Guy thought about Pulleyn. He'd been reluctant to bring in Guy and Kit so young. Only their foolish antics got them in, so it was little surprise he'd not inducted Maria in demonology while he had the chance.

They walked on in silence for another five minutes, and the path sloped upward once more.

"You know where this leads?" Thomas called from the back.

"You'll see." In truth, Guy had no idea, not until he reached a stone barrier at the end of the corridor.

"You better be able to open that," Maria said.

Guy placed his hand on the stone. Yes, there was only one place he could be. This passage had led him to the place of his nightmares: the crypt at York Minster.

Together, the three of them shoved the stone forward and pulled it to one side. When there was enough room, Guy squeezed through. The crypt was as he remembered it, a series of dingy sepulchres, and a labyrinth of stone sarcophagi. Someone had replaced a number of the covers, but had they also placed the remains of the risen dead back in place? There would be no way to ensure the right parts went in the right places... but who was likely to argue?

"We'd better hurry," Thomas said. "They'll likely know we escaped, and if they know where the tunnel leads, they could well be waiting for us."

"Which way out?" said Maria.

Guy led them around the corner and extinguished their lantern. The exit was clear, with the light coming from the nave of York Minster. If that was lit, it was probable someone was above.

Guy took the stairs and stood before the crypt door. He put his hands against the wood, but he couldn't bring himself to push it open.

"What's wrong?" asked Maria.

What could he tell her? In his mind, he kept a demon trapped here, and he feared what opening the door would do. It was the truth, but it made him sound insane even when balanced against the other strange things they had witnessed.

"Nothing," Guy said.

"Open the door. This one's right. The men at King's Manor are likely to know where we are."

Guy placed his palms against the wood but again could not find the strength.

"Let me." Maria brushed past him on the steps and gave the doors a shove. With a crack, it opened. Blinding light left Guy dazzled and blinking wildly, but Thomas dragged him onward with a frustrated cry.

The three of them ran through the nave and out of the main entrance, ignoring cries from somewhere for them to stop. Whoever they'd upset, (history suggests Archbishop John Piers) may have yelled the word "vandals." but none of them could swear for sure what insults they'd suffered.

Once outside, the trio gasped at the fresh night air, but the sound of a whistle told them they couldn't tarry for long.

"Where now?" asked Thomas.

Leaving the city would be problematic. The guards in the gatehouses liked to stop and question anyone suspicious who passed, and given the rancid demon blood covering them from head to toe, they looked pretty suspicious. Staying where they were meant certain capture.

Again, he thought of Kit. He'd know of a way out. When they used to roam the streets, monitoring illicit activity at the properties purchased by Hastings and Sandys, Kit knew of all of the secret passages. Guy though, could only think of the river as an unmonitored route out of the city. Once beyond the walls they could rest and slip back in inconspicuously the following day; Walsingham's guards would not be paying heed to those entering the city.

Guy mapped out the path of the river in his mind. It passed through the city nearby, to the west close to King's Manor. Exiting that way would not only put them closer to danger, it would also entail swimming upstream. The south exit would be better. He also knew they were looking for three. If they split up, less suspicion would fall upon them. As Guy knew York best, he decided he'd be the one to take a different route.

Guy whispered the plan to Thomas and Maria as they loitered in the shadows. He directed them to the Ouse Bridge where they'd wait in the cover of the grain store. Guy watched Thomas and Maria leave together, cursing himself for a plan which separated him from Maria so soon after meeting her.

Once he could no longer hear their feet on the path, Guy took off along those once-familiar streets, streets on which he'd walked with great vigilance so many times before. There were few people around at that hour, and he kept to the shadows to avoid suspicion. He listened for the sound of footfall, which helped him determine his route. When as far away as he planned to get, a whistle sounded. He froze, fearing the worst. Had Walsingham's guards caught Maria and Thomas? No, the whistle sounded from the west, a couple of streets over. His companions travelled south. Still, he quickened his pace, remaining far from where the whistle was likely to draw more guards. He slowed before the bridge. This was often a point where guards would stop and ask questions, but the guard's emergency call had drawn them away, clearing Guy's path. Within a minute, he was at the riverbank behind the grain store alongside Maria and Thomas.

"Ready?" he asked.

"After you," said Thomas, giving Guy an assistive nudge into the water.

Chapter 11—In Which Guy Fawkes and Friends Return to Scotton

For a man associated with one of the most diabolical plots in the history of time, Guy had to confess that as far as plans went, this one was terrible. He clambered out of the river once he'd emerged on the other side of York's walls. There were no guards stationed there, but it wasn't pleasant terrain, and only got worse further south with the boggy marsh of Knavesmire. While there were plenty of trees to hide within, there were few dwellings. But sometimes the simplest plan, however terrible, is the right one when time and options are short. There's no point formulating a genius idea when already in irons.

Thomas wriggled onto the bank next to him.

"Where's Maria?" Guy asked.

"So that's how it is now. No 'how are you, Thomas?' after that plunge into the icy cold water?"

Maria gasped as she emerged from the water a little farther along the bank. Guy held out a hand to help her, but she didn't see it in the darkness. That's what Guy told himself.

"So, what now?" Thomas asked as he stood dripping by the water.

Guy pointed. "We make for the trees and build a fire."

"Won't someone spot it out here?" Thomas asked.

Guy scanned the horizon as best he could in darkness. "Not if we build it right."

Guy led the way, selecting a spot where there was a dip in the ground and the layout of the trees made screening the fire possible.

With a couple of branches, Guy constructed a weak frame.

He pulled off his saturated jacket and breeches and draped them over the wood. "Thomas, I'll be needing the same from you."

Once the screen was in place, Guy set about lighting a fire. He ignored the discomfort of his wet hose and shirt clinging to his body. The sooner they had fire, the sooner he could banish the cold. Despite the wetness of the area, the fallen branches had been there long enough to have sufficiently dried out in places where they weren't in direct contact with the ground, and soon Guy had a small fire going.

Maria's teeth chattered as she stood with her arms crossed.

Realisation struck Guy with a pair of quick blows: he wished to help Maria, but he was powerless to do so in any meaningful way. "I'll not suggest you remove your dress, but it might help if you sit as close as you can bear to the fire, to dry out."

"No, it's okay. It needs to dry. I'll remove it."

Maria had lost her apron in the river, and her dress was heavy with water. She struggled out of the heavy material.

Neither Guy nor Thomas looked Maria's way, staring into the distance instead.

"It's daft, you two trying to avert your gaze. You'll crick your necks."

Both men faced one another instead. Was Thomas's head turning toward Maria? Guy cleared his throat, drawing Thomas's attention, and indicated that they should sit.

Maria sat in her smock and petticoat, shivering, unable to get warm.

Guy checked the frame once more, and removed his jacket. For a considerable time, he held it over the flames, turning it one way then the other. After several minutes, he checked it carefully. While damp in places, it held a degree of warmth. He handed it to Maria. She nodded and pulled it over her shoulders.

"You two try to get some sleep. I'll keep watch," Guy said.

"You don't need to play the hero to show off to the young lady. We could all do with some sleep," Thomas said.

Guy blushed.

"He's right," Maria said. "If there's anyone or anything out there, we'll hear it before it gets close."

Guy agreed and rested against a tree. He had no intention of falling asleep, though. He was afraid of what he'd find in his dreams.

• • • •

WHEN DAYLIGHT ARRIVED, Guy stood and stretched. Having fallen into a light sleep, it took a second to shake the waking day into himself. He stood and felt the clothes on the frame. They'd dried out in most places as much as they were going to, carrying only the damp of the early morning. And while those clothes would never be sufficient for polite company again, they no longer looked like they'd bathed in blood. He pulled his breeches back on.

Thomas roused next with a stretch.

"We need to fetch our horses as soon as possible," Guy said.

"Aye," said Thomas. "But collecting our gear from the tavern is out of the question. They may know where we stayed. Will it be safe to collect the horses?"

Guy had left them at his usual stable, a place where he was known by the name Blake, not Fawkes. There was no way they link those horses to the events at King's Manor. There was no way he'd leave Pewter behind. "Aye. Would you like me to venture in first to test the process? I know the city better than you."

"No. I'm famished. I'll head in, get some breakfast, and bring my horse out through the east gate."

As Thomas walked away, Maria stretched out. He didn't let his eyes linger on her the way he wanted to. She didn't need that after the evening they'd had.

"Sleep okay?" he asked.

"Better than you."

"You think?"

"Every time I woke, your eyes were open."

Guy moved over to the frame and checked Maria's dress, avoiding conversation about his desire to avoid sleep. "Aye."

"Is Thomas collecting the horses?" Maria joined him at the frame. Where they'd wrung much of the water from the dress and placed it close to the fire it had mostly dried, though it would never quite be the same shape again.

"Only his. We don't wish to arouse suspicion."

"Then what?" Maria shook out the dress.

"We return to Scotton."

Marie pulled the dress over her head, shivering as the cold hit her again. "I cannot return so easily. I work at King's Manor. Or worked. I can't go back. I can't get my clothes or even my money."

"We'll take you back to Scotton with us."

"I am not some trophy you can carry over your shoulder like the spoils of war, Guy Fawkes."

Guy smiled at the way she drew out the syllables of his name. "Well, we can take you back to Harrogate if that's what you desire." He threw another branch on the fire and gave it a poke to wake the flames, hoping the renewed warmth would stop Maria shaking.

"I'm sure Scotton will suffice."

"Can you ride?"

Maria crossed her arms. "Aye. I can ride."

Maria looked down at herself, then at Guy. "With both you and Thomas looking like serving men, and me dressed as a maid, we're not well disguised."

"When I go into York, I shall find us something with which we can cover ourselves."

Maria nodded. "You look tired."

"I am." Guy sighed and turned his gaze to the ground.

"Are you sure you don't want to sleep until Thomas returns? I'll watch over you."

Guy didn't fear his dreams when he knew Maria watched over him. He closed his eyes, and soon he was asleep.

• • • •

GUY OPENED HIS EYES to find a hunk of bread thrust into his face. He had an idea something vicious had been circling his thoughts, but whenever it came too close, Maria's presence kept it at bay. He realised whatever happened, he had one desire: to keep Maria in his life. At the same moment, he realised the next thing he had to do was walk away from her.

He made his journey into York as fast as possible, breaking into a run at several points until he was at the city walls. While guards scrutinised anyone looking to leave the city, they paid little heed to those entering. Guy's first port of call was Pavement. There was always a merchant present who traded in clothing. Guy had sufficient coin to buy three meagre robes and leave him enough to purchase a horse. When Guy collected Pewter, he asked the stable boy about the best place to purchase a horse. He told him of a stable a twenty-minute ride north. Perfect.

It was three hours before he was back with Maria and Thomas. Guy chose to circumnavigate the city rather than risk passing by its guards once more. He handed them their cloaks and the reins of a black mare to Maria. "For you," he said. "I chose her because she reminded me of the colour of your hair."

Maria smiled. She stroked the beast's mane. It huffed and curled its top lip, revealing its large teeth. "Thank you. Does her smile remind you of me, too?"

Guy's mouth fell open, but his mind hunted for a response without success. Instead, he stroked the horse's mane, which only made her expose those enormous teeth again.

Thomas placed one hand on his shoulder. "Isn't it time we got as far away from here as possible?"

• • • •

EN ROUTE BACK TO SCOTTON, Thomas solved one of Maria's problems and with it one of Guy's too; he invited her to become staff in his home. His mother, he alleged, had been considering taking on a new servant for some time, to help out their belligerent housekeeper and he would be thrilled if she would take on the role. Guy had suspected that she would consider it charity and refuse, but much to Thomas's pleasure, and more so to Guy's, she accepted. He almost lost his balance and fell from his horse when he realised he'd be able to see Maria regularly.

But when Guy returned home, conflict awaited. Anne stood in the kitchen, arms folded, a sullen look on her face. With the household servants in proximity, she could not clear her mind as quickly as she desired. She marched him upstairs to his room and checked out of the window to make sure Elizabeth was still in the garden. "You're selfish, you know, Guy."

Guy held up his hands. "I've done nothing wrong."

"Please. I can smell the demon blood on your clothes. How could you go off hunting without me?"

"Is that what this is about?"

Anne stared with piercing eyes. "Aye, it's what it's about. I thought we were a team."

"It's not like that, Anne. It wasn't supposed to be blood and mayhem."

Anne rolled her eyes. "With you, it's always blood and mayhem."

"But Thomas said–"

"Thomas, Thomas, Thomas. Since you met him, you've not given me a second thought. Aye. You'll eat my bread, but you'll not raise a sword with me."

"You know I never want to put you in danger."

"But you don't give me the choice." Anne's eyes blazed.

"If father was here, he'd be furious. I have to look out for you."

"No, Guy. I've not had a father for a long time. I don't need a father. When we fought, side-by-side, that's when I felt alive."

"But what if you got hurt?"

Anne prodded Guy in the chest. "And you know I can handle myself. It's unfair for you to go off in this way. You gave me the gold angel to look after. You told me our grandmother had meant this life for us."

Guy rubbed the spot Anne had prodded. "You've got your baking, now. I thought that made you happy."

"You really are clueless, you know that?" She shoved Guy again, and he fell back to sit on his bed. "Aye, I love to bake. It's relaxing. I love to take those ingredients and create something, especially when I can share it. It feels like I'm giving something back, but my only place isn't chained to the kitchen, you know."

Guy stared at the floor. She was right. He had let her down.

"How can I do it all, Anne? How can I keep you safe and fight by your side?"

Anne sat on the bed beside her brother. "Let me keep myself safe. Let me have a choice. That's all I'm asking."

Guy nodded. "I will."

Anne smiled and shifted her tone. "And who did you ride back into town with?"

Guy looked at the floorboards and felt about five years old. "Thomas..."

"Thomas and...?"

Guy couldn't help a smile spread across his face. "Maria."

"What's that on your face?"

"What?" He touched his cheek.

"You've gone bright red."

"Haven't." Guy could feel the heat in his cheeks.

"So, you went out hunting demons and now you've entered a courtship with a young lady?"

"It wasn't like that." But even as Guy thought of Maria, he couldn't stop his smile spreading.

"Maybe I was better out of this one."

"We're not courting."

"Nay, but you'd like to be."

Guy gazed at the floor again. Aye, he would.

Chapter 12—In Which Dudley's Determination Forces Guy Fawkes into Exile

Whe one is smitten with another, even if they are clueless when it comes to courtship, they find ways to be in the company of the one they admire. As such, Guy took full advantage of the opportunity to visit Maria regularly over the next few months, and another summer arrived and swiftly departed. While she was always pleasant and polite, she kept conversations short, often excusing herself to complete her duties. Guy longed to speak to Maria about Walsingham, and about the part he'd played in gaining revenge on the other men responsible for bringing death upon her great uncle. But whenever they spoke, it went little further than formalities. That night in York had shown Guy the strength of what he faced. How had Maria coped knowing that the man she wanted revenge on had so much power around him, knowing he was almost untouchable? Had the weight of impossibility vanquished her desire for revenge, or did the flame burn stronger than ever?

Guy's excuse for his visits was always to converse with Thomas, who had kept himself abreast of the political situation, while avoiding visits to York. Walsingham frequently visited King's Manor as part of his work with the Council of the North, but it was far from his preferred city. He was often met with opposition, for while York was not unruly, the town folk would not allow themselves to be cowed.

To gain access to those of great wealth, Thomas had allied himself with several reputable tailors, meaning to get into the business. In what other profession could one get so close to powerful figures in vulnerable positions? Often, he found Thomas lingering in rooms where Maria busied herself. He'd be in the library while she dusted the shelves, or in the parlour while she polished the silver on the sideboard. Guy would often come in to catch them in conversation about fine clothes, a conversation Guy found himself unable to engage in.

One such afternoon, when Guy found Thomas and Marie conversing in the library, Guy tried to interject in the conversation without success. He was thankful when the housekeeper called Maria away, allowing Thomas to change the subject. "I've news about Robert Dudley."

Guy wasn't listening. He had watched Maria leave. He turned and noted Thomas's eyes on her too. "Why does Maria always leave so soon after I arrive?"

Thomas smirked. "One would imagine she finds the attraction to you too much to handle and simply has to flee."

Guy smiled.

"Either that or she fears falling afoul of our head housekeeper if she's caught chatting inanely with you."

Guy continued to stare into the hall.

Thomas clicked his fingers. "Attention Guy. I have important news about Dudley."

Guy grimaced. How he hated to be reminded of Dudley. Maybe Thomas had good news for him. He hoped Queen Elizabeth had called Dudley into her service and sent him to war in Europe. Alas, that was not the case.

"He has been heard to speak your name." Any sense of humour had left Thomas's voice.

Guy sighed. "Where?"

"As recently as a fortnight ago, I have a report of him in Wetherby. He is asking in taverns if anyone knows of a young man by the name of Guy Fawkes."

Guy shook his head. "He seeks not the name Thomas Percy?"

"I was not fool enough to go around shouting my name attempting to woo a young lady."

Guy craned his neck in case Maria was anywhere in the hall's vicinity, visible from his position.

"Guy!" Thomas whistled to regain his attention. "He's likely to find his way to Scotton eventually."

"So what?"

"Do not doubt there's a purse on offer for the right information. There are good people here, but I'd wager there are more that could use a bit of extra coin."

Guy sat upright. "What would you do?"

"Me? I'd flee. I don't want my head on a spike. What would I do if I were you? That's what you're asking, isn't it? Which means I'd have to put that fool head of yours on and think like you." Thomas feigned consideration. He stroked his chin. He tapped his temple. Then, he held up his finger and opened his mouth as the answer hit him. "I'd ride to York wielding a banner emblazoned with the words 'I'm Guy Fawkes; come and get me.'"

"That's what you imagine I'd do?"

"Perhaps you're not that much of a fool. You can rarely tell when I'm talking figuratively with you and when I'm being honest, though. I'm saying you're the type to confront a problem head-on."

Guy rubbed his forehead. "And that's what you believe I should do this time?"

"Will you listen?"

"Will you tell me what you think I should do?"

Thomas stared at Guy, ensuring he had his full attention. "Run."

Guy glanced toward the door, hoping Maria was nearby. "Never."

"See?"

"Do you have any more advice?"

"You won't run, that I know, but maybe you pretend to do so. Create an ambush."

A smile returned to Guy's lips. "This sounds like a plan I can get behind."

"Winter's coming. Make it known in the village that you'll be away for a period, planning to return for lambing season. When Dudley calls, someone's bound to blab your location. Sit tight and be ready."

Guy's sheep would be safe. Bainbrigge would ensure that. This plan was feasible. "Where? Do you have a location in mind?"

"Aye. Brimham Rocks. We keep the land there with a flock of sheep on it. There's a shepherd's hut there."

"And the shepherd?"

"He'll be happy for a brief respite."

Guy considered his options. If Dudley came to Scotton, it would put everyone he knew in peril. "And you're sure this is a good idea?"

"Aye. He'll come for you. If he comes here, people will give you away in a second. Your family is here, and he can use them against you."

"Okay, I'm in." It wasn't only his family Guy was thinking of. He wanted to keep Dudley as far away from Maria as possible.

• • • •

AS SOON AS GUY RETURNED home, he found Anne in the kitchen at the long table, her back to him. She hummed a tune as she mixed ingredients in a bowl. Guy watched as she lifted the spoon from the mixture and gave it a shake. Anne poured a little milk into her bowl and stirred once more.

"Anne, I need to speak to you."

Anne turned, the bowl in her hand. Some of the mixture plopped from the spoon back into the bowl. "I can tell by the look in your eye I'm not going to like this."

Guy stepped toward his sister. "Listen for a moment, Anne."

"Don't tell me you're going off on another adventure, leaving me here again, Guy. Don't do that to me." She plonked the bowl down.

"It's not like that, Anne. But... I do have to go away."

"Then what is it like?"

"Remember what I told you about the last time? About York?"

Anne folded her arms.

"Dudley's coming after me."

"Why would you think about going away without me then? We can fight him and whatever army of demons he has off together."

"Thomas has this plan..."

Anne grabbed the spoon and pointed it at Guy. "Don't tell me you're picking him over me again!" Batter fell from the spoon into a dollop on the floor.

"It's not like that." Guy explained Thomas's plan, while Anne huffed. She distracted herself from her frustration by giving her batter another stir and preparing a tin.

"So, you see why it would make no sense if you came with me. Dudley would be suspicious."

Anne placed the cake in the charcoal-burning stove and dusted her hands. "I do get it, Guy. I swear though, there will come a time when I won't put up with being left behind anymore. And I hope you understand that." She left Guy alone in the kitchen. How he wished he didn't have to go through with this plan alone, but what other option did he have?

• • • •

WITHIN THREE DAYS, Guy, with map in hand, and Thomas's vague instructions, was riding as far east as he'd ever been into the Yorkshire Dales. The view here was like nothing he'd seen before: miles and miles of undisturbed countryside, with only the odd remote farmhouse to signify any human activity this far from civilisation.

Guy followed the roads as indicated, though it became more and more clear how seldom travellers used these routes, perhaps only seasonally for driving livestock. He knew he was on the right track when he encountered what Thomas had called, "A peculiar formation of rocks."

It was as if God himself had played a strange balancing game with Mother Nature. The rock formations looked simultaneously deliberate and yet chaotic. They were like hulking beasts, calcified by time and nature. Some were many times his height, others he could climb onto the backs of with ease. The spaces between them created a maze. Some of the narrow gaps between them led into huge clearings, others disappeared underground into what looked like a network of caves.

The terrain itself also rose and fell, wild rock beasts petrified across it all. In the lower places, moss covered the moist ground. Higher up, trees sprouted, life having forced itself through the solid rock. Winter had stripped them bare, with branches twisted at ugly angles as they'd spent generations seeking sunlight through gaps in the rock. This was a magical place, of that Guy was certain. The pungent odour indicated how close he was to the essence of nature. He suspected someone in tune with the order of the earth had harnessed its power to shape the stones. Some rocks contained strange markings, perhaps ancient writing carved by druids from a bygone era. Maybe they contained the secret to finding contentment in life, contentment Guy could find if Dudley's pursuit ended.

Guy continued along the path, which took him close to one particular rock formation. As Pewter trotted by, Guy brushed the stone with his fingers. First, there was only the cold, but there was something more, a spark within ignited and radiated an ancient heat source from within. Thomas had told him it was not more than a ten-minute walk beyond the tallest of the rocks. Guy passed over a peak and came around the corner to discover his abode for the time being, a rudimentary wooden shack built against the rock, right next to a cave that disappeared far into the rock. The bleating of his companions, the sheep, greeted him. He smiled. He'd had worse company.

Thomas had sent one of his men to ride out to release the current shepherd from his duties, so when Guy reached the shack, it was deserted. He pushed open the door. It was a simple abode with two separate rooms. One was the main living space comprising a fireplace, a table and a pair of chairs, and some shelves on which a few cooking utensils sat. The other contained little more than a bed and a small dresser for possessions. Thomas had informed Guy that he'd find certain tools and supplies kept in the dry parts of the cave next door.

As ridiculous as Thomas's plan had sounded, it was likely that Dudley would come for him, and here gave him a good chance of defending himself without drawing his family into it. As bad as he felt about leaving Anne out of another plan (augmented by their conversation in the kitchen) he knew it was for the best. Whatever she said, he still held onto the idea that he had to protect her. In Scotton, she had a chance to escape the nonsense of a life of hunting demons. If he could put Dudley down, maybe he, too, could escape. Maybe that's all he needed to do to give him a chance at peace.

And yet, with Maria, he hoped for another kind of life, the kind of life many people in the small places like Scotton lived, a life in which they could have a home of their own and work the land. Together, they could bring a new life into this world.

But once more, doubts stirred. Could he bring a child into a world ruled over by evil? Would that be fair? Was it an impossible dream to defeat all evil and bring a child into a pure world? What was it Francis Ingleby had been so sure of? Hope lies with the Spanish. And yet their ships lay at the bottom of the North Sea. Some hope that was.

Guy stopped himself from thinking. He had weeks to do that. All he had to prioritise was how he was to defend himself. He would train his body. His sword, he placed on the table. He would train his mind. He took a weighty tome from his knapsack and placed it on the table. After the journey, he would feast, and then explore the magnificent rocks that surrounded what he now called home.

Chapter 13—In Which Guy Fawkes Encounters Isolation

Guy Fawkes had, for as long as he remembered, always had people around him if he needed them. When lying in bed, injured after his encounter with Master Leonard, Anne was by his side. After the death of his Uncle Thomas, when he'd travelled far from home to Saint Robert's Cave, he'd had Ghost. After his father's death, when he spent much of his time alone in the hayloft of his uncle's barn, his family was always right there beneath him if he needed them. At Brimham Rocks, however, Guy was alone, unless he counted the sheep.

Days passed with no sign of Dudley, no sign of any other human. Guy had taken to climbing only the backs of the rocks to find the highest vantage point. Some rock formations were simple climbs with plenty to grab onto. Others were smooth and provided a challenge. Faces appeared in each and personalities formed. Some formations were close together, like a family, allowing him to leap from the top of one member of the family across to another, while some stood as friendless monoliths. From one such rock, he'd look out for any approach from the east. It should have been cold at that time of the year, open to the elements, but those rocks held some kind of mystical heat.

Throughout the area, Guy practised with his sword and read from his books. He remembered the teachings of the past, using his weaker hand, backing himself into awkward positions among the rock and running through scenarios. With the books, he reminded himself of the different malevolent spirits. While he had encountered those known as aerial powers, demons that took the form of great winds, others he had not seen classified in such ways. He read of astral spirits, those borne of ancient places and appearing as ghostly hauntings; he read of igneous spirits, those he recognised as monsters, either creatures not of the earth, or wicked bastardisations of earth-dwelling creatures, often creatures which appeared monstrous; and he read of the terrene spirits, those that took the shape of the earth itself. He had witnessed creatures rise from within the earth, so it was possible they were a type of terrene spirit, but the text also suggested they had not a physical body as we understand it, but make use of the terrain, forming obstacles and weapons of the earth as required to do harm. With that, Guy wondered if the rock formations themselves were the creation of terrene spirits. He felt less at ease on and around the rocks.

That night, a storm blew in. The sheep were hardy; Guy worried not about them. They had the good sense to make use of shelter if the need came. He, however, was unfamiliar with such conditions; the winds, their strength concentrated after working around the myriad rock, assaulted the thin walls of the shack. Even his uncle's hayloft had fared better against the wind. The walls bowed inwards, and every time Guy lit a candle, the wind forced its way through a crack to blow it out again. As such, he found himself in the company of near-darkness. Only the full moon offered solace, shining through breaks in the dark cloud to bathe parts of the room in an indigo glow. Not long after Guy had given up on trying to light a candle, the whispers came, arcane words, a lost language, carried on the wind that pushed through every knothole and tiny gap.

These voices were not the same as those of the restless dead. Guy tried to pick out patterns in their words. From time to time, a deeper moan came, and Guy turned to the window seeking signs of approaching evil. What on earth was he doing? Why had he taken himself away from his family and the home he knew, away from Maria and a life he hoped to have? And still, the whispers came. He suspected they spoke his name, but what came next was too broken, too unintelligible. The more they whispered, the more he worried they were malevolent, the words of aerial powers riding the gales to do him harm, or some astral threat from the druid origins of the place. Perhaps their ancient symbols had summoned something that haunted these places in the darkest hours. Or had that terrene threat risen from the earth to tempt him outside...?

He looked at his sword, placed on the table so he could grab it with ease. Was the edge of the blade glowing blue, or was it a trick of the cloud-filtered moonlight? He grabbed the hilt, lifted its satisfying weight, and with it, the whispers stopped.

It couldn't have been the threat of the blade, Guy told himself. When he moved, the fragile shack had shifted, and it was enough to seal all the gaps. That's all. He could have lit a candle to prove it, but he took himself off to bed where he planned to wrap a blanket around his head too, in case the whispers returned.

· · · ·

MORNING CAME WITH A white light shining into the room. Guy half expected to find an angel hovering in the corner. Glancing outside was almost impossible, the sun reflecting off a dazzling carpet of white. He dressed into his thickest clothes and, after a considerable amount of shoving on the door with a foot and a half of snow against it, stepped outside. He faced the shack. Yes, he'd have a job to get the snow from its roof, but if he didn't, it would only be a matter of time before it melted and dripped through, or the weight of it would collapse the roof altogether.

A distant and weak bleating informed him of a more urgent priority. He glanced toward the cave. Most of the sheep were huddled inside, but the continued weak bleat indicated one lacked the good sense to seek shelter. He trudged through the snow to where the bleats originated and approached a colossal pile of rock. From a gulley, the back end of a sheep, a fluffy outline against the snow, stuck up in the air.

Guy struggled through to the sheep, pushed the snow away from around it, and tugged on its rear legs. The bleating became panicked, and the sheep didn't budge. It had to be wedged in there.

Guy looked back to the shack and the neighbouring cave. He should have grabbed the shovel. That would have made easier work of it. He stepped around the side of the animal and hefted great heaps of snow away. The cold bit at his neck, but he knew he'd be able to get warm again as soon as he returned to the shack.

The poor sheep had suffered for too long already. Guy lifted the creature's head. Weak, it drooped once more and gave a feeble baa. Guy felt for the top of its leg and followed it down and into a gap in the rock. Aye, that was the source. Its front left leg had become trapped in a fissure. Guy shifted position once more so he was leaning against the solid rock to give himself the leverage so he wouldn't snap the poor creature's bone. He reached in again, pushing the bottom of the sheep's foot away with one arm while attempting to wriggle it free with the other.

The second it came free, the sheep dropped its head, its mouth closing around Guy's arm and clamping down.

Guy cried out and tried to pull his arm away, but only pulled the sheep's head toward him. Its eyes bulged to reveal half of the eyeball; clusters of burst blood vessels stained the eye red, and the pupils were an ever-swirling orange. With growing pressure on his clamped arm, and serious doubts about the snow-white purity of the lamb, he jabbed at its head with his free arm. It didn't react. He dragged it closer, dragging his clamped arm toward his body and with his other hand, and punched the crown of its head. Three quick punches were enough to make it release its grip. He shoved it with his punching arm and pushed it away with his foot. It stared at him and spoke in the way of the restless dead and of demons, its voice materialising in his head while the jaw remained motionless.

"Baa-stard boy! Baa-rbarous, baa-stard boy! You'll bleed! The earth will swallow you whole. The rocks will be your tomb."

With that, it turned and hopped away, leaping out of the snow, and when it landed, it dissipated as if formed from the snow itself.

With the threat gone, Guy wrinkled back his sleeve to check the damage. Already the bruising was coming through a deep purple; on the underside, where the sheep's teeth sunk in, were several puncture marks, barely deep enough to break the skin. A little blood marked his arm. The injury didn't concern him; the demon sheep, however, did.

More bleating came from the direction of the cave. Aye, those animals with sense had taken cover there. He took large steps toward them, wondering how much of what had happened was a result of his presence and the fact that one with known demonic properties was seeking him, and how much of it was a result of a much more ancient and deadly evil residing within the earth and permeating through those rocks.

John Pulleyn had once told him that in the demon world, news travelled fast. If this were an envoy of Dudley's he would be on the way soon. Guy would have to renew his preparation, but only after he's made sure the flock were all accounted for, and that Pewter was warm enough and had plenty of food in the cave.

Chapter 14—In Which Guy Fawkes Contends with the Challenge of a Blood Imp

While Guy had encountered many strange things in his years battling demons, he had witnessed only the smallest portion of all the nightmares of Hell. Soon, he would add more horrors to his catalogue of ill experiences, but first, menial chores called. By the time Guy had cleared the bulk of the snow from the roof, darkness loomed and heavy clouds had gathered once more. Despite the cold, he took time to nail a couple more planks of wood to the outer wall to stop the ingress of the wind. Inside, he lit a candle.

For the first time, he examined his wound. A clump of wool stuck to the blood smeared on the underside of his arm. First, Guy tried to brush it off, but it was stuck. Next, he tried to pull it away, but again to no avail. He took some water from the bucket and wet his arm, hoping the wool would wash away with the blood, but still, it wouldn't shift. Guy moved closer to the candlelight to study his skin. This wool wasn't stuck to his flesh, it grew out of the wound. He pulled again, harder. Aye, the tug pulled something within the flesh, nauseating him. Swallowing back bile, he grabbed it between his thumb and finger and yanked. Pain spiked in his arm as the wool left the skin, taking a chunk of flesh with it. It was as if that demon sheep had sunk his teeth into his arm anew. Blood sprayed from the wound, over the walls and the floor until he bandaged his arm with some cloth. Relief washed over him as he sunk into the chair.

Peace was fleeting. He peeped at the wound to see more wool coming from the adjacent puncture mark. The idea of leaving it was worse than revolting. He needed to apply some of the healing salve to the wounds to stop infection setting in. After shuffling his bandage as low as he could to access the next woollen growth, he yanked it out, causing searing pain to soar up his arm as blood ran down it and dripped from his fingers. With tears streaming, he rubbed the salve onto the wounds and wrapped the bandage around once more.

Breathing heavily, he collapsed onto a chair which groaned under his weight. His eyes fell on where his blood had pooled. Blood had jetted from his wounds and splattered the walls. It ran in rivulets down, onto the floor, to a position close to the fireplace, mingling with the rest of the spilt blood, some pooling on a particular floorboard, but the rest disappearing beneath the cracks to drip below.

As he stared at the blood in front of the diminishing fire, little more than a gentle glow from the edge of a blackened log, Guy's eyes became heavy, his body exhausted from the rush of energy and pain, and soon, he was in a deep, troubled, uncomfortable sleep.

York Minster, night, the nave illuminated by oil lamps. Laughter rings out from the pulpit, but there's no one standing there. The lamps burn brighter, and Guy shields his eyes. The laughter becomes louder, and the source easier to identify. It's coming from below, from the crypt. He wants to rush to the door, to bar it once more, but the nave is suddenly full of snow and walking takes an age. It's like he's wearing a rucksack filled with rocks, each step draining the energy from him.

He continues to trudge toward the crypt. The door still holds firm. The symbol of the ash tree, though, is illuminated orange with licks of flame expanding beyond the edge of the door. Guy knows if he gets there, if he presses his hand to the trunk of the tree, it will restore its power; it will hold back the demon once more. Each step closes the distance by less and less. He persists, stretching out his hands. Before he can touch it, with an earth-shattering crack, everything before him obliterates. A splinter of the door scratches his cheek, stone fragments strike his torso, and he raises his arms to shield himself as debris rains upon him. Before him is only swirling dust which he wafts at with his arms. As it clears, in front of him is one of the rock formations that surrounds him during his days.

Turning around, he sees the walls of York Minster are no more. He glances up; the ceiling is gone, revealing only a sky heavy with grey clouds. When he gazes downward, he sees not the decorative floor, but more rock. Once more the world judders, and the rock beneath him flies up, carrying him into the clouds where another rocky platform floats in the sky. On it stands Master Leonard, the red-skinned, four-armed creature wielding the whip and sword that almost ended him.

To his left, he sees his sword, ready for action. He reaches for it, but cannot close his fingers around the hilt. Instead, he knocks the blade away, and it tumbles from the edge of the rock. He looks at his hand, but the limb ends in a cloven hoof.

Guy woke and stared at his hand. Aye, it was there. To confirm, he touched the flesh with his other hand, squeezing each finger, feeling the smoothness of the nail in contrast to his rough skin. Outside, the howl of the wind accompanied the creak of the shack. No light entered, as thick, snow-delivering clouds blocked out the moonlight. The fire was out, and Guy had no natural light with which to see. He set about relighting the fire. What was in the fireplace was damp. Snow must have come down the chimney. He dragged out the sodden ashes and shoved the broom up the chimney to clear it. A clump of snow fell, which he clawed out of the way. He added new logs to the fire and used his flint and steel to create a spark which soon took on the dry logs and brought an instant burst of heat to the room and alongside it light, which reminded Guy of the intense light of York Minster from his dream.

An urgent need to check his wound overcame him. Guy unwrapped the bandage, only to find the dried blood had pasted it to his skin. He had no great desire to open the old wounds once more, so he dipped his cloth into the water bucket. The cold water brought a grimace when it touched the wounds, but the bandage loosened. Dried blood on his arm was better than his greatest concern: newly sprouted wool, but he was happy to report no signs of that bizarre corruption. He added a little more of the salve to the wounds, hoping to cleanse whatever ill was inside and stop any potential infection. With a new piece of cloth, he wrapped the injured arm once more. He sat back in his seat and pondered sleep, but the wind buffeted the shack and every plank creaked. Even the floorboards squeaked. Guy leant forward, studying them. His blood had pooled in a spot in front of the fire, but now there was no sign of it, not so much as a stain on the wood. The walls too were blood-free, no streaks of the blood that had liberally run down them only hours earlier.

Again, the wind came. The roof creaked and the walls bowed, but it was the scrabbling below that interested Guy. It sounded too small, too insignificant to be any kind of demonic threat. Had some kind of small animal taken shelter beneath his shack? He knocked on the floorboards and again heard a shuffling noise. There was something under there. He tapped again. This time, it tapped back. He tapped in a different place. It moved beneath the floor and again tapped below where his hand was. Amused, Guy made random taps on different floorboards and waited for the response. Perhaps it resulted from having spent so many nights alone that this felt like the most significant interaction he'd had in some time.

"Hello," called Guy when he knocked again.

From beneath the shack came a giggle.

No, it can't have been. "Hello?" he called again, accompanying it with a knock. The scrabbling sound came from several places beneath him at once, and there was the sound again, like the gurgling giggle of a baby, only with an even higher pitch. No animal he knew made that sound. From beneath came a thump powerful enough to lift him from his spot on the floor. Several thumps came as the thing below moved toward the fire. It came to a stop beneath the spot where the blood had pooled and thumped several times in quick succession. The end of the floorboard rose by a fraction of the inch, the nails rising. With his eyes still on the floor, Guy reached for his sword. He clumsily caught it with his fingers, causing it to twist away, as in his dream. He had to glance at his hand to make sure it hadn't become a cloven sheep's hoof. It hadn't.

Another pair of thumps came from below, and the end of the floorboard had risen by a couple of inches. He heard a strained sound, and a shape squeezed out between the floorboards. The creature was no larger than three inches in height and human-shaped and made from some sort of gelatinous red substance.... And that's when Guy realised this creature consisted of his congealed blood.

The creature, a blood imp, he dubbed it, took a couple of tentative steps toward him, leaving a tiny blood smear on the floorboards. It stopped and held out its minuscule, bloody hands. As it tried to part those microscopic fingers, spider-web-thin wisps of blood hung between them. Guy pointed the tip of his sword at the creature.

The blood imp raised its hands higher, stretching on its tiny tiptoes in surrender. "Please." Its voice was high but also muffled as its lips stuck together.

Guy kept his sword pointed at the creature, though felt less inclined to cut it in two. Whatever the thing was, Guy was certain of one thing: there was devilry at work. He scanned the room. His water bucket was full, and he didn't like the idea of drenching the cabin with the outside temperature being so low. There was, however, a tin cup on the table which Guy used for drinking. Keeping the tip of the blade aimed at the little blood imp, he grabbed the cup with his other hand and lowered it over the creature, which was no larger than a shrew stretching up on its hind legs. He placed his hand on top of the cup to hold it in place. A thump from inside caught him unaware, and he had to apply more pressure before it could escape under the gap.

"Let me out!" came the tiny voice, now echoing within the cup.

Guy leant closer. "What do you want?"

"I want to help you."

Guy wondered about the rationality of his actions, engaging with a tiny creature made from blood that he'd trapped under a cup. Was the isolation getting to him? "Why would you want to help me?"

"Where did I come from?" the blood imp asked.

"What do you mean?"

"What am I made from?" The blood imp spoke slowly, patronisingly, as if trying to gently guide Guy toward the answer.

Guy glanced at his wounded arm. "My blood. Something made you from my blood."

"No. I was born from your blood. I'm part of you."

"There's devilry in you."

"Not all magic is bad." The creature leapt within the cup again, but Guy held it firm.

Guy sighed. "How did you come to be?"

"I don't know," the blood imp said.

"What do you want?"

"I'm here to help you."

"How can you help? I don't mean to be rude, but you're no bigger than my forefinger."

"I can tell you things."

Guy glanced at the door, half expecting to see someone watching, laughing at his actions. "What can you tell me that I don't already know? As you say, you are a part of me."

"That's why I'm the best person to tell you."

"To tell me what?"

"The things in your head you haven't worked out yet."

Guy looked at the cup with mistrust. Part of his mind told him to bail on this questioning, to destroy the creature, but curiosity won. "Like what?"

"Like why you're here."

"I know why I'm here." Guy had been certain of his purpose ever since he mounted Pewter and left Scotton.

"Do you?"

"Aye, I'm waiting in ambush for Robert Dudley."

"And whose idea was it for you to come here?"

"Thomas Percy's." Thinking of his friend made Guy smile.

"While you're here, who does he have the chance to be all alone with?"

"Maria." Guy gasped and loosened his grip on the cup.

The second Guy's hand left the vessel, the blood imp thumped it into the air. Guy's eyes were on the cup, and before it even reached the apex of its arc, the imp crouched and launched himself into a jump. Guy saw it too late. He batted at the air, at the space it had left, and couldn't stop it from flying up his left nostril. It oozed along his nasal passage, and he grabbed the end of his nose and pinched, but the imp was already beyond that point. He covered the right nostril and blew hard through the other. A few bloody speckles and strands of snot spattered onto his hand, but not enough to suggest the imp had come out in its entirety. And he knew it was still there a second later when that scrabbling he'd heard under the floor recommenced in his head.

"What are you doing?" Guy called.

A twinge came from somewhere behind his right eye and he squeezed it shut, rubbing the outside with the meat of his hand.

"Taking control." He could hear the voice from inside his head weirdly muffled.

"You can't. I won't let you."

"Someone has to, or you'll be out here until you freeze."

"No, I'm in control. I make my decisions." No sooner had Guy spoken than pain needled the base of his skull. His right hand rose and punched him in the cheek. He winced. "Don't do that."

"Admit I have control of you," the blood imp called from inside Guy's head.

"Never."

Guy swung his right fist again, but he blocked it with the left. The right hand twisted and tightened against his throat. His left hand lacked the strength to pull it free as his fingers tightened around his windpipe. He tried to cough, but couldn't. He struggled to his feet, and as his vision clouded, he dropped his head and ran straight for a supporting beam against the rock at the back of the shack. The second his skull crashed against the wood, his right hand stopped functioning and he collapsed to the floor in a dazed heap.

Chapter 15—In Which Guy Fawkes is Besieged by Ill Thoughts

Stars danced before Guy's eyes. He'd not knocked himself out, but he had brought quiet to his brain, throbbing pain excluded. Dazed, he struggled to his feet, using the wall to steady himself as the room tilted one way then the other. A wave of nausea washed over him. He swallowed back bile and took a small step toward the fire. It had dulled, so he threw on another log and jabbed the fragments of the previous piece of wood with the poker to arouse the flames.

He listened to the wood crackle and watched the flames rise as he tried to calm himself. He touched the spot on top of his head where he'd collided with the beam: a touch tender, but no lasting damage. His throat felt worse. He took the cup from under the table and wiped it with his sleeve and poured himself a little ale from the barrel. There was no sign that the blood imp was still present. Maybe knocking himself down like that exorcised him of its dark influence.

Did that little blood imp have a point, though? Guy thought back to all the times he'd arrived at Thomas's house to find his so-called friend loitering in Maria's presence. He was bound to fall for her being so close all of the time, but the swine had not mentioned a word of his affection! The double-crossing villain! Thomas had sent him away to allow him to spend more time with Maria. Of course, she had free will, and just because Thomas was interested in her, she wouldn't necessarily feel the same way, but what was to stop Thomas from poisoning her against him? He had a way with words.

The flames flickered and twisted into the shape of Thomas, a wicked grin on his face. He saw Maria, and the half-smile she always gave him. As the flames flickered again, it was Thomas and Maria together, held in a tight embrace. He looked away and stared at the wall instead. Written in blood was a single word: 'fool'.

Guy stood and grabbed a cloth, looking to wipe the word away, but as soon as he moved, it was gone. It was right, though. He was a fool to let Thomas send him away. What evidence did he even have that Dudley was after him? Even that was the hearsay of Thomas. Was his so-called friend the kind to orchestrate such a plan? He was a devious one, all right. And would he be interested in Maria? Of course! What single young man wouldn't be interested in the prettiest girl he'd ever seen? He needed to get back and confront him.

Guy glanced out of the window. Even in darkness, it was possible to see the snow continued to fall, and heaped high outside the window. The first challenge was to escape the shack. And Pewter? Would she be able to handle a journey through heavy snow? It was unlikely to have fallen so heavily on the lower grounds, but he had to get there first, and that meant digging a path all the way there. At best, he'd have to wait for morning. But every moment that passed was a moment for Thomas to prey upon Maria. What other option did he have?

Another cup of ale. Aye, then another. There was a heat in his belly that bubbled and roiled every time he pictured Thomas and Maria together. Maybe more ale would cool it. Guy peered out of the window. Perhaps he could force his way through. He couldn't wait and let that fiend ravage his beloved, could he? He pushed on the door, but it wouldn't budge by more than a few inches. A cascade of snow fell through the tiny gap. He pulled the door closed again and dumped the excess snow to top up his water bucket. So, he was stuck with the shack, the fire, and his imagination. And a little more ale. He drained his glass and poured another before collapsing on the chair to stare into the fire once more.

Eventually, Guy's thoughts came back to the idea of him and Maria together. What did he have that would make him worth marrying? Nothing. Every friend he'd ever made, he'd let down. Kit and Jack hated him for not joining their quest to Durham, and blamed him for the death of their uncle, Francis Ingleby. So many deaths resulted from either his actions or his lack of them. Now his only remaining friend planned to betray him. Was it even a betrayal though, if Guy had never made his feelings known? Was it not once more his lack of action that cost him? He tried to finish his ale, missed his mouth, and the shock of the liquid splashing onto his clothes and seeping through made him stand, gasp, and fling the cup at the wall. He staggered a few steps into the bedroom and collapsed onto the bed.

• • • •

A FAMILIAR VISITOR came that night, the floating head of Thomas Percy, another whose words only ever led Guy toward his darkest days. Guy sat when that incandescent light from the skull of the long-dead rebel shone into his eyes. The brightness made his head throb, and as much as he wanted to look away, he couldn't. At first, two skulls floated in front of him, but, after circling each other several times, they solidified into a single entity.

"Leave me alone," Guy yelled.

"You are in great danger."

"You're singing the same tired, old song. Go away." Guy leant forward to swat the skull away, but it drifted out of range, used to Guy's annoyance. The movement made Guy's entire body ache. Inside his head came the constant pounding of hammers and chisels chipping and scraping away at his sanity.

"It's still trapped within you," Percy said.

Guy considered the noise in his head, that sense of something alien inside, but then the solution hit him. "It's the ale."

"And from where did you get that idea?"

Guy climbed out of bed. No, he wasn't listening to the nonsense of some long-dead buffoon who'd lost his head due to his own foolish mistakes. Guy stepped forward and swung a punch that missed Percy and cracked the wooden plank, allowing in the louder howls of the wind.

"Guy, listen," called Percy from the opposite corner.

"No, you listen. I'm finished with you and your 'danger' and your 'path' nonsense. I'm doing what I want from now on."

Guy ran at Percy again, but he swooped out of the way. Guy refused to give up his pursuit, swinging his fists through the empty air. Percy circled the room, never in danger from Guy's blows, and, after countless failed swings, exhausted and dizzy, Guy collapsed back onto the bed.

Percy was not finished. He left Guy with a last question, hoping to plant it as a seed within Guy's battered brain. "Which are the two lowest ranks of demon?"

• • • •

WHEN GUY WOKE, HIS mouth felt crammed with wool. He ran his tongue around, but there was nothing there. Guy stood and horse hooves clattered inside his head. It was easier to crawl. He made it to the main room. The water bucket he'd topped with snow looked tempting. He plunged his whole head inside. The cold of the water caressed his head like the touch of an angel. But he couldn't remain with his head in a bucket for the rest of his life. Well, he could, but it wouldn't last long.

He scanned the room. The fire once more was out, but light, and with it, some warmth entered the room. The floorboard which had battered its way up was back in its original location. Of course it was. None of that happened. He didn't converse with—and snort—a blood imp. No, his mind had tried to get things straight and created a complex visual aid to help him. He needed to get away from Brimham Rocks and back to Scotton to stop Thomas from wooing Maria.

He'd dress, he'd feed the animals, groom Pewter and make sure she was ready for the journey before he'd set about digging a path out of the hills, freeing him to ride back to Scotton.

But getting dressed was a problem. His balance was gone and raising one foot to pull on his hose without falling proved a challenge. On the third attempt, he placed one leg in them, and several attempts later the second leg was in too. He pulled on his thick, woollen stockings with a little less difficulty. An incredible sweat formed on his legs and lower back right away, but he had to tolerate it. Next, he checked the puncture wounds on his arm. There was no clear sign of infection, no tufts of wool. Once clothed, he set about leaving the shack. The front door would be impossible. That he'd known the previous night, and more snow had fallen since. The front window was large enough for him to squeeze through. From there, he could get to the cave to tend to the animals and fetch the shovel to dig a way out.

He opened the window and dropped out feet first. At its deepest, if he sunk to touch the ground, the snow would be at his waist. He didn't so much trudge through the snow as wade through it. Once more, the sheep had found cover, and it was in the cave that he spread their feed before finding Pewter, also wise in avoiding the snow. As he gave her a brush, a pang of guilt about the prospect of riding her through snowdrifts struck him.

He took a shovel and cleared a path from the cave entrance to the door of the shack. The snow was soft and light where Guy had not touched it, but soon became impacted when trodden upon, and it didn't take too much use before Guy's fingers froze to the shovel. He returned inside to make the fire, knowing he'd need frequent returns to the heat before escape was possible.

He was only inside for minutes, but when he stepped outside once more, it was as if the snow had fallen fresh. While the wind blew continuously, it seemed insufficient to undo all his hard work, but undone it was. He leaned on the shovel and sighed. How on earth was he going to escape if the snow itself turned on him? Before they parted, Thomas warned that snow may come, but also that it was unlikely to stay for long this early in the winter, so it hadn't been unexpected, but to what extent had his supposed friend led him astray here too? Perhaps telling him any snow would be untimely and would pass was another ruse, something to stop him from fleeing at the first sign of snowflakes and trapping him far away for an extended period.

He gazed at one of the nearby rock formations. From there, he might see how widespread the snow was–a localised flurry on the hills or something more widespread across the region. His fears that the rocks themselves were malevolent had not passed, particularly after being attacked by demon sheep, but doing nothing was not an option. Guy trudged through the snow and headed for the drier side. He'd scaled this monolithic rock only a few days prior, and it had not been a challenge, but on this day, the rock had lost its warmth, and his hands cramped every time his fingers came into contact with the cold stone. He flexed his fingers several times before committing to each new hold, slowing his progress.

When close to the top, and looking to secure a grip to pull himself up, he worked his fingers in readiness. Alas, once he began this action, he could not stop. He gave the hand a shake and forced it into a fist, and it stilled. He placed the hand onto a solid hold at the top of the rock formation and pulled himself up, pushing his feet into higher secure gaps. As he made to move his other hand, it jerked back, out of his control, with almost enough force to throw him from the rocks. With one hand he pulled himself up enough to let his feet do the rest, and he collapsed into a heap on the snow gathered on the plateau. He rolled onto his back and drew in several deep breaths.

Guy punched himself in the face. He lay there for a moment, overwhelmed by his smarting cheek. Was the blood imp real? Was it still inside him? To answer the question his fist lifted itself into the air again.

"Stop," Guy cried as he grabbed his fist with his other hand.

"No," called the blood imp, the voice resonating inside Guy's head. "I'm in control, and I say we're throwing ourself from the top of these rocks."

Guy gulped. "You are *not* making me do that."

"If we aim right, we might hit those jagged rocks. What a delightful mess we'll make."

An involuntary twinge came in Guy's leg, but his hand felt like his own once more.

"Why are you doing this?" Guy called.

"For your own good."

"How is throwing myself to my death going to do me good?" Guy's leg spasmed trying to force himself into a standing position.

"It'll put you out of your misery. It'll stop you from spreading your misery to others."

For a second, Guy saw his point. He pushed himself to his feet, and let the one he lacked control of shuffle closer to the edge. He knew the imp could take control of the other leg in an instant, though not more than one limb at a time. And there it was, the twinge in his muscles as an involuntary movement occurred before him. With control back of his right leg, he shuffled that one back a step.

"Stop. I'm in control of your destiny now," said the blood imp.

It was the word 'destiny' that sparked the memory of his nocturnal visit from the floating skull of Thomas Percy. He'd challenged him to remember something... the lowest order of demons. What were they again? He tried to take his mind back to his secret schooling in the hidden places below Saint Peter's. However, trying to use his memory while also keeping track of which limbs he controlled and undoing the work of the blood imp proved taxing. To buy himself a second, Guy threw himself backwards to land on his bum. Now, the imp had work on his hands. He forced a one-cheeked bum shuffle, giving Guy a chance to plot while the demon switched attention to the other cheek.

The lowest order of demons? At the bottom were the tempters and ensnarers, and next came the accusers. Guy pictured his former headmaster, John Pulleyn, before him, those magnificent eyebrows arcing toward the sky. "Now come on, Master Fawkes, what is it the Accusers do?"

Guy squeezed his bum cheeks together hard to stop any further shuffling. "They're the spreaders of bitter envy. They make people feel ill of their fellow men."

That's what this blood imp was! It had entered his head with the sole purpose of making him think Thomas had misled him, trying to stir feelings of despair and misery.

Guy's arm lifted, but he caught his fist before he could strike himself. "I know what you are, and I cast you out!" Guy cried. The weakest of demons possessed no resolve to remain within a host when no longer welcome, and with these words, and the knowledge of what he faced, the creature commenced its departure, but not without a final burst of frantic activity, throwing Guy's body into wild spasms until the imp pulsed high in his nasal passage.

Letting it get away wasn't an option. He covered one nostril, giving it no choice but to exit via the left path. With his other hand cupped, ready, beneath his nostril, he blew hard. The blood imp landed in his palm, covered in snot. Guy squeezed his hand tight, and congealed blood squirmed through the gaps in his fingers. He crouched and wiped the rest of the mess off on a snow-covered rock. He stood. Finally, he could focus on his purpose, and check his surroundings. That's when he realised he was in much greater danger than he ever feared.

Chapter 16—In Which Guy Fawkes Faces the Threat of Aerial Powers

While Guy's formal education was some time ago, he had not forgotten all of the lessons he learned at Saint Peter's. His Latin was weak at best, but his demon knowledge remained strong: *The sixth order of demons is the aerial powers, the bringers of storms.* Guy remembered Pulleyn repeating the list, and now, looking beyond his immediate area, it was apparent he was at the mercy of someone controlling one of these demons. Not far away were evergreen trees and vegetation untouched by snow. The snowstorm had been localised around him, designed to pen him in, either to drive him insane or to keep him pegged down until someone arrived to confront him.

Guy had dealt with aerial powers only once: when Hastings had liberated a controlling stone from Selby Abbey and used the power of the wind against him. It was only by destroying the stone that he'd been able to rid himself of that threat. Someone had to be lurking nearby with similar powers.

Snow swirled in miniature storms around a perimeter in which his shack was centre. At any potential point of escape, they whorled around, threatening to pull anything into their path. Dancing snow filled gaps between rocks, and great drifts blocked paths between the trees. An ice-coloured shape comparable to a Chinese dragon or an enormous flying fish patrolled the perimeter. Its long neck craned toward him, and the body twisted from its path. The head turned his way, glowing orange eyes standing out against so much white. It propelled itself toward him, malleable ice manipulating the wind. With his formidable foe carrying the power of wind and snow, Guy knew his chance of remaining atop the plateau was slim. He'd rid himself of the imp, but it had left a residual mistrust of his limbs. Regardless, he had to use them. He slid, on his belly, backwards off the opposite side from which the ice demon approached. His feet found a piece of rock jutting out strong enough to take his weight.

No sooner was he clear of the top of the rock than the creature passed above, drawing up the fallen snow and blasting it over the edge. It cascaded over Guy, flakes falling onto his neck and into the gaps between his undershirt and his skin. His body tensed with the cold, every impulse reacting at once, but he dug his fingers into the rock. When the sensation passed, he continued to seek footholds, looking for a safe way down. The ice demon passed again, breathing an icy blast, tiny particles of ice striking the exposed parts of his body. With a screeching wail, another gust hit, ripping at his fingers, first pulling one from the rock before attacking another. Ice formed in the palm of his hand, growing, pushing it away from the rock. But as his fingers lost grip, he grabbed on once more with his other hand.

As it circled again, Guy continued his descent, trying to move at a quicker pace, but the ground appeared no closer. When he studied the rock for safe places for his feet, he understood. The rock folded in on itself, the jutting foothold smoothing. It shifted as it rose at a rate that matched his descent. He grabbed a lower piece of jutting rock and scrabbled with his feet until they found purchase. His fingers wrapped around a piece of smooth rock shaped like an inverted cone. He glanced at it before trusting his hold, for it felt like an icicle. He held this only long enough to allow him to swing to a lower lip. More of these sharp icicles hung in a row, and beneath them, matching stalagmites. It was like he was looking into a giant mouth. That's when he understood the lip on which he stood was exactly that. The rock behind those sharp teeth disappeared to form a cavernous mouth.

Behind him, the ice demon appeared. It blew another icy breath at him. The teeth above lifted to allow him into a place he had no intention of entering. Guy held on to the teeth to stop himself from falling but braced himself with his feet to stop the rocky mouth from pulling him in. The force of the blast buffeted his body. The rocky mouth inhaled, attempting to pull him into oblivion. Fearing those rocky teeth, Guy dropped to a prone position on the lip. The gust pushed him into the bottom row of teeth, but not within them. The ice demon could not remain still. Its strength came from the wind, so it had to circle once more to build power for another attack.

Free from the icy blasts, Guy rolled his body off the lip, reaching back to cling to a jutting rock. As his feet scrambled for purchase, the ice demon returned. Another icy blast came picking at his fingers, and this time his grip failed. He tried to claw back at the rock, at anything, but it was out of his grasp. An instant later, his back struck the ground and all the air left him.

Winded, he groped at the snow, trying to sit up. The rock's teeth were but a few yards above. He'd not been as high as he'd feared. He struggled to his feet and gazed at the human-shaped impression in the thick snow. He scanned the horizon. The shack offered hope, it offered shelter, if offered the warmth of fire, and better, his sword lay on the table. Someone had to be controlling that aerial power, and Guy suspected Dudley. It was time to end this.

The ice demon swirled around once more, passing the mouth of the rock formation. An icy tendril wrapped around the largest of the teeth. With a crack, the tooth broke free, and the ice demon hurled it at Guy.

Guy dived to one side, and the impact beside him shook the ground. The demon had already armed himself with another tooth by the time Guy was back on his feet. Guy ran for the shack, struggling to gain pace through the snow, trying to brush it out of his path with his hands as he ploughed onward. Another demon breath peppered his back with chunks of ice. The creature had pulled its clawed arm back, ready to throw the tooth. Guy waited until the second it left his hand, then dived into a bank of snow on the right. It soared harmlessly past him and embedded in the ground.

Instead of waiting for the demon to strike again, he scrambled to his feet and continued for the shack. The door was only a couple of yards away. The cold wind stirred once more, but before he felt the effect, he reached the door. He yanked it open (glad that the snow he'd cleared through shovelling hadn't completely refilled) and slammed it closed once on the other side. Pellets of ice battered the door.

Guy first grabbed his sword and placed it in its scabbard, which he attached to his belt. He wouldn't be going out there without that again. A thump against the door signalled more activity, probably another hurled tooth. The walls wouldn't withstand much battering. He moved to the fire and threw on another log and took a thinner piece with which to make a torch. With a piece of cloth, he bandaged the length of wood, dripped oil over it, and ignited it. Now he was ready.

He stepped outside and drew his sword. The ice demon had resorted to circling while it awaited further action. Upon seeing Guy, it spat out another torrent of ice. Guy raised his sword and deflected most of the larger chunks, the smaller parts striking his jacket and melting. The ice demon flew at him, its claws long and sharp. The sensible action for those wishing to preserve their life may have been to seek cover. Guy stood his ground, looking into the creature's mouth, studying the sharpness of its icicle teeth, glaring into those fireball eyes, calculating every movement to give him the best chance of success. Guy counted down from five, resisting the temptation to swing too soon, only acting at the count of one. He slashed forward with the torch. The ice demon twisted around to one side, a sharp turn that made every joint in its body crack.

Guy held his sword before his face and spoke the words that imbued it with great power. Blue flame ran along its edge.

The creature again breathed ice, but Guy held the blade out before him and it melted.

The creature raised its claws, and swirls of snow on either side lifted from the ground and flew at Guy. He spun, twirling his blade to melt the snow.

A roar came from the rock formation, and the ground cracked close to where Guy stood. He took a step back and gazed into the fissure below. The red glow told him the flames of Hell awaited his fall.

In his younger days, at this point, his friends would have ridden to his rescue and stood and fought beside him. He gazed into the distance and confirmed that the chance of that happening was slim.

But there had to be someone to perform the summoning. There had to be someone with an artefact controlling the aerial and terrene powers who combined against him, and they had to be close. Perhaps they lurked on the rocks above to the west, but that seemed unlikely given they would have approached from the east. Guy had passed beneath an arch to arrive at the shack and had noted how smooth the rock was, imagining thousands of people pressing their hands against it as they passed. Maybe it was a place where one could commune easily with the underworld. With his flaming sword and torch swinging, Guy melted the snow away before him and he moved much quicker through the terrain. The ice demon was wary of fire, and kept its distance, periodically hurling balls of ice, but it was biding its time, waiting for a real opportunity to attack.

The ground shook once more, and another gap appeared, a stalagmite avulsing through the earth.

Guy kept his eyes on the ice demon, mindful of its demonic tricks. A storm of ice swirled before it, and it busied its claws, fashioning something from the ice.

The fissure was only narrow, but as Guy stepped across, a gust buffeted him from the side. His foot missed the opposite edge and fell into the gap. He fell forward, his hands grasping the rock on the other side. The earth rumbled again, and as Guy snatched his leg out it came together, snapping closed, with his foot less than an inch from its grip. The path ahead took him between more rocks. He tried to spy another path, but the ice demon lurked to block other avenues and scattered rock posed a threat everywhere else.

The sound of crumbling rock was all too familiar. The top part of the tallest monolith, the one he'd earlier scaled, the one that had tried to consume him, had cracked away from the body and slid toward him. Guy tried to break into a sprint, but the snow slowed him again. Rock smashed into the ground behind him. It shattered, and a large chunk hit him in the back, knocking him down. He heard the sizzle of his stick as it extinguished. He struggled back onto all fours, and a ball of ice hit him on the side of the head, knocking him into the snow once more. His head throbbed. Again, the ice demon swooped through the air, the temperature plummeting. Guy lifted his sword arm. The fire had left the blade, though it retained its blue glow, signalling its thirst for demon blood.

From above, the ice demon swept down, shooting balls of ice. With his arms, Guy deflected a number from his head, but when a large chunk of ice caught him in the gut, he had to take a sharp intake of breath. The ground cracked beside him, a jet of air blasting out a sulfuric stink.

Cradling his stomach, he considered his options. With further cracks appearing in the ground, Guy had no choice but to make for the gap in the rocks. The grinding of stone began before he got close. It was only a few yards to the other side. What other choice did he have? Beyond, the land opened before sloping into an area of smaller rock formations. He'd seen beyond these areas, to where the snow stopped. If he made it outside the perimeter, he'd be safe.

The second he was beside the stone wall, it shifted. Small stones fell on him as the rocks quaked, some splitting. Larger pieces toppled from the top. Guy raised his arm to shield his head, crying out when a chuck clattered into his forearm. The gap in front of him narrowed. He broke into a sprint and launched himself forward.

As he fell into the snow on the other side, the rock crashed together. But from there, Guy saw where the influence of the aerial power waned, the lack of snow at the base of the hill on the other side.

Dudley stood attired in heavy armour, as Guy expected, by the rocky arch, his hands pressed to the rock, drawing its power. With him were two guards. He had to have an amulet to control the ice demon. He had to have a familiar to commune with the terrene spirits to manipulate rock from beneath the earth. Neither of the guards looked like the familiar sort, for they were too well-built; most familiars when they took human form were frail and slender so they could shift form swiftly.

Guy felt the cold of the ice demon as it closed on him. It exhaled, and his body tightened. He tried to draw in breath, but only ice particles filled his lungs, stabbing from the inside. He turned. The demon swooped low. He could barely swing his sword, his arms numb with cold. The ice demon's body twisted as it lunged out with a claw. Summoning strength from the pit of his gut, radiating heat into his limbs, Guy threw himself to one side, twisting his blade, catching the tip of the ice demon's claw. It reeled back, breathing a blast of ice at Guy's feet as it retreated. The ice solidified in a block, trapping Guy where he stood. He had no choice but to crash to the floor, bracing the impact with his left hand. At least he knew wounding this demon was possible. There was more to it than the entity made of wind he'd faced in the past, but while he was prone, he was vulnerable to the earth. As a crack came, he rolled to one side, the fresh stalactite missing him only by inches.

All the while, Dudley and his guards watched.

Guy cast his eyes around the sky, seeking the ice demon, knowing an icy blast to the head would kill him, but it remained out of sight, perhaps nursing its wounded claw. He listened for further murmurs from the earth, and hearing nothing, he lifted his ice-encased legs in the air. He twisted and brought his legs down hard against the fresh stalactite. Shards of ice flew in every direction. Guy turned his head to avoid being blinded.

The earth rumbled again, and Guy rolled into a bank of snow. The earth opened before him, again unleashing its Hell stink.

Guy pointed his blade toward Dudley and his men, who were still some distance away. "You," he cried. "Call off your demons, go home, and leave me in peace. I'll not concern myself with you. You need not concern yourself with me."

Dudley stepped away from the rock and stood with his hands on his hips. "You made a fool of me, boy, when you gave me the slip in York. For that, you'll pay."

Around Dudley's neck were two chains, one with an ice-blue amulet attached to it, the second containing some kind of pendant.

Guy glanced over his shoulder. The blue tinge in the air suggested the ice demon was readying another assault.

"I can wound your creature. And I know for sure I can hurt you." Guy blessed his sword once more to show he meant business.

Dudley grimaced and touched the amulet. Behind him, one of the guards loaded a crossbow. Guy was ready with his sword to deflect a bolt away. But still, he did not like the odds he faced. Three human enemies would be tough enough, but an ice demon, albeit a wounded one, and the power of the rocks, was a different matter altogether. If only he could weaponise his sheep.

The guard shot the bolt. It flew wide of its mark. Dudley glanced at him and rubbed the amulet.

From behind the rock formation, the ice demon emerged. Guy noted it protected one claw as it flew. Aye, he could hurt it if he could get close. Guy had a plan. It was a terrible plan, but a terrible plan was better than no plan. He ran back in the shack's direction. The collapsed rock before him meant passing through it was impossible, but he had no intention of passing beneath the rock, not yet. In his first days at Brimham Rocks, before the snow fell, he had leapt from rock formation to rock formation where they were closest. Their desire to see him fall, he would turn to his advantage.

The ice demon was, however, faster than Guy. After leaping over a couple of rocks which groaned when he landed upon them, Guy turned and raised his sword. Heeding the warning, the ice demon rose higher, ready to circle back for another assault. Guy checked the terrain once more. Now there was the perfect angle for the ice demon to swoop in. He leapt, choosing his rocks with care. Each took such offence to his presence that they collapsed upon themselves, hoping to draw Guy to his destruction. Guy remained one leap ahead. He gazed back. Where rocks had fallen, he'd created a channel. The way the rocks came together at the top cast Guy's mind back to the shops of The Shambles, that street in York where he'd spent so many of his younger days.

Guy waited until the ice demon circled to the right position, sheathed his sword and leapt from the rocks, letting the snow break his fall. With the threat of the sword removed, the ice demon surged toward Guy. He stood and broke into a run, heading into the channel between the collapsed rock formations. When the temperature dropped, indicating the beast was close, Guy increased his pace, focusing on his balance on the slippery ground. From his left, from the rocks, came a rumble. Behind him, balls of ice exploded against the rock as the ice demon continued spitting projectiles at him. Some struck his back, but he struggled onward, ignoring each blow.

Guy turned briefly to check how close the ice demon was. So close, nothing but it and the rock was visible. If it slowed and took in enough air to blast him, Guy would be frozen to the spot. Guy had to hope its intense pursuit had rid it of all logic.

Loose rock tumbled into the path before him. He pushed all of his force into his legs and gained a little more speed as he approached the tallest of the remaining rock formations. A crumble became a crack, and a tumble of rocks became a great cascade. Guy ducked out through a crack in the channel that slammed together behind him, and as the rocks toppled into the channel, a sound like the shattering of glass rang out. Guy ducked as shards of ice flew over his head. Yes, it had worked, the terrane power had toppled rock onto the ice demon, smashing it into a thousand pieces.

Guy's odds against Dudley had improved. With no ice demon to freeze him to the spot, spear him with a shard of ice, or smash his head in with an ice cannonball, he only had Dudley and whatever he had up his sleeve, and his guards (one of whom had a crossbow with a poor aim) to worry about. And Dudley still had his amulet, so the chance of summoning another creature of the elements was a distinct possibility if he didn't confront him immediately.

He looked back beyond the fallen rock to the shack. There he had some of his curious liquids which might help ward off some of the demon threat, but the sulfuric stink pouring from the fissure between him and it warned him something lurked there he did not want to tempt out.

Instead, Guy hurried back toward Dudley. It was time to end him.

Chapter 17—In Which Guy Fawkes Takes on Dudley and his Chums

As much trouble as aerial powers had caused Guy in his life, he always felt a touch of relief that they were never in the hands of a truly competent man. As Guy clambered over the rocks to find his way back to Dudley, he swore that he'd bring the life of another demon-loving buffoon to an end. Again, he found a crossbow pointed in his direction. As inept as the guard had been, there was always a chance he'd get lucky with a shot.

"We thought we might have to come find you," Dudley called.

Guy cupped his hands around his mouth to amplify his voice. "You're quite the fool, aren't you?"

"Are you sure that's what you want to say to the man with your life in his hands?"

"It's only a matter of time before you fumble it."

"Insolent boy!" Dudley nodded to the crossbow-wielding guard.

The bolt, this time, was at least coming toward Guy. He could have lifted his foot and kicked it, but he didn't want a bolt sticking through his foot, so he sidestepped and let it thud into the ground beside him.

"You may have great power, but you don't have a clue how to handle it."

"And you do, I suppose?"

"Aye." Guy held his sword before him and ignited it, summoning it to its largest size. While the guard tried to reload once more, Guy ran toward them. He'd almost got the knack of running over the snow, angling his feet so they didn't fall so deeply and leaping to cover more ground. He was upon the first of Dudley's guards much sooner than he'd expected.

The guard had time to raise his sword and block Guy's downward slash, but before he had time to do anything else, Guy kicked him in the side of the knee and brought him to the ground.

As Dudley backed away, the second guard still fumbled with his crossbow. Guy sped to him, swinging his sword and knocking the crossbow from his hand.

Dudley mumbled as Guy ran at him. From behind came wailings of inexpressible despair, and a rush of air that forced him to turn around. Like the guards at King's Manor, these two floated through the air, their faces corrupted by demonic possession.

"You do this to all your guards?" Guy called as he readied his sword for the first demon. With hands mutated into demon claws, hoping to bury them deep into his skin, they flew at Guy.

The nearer cried out: "A turd in thy mouth, pilgarlic."

While the follower called: "I'll foin ye tewel, imbiber of gurry."

As the first swooped through the air, Guy ducked and rolled out of the way, standing as the second closed. He slashed with his sword, but the demon-guard swooped lower still, bursting through a bank of snow ready to loop around again.

"It's no surprise your guards can neither aim a crossbow nor swing a sword," Guy yelled at Dudley. "How many times have you had them possessed? You've rotted their brains!"

Dudley fingered the amulet, which rested against his armour. He stopped to glance at Guy. "What does it matter? Plenty are willing to take the Queen's coin to replace them."

Guy glanced at the two demons, noting their position. Was it possible to rush Dudley? Still, there was no sign of the familiar with whom he'd have to be in cahoots. Severing the tie by killing the familiar would also render Dudley powerless. There was no sign of a small animal close to him, and no birds loitering on the rocks communicating with him.

"Crooked jibber! Your soul's my swill!" The first demon was back again. Guy flashed his sword, but it clashed with the claws of the creature and bounced off. The demon exhaled a cloud of stink, making Guy reel back.

From behind the other called: "I'll gobble your costard, puttock prigger!"

Guy spun around and lunged, catching the demon unaware with a blade that entered the body south of the neck. He used the momentum of the creature, levering it over his head to crash into his kin. With a thrust, he slid the sword in deeper, pulled it out and likewise speared the second demon.

Dudley, however, was unperturbed, the smile on his face indicating that, if anything, he'd enjoyed the show.

He took the pendant from around his neck and hurled it against a rock. It cracked and fell in two, a small black swirl dropping from it. Freed from its cage, it grew until Guy realised why he'd been unable to locate Dudley's familiar. It was a tiny spider imprisoned in the pendant. A tiny spider, alas, it was no longer: the pulsing abdomen at the rear was the size of a cartwheel, and each leg comprised three sections, each a good yard-and-a-half long. It scrambled toward him.

The creature's reach was infinitely superior to his. He's seen this type of spider dart from the corners many a time to know that at an inch they were swift, at this size, there would be no fleeing from it.

It stopped. The abdomen and back four legs remained grounded while it raised its head and thorax, wiggled the front legs, and opened its mouth to expose its fangs.

Guy gazed at the rocks, hoping the terrine beings would be so disgusted with the abhorrence before them they'd crush it, but the spirits, as always, were against him.

Dudley giggled.

Perhaps it was this that stirred Guy into action, the need to wipe the smile from the face of that cocky bastard. A plan formulated. The felled bodies of the demon guards would make an effective barrier. Nearby lay the guard's weapon: the crossbow. Taking a direct route would be suicide, but if he rounded the bodies, the spider might misinterpret his intentions.

Guy knew a thing or two about spiders, so he was unsurprised when it switched position, head and front legs low, and abdomen twisting upwards. A jet of sticky silk shot from its spinneret glands. Guy dived for the bodies as the web hit the snow. Once more Dudley's foolhardiness was apparent for web didn't stick well to snow. If anything, it would do Guy a favour.

The spider rushed toward him, fangs exposed, but he was on the right side of the bodies. When the abdomen quivered again, he dived for the cross-bow and the bolt that had fallen beside it.

Dudley laughed again and fiddled with the amulet.

The spider scuttled round to face Guy.

Most people would fire at the greater threat. That would be the correct course of action. Most people, however, would misidentify the primary threat. Guy didn't. And while Dudley tried to speak an incantation through his chuckles, Guy released the crossbow bolt which sailed through the air and found a home in the centre of Dudley's throat. When wielded properly, there was nothing wrong with the crossbow's aim at all.

Guy had heard a theory, not from his schooling at Saint Peter's with Pulleyn, but from Margaret Clitherow. She was always more interested in teaching through tales than lore and such tales had told of powerful demon masters and their familiars, and what became of them when said demon masters passed away. The familiar of a truly great demon-master who had nurtured the creature, used its power, and given it the freedom to develop its own initiative and resilience would often survive the death of its master, and thrive, retaining any power invested in it and inherit the ability to perform great feats of magic themselves. Alas, Robert Dudley was not a great demon master. Aye, he had access to a great many spells and the assistance of the best artefacts, but he was like a child toying with powers he had no understanding or appreciation of, and his familiar he had kept caged. Lacking the emotional connection to Dudley, the spider gave up on its endeavour, and the magical tether having been severed, it shrunk back to its original size. While Guy could have crushed it under his boot, he elected to leave it. Instead, he rushed to Dudley, grabbed the amulet, threw it to the ground and stomped it beneath his boot.

On the back of his neck, Guy felt something he'd not experienced in some time: the sun emerged from behind a cloud, a clear signal it was time to head for home.

Chapter 18—In Which Guy Fawkes Goes Home to Confront His Fears

Vanquishing the demon threat had not entirely dispelled the wrongs the blood imp had whispered into his Guy's mind. Aye, he worried that when he got home, he'd find Maria in Thomas's arms. If that were so, he'd wish them the best. It might hurt for a while, but Guy had made no effort to woo the young lady, other than a few awkward and cringe-worthy conversations. But the idea of Thomas and Maria together was a seed planted by a demon that had sprouted into a sick thought. It needed to be uprooted and destroyed. The job of the lowest order of demons was to sow the seeds of discord with mistruths, not to warn men of betrayal. They specialised in the affairs that weren't happening, and false treason. So, when Guy made it home, he intended to ask Maria to be his wife. He would waste no more time without her. His experience with Dudley told him his days of hunting demons would never be over, but why couldn't he have love in his life, too? If he was doing so much good by ridding the world of such intense evil, didn't he deserve a little happiness?

As he rode Pewter home (who was glad of the chance to get some warmth back into her limbs), he ran through different scenarios. Would he sweep into the Percy household, seek out Maria while she performed her duties, and fall upon his knees and proclaim his undying love for her? Would he wait until she came outside, take her by the hand and propose marriage? Should he have decapitated Dudley and dropped his severed head at her feet as a sign of his superiority and wait for her to declare her love for him? No, he'd do nothing so rash. It wasn't his style. He'd call in at home and tell everyone he was safe. He'd let Thomas know what happened and make sure they sent someone back to Brimham Rock to tend the sheep. Maybe he'd speak to Thomas about an opportunity to speak to Maria alone. Then he'd ask her to marry him. His confidence drifted further away each time he ran the scenario through his head. But he'd ask her that day. Unless there was a good reason not to.

His first port of call as he rode through the village was home. Darkness had already fallen, and given that it was a cold and damp evening, no one was out on the street. He stabled Pewter and entered through the back door. As always, Anne had been the one listening for his return. She rushed to him and he took her into his embrace. She released him and led him into the kitchen where soup bubbled in the pot over the fire.

"Oh, Guy, I've been so worried ever since that awful man and his guards rode through the village asking questions. Did he find you?"

Guy pictured the crossbow bolt piercing Dudley's throat. "Aye. A poor move on his part."

"Is he... dead?"

"Aye." Guy leant on the table, tiredness striking him when he realised this episode was over.

"And are you hurt?"

Guy shook his head, but the more he thought about it, the more he felt the bruises from where the ice demon had pelted him with balls of ice. "The man was a fool. He had no idea of the power at his fingertips. With a little wisdom, he could have put me in the ground."

Anne stepped forward with a kitchen rag and whipped it at Guy. "You're the fool for going through that on your own. You know I could have helped."

"Aye, but would I have wanted to be trapped in a shack with you all that time? I preferred the sheep for company."

Anne whipped Guy once more. "Without jest, though, brother, I wish you'd have faith in me."

Guy thought of all of the ways he'd suffered while isolated. Why had he made that choice to go alone? Yes, the ruse may not have been so convincing had people known Anne had gone with him.

"Aye," said Guy. "We should have done it differently. I could have used your help."

"Then next time, trust me!"

"I'm hoping there won't be a next time."

Anne sighed and returned her attention to the soup.

A pang of guilt hit Guy. For so many of his junior years, he'd tried to shake off Anne's affections, but she was the one who was there for him when he needed someone. She'd shown her skills and hunted with him when he had no one else. She'd tried to keep him sharp when his spirit dulled. Not only had he left her behind again, but he also planned to abandon her once more by seeking a married life.

As Anne stirred, the delicious aroma of winter vegetables and a range of herbs flooded Guy's senses. Maybe he didn't have to hurry over to the Percy household to see Maria... but if he put off seeking his heart's desire, when would he ever do it?

"Can you save me some soup? I need to pay a quick visit to the Percy household."

Anne smiled. "To check in on Miss Pulleyn?"

"Aye? No. What? What would make you say such a thing?"

Anne raised her eyebrows. "She's missed you."

"How would you know?" Guy studied his sister's face for signs of some kind of trick.

"I do speak to people outside this household."

"What did she say?"

"Not a lot. Thomas has as good as talked her ear off and she said she'd be glad of some sensible conversation."

Guy smiled. He'd give her some sensible conversation, and a little more too: an important question to ponder.

He exited the house and walked back toward the Percy household. Aye, he could turn up under the guise of needing to converse with Thomas and seek Maria once there. He wiped his hands on his jacket. Where was all this sweat coming from on a cold evening? The closer he got to the house, the shorter his stride became until he was almost shuffling along the path, his legs spasming out of control. He swallowed hard and gently, ponderously, fearfully, knocked.

It was the Percy's stern housekeeper who answered. "Fawkes. How can I help you?"

Guy's tongue had been replaced with a lump of wet moss, and rather than speaking he opened his mouth time and again like some kind of human-goldfish hybrid.

"Spit it out, man." The housekeeper folded her arms.

"I..." He'd managed a word. That was a start.

The housekeeper stared at him.

"I..." That was no better.

Sick of his stupor, the housekeeper intervened. "If you're here for Thomas..."

Guy took a gasp of breath, thankful to be put out of his misery.

"You'll find him in the library."

Guy stepped inside, and the housekeeper closed the door behind him. He walked through the hall. How on earth did the Percys keep their home so warm in winter? It was like the sun itself was a guest. Guy glanced at the oil lamps spaced along the hall. Surely, they provided only light; such a little flame shouldn't draw so much sweat from him? He mopped his soaked forehead with the sleeve of his jacket. He made his way to the library door, which was open, and as usual, Thomas sat in an armchair with a weighty tome in his arms.

Hearing Guy's heavy footsteps, he gazed up. He closed the book and stood. "Good lord, Guy, are you all right? You look like you've suffered from sights that even Dante couldn't dream."

"Aye," said Guy. He clutched the doorframe and started his speech over. "Aye, I..." Wait, was he saying the same word twice, or did it only sound like it?

"Take a seat, my man. Are you hurt? Do you require aid?"

Guy shook his head. "Aye."

"Well, which is it? Aye, you need aid, aye, you are hurt, or aye to both?"

Guy's mouth dropped open once more, but this time no words came—back to the old fish routine. He let Thomas take him by the hand and lead him to the chair in which he'd been sitting.

"You don't appear to be bleeding, so I'll not have to bury you in the backyard. How about I get you a flagon of ale from the kitchen? Perchance, that's what you need to rouse you from this stupor?"

Guy nodded. "Aye."

Thomas stared at him for a moment, sighed, and hurried off.

Alone, Guy had a moment to ponder. Perhaps this was what it meant to be lost for words? He only needed but four with Maria, but four may as well have been four million given his inability to utter more than a single syllable, albeit one that made two discrete words. Sitting helped. Perhaps it wasn't the right time to speak to Maria. He had been through an ordeal, after all.

Thomas returned. He set the ale on the low table and collected a pair of decent-sized tankards from the sideboard. He filled both before pushing Guy's drink toward him.

Guy grabbed it and drank thirstily.

"While you're enjoying that, I'll tell you what happened at this end. When you're feeling capable, you can fill me in on your part, and as long as the bulk of the flock is okay, I won't have to box your ears."

Guy put the half-drained tankard down and listened as Thomas told his tale. As always, it started a good day and a half earlier than it needed to with the arrival of a few irrelevant travellers in the village who stopped the night in the tavern, and a delivery of cloth that Thomas planned to make use of as part of his tailoring endeavour. Eventually, Thomas reached the part of the tale in which Dudley appeared.

"So, he rode into the village with this pair of gormless guards by his side, demanding to know if one by the name of Guy Fawkes lived in these parts. Of course, more than a few spoke up, and it wasn't long before someone pointed them toward my old abode. There, Bainbrigge did his part and said you were shepherding at Brimham Rock for the winter. Off they raced, straight into the trap we'd set. I take it you dispatched them with ease?"

The ability to speak came rushing back to Guy. "With ease? With ease? Have you ever had someone create snowfall to isolate you and turn you insane? Have you ever had the very earth beneath your feet turn on you? How about snow and ice forming into a spirit of malevolence? Has your blood turned your body against you? A demon sheep bit me, Thomas. I had wool growing out of my arm. If Dudley hadn't already turned his guards' brains to mush, if he hadn't been so unwise in using his powers, I'd be dead. So, no, Thomas, while you were sitting here in your baking hot home, I was not dealing with the problem *with ease*. But it's done now, and you can rest–with ease."

"Oh, good. Maria will be pleased."

And the words were gone once more, Guy's mouth moving as if he should be talking, but no sound came.

"Ah, so now I come to understand the crux of your problem. You didn't come here to see me, did you? Your first port of call upon your return was to visit Maria, wasn't it? No, no, don't speak. I can't stand the thought of looking at that vacant face of yours as you stammer and splutter. Well, I've got news for you. She was so distressed about the peril you were putting yourself in, that we gave her a leave of absence. She's back with family in Harrogate. I know, I know, she was reluctant to go back there after the nightmare at the King's Manor, but she's staying with an aunt. And yes, I will give you her address, but for heaven's sake, man, pull yourself together before you go. If you stand before her with your flaming hair on end and drool smeared all over that fluff on your chin you call a beard, any affection she has for you will soon wane."

Guy's jaw dropped, and he raised his hand to feel the self-inflicted wetness in his beard.

"And yes, man, you heard me right. Maria does indeed return the affection you have for her. Any fool can tell, though Lord only knows why she'd want to form a union with one such as you. I suggest you hurry to her at first light and make that proposal before she sees sense."

With that, Thomas drank his ale. Guy mimicked his action, and Thomas rose, dragged Guy from his chair, guided him back through the hall and gave him a gentle shove back toward his home.

Guy played Thomas's words over and over in his head. "She has affection for me?" he muttered as he made his way back home. All he had to do was ask the question. Knowing she was likely to respond positively made that easier, right?

Chapter 19—In Which Guy Fawkes Makes a Proposal

All of Guy's prior journeys away from home had involved peril–either to avoid it or end up in it. And yet, none made him as nervous as this one. Pewter knew it too, for she could feel him sweating through his clothes, and it dripping from the saddle onto her. She forgave him, though, even trying to bring him calm by making the ride as comfortable as possible.

Maria's aunt lived close to Tewit Well, a place which had become popular over the previous twenty years as a result of the discovery that its waters were rich in healing mineral properties. While its ferruginous colour put many off drinking the water, those brave souls that did boasted of increased vitality and a fuller head of hair.

Several new properties had been built in the area and the signs of development were abundant, but the land the Pulleyns had owned and farmed for generations was in stark contrast: simple stone buildings showing their age. Guy tried to imagine the area without the recent development, imagining the place where his former headmaster, John Pulleyn, would have been as a boy. Aye, there was an appeal to this landscape. He could imagine him working the land one moment, and turning his attention to his studies another.

He approached the small farmstead belonging to Maria's aunt and knocked upon the door, feeling far calmer than he had when approaching Percy's door the previous evening.

A small woman with a round face and tired eyes opened the door. "How can I help you?"

"Is this the abode of Agnes Pulleyn?" (For that was the name Thomas gave to Guy.)

"What business have you with Miss Pulleyn?"

"None, but I understand Miss Maria Pulleyn is staying with her?"

The woman huffed. "She'll not be interested in you."

Guy took a step back. "I'm sorry? How can you know that?"

"I've spoken to her. She's smitten with some adventurous young man from York."

"But that's–"

She shook her head. "So, she'll not want to speak to the likes of you. What are you, another of those labourers working on the houses?"

"No, I'm–"

The woman rolled her eyes. "You're not the first to try your luck. No doubt you saw her ride in. She's the sort to turn heads, I'll give you that, but as I say, her heart already belongs to another."

"I'm him."

The housekeeper leant in to study Guy closer. "No, she said he was a handsome chap."

Guy placed his hands on his hips. "Still me."

The woman leant forward to look at him better. "She said he was strong and quick-witted."

Guy placed a proud hand on his chest. "And that I am."

She frowned. "Can't see it meself, but if you are who you say you are, no doubt she'll be happy you're here. And in case you're not, I'll stick the poker in the fire, ready to brand you a liar."

She stepped aside and welcomed Guy into a large kitchen filled with shelves containing jars of produce, and several bulging sacks in one corner. A fire blazed at an interior wall. Ahead was another door, but the housekeeper guided Guy to the right, through a room which contained only a small table, a comfortable armchair, and a bookcase. Again, he imagined a young John Pulleyn sitting in that chair reading from a book with the aid of the light pouring through the window. Another door led to a comfortable sitting room.

The woman who had answered the door announced his arrival. "This..." she turned to Guy with a look of disdain, "gentleman, claims to be an acquaintance of yours, Maria?"

Maria glanced from the text in her lap, and when her eyes fell on Guy, the reaction was the opposite of that of the small woman. She smiled.

Guy felt his mouth dry once more, and his palms became sweaty. He couldn't lose his words again, not now.

Maria stood and approached the other woman in the room, an elderly lady, her hair thin and white. Her armchair dwarfed her.

"Aunt Agnes, I'd like to introduce you to my friend, Guy Fawkes. He studied under your brother at Saint Peter's."

Guy stepped into the old lady's line of sight. She had the family eyebrows. "It is a pleasure to meet you. Mr Pulleyn was an extraordinary teacher. I owe him a great deal."

Maria indicated a chair and urged Guy to sit.

Agnes parted her lips. Her small tongue darted out to moisten them. "That he was," she said with a nod. "Always looking to do good, always seeing the good in others."

"Aye." There was so much Guy could say about Pulleyn, but it would never be enough. "I came here today to speak of a matter of some importance with your niece."

Agnes nodded.

Maria leant forward in her chair. "The business with Dudley, is it done?"

"Aye, we have concluded our business."

Maria took a couple of deep breaths.

Guy knew the custom was to speak to the father before proposing marriage, but Maria had been orphaned young. There was no remaining senior male in the family.

Guy looked from Agnes and back to Maria again. Age before beauty was another line someone had fed him at some point, though perhaps that came from Thomas and was less of a reliable guide to leading one's life.

He turned to Agnes. "My primary business in coming here today was to ask for Maria's hand in marriage."

He heard a huff from behind him and the shuffle of feet as the small woman left.

"Go on," Agnes said. Clearly, they were not a family who needed everything done by the book.

Guy crossed the room and knelt before Maria. "I know I have not had your acquaintance for long, but I feel like I have known you my entire life. You have resided in my dreams, and it would be an absolute honour if you would make those dreams a reality. Maria Pulleyn, will you marry me?"

Maria took Guy's hand. A single tear rolled down her cheek before another came on the other side to match it. Others followed, and now it was her turn to be lost for words, but she nodded, and that was enough for Guy.

• • • •

YOU'LL FIND NO RECORD of a wedding between Guy Fawkes and Maria Pulleyn in any of the history books, for it was a Catholic priest that wed them in a ceremony that took place the following spring in private at Percy House. The wedding was witnessed only by Guy's mother and his step-father, both of whom were happy Guy had realised it was time to say good-bye to the wildness of his youth; by his sisters, Anne, who baked most of the food for the celebration, and Elizabeth, who produced a beautiful display of spring flowers; Thomas Percy, who Guy would always insist invited himself; and the members of the household staff. Ask anyone there, and they would have said it was a joyous occasion. There was not so much a seed of doubt in Guy's mind, no lingering fear of evil.

In the months preceding the wedding, Guy had busily prepared for married life. With a promise of part of his inheritance when he became entitled to it, Guy purchased land from Bainbrigge, for he wished to establish himself on his own terms. On this land, he would keep his sheep and plant crops. He would be self-sufficient, trading with others and selling at the markets in nearby cities when the need came.

He had a small dwelling built, single storey, with a large kitchen, a cosy living room and a bedroom. It would be more than sufficient for the early years of their married life. With each stone he placed, Guy sensed future memories being built as they revelled in each other's company until such a time that their family blossomed from two to three and in later years more.

Guy had enlisted Elizabeth's help to plant parts of the garden. While he expected Maria would wish to tend to it herself, he wanted a place that had some colour, a place worthy of her beauty, from the start. Many of the details of this abode he kept from Maria, and while he could not stop her from peering at it from afar, he wanted their home to be a surprise when they entered for the first time after the ceremony.

Guy would have been lying if he claimed his head was free of demons in the days before his wedding, and when building the house, he'd put in place every manner of protection. He remembered what he'd learned about warding off evil spirits and placed pots containing various herbs within the walls. The hedgerow he'd planted around the perimeter of his property had holly at every corner. He knew it was ridiculous, but the ancient teaching suggested that evil entities ran along the tops of bushes and hedges, but a prick from a holy bush made them fall off.

He did not forget Walsingham. It was Maria's anger with him that had brought them together, after all. Guy could not marry Maria without first knowing her thoughts about that master of demons.

"Don't get me wrong, Guy," Maria had said. "Rarely does a day go by when I don't wish him dead, and if the opportunity arose to sink a dagger into his chest, I'd take it in a heartbeat. But the last thing I want is either of us putting our necks on the chopping block for something that happened in the past. We can't go back and change it, but we can make a future worth living."

That was good enough for Guy. If only he'd known.

Aye, Guy put every protection from evil in place, and he'd cleansed his mind before the day of his wedding. But when he entered that house, when he celebrated his new union, his new home with his new wife, after they had consummated their love on the new bed, an old spirit, though one without malevolence, found its way through, nonetheless. When Guy opened his eyes in the middle of the night, roused from a deep and relaxing sleep with the woman he loved by his side, the floating head of the rebel Thomas Percy appeared before him once more.

"You two are now intrinsically linked."

Guy sat. He stared at Maria, who remained asleep. "Aye," he said in a low voice. "For better or for worse."

"Worse," said Percy. Somehow, despite being a translucent version of a skull, the bone structure suggested a deep sadness.

"No," Guy said. "I'm settled now. All that is done."

"You don't get to make that choice."

"No? I'll not take hold of the hilt of a sword again, not unless it's to protect my wife, my family to be."

"I wish it could be different. I warned you not to take this path." Percy drifted into a corner. "I wish it could be different."

Percy continued to utter those words long after Guy had closed his eyes and forced himself back to sleep.

Chapter 20—In Which Guy Fawkes Experiences Peace and Joy

For a time, Scotton was a place of peace, and from there it radiated out into the wider world. Guy stopped worrying about the repercussions of Dudley's demise. Walsingham, seemingly, had forgotten about the attempt on his life at King's Manor. Perhaps he dealt with such threats all the time. As long as Walsingham didn't come looking for Guy, he saw no need to seek trouble.

The skull of the rebellious Thomas Percy remained quiet after the wedding night. Guy kept his words, always, in the back of his mind. His fate may have been inevitable, but it didn't mean he couldn't keep it at bay, perhaps even for years, and build a satisfactory life. The other Thomas Percy, wearing ever more elaborate attire as he continued his tailoring endeavours, kept Guy abreast of major events in England, but there was no more talk of an invasion from Spain. More English troops were in continental Europe than at any time in Elizabeth's reign as she asserted her authority and made it clear England was not a land that one could set so much as a foot on with bad intentions.

In England, there were no further plots to overthrow Queen Elizabeth. The Council of the North existed, for a long time, only to ensure the efficient collection of taxation to support the cost of conflict. And while Guy was glad to listen to all of this, he wanted no further part in it, and Thomas respected that. But for Thomas, knowledge was always calling, and he found himself drawn away from Scotton more and more regularly until he finally bid Guy farewell when he had purchased a property in London, ready to take his joint tailoring/spying exploits further. If anything, Guy felt a little glad when he left, for he realised that any time he spent with Thomas was time away from Maria.

And Maria needed Guy by the time Thomas left in November 1590, for she was heavy with child. Guy had made a success of his smallholding, with ample produce harvested, and wool and meat and parchment from his sheep for them to have plenty to trade within the community to get all they needed. With winter fast approaching and the days short, Guy found himself with long evenings spent by Maria's side. Often, they lay in bed, Maria resting her head on Guy's chest. He'd run one hand through her hair, sometimes take in that scent of apple blossom he always picked up from her. When he rested his hand on the rise of her belly, sometimes feeling the movement of his child within, he'd imagine holding his child. He pictured himself counting ten tiny fingers and ten tiny toes. He thought about the idea so much he could almost feel the warmth of his child against his chest as he pulled him close. Guy thought of his father, and how much he'd learned from him before those evil men cruelly ended his life. He wanted that same opportunity to share his knowledge.

At these times they'd talk about their hopes and dreams for the future, how that one young life would be the first of many, how they'd raise those children and educate them, and how they'd keep them safe and save them from the hardships that blemished so many lives. In his mind, Guy pictured how they'd expand the house. There was plenty of land on which to do so. Bedrooms would all expand from the kitchen, so they'd always be close to one another. Guy and Maria spent so long in conversation. Maria longed to do something practical but baulked at the idea of sowing or baking. Maria spoke of her Aunt Agnes, and how she'd shown her how to work with leather. They travelled back to visit the old woman (who was delighted to see Maria with child) and picked up the tools so Maria could again go about creating something practical. Some nights, Maria and Guy would speak until the sun came up, then rush to bed, knowing sleep was necessary before another day's work but unable to resist one another. And yet, they never felt tired.

Perhaps Guy spent such long hours with Maria because he couldn't escape that nagging doubt, the skull of Thomas Percy's warning of the wrong path. And while his sleep had been restful for so long, in his dreams, Master Leonard returned, freed from his prison in the crypt of York Minster, the ash seal on the door broken. It was no longer Guy that was the object of his desire, though. No, in Guy's dreams, he explored York Minster, and from the nave, crying came, always at the opposite end of the cathedral. Every night he ran toward a crib from which an ethereal light glowed, but thunderous footsteps signalled the start of a race he eternally lost. Master Leonard always reached the crib first and snatched the child, swallowing him before Guy could even set eyes upon him.

As a result of these nightmares, every twinge of pain Maria shared led Guy into a panic, fear that his destiny was never to hold his child. Guy and Maria found a reliable midwife in the village long before the birth, and sought advice, even from his mother, to ensure a safe delivery.

Such worries proved unnecessary, and on December 25th, Maria Pulleyn gave birth to a baby boy.

They'd not discussed a name, but as the parents looked upon the child, they spoke in unison: "John."

While Guy had imagined holding a child for so long, the reality was so much better. Holding his son close to his chest brought him not only the warmth of his skin but a feeling of pure love. Sometimes whole minutes passed with Guy doing nothing but staring at a small part of his son's body, the bottom of his foot, the curl of his fingers, those blue eyes.

John was a peaceful and curious child. Rarely did he cry for any unfathomable reason, and he was content to lie on his back much of the time. Whenever Guy held John, he was always fascinated by his son's busy eyes, looking from one corner to another to take in every tiny detail, to absorb every colour and shape. For Guy, it was always a pleasure to come home from a day's toil and take his son in his arms and revel in the wonder of the new life that he and his wife had created.

Aye, if everything could have remained that way forever, the gunpowder plot may never have come to pass. Of course, destiny was always going to find a way.

Chapter 21 – In Which Guy Fawkes Goes to Market

Guy was blessed with the miracle of birth during lambing season too. Or perhaps it was a curse. The only difference between the two is perception. With many more of his newborn lambs surviving than was typical, his flock was much larger than he could tend without altering his method of operation. For an ambitious man, with the desire to take on more land, the opportunity was ideal. His stepfather, Bainbrigge, told him he should grasp the opportunity with both hands. Maybe, had young John not so recently come into their lives, they would have taken that chance. Maybe everything would have been different. Instead, Guy decided to part with some of his young lambs in Knaresborough, the nearest market town, a mere two miles away.

It was common for the farming folk of Scotton to make the journey to Knaresborough on a Wednesday for the market. While Guy had not visited himself, he often traded with villagers who made regular trips to town. A well-worn droving route followed the path of the River Nidd into Knaresborough, and two other Scotton farmers, George Hartburn and Henry Shufflebottom, invited Guy to accompany them one week in late June when they too wished to part with a few excess lambs. It was customary to travel to market in small groups. While it was rare to be stopped on the way to market by one with malevolent intent, the road back was a cause for concern, with increasing stories of dark-hearted thieves looking to rid lonely farmers of their profits.

Both Hartburn and Shufflebottom had over fifteen years on Guy, who found himself on the periphery of their conversations every time they rested during the journey. He took the role at the rear of the party, guiding any of the distracted lambs back into the flock, and it wasn't long beyond the idyllic tranquillity of the droveway by the river merged with the road to Knaresborough, and the sounds of horses and carts replaced the calm of nature.

Shufflebottom had explained to Guy how the livestock auction worked, and where they were to pen their flock upon arrival. Once they arrived at the market square, they herded their sheep into three separate pens.

Hartburn gave Shufflebottom a nod. "A lot in today."

"Aye, we should get a good return. Might afford us a sup in the tavern."

Hartburn caught sight of someone he recognised across the square, waved, and trotted over to him.

Shufflebottom put his hand on Guy's shoulder. "What did you make of the journey, Fawkes? Is the market life for you?"

A crash broke their conversation. A wooden crate of onions lay overturned next to the barrel from which it had fallen. A young man fled the scene, pushing past a pair of onlookers and disappearing between two buildings.

"I prefer the peace of Scotton, these days." Guy glanced at his lambs. They'd not be his much longer.

"Are y' looking to return with anything other than a little extra coin in your pocket?"

Guy shrugged. "I can't say I'd given it a great deal of consideration."

"Now's the time to give it some thought. A dairy cow would keep you in milk. A wise investment, I'm sure. Old Edwin Rimer would trade you a butter churn for a bag or two of wool when the time comes."

Guy gazed over his shoulder once more while the farmer gathered the last of his onions to return to his crate. "Could you point out a decent one?"

"Aye, my lad. That I will."

Hartburn return. "No surprise there's a lot about today."

"Why's that?" Shufflebottom asked.

"Special visitor is blessing the town with his presence. Only, Francis, bleedin' Walsingham himself."

Shufflebottom cooed in surprise. "Well, aren't we a lucky bunch? How d'you like that, Guy? First visit to the market and you're treated to a visit from one of the Queen's closest advisors."

"Maybe they heard you were coming, Guy?" Hartburn grinned.

Guy didn't even hear him. Instead, he was back in York as a child the first time Walsingham appeared in the city. He remembered gazing upon Walsingham, Sandys, and Hastings outside York Minster, pure hatred in his eyes. And it was his failure to follow his friends to seek Walsingham in Durham that had brought a rift between himself and the Wright brothers. Their friendship now felt like something from a distant age. There was one fact Guy was one hundred per cent sure of: his father, Edward Fawkes, had written to Walsingham to report on the corruption in the city, and within weeks he was dead.

He remembered his many conversations with the skull of Thomas Percy, who insisted time and again that he could never avoid treading his destined path. How could an innocent journey driving sheep to market in one life have put him on the same road as the flaming-sword-wielding demon hunter he once was? He'd long ago put that sword to rest, and carried no weapon but a short cudgel on the advice of Shufflebottom in case a bandit jumped them on the road home.

He thought back to the earlier commotion, the dropping of the onions. Had it not come immediately after Shufflebottom spoke his name? Were Walsingham's spies already in place? Had Dudley spread his name among his associates before he set off on his own relentless and failed pursuit?

Mysterious faces leered from every stall, every doorway, every alleyway. Surely most were there for the market, men with produce to sell, deals to be done, men looking for a bargain, but too many had hidden their faces in hoods. He noted the way cloaks sat at men's sides, the telltale sign of a scabbard, and where there was a scabbard, there was a sword.

The movement of one man across the market square, almost drifting through the crowds, caught his eye. He was tall and rakish, and when he stopped and looked directly at Guy and moved into an alley, he knew his old life had caught up with him.

"Excuse me," Guy said, leaving Hartburn and Shufflebottom deep in conversation.

Guy moved past a pen of pigs and rounded a stall selling tarnished metal trinkets before coming to the entrance to the alley.

"How are you, old friend?" Guy asked.

"So, you recognise me. The old Guy Fawkes isn't completely lost." Ralph White, another member of the Saint Peter's alumni, remained in the shadows.

"Have I changed that much?"

"You come here today in the presence of our greatest enemy without a weapon, with your face on full display. I'd say you're not the Guy Fawkes I fought beside."

Guy looked Ralph up and down. "You're much the same Ralph White, still lurking among the shadows. Do you remain in touch with Kit and Jack?"

Ralph spoke through clenched teeth. "Aye, and you should be glad it's me before you and not Kit, for I swear he'd run you through if he saw you like this."

Guy took a step back from the gloom of the alley into the sunshine. "I'm happy! Is that so much of a sin these days?"

"If you can be happy while ignoring the suffering of others, aye, it is."

Guy shook his head. "Are Kit and Jack here too? Need I watch my back?"

"They are far from here."

"Is it Walsingham's presence that brought you here?"

Ralph tipped his head back and looked at the sky. "You knew the great demon master was coming here today and still came unarmed?"

Guy shrugged. "I knew not until I was already here."

"You are either doing a wonderful impression of Guy Fawkes: foolish sheep farmer, or the boy I knew truly died."

Guy turned to walk away but changed his mind. "When I saw you, I was eager to speak, but I can tell I'm best out of it; a life skulking in the shadows has turned you as twisted as those who summon demons."

"Be careful, Guy Fawkes." Ralph backed away. "I've heard your name whispered on the back streets. There's an interest in you, and you're walking blindfolded into a trap."

They parted. Guy returned to the market square and situated himself by the pen which held his sheep. Hartburn and Shufflebottom estimated sale prices for various flocks and beasts. Guy made no attempt to join the conversation; he waited, forever alert, wishing time away so he could return to Maria's arms in Scotton, where he could cuddle young John and breathe in his delightful infant scent once more.

. . . .

THE AUCTION HAD STARTED before Walsingham arrived. Hartburn and Shufflebottom sold their flocks for good money. No sooner had the second bid come in on Guy's flock, than a great hubbub turned the crowds away. The thunder of hooves drowned out the sound of bidding. Guy fixed his focus on the sound as it grew closer and closer, louder and louder. Through the parting crowd on the opposite side came a black mare, upon it, Walsingham himself, his face skeletal, bearing the signs of a life of increased depravity. He crossed the market square at pace, oblivious to anything in his path. When a figure dressed in grey stepped out before him, Walsingham didn't so much as slow, the mare knocking the man down, his bones audibly cracking under the weight of the horse's hooves. In an instant, Walsingham was gone, the crowd backfilling the space he'd torn through.

Much of the attention had turned to Walsingham's arrival, and Guy didn't even hear the auctioneer bang his gavel. He only realised it was over when Hartburn and Shufflebottom shook their heads.

"What is it?" Guy asked, expecting a comment on Walsingham's arrival.

"That's a rotten price for as good a flock as you had there. They didn't sell for half as much per lamb as my lot." Shufflebottom gave Guy a tap on the shoulder in commiseration.

"No?" Guy tried to sound interested, but his mind followed the crowd toward Walsingham's destination.

"Still, it should be enough for a decent milking cow if the crowd's thinning." Hartburn pointed at the people turning to walk away, no doubt making for Knaresborough's town hall. A couple had dragged the trampled body out of the way and stood over the man, though whether he was alive or dead, it was impossible to tell.

"Shall we give the cows a quick eye?" Shufflebottom asked. "You don't want to buy one blind, do you?"

Guy gazed across the market square as Shufflebottom dragged him away. From the alley, Ralph stared.

Let him stare. Walsingham wasn't his business. Guy had his own life to lead. He had a cow to buy.

Chapter 22—In Which Guy Fawkes Tastes Sour Milk

All the way home, Guy grasped the rope of the halter and led his cow, ignoring Ramsbottom's quips about his newfound love. It was true. Guy did feel pride in bringing home such a gift for his wife. When he arrived home, Maria gasped. She approached the black and white cow, her upper half almost entirely black, the legs and belly white, and stroked her head.

"It will be nice to have fresh milk. Maybe I could trade a couple of bags of wool for a butter churn." Guy gazed along the lane toward Rimer's abode. The sun was setting, and he could see only a silhouette of the cottage.

"Good thinking." Maria bent to inspect the udders. "Oh, she's a delight. How was Knaresborough?"

Guy recalled Walsingham on his black mare trampling that poor man, leaving him as good as dead on the street. "Aye, it was fine."

"How did you come to bring this precious girl home?"

Guy explained how he had lost out on the cow. "But the winning bidder had trouble with some unpaid fees. As the next highest bidder, they asked if I wanted to match his bid, and I did."

Guy didn't explain how the mood had soured in the market when those guards took the man away, or that he had to answer a significant number of questions that he would prefer not to have answered. He had no intention of leaving so much as his name, never mind the address they demanded for their records, but Shufflebottom had stood alongside him the whole time, and blurted out the answers on Guy's behalf.

"How was the journey back? What's it like to drive a cow?"

"She wasn't a problem. The other two bought a pair of pigs each, and they weren't so keen on following the path."

Guy didn't tell Maria about the constant feeling he had of being watched, and how he kept checking over his shoulder, seeing nothing other than reeds bowing in the gentle breeze, or swans gliding along in the water.

Maria stroked the cow again. "Reminds me of when I was a girl. Aunt Agnes used to send me to milk our cow."

Guy smiled. "Well, I'm glad one of us knows what they're doing."

"I wouldn't go that far." Maria smiled. "I'm sure it'll come back to me."

"How's my boy?" Guy wished he'd reached home while his son was still awake.

"Aye, he's had a good day. He's eaten well, and settled down to sleep."

"I'll go in and wish him a goodnight once I sort her out." Guy had not planned to bring a cow home, and his barn would need some adaptation, but it would suffice for one night to home her in.

Once the cow was secure, Guy entered his house. Maria was preparing a late dinner, and Guy went into the bedroom where John lay asleep in his crib. Guy looked at John's peaceful face and smiled, wishing he could escape the feeling of eyes on him.

• • • •

GUY WOKE FROM A RESTLESS sleep in which he dreamt of Walsingham charging through Scotton on his horse, with John's crib before him. He'd woken before the two had come together or before he could pluck his son out of harm's way. His legs ached as if he'd spent the night running for real. Maria was already up, but John remained in his crib, flat on his back, fast asleep, hands beside his head, looking perfectly content, perfectly perfect.

Guy moved through to the kitchen where Maria sat at the table, a cup of milk before her.

Guy glanced from the milk to Maria. "You haven't?"

Maria smiled. "Aye, I thought I'd get back on the old milking stool."

Guy took the cup. "How's it taste?"

Maria frowned.

"Not good?" Guy asked. He raised the cup to his lips, regardless. The sourness drew a frown to his face.

"What do you think's wrong with it?"

Guy struggled to keep the disappointment from his face. "Speaking to Shufflebottom yesterday, he said the first milking after a while can be a little... fusty."

"Fusty? Is that the word he used?"

"Aye, fusty. We don't know what her diet had been. Get her on the fresh grass and in a few days, she'll produce milk worth drinking."

"What shall I do with this fusty stuff?" Maria smiled. There was a decent-sized jug of the stuff on the table.

"I'll run it over to Anne. She might have a recipe she can use it in."

"You off now?"

"No time like the present. Plus, she might bring us some of what she bakes if I get it to her quick."

"Aye," Maria smiled, making Guy reluctant to leave her side, "as long as that doesn't taste fusty too."

It was only a short walk from his door to Percy House. Guy was still welcome to let himself in and moved through the house, past the sitting room where Mother and Bainbrigge sat engaged in conversation, to the kitchen where Anne was already working her magic.

"Good morning, sister," Guy called.

Anne whipped around, wiping flour on her apron as she did so. "Guy! It's not often you visit us mornings. How'd it go in Knaresborough?"

"I guess this is testament to that." He offered the jug.

Anne took in and stared at the milk before looking quizzically back at her brother.

"Sold the lambs and brought home a dairy cow."

"And this first milking is a touch off, am I right?"

"Aye." Guy sighed.

"That's more than the sigh of a man upset about some questionable milk, Guy. What's happened?"

Guy shuffled over to the table in the corner and sat.

Anne placed the milk on the side and approached the table. "Is John okay?"

Guy closed his eyes and relived the horror of his nightmare once more. "Aye, John's fine. No, it was something in Knaresborough."

Anne sat. "What was it?"

"Walsingham was there."

Anne nodded. "Did he see you? Did he know you were there?"

"Ralph was there waiting for Walsingham. He said he'd heard my name whispered in the dark alleys."

Anne dusted her hands again. "Listen, if you need to act, if you need to strike out before danger comes your way, I can help."

Guy shook his head. "I don't think that's necessary. It lifted me away from..." he pointed in the direction of his house, "all that."

Anne closed and placed a hand on Guy's shoulder. "What you've got is something special. Treasure it."

"But what if he was watching me? What if he had someone follow me home?"

"You do what you've always done. Stay vigilant, and be ready to fight."

Guy thought of his sword buried deep at the bottom of the chest in his bedroom.

Anne ventured across the kitchen. "And don't forget I'm still a dab hand with a blade outside the realm of the kitchen if you need me." She plucked a knife from the side and pointed it at Guy.

With that, Guy stood.

"You'll be off?"

"Aye, the land won't farm itself."

"Maybe I'll whip this sour milk of yours into a treat and drop it off later."

"That's what I was hoping you'd say." Guy hugged his sister and headed home, checking several times over his shoulder on the short journey.

Chapter 23—In Which Livestock Troubles Guy Fawkes

By the time Guy had finished all of his farming duties (with a little catch-up required after spending the previous day at the market), he'd missed Anne's visit. She'd dropped off a quick bread sweetened with honey, which Maria served with a chicken and vegetable stew.

"Did she use the milk?" Guy asked.

Maria shook her head. "No, she said it wasn't good for anything."

"But she made us bread anyway?" Guy took a bite.

"Any excuse to visit our boy."

After eating, and once Maria had put John to sleep, Guy went out to his barn. He'd built a comfortable stable for Pewter within it, and first, he spent some time grooming her, chatting nonsense as he always did. Next, he looked in on his dairy cow. He'd construct a simple pen, but it wouldn't suffice for long. He gave her a brush before heading in to retire for the night.

Nightmares plagued Guy's sleep, the setting York Minster once more. Again, he was in the nave, and again John cried in the distance. Once more, he'd broken into a run across the ever-lengthening hall, John's cries becoming more urgent and yet more distant. From the crypt came an awful banging. Dents appeared on the ground before him, as if something tried to batter its way out. The location shifted. He was in his bedroom, and the knocking from below came from a non-existent cellar. The hatch was chained shut, but the banging lifted it a few inches, a red glow beaming out. Something slithered from the gap, curling toward the crib.

Guy woke, but without certainty as residue from the dream clung on and invaded his consciousness. It took him a second to realise John genuinely was crying. As Maria stirred, Guy shuffled to the end of the bed. He peered at the spot where the imagined cellar hatch was and took a second to compose himself before he slid off the bed and took John in his arms.

The thumping came again and John's crying intensified. Was Guy still dreaming? In the darkness, it was impossible to make out the floor. There couldn't be anything below. He'd built the house with his own hands. He'd dug the foundations, and laid the floorboards.

The bang came once more, and Guy could better locate it this time—somewhere outside.

John roared again as Maria sat up beside him. "Here," she said, holding out her hands to take her son.

Guy passed John over and hurried to his chest. He'd moved the sword to the top after his conversation with Anne, but had hoped not to need to wield it.

Another bang.

"What is it?" Maria said.

"I'll check. You stay here."

He edged out of the bedroom and pulled on his boots. He took a deep breath and opened the door. The banging was much louder, the barn its source. Guy hurried over and threw open the large door. His eyes had adjusted to the darkness, and with the sound of the banging, it was clear what was going on: Pewter kicked at her stable door with her rear legs.

"Pewter, girl, shush, shush," Guy called. Another bang came, followed by a scrabbling from the hayloft above.

"Pewter," Guy called in a soft voice.

She snorted. He called her name once more, and she snorted again. The assault on the door was over. There was a scratching on the outer wall which caused another snort, but when Guy stroked her mane, she calmed. Guy considered the sounds above and on the wall. It must have been a rat. He opened the stable door. Pewter turned and nudged him with her head. He wrapped his arms around her and continued to make calming noises. He felt the rapid beat of her pulse. She'd encountered much worse than rats, and it had not bothered her before. Why had this one agitated her so much? Guy worried his recent high anxiety was rubbing off on her.

He remained with her for some minutes until she had calmed. When he left, he examined the stable door. Some of the wooden slats had splintered and the whole door was bent out of shape. Another couple of kicks and she would have been away. What harm would she have done to herself among the various tools loose in the barn? Before leaving, he checked on his cow. She slept on her side in the straw, undisturbed by the whole encounter.

When Guy left the barn, the first hint of daylight was apparent in the east. While it was still a while before his usual time of waking, Guy knew he'd get no more sleep. First, he returned to his bedroom, where Maria was feeding John.

Guy stared at his wife as she cradled their child in her arm.

Maria looked up, her face full of worry. "What was it?"

"Pewter."

Maria's brow wrinkled. "She okay?"

"Aye, a rat scared her."

"That's not like her."

It wasn't. Guy couldn't shake the anxiety that had taken a hold of him ever since he'd seen Walsingham. He didn't want to trouble Maria with it. "I'm going to go check on the sheep," he said. "Try to get back to sleep."

At this time of the year, the sheep grazed on the hill pasture. Guy liked to roam among them from time to time to check all was well. As the sun continued to expand its reach, he spied them, clustered together in a series of small herds, as they always were. As he approached one herd, agitated baas rang out. It was usual for them to be a little vocal when he was near, but this did not sound like their usual pleasant greeting. The small herd gathered by the wall dispersed, leaving a solitary, stationary lamb. Guy rushed over and crouched beside the poor creature. Its breathing was shallow, and it appeared skinny. It was light enough to carry in one arm.

He'd take it back and place it in the barn too, make sure it ate. If got some nourishment, it might still survive. He noted another lonely lamb a hundred yards farther up the hill. He jogged toward it and found it in a similar condition. This one he took in his other arm. They were too weak to resist being manhandled and carted around.

As Guy set off for his barn, he spotted a third fallen lamb. When he reached it, he placed one of the original pair on the ground to allow him to reorganise: one lamb on his shoulder, and one in each arm. He made his way downhill and into the barn. Once inside, the lamb on his shoulder bleated and kicked its legs. Guy bent and released the other two sheep. He plucked the third from his shoulder. While glad it showed signs of life, and as gentle as sheep were, he recalled the time one (albeit a demon) had bitten him and given him a woolly infection.

Within the stable, Pewter huffed. The dairy cow had woken but seemed unbothered by the fuss.

Back outside, he pulled up some grass and took it back to the lambs. The one which had been vocal after riding on his shoulder stretched her neck to gobble some up, and the other two moved their heads slightly but made no effort to open their mouths. He moved to the trough he'd placed for the cow and cupped water in one hand. With this, he moistened one sheep's lips until it opened its mouth. He returned to the trough to collect more water and did the same with the other. After, it took a little of the grass as Guy hand-fed them.

Guy eyed what was in his barn. Aye, there was enough wood to make a small trough for the lambs. He'd have to pen them in too, to keep them inside for a few days to give them the required nourishment. He made a rudimentary pen, balancing a single plank on either side to stop the lambs from wandering off. (His primary concern was them injuring themselves by getting under the cow's feet.) As he was about to head back out, Maria entered, the jug in her hand.

"What's going on here?"

"Couple of feeble lambs out in the pasture. I'll keep them indoors, fatten them for a bit."

"That's come on quick."

"Aye, it has." Guy had made sure the lambs he held onto for the season were fit and healthy. How had these three escaped his view? "You giving the milking another go?"

"Aye. Even if it's still off, it's no doubt better out of her system. The good stuff will come in time." Maria sat on the stool by the cow.

"Right you are. I'm going to take another sweep of the pasture, make sure I've not missed any others." Guy gazed around his barn. "I've got some work to do in here to make it manageable."

"Anything I can do to help?"

"Aye, water the herbs in the garden, and if you get the opportunity, some of the broad beans should be ripe for plucking."

"I'll get on it once I've filled this." She smiled and gave the jug a shake.

Guy wasn't more than a dozen yards away when he heard Maria scream.

She was on her way out of the barn. Her hand, which she held away from her, was stained red with blood.

Guy rushed toward her. "What have you done? Put pressure on the wound." Guy took hold of her hand and turned it over.

"Not my blood," Maria said through panicked gasps of air.

"Whose, then?"

Maria turned back to the barn and pointed.

Guy examined Maria's hand to make sure there was no injury, that the blood wasn't hers. The upturned milk jug lay on the ground, a small pool of blood welled in the bottom.

Chapter 24—In Which Guy Fawkes Livestock Situation Grows Worse

Guy Fawkes had formed no aversion to blood despite all he'd seen spilt over the years. He was, however, disturbed to find Maria so upset, and after securing the barn, joined her in the kitchen.

Maria wiped her hand with a cloth. "It's not natural, Guy." She tossed the soiled rag to the ground.

"It may not be used to being milked, that's all. I'll speak to Shufflebottom, get some advice."

Maria held her hand away from her, fingers parted. "I want it gone. The sour milk was one thing; this is plain wrong."

"It would have been good to have our own milk, to make butter, maybe cheese one day."

"Aye, that's not the part I'm against." Maria looked Guy in the eye. "It's that cow. There's something peculiar about it."

Guy understood. His enthusiasm for what the beast offered as part of his farming life had hidden what Maria now made clear. There *was* something strange about that cow. Pewter had never been so unsettled. That meant something in itself. "If you want it gone, I'll get rid of it. I'll ask around in the village. Someone must want a cow."

"I know it sounds like nonsense, Guy, but it doesn't sit right."

Guy rubbed Maria's shoulders. "I'll tell you what I'll do. I'll take another wander around the pasture in case we have any more feeble lambs. After that, I'll make some inquiries."

Maria gazed out of the window. "Didn't you say the first potatoes were ready for harvesting?"

"Aye, and they'll be as ready tomorrow, and the day after, and the day after that, too."

"I don't want you getting behind because of my silly whim."

Guy took hold of Maria's hand. "I chose this life to be close to you, so I could make you happy. The worst-case scenario is a few potatoes go bad in the ground. If you don't want that cow, consider it gone."

Maria and Guy embraced, and after looking in on John, Guy headed back out to the pasture.

• • • •

BY NIGHTFALL, GUY HAD built a basic pen for the sickly lambs (which now numbered four) and had hand-fed them all. His plans to build a pen for the cow proved unnecessary, but Pewter's stable door remained broken.

He had called first on Shufflebottom, who was open to the idea of taking the cow, though at a reduced price. Under his advice, he called in on the Percys, but they did not need a cow, and next on Hartburn. He was interested, but like Shufflebottom would not pay the full price. Such was Guy's desire to rid himself of the beast, that he went with the man who would take it soonest, and that was Hartburn who'd be ready the next morning.

When Guy got into bed, it was with a tinge of sadness for his failed endeavour, but as Maria reminded him, there would be other opportunities. At that point, Guy was hoping only for a better night's sleep.

We rarely get the things we desire.

• • • •

THE BANGING CAME ONCE more with the night at its darkest. Such was Guy's level of exhaustion he had been in a dreamless sleep when Maria woke him, the firmness of her shove suggesting it wasn't the first.

Guy twisted off the bed and stood. As he tried to stretch a little life back into his body, sparks of pain hit his shoulders, his back, and his hips, like an echo of the pain he felt for days after battling Master Leonard. The rhythm of the strikes differed from the previous night, a more chaotic series of bangs as if Pewter was alternately throwing hoof and head at the stable door. On his way out, Guy eyed his chest. A faint glow ebbed from its lid. A gasp caught in Guy's throat as he dashed over to the box and it threw open. His sword had that familiar glow when hungry for demon blood.

The banging continued outside, alongside warped animal noises. There was something out there, something malevolent, something that intended to do Guy and his family harm. He couldn't let that happen.

Guy grabbed Maria's arm. "Once I leave, barricade the door."

"What is it?"

Guy stepped away, heading for the door. "I don't know, but it's not good."

"Be careful."

"Get John away from the window."

No sooner had Guy left the bedroom than he heard the shuffling of furniture. He hoped it wouldn't be long before he called to Maria, begging her to lug it back the other way.

With a couple of steps, he was outside, staring at the barn. The red glow from the hayloft suggested fire. It would account for the panic, but the longer he looked, the less that appeared likely, for there was none of the flickering that came with flames.

With each step toward the barn, the sounds of stricken animals became louder; strangled baas from lambs accompanied Pewter's occasional distressed whinny. Another kick at the door came, followed by the sound of splintering wood. Surely that was Pewter free of her stable. Guy increased his speed, reached the barn door and threw off the bar.

In his life to date, Guy had seen his share of horrors. He's seen men's bodies twist and corrupt as demons overcame them, he'd seen enormous demonic amphibian creatures with tongues that cut through stone, he'd seen additional limbs sprout from a demon's torso and felt them batter at his flesh, but when he pulled open the doors, he saw a horror that outweighed them all.

The redness was not fire, but a light shining from the fiery pits of Hell, and the scene before him was every bit as hellish as the worst conjurings of his imagination. His cow's head was missing. From the cavity several thick tentacles sprouted, all of differing lengths, stretching out to points all over the barn. One flapped over the rudimentary pen for his lambs, one of which bleated from mid-air where the tentacle held it. The tentacle tightened and as the lamb's rib cage crushed inwards, the bleating stopped altogether. From the opposite side of the barn, having seen his master open the door, Pewter broke into a sprint. Guy pulled the door open wider. Seconds later, Pewter's head emerged, but her progress stopped. She snorted and a hideous whine came from her throat. Guy stared back inside. The cow's body remained motionless while the tentacles flapped around with an instinct of their own. One had a singular purpose: to drag Pewter back inside. It stretched out and curled around Pewter's fetlock and pulsed as it continued to wind itself around the horse's flesh.

Guy drew his sword and slashed downwards, scything straight through the demon appendage.

Freed, Pewter turned back to look at what had held her.

"Run!" cried Guy.

Another tentacle flew out, thin and vine-like, from the neck cavity of the cow and caught hold of Pewter's other rear leg.

Gut raised his sword to slash once more, but when his sword was at its highest, something smashed into his side. A shovel bounced to the ground before another of the tentacles flicked a further implement at him: a broken hoe he'd been meaning to repair. He knocked it away with his sword as Pewter whined again, beneath it a resigned snort.

Guy scanned the air for further flying tools and ducked under a trowel. He took a step toward the cow as it hurled one of the sheep toward him. Deflecting it with his sword was impossible, not unless he wanted to splice it in two, so he dropped his sword and shifted his position to catch the sheep and place it on the ground, shoving it toward the door. In catching the sheep, he didn't see the tentacle darting for him. It wrapped around his lower leg, sending searing pain cascading through his body. The tentacle snatched back, pulling Guy off balance. He crashed onto his back and all the air went out of him. For a second, he stared only at the rafters, stained red with lamb blood and bathed in the spectral and baleful light that radiated from the ground itself, as if cracks had opened in the world below and Hell itself poured forth. It wouldn't be the first time.

The red light flickered above him. Guy grabbed his dropped sword and raised it to slash at the descending tentacle, severing it in two. The end flopped onto his face, and despite no longer being connected to the cow, or whatever that damned headless cow-looking creature was, it curled around, as if trying to scrunch at his face. Guy flapped his hand and knocked it off, but could do little about the sticky residue it left. His skin beneath it tightened.

Guy pushed himself up with one hand, ducking under a piece of wood hurled by another tentacle, and dashed toward the cow. The tentacles seemed endless, but maybe if he attacked the body?

From behind, Pewter gave another agonised snort and a pained whine. A pair of tentacles wrapped around one of her legs, one high, one low. The upper tentacle was embedded deep in her flesh.

Caught in two minds, Guy didn't know whether he should hack at the tentacles to free Pewter, or the body of the beast itself and bring the whole pantomime to a conclusion.

Pewter's final cry made Guy's mind up, for the tentacles wrenched back, taking Pewter's whole leg with them.

Guy grabbed the hilt of his sword with both hands, raised it high above his head and brought it down with the strength of every muscle in his body onto the back of the cow. Forced between vertebrae, and snapping the spinal column, the blade entered the body, and all resistance ended.

Before Guy could take in the scene before him, Pewter's rear leg smashed into his side, sending him to the dirt once more. Guy scrambled up. Carnage lay before him. The cow, or the cow's hide, was little more than a disguise, or whatever occupied it had grown to consume everything inside the creature. Now, those things were free. Decorated in the residual feast of the cow's innards, a fleshy afterbirth, they stretched in a way that their confinement had restricted. Guy had neither the words nor the knowledge of nature to describe them, and having never seen a cephalopod, how could he? Three creatures blossomed on the ground before him, and only when they parted could he comprehend them. Many tentacles of no uniform length emerged from a swirling conical shell which surely had the purpose of protecting the weak part of the creature. The thicker and stronger of their tentacles they used as legs, pulling themselves away from each other. Thinner but longer tentacles acted as feelers, and they used several others to grab, and pull, and twist apart. They moved ponderously, not used to the freedom after so long confined to a cowhide prison. If the creatures had eyes, they were enclosed somewhere within the shell. They sent their feelers out now in different directions.

Desperate bleating came from the remaining lambs in the pen. The creature closest to Guy had located him. The feelers were closing, but not near enough to confirm his physical presence. What else could they do? Did they react to his movements or his body heat? Guy didn't have time to worry about biology. Instead, he pulled his sword close and bade it grow in size and power.

As it whooshed to life, the tentacles of the creature nearest twitched into alertness. All but two searched for objects to hurl. Those two came for Guy, one coming for the legs, the other for the face. Instinct told him to defend his face first, but one of these creatures had earlier pulled him to the ground with ease, and knowing they'd swarm him if undefended, he fought that instinct, ducked, and slashed at the lower tentacle. What remained recoiled, and the higher attack slashed at his back, wriggling at his side, feeling for his ribs, looking for purchase. Guy spun round, letting the tentacle wrap around him. A block of wood missed his head as he twisted. In this manner, he closed on the bulk of the beast. After two spins, a length was wrapped around him, tightening all the time. It focused all of its energy, all of its effort, all of its strength on this tentacle, and as Guy felt the pulse of its muscles, he lunched forward with the sword, toward the opening of the shell and the main body of the creature. As his sword sliced through the flesh, tentacles dropped to the ground, and as he pushed the sword deep into the shell, it stilled. He brushed the rest of the tentacle from around his waist and spun around to face the others. One had made its way over to Pewter, the other had retired into its shell by the lamb's pen. Perhaps it was wounded earlier in the skirmish, or perhaps it was biding its time to emerge and attack. Either way, Guy's immediate focus became the creature by Pewter. While Guy retained no hope of saving the life of his long-time equine companion, he couldn't let that creature feast on her. Many of its tentacles were wrapped around Pewter's flesh, trying to pull parts of her body into the shell. Its mouth had to be in there.

Guy glanced at the table at the side of the barn. Many of his tools had already been flung around by the tentacles, but his mallet hammer remained in place. Guy thought about the damage it would have done to him. He'd been fortunate. He grabbed the hammer, felt its satisfying heft, and strode to where Pewter lay in the doorway. A feeler tentacle flicked out of the rear of the feasting beast, but before it sent a signal back to the brain, Guy flung the mallet hammer. It struck the conical shell of the beast about halfway up and fell away with the chuck of obliterated shell. Guy continued forward, lunging with his sword, sliding it through the open window of the shell and into the creature's body.

When it stilled, Guy kicked it from Pewter's body. The blood loss from the torn rear leg was significant, and the tentacles had lacerated and pulled open her flank. Guy stared in disdain at the fallen demon creature.

Pewter gave a weak snort. Her eye flickered. Guy fell to his knees beside her, sheathing his sword. One hand he ran through her mane, with the other he rubbed her snout. Her eyes made contact with his. He wanted to tell her it would be okay, but looking at her, he couldn't lie. He knew not how she'd clung on to life through the ordeal, but she had always been a fighter. She'd proved that through everything they'd been through. He swallowed back the lump in his throat, fearing he'd have to put her out of her misery. But Pewter, as reliable a servant as ever, gave up the fight. It was as if she had held on only long enough to know that Guy was okay.

But Guy was not okay.

He raised his sword once more. Two of the creatures, he was certain, were dead. The third he needed to make sure of, too. Guy grabbed his sword, took up the mallet hammer, and made for the final cephalopod. He sniffed and raced for the last one. Ready for the creature to emerge, he fixed his eyes on the open end of the shell. With no sign of it, he assumed it was hiding in the end. It was there he hurled the hammer. The top of the shell exploded, sending shards in every direction and causing more panicked bleats from the remaining lambs. The rest of the shell rocked on the spot, with no sign of the flesh of the creature at either end.

He kicked the shell, hoping to turn it so he could strike inside it, but its lack of weight indicated it was empty.

Guy gazed around the area, looking at the mayhem all around. Shells and tentacles littered the ground. Blood stained the earth. What happened to the third creature?

That's when Guy caught sight of the red glow coming from his home.

Chapter 25—In Which Guy Fawkes Goes Home

There are times when nothing happens quickly enough. Every movement takes an age, and however fast one acts, the rest of the planet moves at a quicker pace. That's what it was like for Guy as the moon peeped out from behind a cloud to illuminate a glistening trail across the dirt, leading into the grass. Guy raced to it, noticing the trampled path where the creature had pulled itself along on those powerful tentacles toward his home, toward his wife, toward his son.

Guy broke into a run, the ground pounding beneath his feet. When he was close, he heard Maria's screams, a cry of absolute horror that either came time and again or echoed in Guy's head. He stormed into his house and through the kitchen. He barged into the bedroom door and bounced off it. Of course, Guy had demanded Maria barricade the door.

"Guy!" came a shout from the other side.

"Maria, I'm here." Guy shoulder-barged the door again.

From inside came another scream.

"Unblock the door!" Guy yelled. Once more he went into it with his shoulder, but again it barely budged.

Another scream came.

It was no good. If something was in there, it had to have come through the window. Guy turned back, but as he made his way through the kitchen, a tentacle, thicker than any of those that came before, pulsed past the window. The front door slammed shut. Guy raced for it and tried to push it open, but a more powerful force was on the other side, its weight against it.

On the other side of the bedroom door came only more screaming. He tried that door again, but it wouldn't shift. How he wished he'd taken the mallet hammer before he rushed to the house, or the axe with which he chopped firewood, but both were in the barn, which might as well have been a million miles away. A rush of debris fell down the chimney. His blade glowed in anticipation as a thick tentacle squirmed out of the fireplace. There was a slight sizzle from the residual heat from the fire that had burned there to cook dinner, but the creature was undeterred. Beside it came several thinner feeler tentacles, but the fat one wasn't waiting for its intelligence; instead, it pulsed up to the ceiling and slammed back to the floor. The blow scattered a pile of firewood. As it flicked up it caught a shelf, knocking pans to the floor. From the bedroom came a wail of such anguish that Guy felt his heart momentarily stop. He ran for the door again, thumping at the solid wood. "Maria!" he cried.

In response came only more wailing. He could not distinguish the difference between John's cries, so much more desperate than his usual demand for feeding, and Maria's anguish; he desired to comfort both of them, but from the other side of the door he was powerless to do so.

Guy rammed his shoulder into the door again. Once more, it only parted an inch before slamming shut again. He tried again, as one of the feeler tentacles groped for his neck. He turned and with a flash of his sword lopped off the end, but it had already served its purpose as the enormous tentacle rose above him and came flopping down. Guy dove out of the way, escaping the bulk of the tentacle which shattered a side table to smithereens. A shard of wood lay beneath Guy's dive. He landed and screamed as the point of the wood embedded in his thigh. More feelers probed at his feet. His instinct was to roll, but with a stake sticking out of his leg, rolling was impossible. He cried out in advance of the expected pain, but it did little to ease it as he yanked the wood free. A burning sensation came as blood spurted out like a volcanic eruption, running like lava, a searing hot pain spreading down his leg. Yet still, he moved into a roll, feeling only the slam of the tentacle reverberate from the floor next to him.

He tried to strangle another cry of pain, but in his silence, he heard a much worse one: no cries came from the bedroom. He tried to bring himself comfort with impossible thoughts. Maria had fought off the threat and had comforted John. That's why there was no sound. Anything else was too awful to imagine.

He hobbled toward the door and pounded on it. "Maria! Let me in. Maria!" He barged it with his shoulder but bounced off it again. Too late, he realised his actions had alerted the tentacle, a rush of air upon him seconds before the strike. Such was the angle of the blow, it hit the back of his head, then crashed against his back, knocking him, face-first to the floor. Pain exploded in his face: his nose broke, and he bit through his lower lip.

The tentacle would come again, bludgeon him on his floor. He rolled to the left and further agony came as something lacerated his arm, more debris from the tentacle's destruction. The tentacle walloped down again, the edge catching Guy and forcing his face into the floorboards again. Feelers groped for his feet. He drew his legs up and shuffled into a sitting position. Every part of his body hurt. If the fattest of the tentacles caught him again, he was done for. He shuffled to the corner and spied his sword. The leg of a broken chair rested by his foot, a nail sticking out of one end. He tossed it to the other side of the room. A second later, the tentacle thrashed the ground there. It was the end of this tentacle that was causing the damage. If he could get closer to the source, he might have a chance. He threw another piece of wood, and as the tentacle smashed into the floor, he grabbed his sword.

Guy edged around the room using any piece of debris as a decoy, drawing the feelers and the master tentacle in the wrong direction. At the fireplace, he threw another decoy. He raised his sword and when the tentacle crashed down, he hacked into it. This one was so much thicker than what he'd severed before. While his sword had sailed through the empty sack of cowhide, with the blade but a third of the way into the tentacle, it stopped. The awful pulse of the creature reverberated along the cold metal, into the hilt and along his arms. Guy hacked with his blade again, but as the tentacle withdrew, he caught a different spot, again going no more than a third of the way through. With a squelch and a spurt of demon blood, he withdrew his sword.

"Guy!" a shout came from outside, a voice he knew, but impossible.

"Are you in there?" Another voice he recognised.

Through the window, shone the glowing lanterns of those who called him.

"Ahoy!" called Guy. "Get to the bedroom. Check on my wife and child."

The tentacle retracted, flicking out at Guy one last time before it withdrew, but it tasted little more than steel which parted its tip.

From outside came cries of shock and anger, cries of battle. He hurried for the front door despite his injury. Still, the creature blocked that exit route. He'd seen lanterns through the window, though. Nothing covered that exit.

He grabbed a broken chair leg, hobbled to the window, and swung it at the glass, smashing it. Cool air rushed through, bringing comfort to his bloody and battered face. With his elbow, he knocked out any jagged fragments and climbed out crashing into the night. Before him, Kit hacked at the creature's tentacles. Ralph unleashed flaming arrows into the creature's body. This one had grown to multiple times its size, its body twice the size of a horse. No shell restrained it. Countless tentacles lashed at his friends. But they were all focused on the front. It had no protection from the back. Guy didn't want to alert the creature. He stepped toward it, keeping an eye out for feelers that would give him away. He raised his sword, his wounded arm aching more and more each time he moved it. But where to strike? It didn't have a head he could sever, a heart he could pierce, but it had to have some kind of nervous system which controlled its impulses. He chose a spot in the body of pulsing flesh, and lunged in deep with his sword, embedding it to the hilt. All tentacles rose into the air before slamming to the ground, and the creature was still.

Guy's leg flamed with agony as he turned back to the house. Blood ran down his arm. All he could taste was the blood that streamed from his nose and his lower lip. He placed his hands over the wounded leg, for it was his legs he needed to make the brief journey to his bedroom window.

Kit raced to him. "You're okay?"

Guy placed an arm around his old friend, part in affection, part to take his weight as he continued to move toward the window.

Ralph was already there, looking in. He shook his head.

"No!" Guy pushed himself away from Kit and toward the house.

Ralph held up a hand. "You don't want to look inside."

"No!" the word scratched inside his throat. The impossible inference of Ralph's warning tore inside him, spiking every organ, every muscle, every nerve.

"No!" this time, his word came as little more than a whisper, as he placed his hands on the stone outer wall and shuffled toward the window.

Kit grabbed his shoulders to hold him back. "Don't do it."

Guy shook him free. "I have to see. I have to know."

Realising it was pointless to fight, Kit and Ralph stood aside. Guy peered in through the glassless window. His eyes fell first on Maria, cradling John to her, still. Several severed ends of tentacles littered the floor. Blood painted the walls.

If there was a hint of movement, maybe hope remained. Stillness was hopeless. And yet, Guy climbed through the window. He gazed at his chest which Maria had wedged into the corner to create a barricade, now buckled in such a way that the guilt-ridden bastard that resided in Guy's head told him it might have given way if only he'd given it another firm shove.

He stumbled into the corner and fell beside them. Warmth lingered in their bodies, but when he looked into Maria's open eyes and saw not so much as a spark of life, he knew it was over. He glanced at the fatal wounds on the pair that had not been so obvious from the distance: tentacles had crushed their centres. Thick cuts covered Maria's hands and a shard of glass lay beside her. She'd fought to the end with the only weapon at hand. Again, guilt quizzed Guy about his decision to leave his beloved without the means to defend herself.

He shoved himself into the corner with them, pulled Maria and John into his arms and held them, again and again muttering the word, "No," but it wasn't in his power to refuse to accept this reality, no matter how many tears fell. Eventually, anguish, or possibly blood loss, overcame him, and Guy fell into the blackest guilt-ridden sleep.

Chapter 26—In Which Guy Fawkes has A Vivid Recollection of Maria

Guy was unaware of much that happened over the next couple of days. He had no memory of leaving Maria and John behind, and he hated himself for having no recollection of that last moment with them. At some point, someone had moved him to Percy House, and stitched, bandaged, and salved his wounds. Sleep came and went, and with it, the moment of the death of his family played over and over. His mind would not forgive him for missing the event and took pleasure in presenting a range of alternative ways in which his family had died. In the worse, he saw the suffering on poor John's face as a tentacle lifted him from his bed and wrapped itself around his waist. He watched John's face grow redder as Maria slashed at the tentacle. Next came the sound of bones breaking. In this dream, Maria stared at him with a look of disgust, all signs of love evaporated forever. And it was while making eye contact with Guy that another tentacle had taken her, too.

In his waking moments, he punished himself, running the events through his head. Had he rushed to save his horse and left his wife and child defenceless? The rational part of his mind told him it was acceptable to go out as he did, as the previous night rats in the barn had upset the animals. His brain found another way to attack him. Had Maria not urged him to get rid of the cow? But Guy had dillydallied, allowed it to spend another night so close to them. The deaths of Maria and John were a direct consequence of Guy's inaction. Whatever way he played it, he'd failed as a husband and a father. He'd let his wife down in the worst way possible, and fatally so.

At some point, Guy knew not what time of day (or even what day), Anne permitted Kit into Guy's bedroom.

Kit stood at the door for a moment. The years had thinned his face and lightened his hair. "I'm not sure I'm welcome."

"Aye, you are. Take a seat."

There was a chair in the room, but Kit elected to sit on the end of the bed, sending a flare of pain into Guy's leg. As he grimaced, Kit's mouth dropped open, and he was that same seven-year-old Guy had first known. "Sorry," he muttered and moved to stand.

Guy held out a hand to stop him. "Don't get up. It'll only make it spike again."

Kit settled. A silent moment passed between them. Kit swallowed hard. "I know it's pointless saying so, but I'm going to say it, anyway. I'm sorry this happened. I'm sorry we didn't get here sooner."

Guy gave a slight nod. Aye, he was sorry too. "How did you know?"

"Ralph said he'd seen you in Knaresborough. Walsingham got word of your presence. Whatever you did to Dudley upset him. This was his revenge."

More pain hit Guy. He'd known Walsingham's presence so close was a threat, but he'd ignored it to play happy families. "How did you get here?"

"Ralph sent word. I was back at St Robert's Cave of all places, preparing to head to the continent. We didn't know they'd strike so quick, and not like this. I wanted to come and make amends. Then we saw the glow from the road."

Knowing his friends had been so close plunged a knife of regret into Guy's chest which dragged down and sliced him open. "I won't pretend I didn't wish it was different, that I didn't wish you got here ten minutes earlier, but none of that's on you. You came; that's what matters."

Kit shifted awkwardly on the bed. "Guy, it's not on you either. You didn't do this. Walsingham did."

"I might as well have done."

"I'm going to stick around for a few days. Ralph and I are at the inn. As I say, we're heading for the continent. Maybe it would be best for you to join us."

Guy opened his mouth, but he had no idea what to say. The thought of the next part of his life, that anything could come after, was impossible to comprehend. All that was left was the pain and suffering of this moment for eternity.

Kit edged off the bed, looking for any sign that he'd caused further pain. "The offer is there."

Guy nodded, and as soon as Kit was out of the door, he let himself fall into the punishment of sleep once more.

• • • •

GUY DRIFTED IN AND out of vivid dreams as darkness fell, each more brutal, more harrowing, more devastating than the last. He pushed himself into a sitting position and gazed out of the window into the blackness. It had to be some time beyond midnight. He sat forward and listened. The house seemed quiet, but was that a hint of footsteps in the distance? Aye, and, those footsteps approached, coming to a stop outside his door. He suspected Anne was checking in on him. She'd done that a lot, much as she had after his encounter with Master Leonard. But when the door crept open, an unexpected sight stood before him. Wearing the white chemise she'd worn on her wedding night, Maria stood at the door. His mind raced through a thousand different thoughts. Had he been mistaken when he climbed through the window? How else could he explain his wife's presence before him now?

"Maria?" Guy's voice was barely audible.

Maria smiled. She closed the door and stepped toward him. Guy caught the scent of apple blossom. The thin fabric of her nightwear rippled, and from beneath it came an ethereal glow, an effect of her holding a lantern in one hand. The ripples continued as she walked, and a realisation came to Guy. He was still dreaming. That moment in which he'd clutched his wife's still body was too real to have been a fabrication. But if this was all he had of Maria now, it was better than the terrifying dreams that had plagued him since her death. He told himself not to think about it too much, not to dispel the illusion.

Maria stopped beside the bed, placing the lantern on the dresser. She turned her head to one side, then the other to allow her long raven-black hair to fall in front of her, draped across her collar bones. With one hand, she stroked it, drawing Guy's eyes toward her chest.

Guy shuffled back on the bed. How he longed to caress Maria's soft skin, but he barely trusted what was before his eyes; he didn't want his hands to run through empty air and destroy the moment.

As if to prove her existence, Maria grabbed the blanket and pulled it to the bottom of the bed, exposing Guy's body. He quivered. Maria climbed onto the bed, and on her knees sat astride Guy's lower legs. She arched her back and raised her arms to lift her hair behind her, exposing her slender neck and pushing her breasts forward.

Guy gulped. He could feel the warmth of her legs against his. This was too real, too vivid to be a dream, he tried to tell himself before he closed his mind to doubt. Ideas like that could dematerialise the illusion.

When the warmth of her hand fell upon his underwear, he gasped, and she shuffled further forward, sitting astride him. She gently took hold of his arms, placing them against her thighs. All his fears of the dream dying eased as his fingers dug into her soft, warm flesh. He ran his fingers along her legs and to her waist, enjoying the feel of her form. She rocked upon him, and he groaned. His heart pounded as blood rushed to his loins. She lifted herself from him and released him from his underwear.

The door flew open. Guy turned as Anne flew across the room, hurling the liquid contents of a jar at Maria. In Anne's mouth was his grandmother's best whistle, and her cheeks bulged as she blew into it. As the liquid drenched Maria's skin, it sizzled. Covering her ears against the shock of the whistle, Maria hissed and rolled off the bed toward the window.

"Succubus!" Anne cried, rushing to the other side of the bed, drawing a dagger from her waist.

Guy tucked himself back into his underwear and turned to the being he'd mistaken for his wife. Still, she maintained the beautiful shape of Maria, but curved horns protruded from her head, and her eyes glowed yellow. She ran for the window, smashing the pane with her forearm. Her tail too had materialised, and as she tried to climb out, two black wings sprouted from the centre of her back.

Anne grabbed one of her feet. "Help!" she cried as the Maria Succubus bucked and kicked.

Guy rolled out of bed and grabbed her other leg, and together, they dragged Maria's demonic double back into the room. They pushed her to the floor, face first. Switching roles, Guy sat astride her, pinning her arms at the elbows.

Her wings retracted, and she squealed. "We could have had such fun."

"Kill it, Guy," Anne called.

The succubus turned its head one-hundred-and-eighty degrees to stare at Guy. Once more, the horns were gone; the eyes resembling Maria's. "Don't hurt me. I'll do anything. Please don't hurt me."

Guy shook his head. He knew it wasn't his wife; it couldn't be, and yet, he couldn't do a thing to hurt this creature that wore her resemblance. "I can't. Please, Anne. Finish her."

Anne gulped, and as Guy leant back, Anne plunged the dagger into her chest. The creature mimicked Maria's screams from the night of her death, echoing them over and over and over, and it was all Guy could do to scream himself to drown her out until she too stilled forever.

Chapter 27—In Which Guy Fawkes Starts the Wheels of a Revenge Plot Turning

Sleep never forsook Guy. Often it was time for his mind to torture him. This time, it left him alone. Perhaps, for once, he'd been tortured enough. So, while Guy did not expect to get any sleep, he ended up sleeping well. When he woke the next morning, Guy left his room to seek Anne. She had taken the body of the succubus away, but they had not spoken about what had happened. He found her in the kitchen, kneading dough so hard he sympathised with it.

He sat at the table and watched her as she turned it over and pounded it once more. "Thank you for last night."

Anne pushed her fists deep into the dough. "You've got to be wiser, Guy."

Guy stared at some spilt flour on the floor. "I know."

"What happened to Maria and John was awful. We're all hurting from that. We can't lose you too."

"How did you know?"

Anne turned away from the dough to face Guy. "Remember the gold angel?"

"Grandmother's angel?"

Anne nodded. "I keep it on my shelf. It vibrated so hard it woke me. I had to check on you. I grabbed the whistle for protection. You know the rest."

Guy sighed. "I feel such a fool."

Anne stared at him. "We all make mistakes. Fools are the ones who repeat them."

"I have to end this."

"End it how?"

"Walsingham. I need to stop him."

A voice came from behind them. "I'll help."

Guy turned as Thomas Percy (the alive one) strode toward him attired in a lime green doublet with matching hose and cavalier hat (the first such hat Guy had ever seen) decorated with an elaborate feather. He pulled Guy into his embrace.

"What are you doing here?" Guy asked, releasing his friend.

Thomas held his hat to his chest. "I received word of the tragedy from my mother, and I had to come to pay my respects. You know how fond I was of Maria, and it is a tragedy that we shall never draw swords with your son and train him in the art of fencing. Your loss, Guy, is extraordinary, and I am here to ease your burden."

Alas, Thomas's words had the opposite effect. Being reminded of how much he had lost was not the tonic Guy required and he buried his face in his hands to hide his tears.

Anne scowled, demonstrating her annoyance by returning to her dough and pounding it once more.

Thomas placed one hand on Guy's shoulder. "When will I learn not to flap my tongue in such ways? I forget the power of my words sometimes. What I meant to say, what I should have said, is that if you wish to undertake an endeavour against Walsingham, I'll be at your side. Maybe not directly at your side when the spawn of Hell rises from beneath us and tries to drag us back with them, but I'll do what I can to help, within reason."

Guy touched his friend's hand and looked him in the eye. "I thank you for your assistance. You will be an asset."

"Don't you dare leave me out time one, Guy." Anne readied her hands to scrunch into the dough once more.

It had always been Guy's job to protect Anne, but she'd proven herself time and again. So often she had been the one to save him from disaster or to nurse him back to health after narrowly avoiding it. "Aye," he said. "I'll want you there. Kit and Ralph too, if they're still around." Guy turned to Thomas. "They're staying at the inn. Would you like to join me in calling on them to ask for their assistance?"

Thomas's mouth fell open.

"What is it?"

"You wouldn't be talking about Kit Wright?"

"Aye. What of him?"

Thomas placed his hand, still holding the hat, against his hip. With his other hand, he scratched the top of his head. "Well, there's every chance he might not be aware..."

Guy's brow furrowed. "What?"

"I happened to make the acquaintance of his sister, Martha..."

Guy frowned. "If Kit finds out you've acted inappropriately–"

"I assure you I was every bit the gentleman. I even proposed marriage."

"And?"

Thomas stared at the floor. "She has yet to respond to the note I left."

Guy shook his head but failed to keep the smile from his face. "It is a blessing to see you once more in these darkest of days, my friend."

"How I wish the days were less dark."

"When we bring Walsingham's pitiful life to an end, that's when we lift a little of the darkness."

Thomas pointed to the door. "Lead on to the tavern. I shall be on my best behaviour."

• • • •

GUY COULD NOT HELP but think of the last time he'd sat with Kit in a tavern, before Guy made that choice which brought a pause to their friendship, choosing to take on Sandys alone rather than following his friends to Durham. How might the course of their lives have changed if he had joined Kit? Would they have saved Francis Ingleby from the noose? Would Sandys still have a hold over the city of York? Would Walsingham already be in his grave, and would he have met Maria in safer times? Was this the fatal error that had darkened his days?

With his mind full of scorpions and tears welling in his eyes, he sat opposite Kit.

After a mumbled greeting, Guy introduced Thomas, who sat on the same side of the table as Guy.

There was no reaction from Kit that suggested the name of Thomas Percy was familiar.

On the table in front of Kit were the runes that he spent much of his childhood fiddling with. Guy had never seen them spread out like that before, only ever seeing one at a time when Kit pulled them from his pouch.

Guy gazed around the tavern.

Reading his thoughts, Kit said. "Ralph has gone ahead."

"Gone ahead? So, you know where to find the Queen's spymaster?"

Kit stared at his runes. "In Durham."

The past rushed through time to punch Guy in the face.

Kit flipped a rune over. "The people of York seldom make Walsingham welcome; his visits are always brief."

Thomas cut in. "I have the perfect ruse to get us into the castle."

Chapter 28—In Which Guy Fawkes' Revenge Wagon Arrives in Durham

Three days later, Guy, Anne, and Kit were in Durham, on the market square, modelling the high fashion of the era under the ruse of running a market stall, awaiting the return of Thomas and Ralph from the castle. Anne and Guy stood in front of a table stocked full of fine fabrics, while Kit loitered in the shadows.

"Why do we have to be dressed like this?" Kit stroked the blue feather in his cavalier hat. He wore a silk shirt, also of a royal blue, and some tight-fitting breeches.

"Either we get into the castle under the guise of tailors, or we fight our way through the guards, put the castle on high alert, and get chased by every soldier in Durham." Guy too wore a similar hat, but his colours were a more discreet sandy brown. He had drawn the line when Thomas suggested a ruff to complement the outfit.

Kit sighed.

Guy recalled dozens of occasions in which his friend had advocated immediate action. "All these years later, you still favour running in headfirst."

Kit peered out from the shadows. "It's not only that. Why do we have to be here on the market square where everyone can see us?"

"As Thomas said, if we're coming this way, we may as well try to turn a little profit."

"Thank you," said Anne, taking coins from a customer as if to prove Guy's point. She wore a long red-wine-coloured dress with a bodice embroidered with delicate flowers. It hid her knives well.

With the afternoon almost over, Kit still sulking, and the stall having done decent business, Thomas and Ralph returned.

Guy dashed to them. "What news, friends?"

Thomas smiled. "We have an appointment with Walter Dudley tomorrow morning to display our wares."

"Did you say, 'Dudley'?" Guy thought back to his encounter at Brimham rocks.

"Aye, the one the same. The older brother of the man you defeated."

Guy looked on, stern. "It's not him I desire to see."

"That, I'm aware of, but it will get us into the castle. I advised the court that we would need some time to set up so we could exhibit our finest materials without wasting Walter Dudley's time."

"And they agreed?"

Thomas grinned. "Aye. Before sunrise, we shall enter the castle. Once inside, finding Walsingham will be little trouble, and you shall have the opportunity to put him to the sword." Thomas mocked a thrusting action.

Guy's chest tightened. He thought of Maria and John. Their time as a family had been so short. For those few months, Guy lived a life of tranquillity and joy. While he understood it would never be possible to recapture those moments, he owed it to his wife and his son to make sure he brought the life of the man who had cursed them to so hideous a death to an end.

Thomas slapped Guy on the back in triumph, and they walked back toward the stall.

"Ralph, what's the situation inside?" Guy asked.

Ralph cleared his throat. "Minimal security. The city's gates are fortified. The castle is the same on the outside. As such, they have little need for security inside."

"Will there be many people inside?"

"A banquet is planned for tomorrow, so there will be a lot of activity."

"And Walsingham? Did you have eyes on him?"

Ralph shook his head. "Though Sir Dudley did state that Walsingham would be keen to be measured for a new doublet if our material was as lavish as we stated."

"It is," said Thomas, stroking a length of cloth.

"Did you see anyone or anything that could be a familiar?"

"Walter Dudley has a pet crow, so it's possible."

Guy thought back to the day he'd spoken to Maria for the first time at King's Manor. "What about Walsingham's weasel?"

"I saw nothing of the sort. It would likely have been with the demon master himself."

At the stall, Thomas eyed the remaining merchandise. "You're a natural saleswoman, Anne. I'm impressed."

Anne mumbled in response.

Kit stood. "Can we put this ridiculous charade behind us now?"

Thomas hurried over to Kit and straightened his doublet.

Kit stared, wordlessly, in response.

Thomas gazed at the darkening sky. "Yes, it's an opportune moment to close after a successful day of trading."

Anne handed Thomas the cloth bag containing the proceeds from the day's sales.

Thomas took hold of it and considered its weight. "Feels like dinner is on me."

The party returned to the tavern they had arrived at late the previous night after a hard day's riding. As Thomas headed for a table in a corner, with Ralph following, Guy held out a hand to stop Anne.

"I'm away to my room. I've no appetite."

"For the food or the company?" Anne asked, staring at Guy.

She knew him too well. "A little of both, in truth."

"It does no good to sit in your room alone."

"I need some time to get my head right before I do this."

"You don't have to do this alone." Anne placed her hand on Guy's and squeezed it before letting him go to his room.

• • • •

HAVING BEEN BORN UNDER the clangour of church bells, the voices of spirits carried on the breeze were not alien to Guy. At times, when he heard voices, he often had to ask himself whether they were the voices of the dead coming from another plane, or if they were the product of his imagination. None came in the way Thomas Percy's skull did, breaking through as a vision rather than a voice, but some voices were louder than others. At Knavesmire, many times those newly arrived in the spirit realm spoke to him, often while their bodies still swung from the rope. But when he found Maria and John dead, such was his pain, he did not listen for their voices.

In his room, he listened for Maria. As he could no longer have her at his side, physically, he wanted her essence. If she stood before him spiritually, he wanted her to know the depth of his love for her. But when her voice came, it didn't give a message of love or of home. In her voice, in his head, he heard only a name: *Francis.*

He left his room, passing the entrance to the tavern with his hood up and his head low, not wanting any of his companions to accompany him. He hurried toward the city gates, to the place where he'd seen his mentor, Francis Ingleby, swinging from the end of a rope.

Guy stood on the street, facing the gate. Of course, he'd seen Francis from the other side, having not reached Durham in time. Did Ingleby's spirit still linger? As he loitered, the bells in Durham Cathedral's northwest tower chimed the hour. Ingleby had told him to listen carefully at these times for voices alerted by such a herald. What would Francis tell him now? Myriad voices carried on the wind. Guy scanned the area. A group of young men had gathered at the end of the road in one direction. A pair of guards walked a patrol route heading the other way. But no, it was not their voices he heard. There were too many words jumbled together. Guy focused his listening until a clear voice resonated above the hubbub. *"He's not what you think."*

Guy focused his listening, trying to pick out more, but again, the many voices made it impossible to distinguish any complete sentences. He waited for the sound of the bells to stop and for the spirits to calm before he returned to his room in the tavern to sleep.

Chapter 29—In Which Guy Fawkes Comes Face to Face with Walsingham

With so much expectation built upon the following day, Guy did not expect sleep to come so easy. He expected to be pulled from the darkness by the luminescence of Thomas Percy's floating skull, but of him, there was no sign. Guy woke relieved. The last thing he needed was a long-dead revolutionary telling him about his bloody path. Instead, Guy woke refreshed and firm of purpose. When he discovered his travelling companions gathered for breakfast in a similar state, hope for a simple operation swelled inside him. But when was that ever the case?

Within an hour, they were at the castle, in the fine attire of tailors to the wealthy. The first hint of sunrise peered over the castle's eastern wall, bathing the sky in red. Any anxiety Guy had about breaching the castle walls dissipated when the guards checked their piles of material in the back of their wagon and ushered them through. They came to a stop in the central courtyard already busy with activity in advance of the banquet. A young courtier led them to a small chamber on the north terrace, a room with a large window, making it ideal for the scrutiny of fabric. Several trips were made to ferry the rolls of cloth and the pre-made jackets, doublets, breeches, and hose into the castle. When they were alone, either while walking from their wagon to the chamber, or in the chamber itself, discussions took place about the best approach. For once, Kit had not advocated the sword-first approach.

As Anne lay out a roll of fabric, she checked they were alone and held out the tape measure. "While measuring Walsingham, he will be vulnerable." She placed the tape measure on the table and grabbed the handle of her knife. "One could easily do the deed then."

Guy shook his head. "I want him to look into my eyes and know death is coming."

"It's likely he already has an idea," Ralph said. "Ill news travels on the wings of the damned. If any spirit knows we're here, they'll have informed Walsingham."

Thomas took a step back and looked at his display of material. "Could we not wait at least until Dudley has made a down payment on a doublet?

164

My purse is not bottomless, and if we have to flee, leaving all of my wares behind..."

Kit placed a hand on Thomas's shoulder. "Friend, you forget our purpose here."

Thomas shrugged. "I jest when it is not called for. My resolve, perhaps, is floundering."

Guy stepped forward. "You got us here without us having to raise a hand in anger. I appreciate that and will repay you for your ingenuity. Kit and I will seek Walsingham. You three carry on this ruse. Occupy Dudley for as long as you can. When they send someone for Walsingham, it will be time to exit."

"And Dudley?" Ralph asked.

"We don't want the castle put on high alert ... but should he fall, it would be England's gain, not loss."

Guy headed for the door, but Anne grabbed his arm and pulled him back. She stared into her brother's eyes. "Keep your head. Don't let your rage cloud your judgment."

Guy nodded and made for the exit, with Kit by his side. They crept through the passages of the castle, knowing that the further away they were from the room they'd set up in, the more suspicious they would appear. Ralph's intel had suggested that Walsingham was most likely in one of the places where they were not supposed to be. Either in a bedroom in the tower or the chambers beneath it. Durham's castle dungeons were there, and Dudley had given Walsingham control of the space. Ralph had heard rumours that Walsingham had the dungeon master in his grip, using the prisoners for whatever nefarious purpose he desired.

When they reached the north terrace toward the tower, Kit glanced back. "I'd be wary of your friend Thomas Percy."

Guy paused. "You don't trust him?"

"I am not sure he is... a man of honour."

Having known Thomas for some time, Guy agreed.

Kit continued. "I don't like the way he leers at your sister."

Guy's conscience prickled. "He has known Anne for some time. He doesn't look at her that way."

"You see her with a brother's eyes. Some would say she has become a fine young woman."

They stopped at a door and listened for voices. Upon finding it clear, Kit continued. "I wouldn't want him looking at *my* sister in that way. As your friend, I couldn't remain silent."

The responsibility of friendship hit Guy from both sides. Yes, he knew Thomas was a cad, but if he told Kit about Thomas and *his* sister, he'd run Thomas through. What's more, Thomas had told him that information in confidence. Before Guy had time to decide, a splash came from the outside door. Guy hurried to the window and peered out. A man in dark clothes tossed another bucket of slop onto the floor to run into the grate. The man was short and stout, with lustrous black hair and a strong chin. He turned away and headed down the steps into the dungeons.

Guy and Kit edged out of the door and breathed in the morning air. Before them stood two entrances, each leading to a staircase, one going up to the bedrooms in the tower, the other down into the dungeons.

"Up or down?" Kit asked.

Guy glanced at the tower. While there were only narrow windows, the rooms in the tower would be lighter, the air fresher. They would be almost pleasant, particularly if kept as the best rooms in the castle for guests. The dungeons, on the other hand, would be dark and damp. Foul air would taste of acts of degradation, and unseen danger would lurk in every corner. But of course, that's where Walsingham lurked.

"Down," Guy said. He adjusted his fine clothes to make sure his sword was accessible.

The dungeon master's footsteps echoed from below. Guy and Kit kept their distance, only increasing their pace when the steps from below changed, indicating that the gaoler walked on level ground rather than steps. At the bottom, they peered into the central chamber. Opposite was a large wooden door. On either side were cells. In the centre, a fire burned in a brazier. Branding irons, with one end in the flame, suggested the horrendous torture the prisoners suffered. No doubt, beyond the door were other instruments of torture. From their position, they could see into a couple of cells. The inmates lay on the floor, giving out occasional groans.

Guy and Kit locked eyes and as if one spoke the other's mind, they spoke together: "Rush the gaoler?"

In half a dozen steps, they were upon him. He turned but had no time to draw his weapon. Neither Guy nor Kit would slaughter an unarmed man unless they were certain he was little more than a host for a demon. Guy grabbed one arm, Kit the other, and as Guy swept the legs out from under him, Kit guided the dungeon master to the floor and covered his mouth with his hand.

An angst-ridden wail came from a cell to their left. In reaction, the prisoner on the right took his wooden cup and ran it across the bars of his cell.

"Control your prisoners!" From the other side of the door came Walsingham's distinctive voice.

While Kit pinned the gaoler, Guy scanned the room. His eyes fell upon a pile of rags in one corner, clothing reclaimed from damned men. He tore a strip of fabric and balled up another, shoving the cloth in the gaoler's mouth before gagging him. Kit lifted him to his feet and chained him to the wall. Streaks of blood on the floor suggested this was another location where the dungeon master tortured prisoners. The wailing man's noise grew in intensity and pitch. No doubt he had once suffered in that position, and he longed to watch his torturer suffer the same way.

"I told you to keep it down in there!" came another shout. Guy raced for the door, and as Walsingham pulled it toward him, he kicked it, knocking it into the Queen's spymaster, sending him crashing first against a torture rack and then onto the floor.

Guy and Kit flew into the torture chamber. The full horrors of the room were not immediately apparent to them beyond the rack that Walsingham slumped against. They did not notice the various ropes, chains, pulleys, and weights that surrounded the room to apply pressure on prisoners in imaginative ways. They did not notice the array of implements for clamping, twisting, separating, and crushing different parts of the body. The large wooden wheel upon which many a man had been broken remained out of their immediate field of vision, as did the pot used to boil men alive. Guy's eyes may have fallen upon these things, but he did not register them, for he was looking for something else.

"You're alone." Guy smiled.

Kit, too, scanned the room. "No familiar."

Guy pointed his sword at Walsingham. "Do you know who I am?"

Walsingham bared his teeth. "The maggot from York..." He twisted his hand and curled his fingers together.

Something fell from the ceiling onto the back of Guy's neck. At first, he dismissed it as a drop of water. Castle dungeons were damp places, after all. The wriggling feeling crawling down his spine changed that assumption.

Beside him, Kit patted his back.

Another drop came from the ceiling, falling, this time into Guy's hair. He brushed it to the floor. A pus-yellow maggot writhed on the stone floor.

Walsingham laughed, a catalyst for further maggot-fall. Guy and Kit batted them away and brushed the larvae out of their hair.

No longer under the threat of the point of a sword, Walsingham flew into the corner of the room, his eyes glowing red, his teeth growing to sharp points and his fingernails turning to talons. He pointed to the door and snatched his hand back. In response, the door slammed shut. As the room vibrated, the ceiling dropped the last of its living rain. Around Walsingham's neck hung a peculiar scarf–the skin of a Walsingham's weasel.

Guy turned to Kit. "He sacrificed his familiar! He *is* the demon, now."

They enchanted their blades and felt the power of the bright blue flame reverberate around them.

Walsingham's laugh boomed from the corner. "How's that cow you bought from Knaresborough Market?" With a flick of his wrist, Walsingham roused the knives on the opposite wall to life. They clashed together before flying toward Guy and Kit. With a flash of their swords, they knocked the blades to the ground.

"Your wife resides in Hell now. She serves me!" Walsingham grinned.

Guy dashed toward him, swinging his blade, but Walsingham swirled out of the way and appeared on the other side of the room. A rope lashed out from the wall, but Kit sliced it in two.

On the floor, a chain snaked toward Guy. Oblivious, he plucked a vial from the pouch on his belt and hurled it toward Walsingham. Again, the demon swirled out of the way and headed for another corner, but the holy water dripping from the ceiling would make him think twice about returning to that part of the room.

Walsingham hovered above the giant wheel. He summoned it upright, and the straps unbuckled themselves.

The chain lashed around Guy's leg. He yelped as it tightened. He slashed at the chain, but the solid metal would not yield to the blade. Kit spotted another chain coming his way and leapt over it before grabbing one of his own vials of holy water and hurling that at Walsingham, who swirled away once more.

The chain wrapped around Guy's other leg and yanked back, pulling Guy off his feet to crash onto the floor. His skull collided with the solid floor and the room blurred. A clatter of wood against the floor nearby turned his head. The wheel rolled toward him. The chains lifted him into the air and turned him upside down. His pouch of vials and potions fell from his waist and emptied onto the ground, some shattering on impact. Guy slashed at the metal with his sword, but it only deflected away from the metal links as they swung him closer to the torture wheel. A leather strap flicked out and wrapped around Guy's wrist, and as it tightened, he lost his grip on his sword, and it clattered onto the stone floor. Other straps flapped in the air, seeking his other hand, but he pulled it away, holding it close to his body.

With his vision stabilising, Guy turned to Kit. His friend struggled with a chain wound around one arm, dragging him toward the torture rack. His feet kicked out, connecting with nothing. Kit struck the chain with his sword, but it had no effect.

Walsingham floated toward the floor, laughing as he did so. He held out his hand, summoning a whip to fly into it. He lashed at Kit, knocking him back into the rack. The chain pulled his hand to the strap, which wrapped around it. Walsingham approached him as the chain assaulted his legs, dragging those two toward the straps. Kit swung his sword toward Walsingham, but the demon spymaster only laughed as he lashed out with his whip again, binding around Kit's forearm. Kit turned his head toward Guy, and with the last of his movement in his wrist, flung his sword. Guy stretched out his hand, and as if guided by providence, the hilt fell into his grip. While holding the sword in his left hand felt awkward, he slashed at the strap holding his right arm, then transferred the sword to it, ready to free his feet. He prepared himself for the fall, curling over on one shoulder, and rolling when he hit the floor. He pushed himself onto his feet and surveyed the scene.

Walsingham's focus remained on Kit who had all four limbs strapped to the rack. Walsingham set the machine to work. Guy grabbed an unbroken vial from the floor and hurled it at his nemesis. This time, Walsingham was unprepared, and it exploded over his back.

Guy followed with another, grabbing it from the floor and throwing it at the back of Walsingham's head. The demon kicked at the structure beside the torture rack.

Weights fell from their position, and Kit screamed as pain jolted through his body. The torture rack groaned as the full weight of the device threatened to pull Kit's limbs from their sockets. Walsingham scurried to a corner, screaming as the holy water dissolved the flesh from the back of his head.

Guy grabbed his sword. Walsingham was weak. Finishing him would be easy. He glanced from Walsingham to the agony on Kit's face.

Walsingham mumbled, summoning strength from the depths of the underworld. If Guy didn't strike, he feared he'd lose the opportunity. He glanced back at his friend.

Kit gasped and his eyes rolled back in his head.

Guy swung both his and Kit's sword in tandem, severing the rope that held the weights, relieving the stress on Kit's joints.

Walsingham remained huddled in the corner, his chanting fervorous. Through the gaps between the stone blocks of the walls, a black vapour emerged. Slashing again, Guy cut through the straps at Kit's arms and legs. Kit rolled from the rack onto the floor, curling into a ball, hugging his limbs to himself as he struggled to draw breath.

Guy tossed Kit's sword to him and turned to finish Walsingham.

The Queen's demon spymaster was no longer cowering in the corner. He loomed over Guy, his skull showing, and horns exposed where his scalp had either melted or slid away. Black blood ran down one side of his face, and the remaining flesh pulsated. While the body was failing, Walsingham's eyes still burned with malice. He clutched Guy's shoulders, leaving meat on his doublet, and exhaled a black cloud.

Guy twisted his sword into Walsingham's torso as the taste of sickness and decay hit him.

Walsingham collapsed, dissipating to nothing, leaving only his clothes hanging from Guy's sword. Guy let the pile of cloth fall to the floor. No flesh, no bone remained, nothing but the sickness in Guy's mouth. The idea that the final essence of Sir Francis Walsingham, spymaster to Her Majesty Queen

Elizabeth, and an actual demon was somewhere in his respiratory system was a sickening thought. His stomach flexed, and he vomited on the floor.

Alas, evil is not easily purged.

Chapter 30—In Which Guy Fawkes Leaves Durham and the Party Dissolves

With Guy queasy and every joint in Kit's body aching, they trudged up the stairs, leaving the dungeon master chained to the wall. When Guy stepped into the open, he gulped at the air, hoping to taste some kind of freshness, some kind of relief. Yet vanquishing Walsingham had shifted none of the awful feelings inside him. The way the Queen's spymaster disappeared deprived him of the opportunity to stand over the man who had brought ruin upon him and curse his bones, for there were no bones to curse.

Bits of Walsingham clung to Guy's clothes. Kit couldn't walk without aid. If anyone saw them in this condition, there would be questions. It was only a matter of time before Dudley sent someone to fetch Walsingham, unaware that he was no more. The wagon in the courtyard offered salvation–spare clothing and a place to rest. Guy helped Kit back into the keep. Instead of following either set of stairs, he entered the ground floor building. At times of peace, the keep was quiet, and the many barrable doors were left open for the straightforward operation of day-to-day business particular with the busy preparation of a banquet. Through here, Guy and Kit made their way to the courtyard. Guards checked wagons as they arrived with supplies. Under the cover of the general hubbub, Guy hurried Kit to the wagon and helped him inside.

Only at this point did his attention turn to activity in the north terrace. How were Anne, Thomas and Ralph getting on with Sir Dudley? If they were still inside when Walsingham's disappearance was discovered, they'd have to fight their way out. He scanned the remaining clothing in the wagon and found something his size. Thomas would no doubt tell him it didn't match, but what did that matter? Better to be oddly attired than blood-soaked.

After advising Kit to remain quiet and hidden in the wagon, Guy strode back into the north terrace and into the small chamber in which they'd set up their tailor's station.

Walter Dudley was easy to recognise, for he looked much like his younger brother. He stood over a table, admiring a range of fabrics. Hearing Guy at the door, he turned and frowned.

"You're not the young man I sent after Walsingham. Where is he?"

A crow cawed. The creature perched on a small frame, its head flitting about, watching everything. It cawed again.

Guy sensed there was more to it than a normal crow. If it indicated to Dudley something was wrong, they'd not avoid further bloodshed.

"My colleague saw Walsingham on his way here. He's measuring him in his room."

Again, the crow cawed.

"How unsociable." Dudley shook his head and turned his attention back to Thomas. "Could you have the doublet made in time for the banquet?"

"That's quite impossible," Thomas said, holding up his hand.

Guy hurried over to him. "Well, if we were to make a start on it right away..."

"It's possible?" Dudley tilted his head to one side as he awaited an answer.

Thomas stared at Guy, and as understanding dawned, he nodded.

"Of course, but we'll have to be on our way," Guy added.

"As soon as we take our stock back to our wagon." Thomas grabbed a roll of fabric.

"No, no," Guy said, nodding at Ralph and ushering Thomas toward the door. "We'll leave that here so Sir Walsingham can make his choice. We shall collect it when we drop off your new attire." Guy smiled at Dudley.

Thomas pointed at a couple of fabrics. "These wouldn't suit his colouring at all..."

Anne grabbed those indicated by Thomas, and the four of them hurried back to the courtyard, into the wagon, and out of the castle. They didn't stop moving until the city of Durham was far behind them.

Rather than travel due south, they took a route southwest, following the River Wear. An hour into their journey, they discarded the wagon in a thicket, turning it over to look like highway robbers had assailed it. Thomas mourned the loss of yet more fabric, begging the others to load the best of it onto the horses.

Without the wagon, they rode at greater pace and their choice of routes increased. At Bishop's Auckland, they left the path of the river, continuing southwest, stopping at a tavern at Staindrop, where they elected to stay for the night.

• • • •

WITH HOODS UP AND HUDDLED in a corner, the quintet supped ale.

Kit glanced at Ralph before addressing the table. "It will be safer if we split into smaller groups."

Guy nodded. "What's your plan?"

"Ralph and I will join Jack on the continent. From here, we'll head east and follow the coast around to a port." Kit gazed at Guy. "You're welcome to join us." He turned to Thomas. "That goes for all of you."

Guy glanced at Anne. He couldn't leave her. "I don't doubt that my fate will take me across the sea one day, but not at this time."

Kit frowned. "In the morning, we shall go our separate ways. Stay off the major routes."

Guy raised his eyebrows. "Do you take me for an amateur, friend?"

Kit nodded toward Thomas. "Nay, but I'm not so sure about your companion."

Thomas gave a dismissive wave of the hand, and they returned their focus to their ale.

Later, after much ale had flowed, Guy spied Kit rubbing at his shoulder joints. "How are you?"

"This arm's about two inches longer." Kit nodded toward his left arm as he held his uneven arms out.

"You'll be okay?"

"Aye, no lasting damage. But..." Kit swallowed hard. "I appreciate what you did, turning to me before you finished Walsingham."

Guy didn't know what to say.

Kit stared into Guy's eyes. "He didn't... do anything to you, did he?"

Despite the gallons of ale, the taste of Walsingham's foul breath lingered on Guy's tongue. His chest tightened as he imagined Walsingham's diseased fumes within his lungs. "Nothing."

"I've not seen one disappear like that... into nothing, leaving their clothes behind."

Guy didn't want to think about it. Walsingham's disappearing act had soured his triumph. Perhaps, vengeance is no kind of victory at all. Walsingham's death didn't restore the lives of Maria and John. It didn't undo all the bad. Maybe in time to come, he would satisfy himself with the thought that Walsingham could no longer harm anyone else, but at that moment, he felt only empty. No, not empty. There was something there, but something he couldn't grasp. "Are there many others like him—demons in the form of men walking among us?"

Kit sighed. "Aye. No doubt there are plenty."

"Where does this end?"

Kit placed his right hand on Guy's shoulder, wincing at the exertion. "That's why Ralph and I are making for Spain. Uncle Francis's dream remains alive. Our actions today may help make that a reality. The Queen has lost a powerful servant in Walsingham. Know you much of the Scottish King?"

Guy shook his head. "Only rumours."

Kit withdrew his hand and rubbed his shoulder. "He, too, has an interest in demons, but he's not like these poisonous bastards. His interest lies in eradicating them."

"So therein lies hope?"

"Aye. Working with the Spanish, we may yet remove Elizabeth from the throne and place a powerful ally in her stead."

"Well, I wish you every success in your foreign endeavours."

"And I wish for you to join us on the continent soon."

"Aye, my friend, that day will come."

They embraced and headed for their rooms to get their heads down for the night, not knowing when they'd see each other again.

• • • •

FOUR DAYS' RIDE, STOPPING at various isolated taverns along the way, brought the trio of Guy, Anne, and Thomas back to Scotton. Alas, it was not Thomas's plan to tarry long in Yorkshire. He had clothes to sell in London. He handed Guy a piece of parchment containing his address and lingered a little too long after kissing Anne on the cheek, before setting off to call on his mother. Once more, Guy's strange friend had proved a more than capable companion.

After stabling their horses, Anne stopped Guy before he made for the house.

"Guy, I need to tell you something." Anne gazed at the grass.

"Are you hurt?" He looked her up and down, checking for any potential injury.

Anne took a step back. "I'm fine."

"Then what?"

"Your reaction now. Fear for me. Checking me over. You'll never see me as an equal."

Guy stepped toward Anne and grabbed one of her hands. "It's my duty to protect you."

"That's why I'm done."

Ha! For so long, he'd tried to put Anne off. As a youngster, he'd treated her with disdain. When Anne's unshakable determination shone through, he'd trained her so hard that he hoped she'd quit. Resolute, she remained. Now, when he wondered if the two of them could make a stand together, purging the area of threats, she yanked that hope from beneath his feet.

"You begged me to involve you."

"But for what? There's too much death, too much misery. Every second we were with that awful Dudley, I kept thinking about what I'd do if something happened to you."

"But it didn't."

Anne moved her head to catch Guy's eye. "You can stop, too."

Guy thought of Percy (the dead one). He half expected him to emerge from the ether and laugh at such a suggestion. Alas, the rebel, Thomas Percy, felt strangely out of Guy's reach. He'd always had a sense of his presence, but, again, there was that emptiness. Guy knew it was wrong to call it that, for something lingered within, like a shadow within a void, something clinging to the lip of a chasm of despair.

Guy glanced back to the fields where sheep no longer grazed. "I know my path, Anne."

Anne sighed. "And you know I'll be here to support you if you need me. I'll not ride out again." Anne turned and entered her home. When Guy followed, he knew he wouldn't remain long.

Chapter 31—In Which Guy Fawkes Ventures South

While many factors could have kept Guy in Scotton, the one which drove him away was that people around him would always be in danger. His father-in-law, Dionis Bainbrigge, was involved in a plot to keep a group of Jesuit priests secluded at Scotton's Old Hall. Guy didn't want to do anything to draw attention to the area. That could put Anne, Elizabeth, and his mother at risk too. What's more, five months after Guy's twenty-first birthday, his inheritance, long kept in a trust, came in from his father. Finances were no object. Part of him thought Europe called, but something else anchored him in England.

How he longed for the guidance of (the dead) Thomas Percy! Alas, Percy had deserted him. Maybe that meant his journey had ended. Was he free from the path the spectral skull long insisted he remained on? It made sense. Walsingham was the last of that unholy trinity, and Walsingham was the link that spread his evil influence over the north. With the nobility untethered from him, they were free from his dark influence.

Guy couldn't help but reflect upon all those he'd known over the years who were no longer part of his life. He remembered the time Oswald Tesimond left Saint Peter's to seek answers in Rome. Perhaps it was Guy's time to do something similar.

With that notion, Guy slowly journeyed south. He hoped the great University of Oxford might bring him comfort in knowledge. On the road, he offered his labour at farms for a bite to eat and a roof over his head. He slept in a hayloft or two, but never one so comfortable as that at his Uncle Thomas's farm. Lonely nights pained him. He cast his mind back to the days after Sandys' death when his ravaged body and nightmares of demons left him drained. This was a different pain, equally agonising, equally straining. He longed to sense Maria's presence, but instead, he felt a chasm ever widening between them. He tried to take solace in the idea that she was at peace, that Walsingham's death had taken the spirit of vengeance with it and let her rest. But the restless dead had quietened, too. The chatter that had scored his life had stopped, leaving him with a maddening void. Physical exhaustion saw him through each night, so wherever he found labour, he worked himself to a point where his body would demand the depths of dreamless sleep.

By the time winter set in, Guy had reached Daventry and found work at Canons Ashby, assisting in the building of a tower house using stone reclaimed from the disused priory. Impressed by Guy's dedication to his work, John Dryden, who owned the property, invited Guy to stay for the winter, taking charge of the estate's horses. While civil to the other servants on the estate, Guy eschewed prolonged conversation. He neither sought nor deserved a rapport with his fellow men. In this manner, 1591 gave way to 1592, and when blossoms decorated the trees, he returned to the road, making for Oxford once more, a meandering journey, again finding work on farms for a few days at a time before moving on.

· · · ·

SUMMER WAS IN ITS INFANCY by the time Guy arrived in Oxford. He made for St Mary's Church where he was pointed in the direction of the administrative services.

With a prodigious beard and considerable muscle mass from months of labouring, Guy looked anything but student material, something the registrar clearly thought as he looked down his long, thin nose at him. "And what makes you believe you are capable of study here in Oxford?"

Surprised by the challenge, Guy took a moment before remembering his headmaster, John Pulleyn. Those memories were sharp, edged with pain, but when Pulleyn's words came back, he knew they still had the power to open doors. *A student of Saint Peter's will be welcome anywhere.*

No sooner had Guy mentioned York's best-known educational establishment, than the registrar's manner changed.

"Saint Peter's has provided the University with a number of notable students over the years," he said. "We have one studying here who would have been enrolled the same time you were. Fairfax. You know him?"

Guy lost himself in a swirl of memories of times training in the depths beneath the school and later, at Saint Robert's Cave. The last he'd heard, Fairfax had accompanied their former teacher, Gaunt, to Leeds. "Aye. I've heard of him."

The registrar rolled his eyes. "There are no *ayes* at Oxford. We speak the Queen's English here."

This conversation alone was enough to inform Guy he wouldn't be enrolling any time soon. No wonder, hundreds of years prior, the locals had driven out a group of academics and sent them fleeing for Cambridge.

"Where might one find Fairfax?" Guy asked, softening his voice in mimicry.

The registrar rifled through records and provided Guy with an address.

For the first time in months, Guy had a sense of direction.

• • • •

NIGHT HAD FALLEN BY the time Guy arrived at Nicolas Fairfax's lodgings. He knocked on the door, but no answer came. He turned and sat on the step. As he considered leaving to seek a bed for the night, footsteps echoed on the path. Taller and thinner than he'd last seen him, Nicholas strode toward him. He carried books under one arm and came to a sudden stop when he saw Guy.

Nicholas blinked several times. "I was not expecting to find you on my doorstep when I arrived home."

Guy stood. "Who were you expecting?"

"What? No one." Nicholas frowned.

"Are you not happy to see an old friend?"

"That depends upon what it is you intend to rope me into."

Guy stepped forward and offered his hand. "I assure you, my purpose here is not to cause any trouble."

Nicholas shook Guy's hand. "Yes, well, I'm glad of that."

"They forced the ayes out of you?"

"Well, I guess, yes, they did." Nicholas smiled and climbed the steps to his front door.

Once inside, Nicholas led Guy along a short corridor and unlocked another door on the left, leading to a small room containing a bed, a chair, a desk, and a trunk. Nicholas placed his books on the desk, took a seat on the bed, and urged Guy to sit.

The two exchanged stories, with Nicholas recounting his time in Leeds and of Gaunt's growing pack of demon hunters. Nicholas's purpose in Oxford was to further his studies, and he assured Guy that his demon hunting days were not behind him. "When I saw you," Nicholas added, "I feared you were here to summon me back. I thought we had business. If that's not the case, what brings you here?"

"Chance. I too believed further study might be my best path." Guy stared at the intimidating stack of books. "Now, I'm not so sure."

"So, what's the plan now?"

"I'm not so sure of that, either." It would be easy for Guy to continue on the path he had been as a farm labourer, but while he had done that, there was a meandering path in mind. Could he do likewise with no goal?

"I'm sure Spencer could find you gainful employment with him."

Guy thought of the last time he'd seen Spencer after they'd journeyed from Durham to York together. "You're still in touch with Ghost?"

"Aye, we write from time to time."

"So, university hasn't completely changed you."

Nicholas raised an eyebrow. "Sorry?"

"An 'aye' slipped out."

Nicholas smiled. "He's in West Sussex working at a manor house."

Guy remembered Ghost's plan to head south so he was close to the action when the Spanish invasion came. It seemed so long ago, now, a hopeless dream with no substance. "Cowdray House, is it?"

"Aye, that's the place. He offered me a job only a few months ago. I'm certain he will accommodate you."

• • • •

NICHOLAS WAS RIGHT. Over the next month, Guy and Ghost exchanged letters, and Guy secured a position alongside Ghost. Guy arrived at Cowdray House, in July 1592. The house was owned by Anthony Browne, 1st Viscount Montagu, son of Anthony Browne, a member of parliament and former Master of Horse to Henry VIII. Anthony Browne, 1st Viscount Montagu, had a son called Anthony Browne, (deceased at the point Guy arrived) who had a son called Anthony-Maria Browne. Alas, some years later this chain of Anthonys would be broken when Anthony-Maria's first-born son, Anthony, died young. History is not a friend to the storyteller when the nobility insists upon naming their sons after themselves.

Viscount Montagu was in charge of affairs at Cowdray House. He appointed Guy as a groom to take care of his grandson's horses on the strength of his reference from Dryden. Guy often accompanied his new young master (Anthony was four years Guy's junior) on rides around the estate. Anthony was naïve even for his age, but a lover of stories and Guy regaled him with tales of battles of good against evil. For Anthony, these were a relief from the new duties that had fallen upon him with the recent death of his father. While his grandfather retained the title of Viscount Montagu and carried out many of the duties, more and more responsibility fell upon young Anthony's shoulders.

Another of the grooms, a troublesome chap named Francis Tresham, however, often responded to these tales with disdain. Tresham was four years older than Guy, and his face bore a persistent sneer. His hooked nose and deep-set eyes only added to his constant look of contempt. His duty was to the horses belonging to Viscount Montagu, but in his senior years, he rarely rode, leaving Francis free to join Guy and Anthony and bring a dark cloud to their jaunts. When not riding or attending the horses, Tresham had a habit of studying his knuckles or massaging the back of his hands with his thumb.

Guy spent a great deal of time with Ghost when not attending to his duties. Ghost had changed little. His face had matured: a sandy beard and time outside in the south had given his face a little more colour, so he hardly suited his nickname any longer, but Guy was not one to dispense with a habit quickly. Ghost retained his eagerness to share knowledge. Guy realised this when Ghost pulled him aside in the stables one day and pointed at Francis.

"He's not to be trusted."

Guy had already worked that out.

"Doesn't mean he can't be useful," Ghost continued. "He's handy in a fight, but an old injury troubles him."

"The hand?" Guy asked, touching his knuckles.

"Broke a knuckle in a fight that never healed properly. It's best to keep on the right side of him."

Ghost introduced Guy to another of his friends who worked in Cowdray House's kitchens, Robert Catesby. Catesby was friendly and happy to share provisions rescued from the kitchen's waste, bread rolls returned from dinner untouched and the overdone ends of joints of meat.

"Catesby knows of the darkness," Ghost had whispered in Guy's ear upon their first meeting. And when Catesby turned, the end of a scar on his neck suggested that knowledge came with its share of pain.

When Catesby left to seek more wine, Ghost told Guy more. "Don't deride Tresham before him—the two have history."

Guy's eyes grew wide. "He trusts him?"

"Please! He's no fool. While Catesby is like to name Tresham a scoundrel, he'll quarrel with anyone who says it is so."

"What makes them so close?"

Ghost checked Catesby was not about to return. "Let's say our Queen's former spymaster had them both in his sights. Walsingham had them sent to the Tower together in case they caused trouble when the Spanish last tried and failed to land on our shores."

Over the first month of his employment, Guy found Catesby amiable, and on the times when he secured wine from the kitchen, stories flowed faster than liquor. Aye, Catesby indeed had known the burn of a demon's claw. A sect in Oxford had trained him and he too knew how to handle a blade against a demon.

As much as he grew to like and trust Catesby, he felt the opposite for the ever-negative Tresham. On more than one occasion, Guy had bitten his lip to avoid saying something confrontational.

But there was no time for a quarrel between them, Guy realised, when Ghost found him in the stables and revealed some important information: Queen Elizabeth was coming to stay in the autumn.

Chapter 32—In Which Guy Fawkes Encounters a Wild Playwright

In the weeks preceding Queen Elizabeth's arrival, activity at Cowdray House intensified. While Guy busied himself with the horses and tried to keep a low profile, he couldn't help but notice how much busier everyone was. Among the arrivals was a man Guy recognised very well indeed, a man who had travelled a significant distance if he'd come from Durham: Walsingham's ally, Walter Dudley. Guy had only seen him very briefly in Durham while attired in Thomas Percy's garb, so he had no fear of being recognised. This link to the past made Guy rather uneasy.

"What's Dudley doing here?" Guy asked when he had an opportunity to catch Ghost alone. Guy had already told Ghost all about his encounters with the Dudley brothers.

"Some say he's keen on replacing Walsingham as spymaster."

From his brief experience with the man, and from better knowledge of his brother, Guy considered him utterly unfit to serve the Queen.

At the opposite end of the spectrum of new arrivals was Catherine Stanley, a distant relative of the Queen herself. Guy had arrived back from a ride to Midhurst to collect some supplies at the same time as Catherine Stanley's carriage arrived, and upon seeing her, he'd almost fallen from his horse. The girl, at eight years of age, could have been a twin for his sister, Anne. Seeing the child with a smile on her face and a look of mischief in her eyes brought warm remembrances of his sister.

While Catherine Stanley charmed Guy, the other esteemed guests troubled Guy. While he'd found perhaps not contentment, but silent acceptance on his travels and in his early days at Cowdray House, now nightmares plagued his sleep once more. Master Leonard roamed in his thoughts, flaying the skin from the bones of all he loved and cared for. With Dudley close, he found himself facing Walsingham again, caught in constant conversation with the demon spymaster and being won over by his silver tongue. A poison spread through his dreams, casting the eyes of everyone he faced red and demonic. Where sleep had for so long had restorative powers, again he woke every morning with pain and anxiety.

On the morning of the Queen's expected arrival, a bright, late September day, Guy rode out with Anthony. A low mist crawled along the ground, lying thicker at the ditches that ran around the perimeter of the property and swirling around the protruding roots of the trees that surrounded the grounds. Guy took in the air, drawing it into his lungs and feeling the benefit as it purged him of the night's sorrows. When they were as far away from Cowdray House as it was possible to get within the confines of the grounds, the young nobleman slowed to move alongside Guy. The dilapidated former servants' oratory stood in ruin behind them, hidden among the trees and vegetation long left to grow wild. Tresham was back at the stables, so Guy was more than willing to share a story, but after checking over his shoulder to make sure they were alone, Anthony leaned closer to Guy. "I need your help."

The furrow on Anthony's brow and the sweat in his hair at his temples told Guy he was struggling beyond the early exertion and the morning sun. He'd not known him long, but he enjoyed the young man's company, for he lacked some of the pomposity of the other nobles he'd spent time with. "How can I be of assistance?" In his life to date, Guy had experienced surprises of all descriptions, so he mentally prepared himself for all manner of problems, from an ill-fitting doublet to nocturnal encounters with demons that took the forms of hippopotamuses, giraffes and great apes.

The real question fell somewhere in the middle. "One of our guests wants to ask me some questions, and I don't know what to do."

Guy wrinkled his brow. He wasn't quite sure what the problem was. "About what?"

Anthony whimpered "I'm not sure I can say."

"Are you in trouble?"

"No." Anthony sighed. "At least, I don't believe so."

Guy realised he'd have to take a meandering path to the root of the problem. "If you can't tell me what he wants to quiz you about, could you at least tell me which visitor it is?"

Again, Anthony checked over both shoulders. "It's Christopher Marlowe."

"Marlowe?"

"You know, the playwright."

Guy did not know. Other than a bit of street theatre in York, Guy had never seen a proper play and knew little about those that wrote them. "And he wants help to write a play?"

Anthony bit his lip. "I assume so."

"What is it that worries you about speaking to this Marlowe?"

Anthony paused. A shudder passed through his body. From a distance of around a mile away, the sound of Midhurst's church bells rang out. Anthony took a deep breath.

"So?" Guy probed.

Anthony shook his head as if shaking an insect out of his hair. "This may sound foolish. I'm worried he may take me for a witch."

Guy looked over his shoulder, mimicking his young master, but with greater awareness of what happens when knowledge gets into the wrong hands. "You shudder at the bells. Hear anything interesting?" Asking the question made Guy aware of one thing: he'd not heard the voices of the dead since Walsingham fell.

Anthony sighed and had his horse trot a short distance before stopping and waiting for Guy to catch up. "You can't say anything."

Guy raised his eyebrows. "It's not me you need to worry about. How does this Marlowe know you hear voices?"

"I confided in Catesby. He swore to help me. Now it appears he told everything to that... to that... to that... stagy!"

Guy considered the situation before he answered. "Catesby has good judgement. If he told Marlowe, he must trust him. Agree to meet him, but I shall stay by your side ready to bar any questions should he pry too far."

Anthony tugged on his horse's reins. "Would you mind joining us later this morning? He's due to meet me in the parlour of the east wing."

Guy agreed, and they continued their ride around the perimeter of the grounds, speaking only when one or the other spotted a bird of interest, or a small mammal hopping through the grass. When they returned to the house, Anthony handed Guy the reins to his horse and dismounted. While he hurried inside, Guy took both horses to the stables.

Inside, Tresham fed the stabled horses. "We've got a visitor coming," Tresham said without smiling.

"Attend to them yourself. I have important business with my master." Guy dismounted and led the horses into the stables, ready to brush them.

"Suit yourself. I'm hoping this one will put a good word in with the Queen when she gets here."

From the stable entrance came the sound of someone clearing their throat. A young chambermaid named Jane who Guy had been introduced to the previous day peered into the stables. With her, Guy recognised Catherine Stanley, looking more of a replica of his sister Anne than ever. She turned to Jane, her eyes wide and sparkling. "Can I stroke them?"

Jane looked to Guy for an answer. He nodded and Catherine sprinted toward Guy's horses. Even the way she ran with her fists pumping reminded Guy of his sister until her leading foot hit a stone and her momentum carried her forward. Her arms windmilled, and Guy dashed to grab her before she fell on her face.

No sooner had he lay his hands on the girl than the blood rushed to his head, and he had to reach for the stable wall to stabilise himself. What was that, a feeling of guilt about improperly grabbing the Queen's young relative? She could have him beheaded for that... but what was he supposed to do, let her fall in the dirt? He glanced at Jane, who gave a nod, suggesting nothing was wrong, but her expression suggested he wasn't wholly in the clear.

"Are you okay?" Guy asked, but before she could respond, Tresham intervened.

"You don't want to play with those horses." He stepped between Catherine and Guy. "They're tired and sweaty from their run this morning." As much as Tresham tried to hide his scowl, and speak in a higher, friendlier voice, Guy sensed he believed himself above this task and felt as much disdain for the girl as he did all else.

Catherine stopped and gazed at Tresham, her contorted face suggesting she too remained unconvinced.

"These have been waiting for you all morning!" Tresham pointed toward the stabled horses.

The draw of the horses trumped her mistrust, and she followed Tresham toward one of the smaller chestnut horses.

Guy busied himself with the beasts that were his responsibility and shook the loose hay from his clothes, ready for his appointment in the east parlour.

Guy had spent much of his time at Cowdray House in either the stables or the servants' quarters. He'd not yet been in the parlour, and when he stepped inside, he considered it one of the grandest rooms in the house, with perhaps only the great hall ranking higher. The large windows across one wall filled the room with light and looked out upon the gardens and their remarkable topiary. An oak sideboard ran along the bottom half of the opposite wall, which was dominated by an enormous landscape painting depicting a woman sitting beneath a tree, breastfeeding a child while great storm clouds gathered over the city in the background.

Anthony was waiting in the room, sitting in a single chair opposite a man lounging across a monks' bench. Guy recognised the man, but it took him a while to place where he had previously seen him. His hair was long and wavy, curling away from his face, making him appear infantile. On his lip was a soft moustache, and only on the end of his chin was there the slightest suggestion of a beard. His eyes were large, brown, and almost feminine. His jacket was of a type he had seen his friend Thomas Percy selling, a dark navy, almost black, decorated with a yellow thread in a pattern of slashes that resembled lightning bolts. When Guy had seen similar on Thomas's stall in Durham, he considered it impossible for any man to carry off such a look... and yet here sat Christopher Marlowe.

That's when Guy placed him, and the experience was so jarring that Guy jolted back. This man had been at Walsingham's council at the King's Manor in York. He, too, had been there on the night Guy met Maria.

Guy glanced at the top of Marlowe's head, half expecting to find devil horns poking out.

"Mr Browne," Guy said, rushing to stand between Anthony and Marlowe, "This meeting is inadvisable."

Anthony waited for an explanation while Marlowe sat erect on the monks' bench, mocking indignation.

"Now, now," said Marlowe, in a voice both soothing yet confrontational. A smile teased his lips while his eyebrows turned inwards. "I've yet to have a chance to offend. Please, allow me at least that dishonour."

"What is it, Guy?" Anthony turned from Guy to Marlowe, unable to maintain eye contact with either.

"We need a word in private." Guy glanced at the door.

"Would you like me to cover my ears?" Marlowe made a play of cupping his hands to the side of his head. "Though I suggest it's already too late. Your master's loose lips have informed me we have a special one here." Marlowe crossed his arms and slung his left ankle upon the opposite knee.

"When Lord Montagu learns of your ways, you will no longer be welcome here." Guy's hand went to his side, though he carried no sword.

"Tush! Which ways are they, Guy? Not my playwrighting ways?" Marlowe shifted in his seat, crossing his legs the other way. "Maybe it's my spying ways? Is that right, Guy Fawkes?"

Guy gritted his teeth. "How did you know my name?"

"Please! There aren't so many Guys around that I wouldn't be able to put two-and-two together to name that scourge of demons. But, hey, if you're here, maybe I don't need to speak to your master at all."

"I'm not telling you a thing." Guy grabbed Anthony's forearm. "Come on."

Marlowe glared at Anthony. "He's a feisty one, isn't he?"

"Come on," called Guy again.

Anthony shifted in his seat and pushed himself up.

Marlowe too stood. "If you think I'm like Walsingham, you're mistaken."

"Why should I believe you?"

Marlowe raised his eyebrows and flashed a smile. "If I were, there's no way we'd both still be alive."

With that, Guy was at least willing to hear him out. "Tell me, what were you doing in his company in York?"

Marlowe sat once more. Anthony did the same, and as Guy edged toward the other spare chair, Marlowe spoke. "You may not believe it, but there's not much coin in writing dramas. I earn a little extra by spying for whoever pays the most."

Guy sat. "That sounds like a reason not to trust you rather than the opposite."

"I'm paid to spy, but I don't share everything. There's a certain type that doesn't take kindly to the arts, dear boy."

Guy leaned forward. "But if you don't tell them anything, why do they keep paying you?"

"Oh, I tell them plenty. Some of it's harmless, and some of it—utter fabrication."

"Isn't that dangerous?"

Marlowe raised his eyebrows. "Part of the thrill! There's nothing like a dose of mild peril to keep the creative juices flowing."

Guy glanced at Anthony, then back at Marlowe. "What did you want to talk to Mr Browne about?"

"I'm doing a little research for a play I'm writing. Let me tell you about a certain Doctor Faustus."

Chapter 33 – In Which Guy Fawkes Witnesses the Arrival of Queen Elizabeth

As Marlowe told Guy and Anthony of his plans for a play about the downfall of a man who summoned a demon, Queen Elizabeth sat in a carriage en route to Cowdray House. While Guy advised Anthony it was not the right time to share his experiences, and while he remained tight-lipped about his own, the flamboyant playwright grew on him. The time would come when Guy would happily regale him with tales of demon battles and advise him of the lore that would make his play authentic.

Montagu entered, a couple of guests in his wake. Walter Dudley followed. He wore a red jacket with a stiff ruff at the neck and frills at the wrists that instantly recalled his brother's attire. Behind Dudley was a smaller man. His brown robe covered his upper half, with two spindly legs sticking out of the bottom. His feet had the smallness of a familiar. Feathery black hair poked out of a hat, and Guy couldn't help but recall the caged raven he'd had in Durham. Dudley didn't turn to face Guy as he continued through the room, though Guy was certain he'd seen a hint of yellow about the man's eyes.

Montagu stopped and pointed at his grandson. "Anthony Browne, what have I told you about fraternising with the help?" He pointed at Marlowe. "This one's little better."

Marlowe pointed at himself and smirked.

Montagu looked back at Anthony. "Prepare yourself for the coming of Her Majesty."

He turned to Guy. "And don't I pay you to tend to the horses? If I see you in here again, you'll be looking for a new situation."

Guy bowed and left, heading back to the stables. He'd give the horses a good brush. He wouldn't want them looking anything less than impeccable for the Queen.

Of course, Tresham loitered in the stables, poised ready to look busy in case anyone of note arrived. Given it was only Guy, he remained seated on a barrel biting into an apple and chewing it with his mouth open.

"Your friend gone?" Guy asked.

Tresham made to throw the apple at Guy but chose to take another bite instead, and spoke as he gnashed the fruit between his teeth, oblivious to the juice running down his chin. "The tiddy gel mooned at the nags, going from one to the next and back half a dozen times. By the time she'd walked there and back, there and back, she was sweltering and her maid called the daft urchin back."

"That so?"

Tresham hurled the remains of the apple core in Guy's direction, but a bob of his head saw it pass by.

"Sickly thing she is. Might be hard-a-hearing from the way her maid had to holler."

She'd not struck Guy as sick when she arrived, but perhaps she'd ailed since.

"That maid though." Tresham rubbed his thighs. "She's a tasty sort."

Guy rolled his eyes.

"When she returns you can show the girl the nags and I'll entertain her maid if you know what I mean."

Guy did know what he meant, but he had no intention of conversing about such things. No, he'd finish with the horses and make sure he was in a position to watch Queen Elizabeth's arrival, fearing the company she might keep.

• • • •

QUEEN ELIZABETH HAD reigned for all of Guy's life and some time before that. Approaching her sixties, she was far from the prime years of her life. And yet, she still proved to be a strong leader, trouncing any hint of rebellion.

Ghost, too, had left his post, finding another to cover for him so he could sit with Guy on the hill and watch Her Majesty arrive.

"I know Catesby trusts Tresham, but what do you make of him?" Guy asked.

Ghost groaned. "Not much. He's a man of little brain and little use. I'd not trust him with anything more than acts of barbarism. He can use his fists and carry more than his share, but I'd not share with him a secret or involve him in a meticulous plan."

"Might there be a need to carry out a meticulous plan of some sort during the Queen's visit?"

"Our time here may be better served as sentries. We will have eyes on the Queen, and we can build a picture of those around her..."

"But?"

"There will be a great many around her. Her guard won't take kindly to us lopping the heads off one of her party, demon or not."

While they were in the open on the hillside, Guy still checked his surrounding before asking his next question. "And what about Dudley? Have you seen him?"

"Indeed. Devilry flows in his blood. Catesby has eyes on him, and has heard troubling rumours about the man."

Guy groaned. "And the talk is that he may be the Queen's next spymaster?"

Ghost checked for eavesdroppers over his shoulder. "I've heard another making moves in that direction."

"Who?"

"A man by the name of Robert Cecil. He's not due to be here. Instead, he remains in London, pandering to those in Her Majesty's ear to gain the promotion."

Cecil, aye, Guy remembered him, the little man with the terrible posture and awkward gait he'd seen at King's Manor. He'd toadied his way into a better situation, as Thomas had predicted.

As they continued their conversation, the clatter of horse hooves and trundling carriage wheels neared. Guy and Ghost watched as six carriages arrived, flanked by royal guards. From the first carriage came several servants who proceeded to unload numerous chests and carry them into Cowdray House, past the waiting Viscount Montagu.

From the next carriage came a trio of ladies, all in richly coloured silk dresses and matching cloaks trimmed with fur. Following them came several officious-looking gentlemen, no doubt there to ensure the business of the nation continued to be conducted while the Queen was away from court. Next came gentlemen dressed in a similar manner to Dudley, all looking self-satisfied and extremely pleased with the stiffness of their ruffs. No doubt these were among the Queen's elite, and every one of them looked capable of acts of extreme bastardry.

When the door to the next carriage opened a herald sounded the arrival of Her Majesty Queen Elizabeth. Two attendants rushed to either side of the carriage door, ready to take their Queen's hand to help her down the steps. She wore a black dress with white sleeves. Gold thread ran through the centre. A large ruff framed her face which was made in her customary white which only made the red curls on top of her head stand out all the more. Montagu came to meet her at the carriage, taking her arm and walking with her toward the house. From the final carriage, more servants emerged carrying cases. While the Queen's stay was only to be for a few days, she was more than prepared for any occasion.

But what satisfied Guy and Ghost most, was the lack of one at her ear. Aye, the Queen retained her purity. No familiar spoke the devil's words to her, and as such, hope to cleanse the nation remained.

Guy chuckled at the idea. The rebel Thomas Percy may have quietened over the last year, but he'd been right about one thing: Guy was on the path once more, demon hunting at the forefront of his mind.

Chapter 34—In Which Guy Fawkes Spies Trouble

The next morning, Guy again woke troubled. His nightmares were distant, and only a red haze lingered in his mind alongside the echo of Walsingham's laugh. His arms ached so much that he rushed to his chest to check if his sword remain buried among his things. No, he'd not been out assaulting demons all night in his physical body. As he put his possessions away, he noted one of his butchery knives, a gift from Margaret Clitherow, was missing. He locked his chest and tested it twice to make sure it was not broken.

Guy sat back on his bed and rubbed his face. His personal grooming had been lacking of late, and his beard felt unkempt. Montagu would be critical of him if he didn't make himself at least a little presentable during the Queen's visit. Guy glanced at his hand. Flecks of red sat in his palm. He dragged his fingers through his beard once more and watched as flakes of dried blood drifted to the floor. Had he scratched himself in his sleep? He entered the courtyard and approached the trough, the nearest source of water, and splashed a handful over his face, pulling it through his beard. There was no great red run-off, no indication of any severe wound. He returned to his quarters and dressed, ready to attend to the horses.

Marlowe joined Anthony for their morning gallops, and this time Guy shared a few details about what happened to those that made deals with the devil. "And what do you know of the party that arrived with the Queen?" Guy asked.

"Dull men, one and all, and duller women. Why the Queen keeps them in her company, I know not."

"Include yourself in that, do you?"

Marlowe put a hand to his chest and dropped his jaw, feigning hurt. "I do not include myself among their number. I am here, first and foremost, as an entertainer."

"You perform to dull men and women?"

"For some, it's the only excitement they get." Marlowe winked.

A familiar whistle resonated through the air and Guy felt his heart stop. For an instant, he was back on the roof of Uncle Thomas's barn, evading Sandys' crossbow bolts. A cormorant crashing to the grass, a bolt sticking through its chest, brought Guy back to the moment.

Anthony signed. "Game shooting. It's not often something we partake in here."

He turned to the source of the bolt. Walter Dudley bowed as other members of the Queen's company applauded his shot. A cocker spaniel sped to the bird, grabbed it by the neck, and trotted back to its masters.

"Let's return the way we came," Guy said.

Marlowe continued to stare at the shooters. "I can understand a man taking a life to save his own, but for sport?"

"Concern yourself not with them," Anthony said as he turned his horse around.

"Perhaps a line or two in one of my plays to show my derision..."

"That will teach them a lesson." Guy smiled.

Marlowe scowled.

They'd gone no more than one hundred yards when Guy held out his hand to urge the others to stop. They were by the path that led to the old oratory, abandoned since Henry VIII's days. Guy pointed at some fresh hoofprints in the mud. "Looks like someone has sought a clandestine place of worship."

Anthony closed on Guy and examined the prints. "They're not horses."

"Would you like to undertake a little investigation?" Guy smiled at his young master and their theatrical associate.

Marlowe dismounted. "Lead the way."

The trio tied their horses to a nearby tree and closed on the chapel. From the outside, it barely looked large enough for more than a dozen people. The roof had collapsed (or more precisely, whoever had been in charge when Henry divorced from the Catholic church, had the roof knocked in), and the arched windows were smashed. Prints of both animal and man led to the doorway. Only boot-prints led away.

In front of the doorway, Guy looked back to make sure no one followed. The last thing he needed was an ambush in a small space with two people with no experience of fighting demons while he'd left his sword locked in his trunk in the servants' quarters. Of course, as a former trainee of the departed Margaret Clitherow, he had a knife which would get him out of a pinch, but he'd prefer not to get into it.

Finding the path clear, he turned to the oratory. Someone, or something, had wrenched the door off its hinges many years ago. Guy expected he could dig for it in the undergrowth if he so desired. He peered through the doorway into the darkness. A rank smell of rotting vegetation wafted out, carrying odours of animal waste. Fresher was the tang of blood. Rotting leaves tiled the floor. A branch had grown in through one window. At the end was the altar, but it was too dark to see inside well. There were several things Guy always kept with him in case of an emergency alongside his knife. One of those was a piece of pyrite.

"Find me some flintstone," Guy called. Anthony and Marlowe busied themselves looking for a piece of rock while Guy cleared a space in the centre of the oratory and piled dried leaves and twigs.

Anthony returned with a piece of flint apt for the job, and Guy struck it with the pyrite, throwing sparks onto his miniature pyre. As the sparks hit the dried leaves, he blew, breathing the spark to life, and soon flames danced on the floor of the oratory, bringing light to a place light had long since abandoned.

Guy continued to crouch by the fire, watching the flames flicker ever higher, fascinated by every cracking twig and enjoying the warmth on his face.

Marlowe grabbed his shoulder and gave him a shake. Once he was sure he had his attention, he pointed at the walls. "I'm no ecclesiastical expert, but that's not what you'd call normal, is it?"

Daubed on the walls in a substance that could only be blood were crude symbols.

"Someone has done a summoning here." Guy moved toward the altar.

"Here?" Anthony took a cautious step back outside.

On the altar was a gold cup, the residue of blood ringing the bottom. A string of intestines hung off the edge, squeezed thin in places. Guy glanced to the side where they hung to find the carcass of a goat, its belly sliced open and its innards yanked out. He studied the cup again. It was not the sort of thing anyone but one with extreme wealth could afford to discard. Marks around the top suggested at least three had drunk from it.

Instinctively, his hand touched his beard, and the desire to escape the oratory hit him.

"Come on." Guy stepped toward the exit.

Marlowe continued studying the symbols, tracing the outline of their shapes with his finger.

Guy gave him a gentle push toward the exit.

As Guy made for the door, a glimmer from beside a splintered pew caught his eye. It was his missing knife, the blade stained with dried blood.

The three of them hurried away, back to their horses. Guy's horse reared up upon his approach, and it took a degree of gentle shushing and delicate strokes to calm her sufficiently to be mounted.

"Say nothing of this to no one," Guy said as they made their way back to the stables.

"You believe someone performed a ritual there?" Marlowe asked.

"Aye, without a doubt." What Guy didn't say, though, was that he feared they'd involved him, somehow, stealing his knife, leaving him with blood in his beard... but how could they do so without his knowledge?

The trio remained silent on the journey to the stables, their faces bearing expressions of increased concern with each passing moment.

• • • •

ONCE GUY HAD SENT ANTHONY and Marlowe inside with a promise to remain silent, and after he has fed the horses, he was glad to be interrupted by Jane, with little Catherine clinging to her hand.

Tresham was absent, no doubt on an errand for Montagu. Guy hated the way Tresham leered at Jane, and the crude remarks he made in front of Catherine were inappropriate. He didn't have to worry about the brute now.

Catherine took a couple of hurried steps forward. Guy's eyes went to her feet, half expecting her to trip again. She shuffled along, hardly lifting her feet from the floor, but avoided any impediment. When she reached the horse which Anthony had been riding, she leant forward, almost falling into it, resting her head against its flank.

Guy turned to Jane. "Is the young lady all right?"

Jane frowned. "She's not sleeping well."

Guy glanced back at Catherine. "That always the case?"

Jane shook her head. "Used to go out like a snuffed candle, and we'd not hear so much as a whimper from her until sunrise."

Guy stroked his beard, remembering the blood smeared there. Surely whatever devilry was afoot at Cowdray House didn't involve an innocent child? "Any idea what's causing her trouble?"

"It may be her age. She's growing fast."

"Aye," said Guy, before turning his attention back to Catherine. He grabbed a dandy brush from its hook on the stable wall.

"Would you like to help clean her up?"

Catherine took the brush and swept it across the horse's thigh, the flakes of mud drifting to the ground.

"You can apply a little more pressure. You won't hurt her."

Catherine did as suggested but gave Guy no indication she'd heard him. And Tresham had said she'd been so talkative on her previous visit. Guy glanced over at Jane, who remained at the stable entrance. She shrugged and looked out across the grass.

Mechanically, Catherine completed the task. She let her arms hang limp by her side. The brush fell from her grip and thudded into the mud.

"Let me take that." Guy grabbed the brush and returned it to its hook.

Guy turned back to Catherine. "These horses are meeting the Queen later. Shall we braid their tails?"

For the first time, Catherine reacted. She glanced at Guy and smiled. No sooner had her face lighted, than a tide of yellow washed over her eyes and she slumped to the ground.

• • • •

"AND NOW SHE'S ABED?" Ghost asked, his brow wrinkled in worry.

Guy nodded. He'd sought Ghost in the servant's quarters as soon as Jane and another young courtier had taken Catherine to her room. When she had collapsed in the stable, Guy couldn't rouse her. Her breath was shallow, but her pulse was steady. He'd tried lifting an eyelid, but none of that yellow that had washed over them was present.

"Without seeing the girl, I cannot know for sure, but it appears some kind of enchantment is upon her. Is there anything else you're aware of?"

Guy told Ghost of his findings at the abandoned oratory.

"Splanchomancy." Ghost puffed out his cheeks.

"I beg your pardon?"

"It's a practice I've only ever read about. Witches can forecast future events by reading a man's intestines."

"But these came from the goat."

Ghost looked into the corner and stroked his chin. "It could be something more. If they'd summoned a spirit into the beast to slaughter, they may be preparing a ritual of significant power."

"With what purpose?"

The room darkened as the sun passed behind a cloud. "They can only mean to use this power to usurp the Queen."

Guy rose to his feet. "We have to stop them."

"But do you have any idea who's behind this?"

"No, but I'd put any money on Dudley being involved."

Ghost stood and placed one hand on Guy's shoulder. "Then, tonight, we act."

Chapter 35—In Which Guy Fawkes and Friends Take on Another Massive Demon

Guy felt no great thrill when awaiting a demon investigation and potential encounter. Each had been a matter of necessity. They'd crossed his path, and it had been a case of him or them. As for his path, he kept walking it, assuming he was following it as he should, for the skull of Thomas Percy had not visited him in some time to warn him of his mistakes. He almost missed the old rebel.

Night fell. Ghost had enlisted Catesby to assist. They were to meet in the stables. From there, they could spy on the comings and goings from Cowdray House, and if a party went to their horses to return to the oratory, they could follow.

Instead, they found someone else waiting.

"Guy," came a whisper from behind one of the stable doors.

Either the horses had started talking (which wouldn't be the strangest thing to happen in Guy's life) or a certain young noble with an affinity with the spirit world lurked behind the door.

"Come out!" Guy called. "It's safe."

The door edged open and Anthony emerged, gazing at the ground.

"What are you doing here?"

"I heard about young Catherine. They say she's been bewitched. I came to offer my assistance."

"I don't wish to be rude, Sir," said Catesby, cutting in, "but do you know what we might have to deal with?"

"Guy has told me some tales..."

"These are more than tales." Catesby drew his basket-hilted sword. The intricate golden weave around the handle, designed to protect the hand, looked to be worth more than Catesby would have made in a year as a servant. "Would you so much as know how to hold one of these?"

Anthony gave a half-smile. "I've done my share of fencing."

"A sport, boy. Have you swung a blade in anger?"

Ghost stepped between them. "What Robert is trying to warn you about is that this may be dangerous. We can't stop you if you choose to follow, but you may not like what occurs."

"I cannot sit by while evil men carry out acts of wickedness in my home." Anthony swept his cloak to one side to reveal his scabbard, from which he withdrew a rapier.

Catesby turned up his nose, but Guy knew that, when blessed, it would be as good a weapon as any.

From the distance came the sound of footsteps and muffled voices.

Ghost nodded toward the side of the stables, and the quartet hurried out of sight.

Peering around the corner, Guy counted six men. In the darkness, it was impossible to distinguish who was among their number, though he suspected Dudley was likely to be one. If that was the case, another was likely to be his familiar. He had seen him flanked by two guards for most of his visit, so they, too, were likely among the six. Whatever they planned to do necessitated guards.

Once the six men had taken to their horses and galloped out of earshot, Catesby headed after them on foot.

"Are we not going to ride?" Guy looked back at the stables.

"They will hear us," Ghost said.

"But they'll be so much faster... Who knows what they can do during that time?"

"That's a risk we'll have to take. We'll deal with the consequences when we get there." Ghost broke into a run, staying close to the treeline so the light of the moon that shone through the gathered clouds didn't give them away.

Anthony soon fell away as Guy, Ghost, and Catesby continued to run. The young noble was not used to such athletic endeavour, while the other three had often had to sprint when their lives were at risk. After fifteen minutes, they had reached the far end of the estate, the oratory = the obvious destination. Through the trees came the faint glow of torches somewhere close to the former place of worship. Guy, Ghost and Catesby slowed. Anthony was some distance behind or had realised this endeavour was foolhardy and returned to the safety of Cowdray House.

As they closed on the oratory, the hum of chanting sounded through the broken window. Dark words recalled memories of every summoning Guy had had the misfortune of stumbling upon. Every time, incredible bloodshed followed. Together, Guy and Ghost approached the window while Catesby walked the perimeter to get eyes on the guards.

Inside, the group were bent over something in the centre as they continued to chant. A lit lantern cast light onto the walls. The cabal had scrawled new patterns there. One man stood, his back to the window, and approached the wall. When he came away, a new mark was present, glistening in the light. Guy's first instinct was to suspect another animal slaughter. He tried to rise to peer at what was on the floor, but the demon worshippers hid it. One he recognised as Dudley's familiar. He did not bend over as the others did. He rested his hands on a lump on the ground and stared at the rest of the party. A quick headcount confirmed Guy's fears. They'd slaughtered one of their number. It was with his blood they painted the walls.

A rustle in the trees followed by a thump, and a flicker from the light by the entrance made Guy and Ghost duck away from the window. A familiar call of a night bird confirmed Catesby had secured the entrance.

From the other side, a snapping twig turned Guy's head.

Out of breath, Anthony appeared. "What's going on?" he whispered.

Guy indicated the window.

As Anthony approached, Guy kept hold of the back of his jacket, ready to yank him to safety once he'd had a sight of it.

"Good God!" Anthony muttered.

"You still want part of this?" Guy said, hoping his young master would make a wise choice and walk away.

"One day, this estate will be mine. I cannot allow this."

Guy turned his attention to Ghost. "Storm in? Stop this before they finish their ritual?"

Ghost nodded, but before they could move, a red light poured out of the windows. Guy gazed up. Light radiated through the hole in the roof, and through a gap in the trees, the moon turned red.

"Too late," Ghost cried.

First came the creak of trees splintering from the bottom up. Next came the shaking of the earth, followed by the crumbling of stone as the energy within the oratory threatened to obliterate the building from within.

"Down!" cried Ghost, diving for cover.

Guy leapt at Anthony and pulled him to the ground. The stone blocks of the oratory flew outwards, some colliding with trees and exploding to dust, some clearing two-hundred yards before crashing back to the ground.

When Guy dragged himself back to his feet, he turned to where the oratory once was. Three men and a familiar stood over a mutilated corpse, looking into a hole in the earth where the altar once was. The earth belched, and an enormous scaled hand slapped onto the stone floor of the oratory. A second hand joined it, and a head emerged. Its face resembled a bulldog's, charred red with black patches around the eyes. Two fangs protruded from its mouth. It pulled itself further from the ground, revealing its wings, followed by two thick but short legs–compared to its body, anyway, for the creature stood ten feet tall.

Anthony peered out from his prone position, his jaw nestling into the ground.

"Stay there," Guy urged as he scooted across to Ghost.

The three witches and the familiar had yet to notice the demon hunters observing their actions. Dudley, illuminated by the ethereal and fiery glow of the beast, opened the book he held and skimmed through the pages.

"What is it?" Guy asked as he found Ghost taking cover behind a tree.

"Cynocephalus... could be any shape-shifting demon..."

"Can we kill it?"

Ghost smiled. "We can try..."

Dudley spoke. "Mighty Lord of the underworld, we thank you for gracing us with your presence. Lend us your power of invisibility, and we shall bring you the blood of God's own representative in this land. Make but one of our number invisible, and we shall bring chaos upon this country."

Cynocephalus smiled, baring the rest of his teeth. He polished a fang with his tongue.

The gentleman to Dudley's left arched his back, and a blade punched through his chest. As he fell to the floor, Catesby stepped out from behind him and swung his sword at Dudley.

Cynocephalus reached for the weapon hanging from his belt. He grabbed the handle and swung an enormous cleaver, deflecting Catesby's blow. Catesby froze, glancing from the cleaver, which had a blade at least a yard long, to the creature that growled at him.

Dudley and the other noble, who Guy now recognised as Sir Basil Warthill, drew their weapons and scanned the trees, looking for other threats. The familiar crept to the cover of a tree. Given the nature of the summoning and the dark magic at play, no benefit would come from taking out the familiar. They had used a greater power to bring evil to the world.

Guy and Ghost imbued their weapons with a greater power too and raced toward the beast.

For a second, it closed its eyes. It touched the top of Dudley's head and the rogue noble disappeared.

"Should I go after him?" Anthony called. He had now risen to his feet but still kept his sword in its sheath.

"No point," called Ghost. "If you can't see him, how can we stop him? Destroy this beast and he'll be visible once more."

As the creature stepped toward Guy and Ghost, the earth shook. It slashed with its cleaver as they both leapt out of the way. Catesby dashed to their side and pointed, trying to initiate a plan of attack. The trio touched their weapons together, blue flame lighting up their blades.

Warthill, meanwhile, recognised that Anthony Browne was without protection. He dashed at the young noble.

Anthony barely had time to pull out his sword and deflect the blow.

As Guy circled to the other side of Cynocephalus, he caught Anthony's battle from the corner of his eye. He couldn't leave him to fight for himself.

Cynocephalus, though, was more than a match for the three of them, destabilising their balance by stomping the ground and swinging that enormous cleaver that could split their trunk in two.

Guy signalled Ghost, indicating his necessary retreat.

Ghost gave a nod of understanding, though his worry was more than apparent as he leapt out of the way of a branch that fell with the latest earth shake.

Guy raced to his master as Warthill struck, knocking the rapier from Anthony's hand. Anthony stepped back, and his heel hit an exposed root, and he stumbled. His arms pinwheeled, and as he appeared to be winning his battle against gravity, Warthill kicked out, knocking Anthony to the ground.

Guy was too far away.

Warthill lifted his sword, ready to deliver the fatal blow.

Guy hurled his weapon, and as Warthill was about to make the downward strike, Guy's sword struck his hand. He released his weapon, and it thudded into the undergrowth. Warthill snarled, his eyes alive with fire. He slapped his hands together and rubbed them. Flame materialised between his palms.

Still, Guy ran toward him.

Before he could finish conjuring whatever fire he intended, Guy leapt at him, his hands wrapping around his middle, bundling him to the ground. Warthill placed his hands on Guy's back, and he felt an eruption of pain as the heat ran through him. It was a pain capable of rendering someone impotent. But while Guy braced himself, a spark ignited in his mind, consuming that heat within him. His brain was alive with a thousand simultaneous images of witchcraft and chaos, before thrusting him back into the moment, Warthill pinned beneath him.

Anthony was back on his feet. He'd not only recovered his blade but Guy's too.

"Finish him," Guy called.

Anthony pointed the tip of his rapier toward Warthill.

"No, it will have to be my blade. He's a demon."

Anthony paused, but when Warthill bared his teeth and fire exploded in his eyes again, Anthony grabbed Guy's blade and struck, slicing through the neck and ending the demon's time on Earth.

Guy got to his feet. He took back his weapon and touched the tip of the blade to Anthony's, uttering the words to bring it power too. A blue flame ignited along its length.

"Right," Guy said. "Let's send this dog-faced villain back into the bowels of Hell."

Ghost and Catesby had kept Cynocephalus busy, but the way their bodies heaved and their laboured movements told a tale of the toll it had on them.

Guy whistled. "Over here, hell mutt!"

Cynocephalus growled at Guy, saliva dripping from his teeth. "I'll chomp on your bones, felus catus, mangey malcontent!"

It leapt into the air and slashed down with the cleaver.

Guy jumped back, but Cynocephalus followed with a kick to a tree, which toppled it, the branches crashing onto Guy.

Cynocephalus raised his cleaver again.

Ghost rushed him from one side, slashing into the creature's middle. Cynocephalus batted him away with his free arm, sending him crashing into a pile of fallen blocks from the oratory.

Catesby attacked from the other side, slashing the creature across the back. He turned and kicked, but Catesby dodged out of the way.

Guy wriggled his torso from side to side beneath the weight of the tree, hoping to squirm into a position where he could pull himself free, but his leg remained pinned. Anthony arrived beside him, first tugging at his body to no avail.

Cynocephalus shoved Anthony to the ground and raised its hell-cleaver above Guy's head.

As it swung the weapon, Catesby hacked at its back, causing its strike to miss, splitting the felled tree in two. Pain exploded across Guy's legs as the weight hit the wood, but then came freedom, and he drew his legs up.

Cynocephalus turned his full attention to Catesby. Roaring at him and yelling, "Rotten skamelar! Fishy asinego!" He hurled his cleaver at Catesby's head.

As Catesby ducked, Cynocephalus wrapped its arms around the nearest tree, tore it from the ground and swung it.

This time, Catesby could not avoid it, the blow knocking him to the ground.

Cynocephalus followed, placing the roots of the tree on top of Catesby, pinning him in place and applying pressure.

Ghost had scrambled back to his feet. He raced over and stood on the other side of the tree, pushing against it, keeping as much of the pressure from Catesby as he could.

Guy raised his sword and ran at the creature. It locked eyes with him, and Guy froze.

"Strike him, Guy!" called Ghost.

Still, Guy stood, looking into the eyes of the beast. The fire went out of his sword and he let it hang loose in his hand by his side.

Cynocephalus grinned. It was his final act.

No one noticed Anthony. Not until the point of his rapier was on Cynocephalus' temple.

The creature jerked its head back as soon as it felt the contact, but Anthony pushed on, the flaming tip blessed with the power to sear through demon flesh, through demon bone, through demon brain. It slumped to the ground, its skin giving way, and in the same manner in which the oratory had obliterated, the inside of Cynocephalus did the same. Guy shielded himself with his arms as a chunky stew of meat, bone, and blood washed over him.

With Catesby pushing the weight of the tree from him, and Ghost twisting it from the fallen demon's last grip, they pushed it to one side. Catesby struggled to his feet, but his breathing was raspy. "Go..." he wheezed.

"What about him?" Anthony pointed his sword at the familiar cowering by the tree.

As soon as eyes were upon him, the feeble man disappeared into his rags, and from out of them, a raven flew.

"Ignore it," Guy cried. "We have to get to the house."

Guy turned toward Cowdray House and prayed they'd vanquished Cynocephalus and broken his invisibility spell before Dudley could carry out his wicked act of regicide.

Chapter 36—In Which Guy Fawkes is Dismissed From his Position at Cowdray House and Chased by Dogs

A night of demon-killing rarely went to plan. While the dog-faced beast with the power to grant invisibility had been felled, they'd been lucky no one had been more seriously hurt within their party. But if they'd not dispatched it soon enough... the consequences were unthinkable. They were not all in a good enough condition to head for Cowdray House, though. Ghost remained with Catesby, while Guy and Anthony mounted the horses left by the cabal and raced for the house. The steeds were acquiescent about being ridden by two strange riders covered head to toe in gore. But when the duo dismounted at the front of the house, the screams inside suggested they were already too late.

Anthony led the way, racing up the steps.

"Halt," called the guard stationed at the door.

Anthony drew the back of his hand across his face, wiping away much of the filth. "It's me, you fool!"

"Mr Browne! I do apologise. If I caused any offence, that was not my intention."

Anthony pointed inside. "Why are you standing here? Can you not hear the pandemonium inside?"

"It's Marlowe's play, Sir."

Anthony raised his voice. "The Queen's life is in danger. Quick! Move!"

The guard bumbled inside, and Guy followed Anthony in. The hubbub came from the main hall. Anthony had been present for the earlier banquet but had dismissed himself from the entertainment. From the noise inside, this did not sound like any entertainment anyone would want to be a part of.

Anthony raced to the doors and threw them open. Now it was clear the sound was applause. On the stage, opposite, players bowed. Anthony wandered into the middle of the hall, with Guy behind them, and the eyes of the guests turning from the stage to the intruders.

Montagu pointed at his grandson. "What's the meaning of this?"

Seated on his table, in a chair far superior to any other in the room, sat Queen Elizabeth, her lips pursed as she stared into the centre of the room.

Montagu pointed to the door. "Outside. Now."

Guy looked around the room. At the table adjacent to the Queen, sat Dudley. He smirked.

As Guy followed Anthony back outside, he tried to piece together the events of the last half hour. He considered how long it had taken to slay the demon. Their acts had saved the Queen's life. Dudley must have become visible before he could act, but not at a suspicious moment. Fortune had fallen upon him instead of ruination. But if he'd made one attempt on the Queen's life, he would act again.

Once outside, Guy glanced back to the darkness, where Catesby and Ghost remained.

A moment later, Montagu joined them, with Dudley following behind, several guards flanking them.

Anthony pointed at Dudley. "Guards! Arrest this man."

No one moved.

"He has plotted to kill the Queen under your roof, Grandfather!"

Montagu stepped forward and shook his head. "Do you have any idea of the disgrace your actions have brought upon the family?"

Anthony pointed at himself. "My actions?"

"Appearing before the Queen in such a state is one thing, but cavorting with this hooligan, getting up to ungodly mischief is quite another!"

"Listen!" Anthony turned to Guy. "Tell them."

Disdain filled Montagu's eyes.

Dudley lurked behind, sneering.

"My noble friend told me about your antics." Montagu placed one hand on Dudley's shoulder. "How dare you bring witchcraft onto our lands?"

"Grandfather, believe me!" A chunk of demon flesh slopped from Anthony's hair and rolled down his doublet before plopping onto the ground.

"I know the culprit. I know who has led you astray." Montagu cleared his throat.

Tresham stepped out from the shadows and joined Montagu.

Montagu pointed at Guy. "Is this the servant you spoke of?"

Tresham nodded.

"And you swear it? You've heard him tell tales of demons, tales to tempt my grandson to evil?"

Tresham sneered. "That is correct, Viscount."

"And what else did you see?"

"Blood. He always had blood on him. On his face. On his beard. He's up to no good, I'm sure."

Montagu nodded. "You shall be rewarded for uncovering this rat!" He pointed at Guy. "Guards! Seize him."

Guy considered drawing his sword. The guards he had witnessed in Montagu's employment were not soldiers; combat was not their forte. But these men were not demons, and neither were they in league with them. Dudley had deceived them, but that was not reason enough to kill them. But neither could he let them take him. It would be a short spell in the Cowdray dungeon, a fixed trial that would condemn him as a witch, followed by a date with the scaffold. No, the only option was to turn and run.

Guy didn't want to lead the guards to Ghost and Catesby–though he hoped they were free of Montagu's ire, so he bolted off across the garden. From the first step, Guy struggled. Where the tree had crushed his legs, they felt dulled, and pain throbbed through his body every time his feet pounded the ground.

"After him," Montagu cried. "Bring him to me!"

The moon, only an occasional guest throughout the evening so far, betrayed Guy, creeping outside of cloud cover to illuminate the garden. The sound of footsteps behind him kept Guy going, but when he took a sharp turn, the thud of footsteps stopped. That meant...

Guy darted for the cover of a pair of topiary birds. A second later, the rustle of a crossbow bolt through the leaves confirmed his fears.

A bark indicated that Montagu had released his hunting dogs, too, so hiding out of sight was no option. They'd soon close on him. He looked up, cursing the moon, and broke into a run once more, eyeing the next safe spot in the garden. Montagu's love of peculiarly shaped foliage again came to Guy's rescue when a conical shrub slowed another bolt.

Alas, as the art of topiary had aided Guy in his escape, it too betrayed him. As he fled for further cover, a bolt found a path through a plant that resembled a duck and embedded in his shoulder.

Guy roared in pain, which caused yelps of success from the chasing guards. He powered on, eyes fixed on the end of the garden, where the thick trees would hide him from the moon and give him greater cover. Moving at any kind of pace jolted the wound in his shoulder. His legs throbbed. The bolt stuck out of him, but he knew yanking it out would only cause the blood to gush out of the wound. In no time at all, he'd be too weak to run.

But the fact he was bleeding introduced a fresh problem. Montagu's dogs would pick up the scent even easier. Guy ran again, nowhere left to go but the trees. A bolt thudded into the trunk nearby, but the second he was among them, he felt safer. He weaved between the trees for a hundred yards before stopping to listen: No sound of the thudding feet of the guards, but the barking of the hounds was closer. Aye, the hounds were closing and with every step, Guy left a clear trail.

Guy took off again, trying to get his bearings. On the times he'd left Cowdray House on an errand, it had been toward Midhurst. If he headed due west, the River Rother was close. Passing through the water might help him lose the scent. Checking the position of the moon through the tree canopy, he headed off. His pace had already slowed. The constant throbbing in his shoulder sapped his stamina and every other function, including breathing, required extra effort. His legs became heavier with every step. But each closing bark drove him to increase his pace until he inevitably slowed once more.

Minutes later, the barks were not all he heard, but the dogs' movement through the undergrowth, too. The trees thinned. The river had to be close. Again, he forced his legs to pump harder, fighting against the ground punching up at him with each step. The bloodhounds' barks suggested they were only yards away, the noise tearing into his eardrums and stirring new levels of panic. Trees gave way to grass. The moon's betrayal continued, revealing his exact location for the pursuing pack of hounds. Even if he made it to the water, what good was trying to shake off the scent trail when he was in their sights?

He continued for want of another plan.

A few more steps and he reached the bank. He raced down, increasing his speed until he splashed into the water. It wasn't deep, his feet scraping the bottom, helping him to push across. The river was not wide either, but it was here he'd be faster than the dogs. On the other side, he could make a stand, use the higher ground and slash at them as they scrambled up the bank. To help him clamber up the other side, Guy grasped at the vegetation again causing pain to throb through his upper body. Letting go was not an option. He gritted his teeth, a futile shield against the pain and dragged himself onto level ground. Behind him came a splash as the first dog entered the water. In front of him was the road. Nowhere else to hide. He drew his sword, ready to fight. As he awaited the first dog, holding his sword in a stance that caused the least pain in his opposite shoulder, the wind pelted him, pasting his clothes, which were equally drenched in blood, sweat, and river water, to his body. Aye, he'd had worse odds: fighting supernatural forces at Brimham Rocks, for example. So why did this feel so much more hopeless?

As the strength sapped from his sword arm, through the trees on the road that led from Cowdray House, a carriage trundled, illuminated by lamps. If they'd sent men to cut him off, he had no hope. Taking on guards and the dogs was not an option, not in his condition. The carriage continued toward him, and another dog splashed into the water. A third barked from the other side. The first was halfway across.

Another plan came to Guy: run for the carriage, slice through the harness, and steal a horse. It was his best hope. The cold bit at him as he tried to run. With his clothes drenched, their weight had multiplied. Every step was like running with lead boots on through treacle, with a knapsack loaded with stone.

But when he was close to the carriage, a sound he didn't expect came: laughter.

Whoever rode in this carriage could not possibly be in his pursuit, not while enjoying so much merriment. Guy waved his hands and called out as the carriage approached. The driver paid no heed, whipping at his horses to increase their speed. Even if he wanted to, he'd not be able to slash the horse free. Somewhere behind him, he heard a dog scrambling up the bank.

The carriage was beside him. Aye, there was laughter, a woman's laugh, and the cause, a crude song. A face appeared at the window, followed by a shout: "Woah!"

The driver pulled on the reins, and the horses slowed. A bark in Guy's ear turned him around. Too late. He had to deal with the dog. It lunged at him, and Guy raised his foot to push it away. It came again, but from behind came a shout, "Guy!"

Guy kicked out again, knocking the dog onto its side. The carriage door opened. Another bark came as the second dog reached the top of the bank.

He had to buy himself time. He drew his sword and blessed it, watching the blue flame dance along the blade. Aye, that would act as a deterrent. As he backed away from the beasts and toward the carriage, he moved the blade in a slow figure-of-eight pattern, keeping the dogs mesmerised by the flame. Another bark indicated the third had scaled the bank. As a pack, they could surround him. The fire would no longer concern them. Guy glanced over his shoulder. He was close enough. He slashed forward, causing the dogs to leap back, and before they had time to switch direction, he took his first step toward the carriage. Another leap and his fingers gripped the doorframe, and his feet scrabbled for the steps. He was so close to safety when agony erupted from his ankle. Even through his boot, he felt the teeth of the bloodhound press against the bone and bile flooded his mouth.

A figure in the carriage leant forward. Marlowe! He leant out of the carriage door, lute in hand, and smashed the instrument over the dog's head. Shock released the jaw, and Guy yanked his foot away, though he lost the boot to the hound. Marlowe pulled the door shut and urged the driver onwards.

Guy swallowed back a mouthful of bile and shuffled back into the seat opposite Marlowe. On one side of him sat a young woman that Guy had seen around Cowdray House in recent days, on the other, a young man who looked like he could be Marlowe's younger brother – though Guy swore he too looked like someone on Montague's staff. On the seat beside Guy was a rich array of food liberated from the banquet.

"Looks like we picked a good time to make the journey back to London," Marlowe said. He plucked a grape from the platter next to Guy and popped it in his mouth. Guy stared out of the window at the dogs leaping at the door. It wasn't long before the carriage left the hungry bloodhounds far behind and Guy was free.

Chapter 37—In Which Guy Fawkes Receives Medical Treatment and Experiences London

Opulence was not something with which Guy was familiar. The silver platters on the seat beside him could buy him a house. Fruits sat on those platters that Guy didn't even recognise. And yet, he could enjoy none of it. The bolt sticking through his shoulder meant every jolt of the carriage was agony, and he was soaked through and freezing from his jaunt across the river. Blood continued to flow from the puncture wound on his ankle no matter how much Guy bandaged it with the discarded shirt of the young Marlowe look-alike.

Marlowe tried to bring Guy comfort by promising him he would see the sights of London, but alas, that had to wait. As soon as they reached Haslemere, Marlowe had his driver slow, looking for signs of light in any of the abodes. Upon finding someone awake, he pounded on their door, and demanded the address of someone who could help, with a gold coin paying for any trouble. Marlowe left Guy in the charge of a capable surgeon and continued on his way, leaving Guy with an address in London, and sufficient coin to find his way there.

The surgeon urged Guy to sit on a long bench close to the fire. He stared at Guy, beetling eyebrows reminiscent of his old headmaster's. The surgeon stared at the shoulder, and the bolt sticking through it, first from one side, then the other. He shook his head and checked both sides again. "It'll 'ave to come out," he said and sat on the bench next to Guy.

"And I was hoping to keep it," said Guy through gritted teeth.

In earnest, the old man shook his head, "No, no, no. Danger of going to rot." He checked both sides again. "It'll have to come out."

"And what about this?" Guy lifted his foot, which was red with blood.

"That I can stitch, but your bolt's the bigger problem."

"Well," Guy said, teeth still clenched together, "would you be so kind as to remove it?"

"Oh, I could." The surgeon nodded. "It'll probably kill you."

Guy grimaced with the pain once more. "Is there a... non-killing way?"

The surgeon scratched his head. "Trouble is, I need to pull it through, one way or the other, pack it with dirt, and seal the holes. Both sides. I needs to do it all at the same time. And I only 'ave so many 'ands."

Guy's head pounded, pain and exhaustion combining to punish him further. "Do you not have a young apprentice?"

"'appen, I do." The surgeon smiled, following it quickly with a sigh. "But 'appen he's out with the sweating sickness."

Guy ran his hand across his soaking brow. "Is there anyone else?"

"Me mother's asleep upstairs. I could wake 'er up, but she won't be 'appy."

"Your... mother?" Given the surgeon's geriatric appearance, Guy wondered how old his mother was... and to what extent she'd be capable of assisting with surgery.

"There's no way you can do this alone?"

"Well, there is," said the surgeon. "If I spring another pair of 'ands from me arse'ole."

"I guess you'd better wake your mother."

Guy sat in silence in the front room of the surgeon's small home. Various surgical implements rested on the table, and as the candle flickered, Guy noticed more and more splashes of blood spread along its length. As he waited, he tried to block out the pain, staring into the opposite corner so he couldn't see the end of the bolt sticking out of his shoulder.

A moment later, the surgeon returned, behind him a woman that looked even older than some things he'd seen rise from sarcophagi.

"Mother, wait there, and I'll get everything ready."

She groaned.

The surgeon grabbed a pail from the corner and placed it on the bench. Guy glanced into it, seeing only dirt. The surgeon hurried to a cupboard, hunted for a moment and returned, handing Guy a long root, about the thickness of a carrot.

"Stick this in your mouth," the surgeon said. "Clamp yer teeth on it, but don't bite through."

Guy did so, tasting the earthy bitterness.

The surgeon placed two irons in the low fire. In doing so, the flames kicked to life once more, drawing Guy's attention.

The surgeon approached his mother. "As soon as I yank the bolt out the front, pack the 'ole wi' dirt and seal it wi' the iron, okay?"

Guy clamped his teeth on the root harder, releasing juice from the inside more bitter still.

Wearing a thick leather glove, the surgeon yanked on the bolt, dragging it through flesh and sinew, and scraping it past the bone.

Guy felt every imperfection on the bolt as it passed through his body, pain exploding in his shoulder drawing tears from his eyes. He bit on the root in anticipation as behind him, the old woman slapped dirt onto his shoulder, poking it with her bony fingers into the hole, grabbed the iron from the fire, and pressed it to Guy's shoulder, sealing the wound.

As his flesh sizzled, Guy wailed through his clenched teeth. The corners of the room closed on him and the fire grew large.

The bolt still stuck out of the front of Guy's shoulder. The surgeon peered round and smiled. "Good job, Ma."

The surgeon mopped sweat from his brow with the back of his hand. "Now I'll tug it the rest of the way through. Ready to go again?" The surgeon didn't wait for a response. He yanked out the bolt, tossed it to the floor, and smeared dirt into the wound before grabbing the remaining iron from the fire and sealing that side too.

Guy's flesh sizzled once more. The root snapped as Guy's teeth clenched tighter, and the walls rushed at him and swallowed him into blackness.

• • • •

GUY WOKE WITH LIGHT pouring through a crack in the curtain. He was in a bed, the finest he'd slept in for some time. When he tried to move, he winced with the pain in his shoulder. He probed the wound with the tips of his fingers. The bolt was gone, so that was an improvement.

As he became more aware of his surroundings, he also realised he was not alone in his bed. The old woman, the surgeon's mother, lay next to him, so still, she could have been mistaken for the dead. Guy gasped, taking in a mouthful of stale air. He twisted out of bed. Movement hurt. His first few steps were to the nearest wall. With one hand, he supported himself as he made his way to the door. It opened to a narrow corridor, where at least the air was less foul. Through a door to the left came a strangled cry. That had to be the surgeon's front room. Guy shuffled forward and eased the door open. The surgeon stood on his bench, bending over a patient. He had hold of the end of a pair of pliers attached to a tooth of the wailing man. The surgeon yanked back, and the tooth flew free, a jet of blood followed it to splash onto the bench. The surgeon dropped the pliers on the table and grabbed another of his roots. "Bite on that over where the 'ole is."

The man grabbed it with his shaking hand and stuck it in his mouth.

The surgeon stared at Guy. "You shouldn't be out o' bed. Rest is what you need."

"But..."

"Ma? She don't mind the company."

But Guy did. Not that he desired an argument with the man who had saved his life.

"I must get to London." Guy glanced toward the door.

"Nah, you set off on a journey like that and it'll let the rot it. Bed rest's what you need."

The patient stood and placed a coin on the table before making for the door.

"Is there a tavern nearby?" Guy asked, leaning on the table (careful to avoid the most recent splash of blood) to support his weight.

"Well, I can't blame yer, if ye don't want mother's company. Follow me, I'll show you the way." The surgeon urged Guy on with a beckoning hand gesture.

Guy stepped toward the door, and as he looked out onto the muddy street, he remembered he was one boot shy, having left it in a hound's jaws. "I don't suppose there's a cobbler nearby?"

He noted, too, the thick stitching in his ankle. Somehow, the old chap had made a decent job of it.

• • • •

FIVE DAYS PASSED BEFORE Guy felt able to continue his journey, five days of sweating in his bed, five days of falling into dreams of demons. These were not the dreams in which he was under constant assault, but dreams in which he revelled with them, dreams in which he slaughtered animals and played with their innards, drawing demons to a cabal under his command. Dreams in which he cavorted with Walsingham and Dudley as their kin.

Guy told himself it was his mind battling with the wound, fighting to stave off the rot. What else could it be? And when a night of peaceful sleep came at the end of those five days, he knew it was time to depart.

He paid a last visit to the surgeon, who checked the wounds, admiring his work with pride. He yanked out the stitching, holding his breath as he did so, breathing again only when the wound didn't open anew.

Next, Guy purchased a horse and set off on the road to the capital, stopping for the night in Kingestowne upon Thames. Guy checked Marlowe's instructions. He'd given an address in Bankside, the Rose Theatre. The closer Guy got, the more condensed the population became, with markets placed on any piece of ground large enough for a couple of stalls, and with so many people, it was impossible to pass through on horseback. He retreated and found somewhere he could sell his horse to recapture his outlay before returning to push through the mass of people once more. Many bore scowls and the pinched faces of poverty. And more than a few bore scabs on their cheeks and noses, causing Guy to draw back and avoid them.

Guy stopped by an extravagant building that could be a theatre. "Excuse me," he called to a young man standing outside. "Is this the Rose Theatre?"

"Does this look like a bleedin' theatre to you?"

Guy wanted to answer in the affirmative, for that was the exact reason he'd asked, but figured a simple follow-up would better suit his needs. "Where would I find it?"

The young man narrowed his eyes. "You're not one of those *thespians,* are you?" He seemed to spit out the peculiar word.

A what? "No, I'm looking for a friend."

The man grumbled. "That way." He pointed. "Turn left when the Thames comes into sight. Keep your eyes peeled for Rose Alley or Maiden Lane and you'll find it."

"Thank you."

The man turned away. "You won't thank me when you see what a sort are there."

"I beg your pardon?"

"I wished you a good day." He put up a dismissive hand and walked away.

Now it was Guy's turn to grumble as he made his way past the building. The river ran in front of him and sprawling across it, London Bridge. This was like no bridge he'd ever seen, the structure carrying enormous multi-story dwellings and shops. There was even what looked like a chapel. Alas, Guy's journey was not yet to take him onto the bridge. He followed the Thames in the other direction until he came to Rose Alley. He did not have to walk far before he discovered the theatre, a bizarre almost circular building (while Guy didn't count them, history tells us it was a fourteen-sided building, the shape of a tetradecagon) with a thatched roof. Compared to some of the nearby buildings, it looked almost new. He walked around until he found the entrance. The door was open, and voices boomed from inside. No one kept the door, so he wandered in, past steps which led to tiered seating, overlooking the central pit. Guy stood at the perimeter watching wild-eyed young men read from pieces of paper, throwing their hands in the air at the culmination of each speech.

Guy approached a nearby duo. "Excuse me, do you know Christopher Marlowe?"

The pair continued delivering their lines as if Guy was invisible. He approached the stage, but before he reached it, another threw himself at his feet and delivered an impassioned plea to continue his work and conquer the world. Guy sidestepped him, but only into another man delivering a soliloquy, over-stressing the rhymes.

All around him, men as old as seventy and boys as young as eight, spoke nonsense as if something otherworldly had consumed their minds.

"Guy!" came a cry.

Marlowe stood before him, arms open to welcome him into an embrace. "Or perhaps a shake of the hand would be better. Wouldn't want to damage that shoulder. How is it? All fixed up?"

"Aye, a peculiar surgeon, but he did a fine job. Marlowe, what is wrong with these people? Are they suffering some kind of bedevilment?" Guy's fingers twitched close to his sword.

"Guy, is this your first time in a theatre?"

Guy nodded. "Is this for your play, Doctor Faustus?"

"Alas, no, the good Doctor if not yet ready for the stage."

Guy stepped back as another man threw himself to his knees.

With an extravagant sweep of his arm, Marlowe indicated the men before him. "Welcome to the auditions for Tamburlaine the Great, Part Two!"

Guy still felt as though he was staring at men who had lost their minds to the devil's enchantment.

"Is that... a play?"

Marlowe shook his head. "Is that a play? Is that a play? It's only the sequel to the greatest play ever performed in this fine city."

Guy pointed to a man weeping over the pages he held. "But what's wrong with them all?"

"They're thespians, dear boy!" said Marlowe, as if it explained everything.

"They're what?"

"Actors! Men born for the stage, men with power to become conduits for the characters of magnificent stories... and you Guy, you shall be by my side as we stage the greatest play of all time."

Guy gazed around the room apprehensive about the situation he found himself in.

Chapter 38—In Which Guy Fawkes Reacquaints Himself with an Old Friend and Serves the Queen

Weeks passed, and the days grew ever shorter. Guy's injuries continued to heal, and he made himself busy around the theatre helping Marlowe and his players as they prepared for the premiere performance.

Marlowe put his arm around Guy as they watched a rehearsal. "Believe me Guy, the day this play opens, November 5th, will go down in history. Mark my words, it's going to be explosive!"

It was impossible for Guy not to be consumed by Marlowe's passion and to feel every bit as eager for success as the playwright. Guy came to understand what it meant to be an actor and appreciated their dedication to bringing the role to life. As he watched rehearsal after rehearsal, Marlowe continued to revise the script, until the passion he felt for the characters and the story materialised in the performances.

At Guy's behest, Marlowe had written to Anthony Browne for information about what had occurred at Cowdray House after Guy's escape. Guy found that everyone else he cared for was safe. Anthony had received a severe reprimand from his grandfather and suffered some slight loss of freedom. To help him settle, his grandfather had arranged a wedding for him in the spring. Catesby had recovered from his injuries, though still suffered from a shortness of breath. Ghost continued with his role unaffected, though an altercation with Tresham left both with bloody noses.

Guy had written back–in Marlowe's name and with Marlowe's permission, seeking more information about what happened with Dudley, finishing with a question seeking news on young Catherine's condition, hoping she had made a full recovery. Alas, the news that returned was not hopeful: Catherine had yet to wake from her endless sleep. Jane had been dribbling water between her lips to sustain her, but the flesh was dropping from her bones. Another member of the household staff had taken ill with the same condition, though she passed after a week in such a state. Dudley, after his failed attempt against the Queen, had returned to London.

Of Queen Elizabeth, too, there was news, though this came from another source. From the pit of the theatre, Marlowe caterwauled.

"What is it?" Guy asked as a messenger brushed past him heading for the exit.

Marlowe reread the scroll.

"The Queen intends to be here on opening night!"

• • • •

SINCE HIS ARRIVAL IN London, Guy had spent many hours at the theatre, resting for the night at a Marlowe rented with another playwright named Thomas Kyd. Marlowe didn't so much burn the candle at both ends, but fling candle after candle into the flames, and when he wasn't rewriting and guiding his players, he performed clandestine acts for the shady figures demanding his services. When Marlowe offered Guy the opportunity to join him on one of these jaunts, Guy declined. He was tempted, of course, but his shoulder remained stiff, and his mind troubled.

Marlowe was not the type of spy to go about his business in a cloak and dagger manner. No, he played roles to gain confidence, or feigned pure stupidity so others would reveal secrets in his presence in the misguided belief they would sail over his head without consequence. It was a skill to know how best to act to get the information he needed. And while Guy chose not to accompany Marlowe unless he was visiting a tavern and needed an extra number in his party, Marlowe always gave Guy the latest scoop, whether or not he wanted to hear it. The events at Cowdray House meant Dudley had weaselled his way closer to Her Majesty, often accompanying her on formal occasions. It was likely he'd be present at the opening night of Tamburlaine the Great Part Two. It was this information and nothing else that made Guy thirst to use his sword once more.

The only place Guy ventured other than the theatre, was to Fleet Street, where Thomas Percy operated his tailoring business. His friend had set up shop, doing a fine trade selling expensive doublets to wealthy gentlemen. Once more, Thomas was reliant on the skills of others to make the clothes, but one thing he could do was sell, and on his visits, customers disturbed their chats.

On his first visit, with the usual haste and lack of awareness, Thomas threw his arms around Guy.

As Guy winced, Thomas backed away and sucked air between his teeth. "My most sincere apologies, old friend."

Guy gave a weak smile. "How were you to know I'd have an injury?"

Thomas leant against a table. "In fairness, I should have expected it given your track record."

Guy slapped Thomas on the back and the two of them chuckled.

"So, what brings you to London?"

Guy recounted his time at Cowdray House and his travels before and after. Only when he finished, did he notice his friend's solemn expression. "What is it?"

Thomas moved to the doorway and glanced both ways along the street before returning to his position. "I continue to keep my ear to the ground. Information sells, and what I've heard, this Dudley is involved in some dark deeds indeed."

"Anything in particular?"

Thomas licked his lips. "He razed a medieval priory to the ground at Burnham-on-Crouch, looking for some kind of artefact or ancient jewel."

If it were something with which he could summon an aerial power, he could prove dangerous. "I shall bear that in mind. Thank you." At that point, Guy noticed something on Thomas's hand. "And on the subject of jewellery, is that not a wedding band I spy?"

Thomas's cheeks reddened. "Why, yes, it is."

"Tell me about this unfortunate young lady."

"I've told you about her before. It's Martha Wright."

Guy raised his eyebrows. "So, it wasn't a one-off encounter. I never expected you to marry so young."

"Neither did I, but after I travelled with Kit to Durham, I knew I was as good as a dead man if I didn't make a decent woman of her."

"And are you happy?"

Thomas sighed. "It is a difficult time. She is with child, and the taxman is forever knocking at my door."

"Anything I can do to help?"

"If you fancy purchasing a new doublet, I'd be happy to oblige."

And that's how Guy came to acquire a significant upgrade on his attire during his time in London.

• • • •

IF GUY HAD ANY FEARS about being recognised by Dudley on opening night, Marlowe soon allayed them when he demonstrated his skill for stage make-up. A close skullcap covered his hair, and Marlowe insisted on giving him a close shave with a sharp razor. With some gentle contouring, Marlowe made his cheekbones more prominent, and shadow drew out his chin. Without a doubt, it was far beyond the level necessary, but Marlowe was not a man who did things in half measures.

Marlowe also arranged with the theatre manager for Guy to work for the night, waiting on the Queen and her party, delivering her choice of snacks and beverages. When guests arrived, Marlowe and Guy shared nervous glances, before each took to their positions, Marlowe ready to spring onto the stage to introduce his play, Guy waiting for an opportunity to serve royalty. Maybe this time he could deliver word of the danger surrounding her. Guy's position allowed him to watch the Queen's arrival alongside her courtiers. Dudley remained close by her side, and while he glanced at Guy, there was no flicker of recognition, no tightening of the muscles, no movement of the hand toward the sword. So far, the disguise worked. Close behind was a man who looked the epitome of a witch: dark, sunken eyes–evidence of many nights poring over dark lore–a sallow complexion that told of an affinity for darkness and a rejection of the light, and a chin elongated by a sculpted beard. The years had not been kind, but Guy recognised the man trying to worm his way into the position of Secretary of State and Chief Spymaster as none other than Sir Robert Cecil. He opened his mouth to reveal long incisors, which, when coupled with the shape of his nose, gave him the impression of vermin. When his eyes fell on Guy, they lingered. He could feel them, boring into him, reading something inside his mind... surely Cecil would not remember Guy serving him potage at King's Manor so long ago? No, Cecil was a man whose eyes were busy and probing, drawing confessions from the guilty without a shred of evidence. But Guy *wasn't* a guilty man.

Guy's role was not to address the Queen and her party, but when she made a request, to fetch it and bring it to her. He was not alone on this duty. The royal party had dozens waiting upon them, and they often sent back more food than they ordered.

Guy's first duty was a simple one: pitchers of ale. Four at a time, he brought them to the Queen's party, taking the opportunity to survey the scene. The Queen sat next to Dudley in the centre of the box, looking upon the stage with great interest. Other members of her group chatted and pointed across the theatre to associates, while Cecil continued to probe all. Again, his eyes fell on Guy and lingered. Next was a course of oysters. Guy delivered these and placed them before the Queen.

As he turned to leave, Cecil called, "Hold."

Guy turned back to him.

"How do we know these are fresh?"

"I assure you they were caught today." Whether or not that was true, Guy did not know, but the manager had warned him they would ask.

"Eat one."

Guy took an oyster without so much as thinking. Only as it passed his lips did he suspect he was not wholly in control of his actions. Had Cecil the power of influence? If so, it was likely a gift from the underworld rather than a God-given talent.

"Okay, thank you," said Cecil.

Taking the cue, Dudley picked up an oyster and fed it to the Queen.

Guy hurried out of their box and took several deep breaths.

As he stood by the door, Cecil emerged. "Walk with me."

He led Guy out of the front entrance, toward the Thames. Each step Guy felt was a bad idea, but simultaneously he couldn't resist following.

When a hundred yards or so away from the theatre, Cecil held out a hand, and Guy stopped.

Cecil's eyes bored into Guy once more. While his lips didn't move, he could almost hear his voice. It was like he stood outside his mind, banging on the door.

Cecil broke eye contact and spoke. "A life beyond death. Extraordinary."

"I beg your pardon?" Guy muttered. His head swam, and he didn't feel in full control of his body.

"I've seen the way you look at Dudley. I don't trust him either. He'd betray us all given the chance."

The word "us" lingered in Guy's mind, hissing over again.

Guy struggled to find words while Cecil straightened his jacket. "I know in my position I could have Dudley removed, but the Queen doesn't like it when someone makes to remove her favourites. It could be career-limiting for me, and I plan to play the long game."

"What would you like me to do?" Guy barely recognised his voice.

"Destroy him, of course. And get rid of the body."

Guy stared at Cecil.

Cecil rolled his eyes. "I have it on good authority that he is plotting to take the Queen's life tonight. He has spent the night plying her with wine so she'll be vulnerable."

Guy continued to stare at Cecil, unable to speak. "I have put certain measures in place to ensure Dudley's intent will be clear. But you must stop him before he gets close. Traitor's Gate will be open tonight. A few sacrificial lambs will fall. One will carry the instructions of Dudley, his plan to murder the Queen. She'll realise she's had a lucky escape, and I shall be in her gratitude."

Cecil turned Guy around and headed back for the theatre. "Back to work. Bring wine and figs!"

Chapter 39—In Which Guy Fawkes Visits a Pair of Taverns in Search of Dudley

Guy continued to serve food and drinks to the royal party for the remainder of the evening, paying particular attention to Dudley and his interactions with the Queen. While she watched the play, it was clear his comments and offers of food did not ingratiate him to her. He was, however, frequently refilling her goblet. Guy had heard that the Queen did not suffer fools, and this was more than apparent with Dudley. She liked to have him around, but why, Guy wasn't sure. Neither could Guy understand Cecil's ploy. Uncovering a traitor under Queen Elizabeth's nose may warm him to her, but what motive did he have to get close? Was he too not only interested in supplanting her with one with demonic leanings? By assisting Cecil, was he helping the forces of evil? Or had he misjudged Cecil? Was Cecil on the side of good? That consideration became secondary, for Guy could not shake the compulsion to act against Dudley.

There was one man Guy knew could help him, one man that often played both sides and came away smiling. But he had to wait for his play to be over. The royal party had ordered the last of their delights to consume during the falling action in the final act. Guy had been to so many rehearsals he mouthed each line along with the actors as he counted down the final words.

Upon its conclusion, after ushering out the patrons, Guy rushed backstage where Marlowe hugged and slapped the backs of his players. Guy removed the skullcap to free his ginger locks.

"A triumph, Guy, a rousing triumph if ever I saw one! Tell me, did Her Majesty enjoy the show?"

"Aye, she did."

"Did she laugh at the jokes? Did she weep at the sorrow?" Marlowe mocked each emotion as he spoke.

"She went through the whole gamut of emotions."

Marlowe slapped Guy on the back. "We must celebrate."

"About that..."

Marlowe raised his eyebrows. "Have something particular in mind?"

Guy moved in closer and lowered his voice. "You know where to find certain nobles within the city."

"I'm intrigued. Go on." Marlowe stroked his chin, fiddling with his tiny beard when he reached the end.

"Where would you wager Dudley will spend the next few hours?"

"Out to avenge him for getting you kicked out of Cowdray House?"

Guy checked over his shoulder. "It's not so much my plan... Cecil wants him dead."

Marlowe stepped back and stared at Guy, his eyes wide. "Liaising with one enemy to defeat another! Ooh, Guy! I never thought you had it in you. You're quite the rascal!"

"Can you help me or not?"

Marlowe rolled his eyes. He patted Guy on the back. "I know a few of his haunts if you're willing to join me in my revels."

"Lead on!"

Marlowe grabbed a black cloak lined with red silk from the coat stand, wrapped it around himself, and strode out of the theatre. "I'll warrant they'll sup upon the Thames. We'll make a few steps on the bridge to gather a touch of intel and dispatch this monster together! Perhaps a scene from Doctor Faustus shall formulate in my mind as we undertake this nefarious business!"

Cold hung in the night air, and as Guy and Marlowe passed each building, gusts of wind carrying the chill of the Thames assaulted them. Street pedlars, who had no doubt done a good trade with those leaving Marlowe's show, tried to hawk the last of their spiced nuts and honeyed pastries while mistresses tempted lone gentlemen into their bawdy houses, a safer destination than the narrow alleys, home to cutpurses and cutthroats. Guy and Marlowe continued, marching with purpose, braced against the cold and ignoring the tempting calls from all sides.

After a couple of hundred yards, Marlowe took a sharp turn to the left. The properties grew closer together with each step, and taller too, until buildings rose six storeys high on either side, leaning together high above them, threatening to kiss. Guy glanced up. A glimmer of moonlight did its best to illuminate the narrow gap. The way the buildings came together took him back to his younger days in York, to The Shambles, where the buildings were similarly affectionate. He thought of Clitherow's Butchers, and the awful death of Margaret, from whom he'd learned so much, and as the memory bit, a sharp pain spiked in the side of his head. Guy stumbled, stepping into a deal table on which a tradesman displayed some cheap fabrics. "Watch yerself," he called with a sneer as Marlowe grabbed Guy's arm to right him.

"Surely the water below has not given you sea legs?"

"Below?" Guy glanced either side but could see nothing other than the tall buildings and the trade tables that made the walkways narrow.

"Guy, don't tell me you were unaware we were *on* London Bridge?" Marlowe retained his hold on Guy's arm and sped him through the pedestrian traffic until the tall buildings fell away and a narrower section of the bridge stood before them with a view of the Thames. A chilly wind buffeted Guy as he looked back to the buildings he'd passed through, his disbelief that someone could build such a structure above the water stunning him until Marlowe urged him onwards. "There are a couple of haunts where we may find our quarry this side of the old Chapel of Saint Thomas. To The Ship!"

The Ship, despite its presence on the river, was not a ship at all, but a tavern, one bursting with revelry. Lamps on the pillars illuminated the rosy cheeks of drinkers, while others lurked in the shadowy corners.

Guy cast his eyes around the tavern for signs of Dudley. None of The Ship's patrons looked to be the sort with whom Dudley would liaise. Dudley spent more on one meal than these good folks earned in a year, if not a lifetime. Guy followed Marlowe to the bar. "Our targets are not here," he muttered as Marlowe ordered two mugs of ale.

Marlowe took a huge draught. "I don't doubt that, Guy. You have much to learn about the subtle acts of subterfuge."

Guy stared at Marlowe, blank. "I concur."

Marlowe leant in close, his voice low. "Spying."

Marlowe looked into the far corner. "There are some gentlemen who may point us in the right direction."

Marlowe bustled through the tavern's patrons to a table in the corner, and Guy followed. "Of course, you know Kyd." Marlowe indicated the man sitting in the corner. While he too shared Marlowe's house, Guy could hardly say he knew him, for he spent long hours locked in his room. Beside Kyd sat a balding young man curled over some papers, a quill in one hand. Upon realising people approached the table, he covered his work with his arm.

"Please, William, why would I want to steal *your* work?" Marlowe tugged at a piece of paper.

William dragged back the paper and secured it with his elbow. He glared at Marlowe.

"Her Majesty came to watch my play tonight." Marlowe grinned. "Tamburlaine, Part Two was a roaring success."

William huffed and returned his attention to his script.

"While you've escaped the thrall of the quill, Kyd, I spoke to Henslowe about your Spanish Tragedy... he's keen on staging it at The Rose..."

Thomas nodded with interest, and Marlowe took another swig of his ale. In imitation, Guy did likewise. After a moment, Guy tugged on Marlowe's sleeve. "Please, tell me we're not here only to boast of your success?"

Marlowe smiled. "But it's such good sport!" He sighed and leaned over the table, causing William to once more shield his work. "While we'd love to socialise, we're looking for a noble party with more than a whiff of nefarious intention... any idea where we may find such fellows?"

William huffed. He shielded his script and raised his head. "The Bell." He continued writing.

"Okay, Guy, drink up. Our next destination beckons."

Marlowe drained his mug, while Guy left his half full (or half empty for the thespians at the table) and squeezed through the patrons back into the night. The Bell was further along London Bridge. They passed through a remarkable new building, Nonsuch House, four storeys which looked like someone lifted it from another world and placed it straddling the bridge. Standing beside it at half its size, and the closest building to the Great Lock was The Bell. Illuminated by lanterns which shone through the windows, it lacked the revelry of The Ship, and once they pushed the door open, Guy realised it lacked the warmth too, and not for the lack of any fire. The clientele of The Bell was better dressed, drinking finer ales from finer vessels, and one particular drinker Guy knew well. Wearing a lilac doublet and matching capotain hat, sitting with other elaborately dressed gentlemen, was Thomas Percy. He beckoned Guy and Marlowe to join them. Guy hurried to the table before any of the other eyes in the tavern fixed upon him, while Marlowe went to the bar.

"Guy, my good man," Thomas slurred. "I was hoping we'd see you out on the town."

Guy eyed the others around the table. Thomas was out among his tailoring kin if their attire was anything to go by.

Guy scanned the bar as best he could from the table. "You don't know if Dudley and his retinue came in here tonight, do you?"

Thomas slid his tankard over to Guy. "You have to try this. They call it 'The Dagger'."

Guy pushed the drink back toward Thomas. "But about Dudley?"

Thomas returned the tankard to Guy. "Drink, then we talk."

Guy took hold of the handle and gazed in at the dark liquid before an overpowering smell of hops made his head spin.

"Drink!" called Thomas.

Guy gulped the beer and had to swallow twice to keep down the bitter taste as the rest of the table cheered.

Thomas slapped Guy on the back and reclaimed his drink. "So, what did you need to know?"

"Dudley. Have you seen him?"

"Wouldn't know if I had." Thomas blinked several times, his eyes not entirely coordinated.

"What happened to the man with his finger on the pulse? The man who knows the ins and outs of the Queen's court?"

Thomas stared over to the other side of the room. "Wait, who were you looking for?"

At that moment, Marlowe returned armed with a couple of ales.

"Dudley, the chap whose castle we infiltrated in Durham."

Thomas continued to look blank, the evening's revels having done his memory no favours.

"You measured him up for a doublet."

"Oh! *Walter* Dudley," Thomas's volume turned heads three tables over. From an alcove out of sight, a head popped out.

Marlowe put the ales on the table. "I was about to say he's here, so we have to be discreet, but that bark has well and truly sailed. Guy, when the mayhem peaks, he'll flee. Do your duty."

"What mayhem?"

Rather than responding, Marlowe took off for a table in the centre of The Bell, launching his ale over an unsuspected patron, crying out, "Felon! Thou slept with my sister," before dropping his tankard onto another table. The drenched drinker, the feather in his cavalier hat limp, turned. He saw the tankard on the table, stood, and struck the innocent man, who looked on in shock. Members of both parties stood to defend the honour of their insulted friends, with fists flying before reason took hold. The fuse had been lit. All it took to make it explode was one man to fall back and knock over another table to draw another party in, angry about their spilt drinks. Tankards flew faster than insults, and soon those cries of "Villain," "Mutton-Monger," and "Pox-ridden pettifogger," were drowned out by splintering wood as people fell into tables and smashed chairs over people's backs.

Marlowe was in the thick of the action, throwing a punch at one man and ducking a chair that splintered against the rear wall.

It wasn't the subtle subterfuge Marlowe had promised. Perhaps the art of a spy came from the ability to improvise and to shift focus depending upon the situation. Guy slipped outside. A whistle blew in the distance. No doubt someone has escaped The Bell before him to summon the watch. He stepped into the shadows and waited. There was no other entrance to The Bell. If Dudley and his party were going to leave, it had to be through the back door. Guy knew Marlowe would orchestrate events inside to drive them out, so it was only a matter of time, and before the chill of the night even had time to penetrate Guy's bones, the door slipped open and a party of three left the tavern. The man at the front sheathed his sword as Dudley followed behind him. At the rear was Dudley's familiar, the figure who had transformed into a raven.

Guy followed, the burning desire to vanquish Dudley controlling every impulse.

Chapter 40—In Which Guy Fawkes Confronts Dudley

In his life to date, Guy had sought a number of evil men with the express purpose of ending their lives, men responsible for the deaths of his father, his uncle, his wife. The rage that burned inside Guy as he followed Dudley toward Saint Thomas's Chapel made his past vengeance tame. What had Dudley done to cause such intense hatred? Alas, Guy had neither the time nor the patience to explore the cause or the depths of his fury. With each step, bitterness pulsed through his body, and scorching blood rushed through his veins.

Guy remained in the shadows and bundled through the crowds of people, resisting the urge to shove them out of his way. London Bridge never slept, for there were as many people wandering in and out of the shops and into the various building as there had been in the heart of Bankside, but Guy kept Dudley in his sights. Rather than passing alongside the chapel and to the north of the city, Dudley entered the building.

Saint Thomas's Chapel had ceased to have a religious purpose since Henry VIII's establishment of the Church of England, but it retained spiritual power. Perhaps it was from here that Dudley was to launch his offensive against the Queen. Maybe he was seeking some kind of token from the chapel to call a being from the bowels of the earth to carry out his misdeeds once more.

Guy approached the door. He didn't want to enter immediately, for they would see him come in, but his body throbbed with excess aggression every moment his pursuit slowed. He felt like he could punch through the wall.

Like many of the buildings on the bridge, the chapel only had a single entrance. Years of filth encrusted the windows and offered little guidance until he caught sight of a hint of light, the movement suggesting those inside climbed the steps into the tower.

Guy eased the door open. What was once a place of worship acted as a storeroom. Where once there were pews, barrels stood, some open, some sealed. Guy approached the rear of the chapel, where the steps led up the tower. He could wait for them to return and ambush them, but given their power and desire to do evil, he knew not what they'd return with if left to their own devices. His roiling anger wouldn't let him wait, either. He had to take the steps and stop them in their tracks.

As Guy closed on the second storey, he slowed, listening for voices. Yes, people were talking, but they remained distant. That could mean only one thing: they'd gone higher, either into the belfry or out in the open air. In the darkness, Guy could see little, but a quick search revealed a crucifix and several other religious statues. What looters hadn't ransacked when the building's purpose changed remained stored away. Whether the men he'd followed had gathered something from the room to use in their sacrilegious acts, Guy didn't know, and there was only one way to find out. Perhaps the crucifix would be useful? He reached to grab it, but pain shot from his finger. What was it, a splinter? Before he could check for a cut, voices sounded above once more.

He dashed back to the stone steps. They continued to a floor no bigger than a square yard, a wooden ladder giving access to the pair of bells which hung from the headstock. Rope hung from the wheel at the far end, which bellringers would pull on from far below to ring the bells, though Guy assumed it had been many years since those bells last sounded. More stone steps led to a door, no doubt onto the top of the chapel's tower. His options were few. He'd already considered waiting in ambush to be flawed, which left him only with the Kit Wright approach: run in swinging and deal with the unravelling consequences. That approach appealed to the hulking rage that made his head feel like it was about to explode. Guy drew his sword and breathed it into life, the blue flame bringing light, and he kicked at the door and ran through, almost immediately to his death, for only a yard the other side was a low wall and a long drop into the Thames. He put out a hand to stop himself, cursing his foolishness. What else was he expecting to find at the top of a tower, a grand ballroom?

Even over the howling wind, the voices of those he'd disturbed were distinct. They'd gathered on the opposite side of the tower to carry out their misdeeds, and a roar signalled their disapproval at being disturbed. Guy spun around. Dudley's aide stood ready to challenge him, eyes alive with the fire of demonic possession. Guy stepped forward and swung, cutting off any escape route with the angle of his blade–or any escape route for a mortal man.

The demon leant back against the low wall and toppled from the tower. Guy waited for a splash, but in its lieu came only laughter. Dudley's demonic assistant swooped through the air and landed back on the tower on Guy's other side, dripping wet. He grinned, revealing his sharp canines. As Guy raised his sword to strike once more, a raven, Dudley's familiar, flapped in his face, knocking him off balance.

As the bird fluttered away and Guy righted himself, a drenching force knocked him against the tower and splashed onto the floor. The demon rushed Guy, lunging with its claws. Guy ducked and lunged forward, flipping the creature over his head. Once more, the water placed him back on his feet. Guy too scrambled up, backing away and heading around the corner. He needed eyes on Dudley.

Aye, there was the lord, a gem glowing blue in his hand. He must have obtained an artefact that gave him control over the aerial powers from Burnham-on-Crouch.

Dudley smiled, his grip tightening on the stone.

Guy could only hope he had his brother's level of competence when it came to controlling such powers. But as Guy stepped forward, a jet of water gushed and slapped his face, suggesting Dudley had complete control over his actions. Guy shrugged off the blow. Water vapour hung in the air all around him, threatening to come together and strike him once more.

Dudley's eyes narrowed. "Aren't you the worm that thwarted my plans at Cowdray House?"

"Aye, and I'll stop you again!" Guy lifted his sword, but another gush of water punched into his bicep, causing him to release his grip.

"There's no one to help you this time. You're all alone."

The water formed a fist which lumped him in the stomach, doubling him over. The hands of the possessed minion grabbed his shoulders and pulled him upright once more. Guy stretched his leg, feeling with his foot, trying to drag his sword toward him, but a surge of water gushed to Guy's knees, and higher, taking the sword and dragging it beyond the wall and letting it clatter against the chapel before falling into the Thames.

The demon kicked Guy in the back of the knees, forcing him to collapse onto them. It shoved down on his shoulders, pushing his head into the freezing water.

Guy tried to draw in a breath but only took in water. He flapped his arms to no avail, his futile splashing drawing a chuckle from Dudley. The demon dragged him out of the water, but only long enough for Dudley to kick him in the jaw. As his teeth clashed together, clamping his tongue, blood filled his mouth, but it was washed away when the demonic brute dunked him under again. Every impulse told him to fight back, to force strength into his legs to rise out of the water, but he battled that impulse and gave up the fight. He knew they could drown him if they wanted, but they were a cruel pair and wanted to draw out his suffering. All Guy had to do was wait for the next opportunity. The ire remained, bubbling away, but instead of releasing it, he let it charge for when there was a real opportunity. He tried to forget the pain in his mouth or the aching in his chest, and when he could wait no longer, the demon yanked him from the water again.

As Guy took a breath, he recognised it was time to uncoil his spring of rage. He smashed back with his elbow, catching the creature on the side of the head, forcing him to loosen his grip. Guy turned and followed up with a two-hand shove, and bustled past the unbalanced creature. He took the next corner and hurried through the door, pushing against the wall to help keep his balance. A tide of water crashed into his back before rushing past, washing the bells before cascading to the ground below. Guy continued a few more steps before another wave crashed into him, forcing him to grab the wooden rails.

"You're finished, boy!" Dudley stood at the door, his gemstone glowing blue. Water droplets circled Guy once more. Another push would see him slip from the belfry and fall far below. He had to take matters into his own hands. It was time for rash action. He took one step and focused all of his strength, all of that pent-up energy into a leap for the rope attached to the headstock. His fingers curled around the thick rope, but even with added pressure, he was sliding down at pace. He wrapped his legs around the rope, slowing him, gaining control of his pace. Above, the clapper crashed into the bell again and again, but then came a crack. The chapel had long been abandoned, the rope not pulled in many years. Never had it been designed to support the additional weight of an adult male. When the demon leapt onto the rope, seeking to follow Guy, the force yanked the headstock from its position. Guy was no longer in a controlled slide, but falling at the same pace as everything above. With a jolt, he stopped. The headstock had met that fragile wooden floor never designed to carry the weight of the two bells that now sat on it. Guy continued to slide, aware that the ground floor was not a great distance away. As a crack came from above, he let go, falling the remaining ten feet into a barrel, which exploded as he crashed onto it. Ignoring the pain, he bolted for the door, leaning forward so far he was almost on all fours as a crack came from above. There was a thump as the demon hit the ground, but no sooner was Guy out of the door than an almighty crash came, followed by a final toll of the bells as the tower crumbled inwards. A series of splashes followed as parts of the chapel fell into the river, and as momentum ripped more of the chapel down, Guy felt the whole bridge shake. People from either side fled, some away from the chapel, others running past it, knowing solid ground was closer that way. Guy stood still, watching more of the chapel tumble into the Thames.

Once the last brick had fallen, Guy rushed to look into the water. Perhaps his eyes were playing tricks on him, or perhaps it was wishful thinking, but he was certain a figure, who could only have been Dudley, disappeared into the water, and a faint blue light faded to nothing.

A forlorn raven cawed from the side of the bridge.

Chapter 41—In Which Cecil Rewards Guy Fawkes for his Service to the Queen

As one would expect, the collapse of a building from London Bridge into the Thames generated frantic chatter and rumours of great evil besieging the capital. The best told of an invisible giant punching through the chapel, considering the old Catholic place of worship an affront to all good and right Protestants. As the days passed, news broke that superseded those wild fabrications: Robert Cecil's guards had foiled a plot to overthrow Queen Elizabeth that same night. A vicious band of brigands entered the Tower of London through Traitor's Gate on a raft, but thanks to the swift action of Cecil's men, they did no harm. Intelligence warned of the attack, so Cecil's soldiers stopped and slaughtered the interlopers while Queen Elizabeth slept. As the days passed, more information crept out, each nugget building a greater picture of sensational betrayal, with Walter Dudley revealed as the mastermind behind the plot. His plan, if rumours were to be believed, was to oust the Queen and place a puppet monarch on the throne. The rumours left Guy confused about Cecil's true intentions, for it was he who had constructed this narrative. Certain aspects, such as Dudley's rumoured escape to Spain, existed to drive further resentment of the Spanish. Many linked the collapse of the chapel and the foiled assassination. Some suggested Dudley's men had accidentally set off a stack of gunpowder designated for the Tower of London, and others claimed the toppling of the chapel was an act to draw attention away from the Tower of London to allow the murderers to slip through Traitor's Gate unseen.

Weeks passed, and Guy was unsurprised to read that Queen Elizabeth had thanked Robert Cecil for his vigilance and declared England in safe hands with Cecil announced as her Secretary of State, also taking on the less official role of Chief Spymaster, that role once held by Walsingham.

One day in December, early in Cecil's tenure as Spymaster, Guy arrived at the Rose Theatre (where he supported Marlowe as the run of Tamburlaine the Great: Part Two continued) to find the Secretary of State waiting.

Cecil wandered with Guy around the theatre, speaking of Dudley and his escape to Spain as if both didn't know he rested in the Thames. In a deserted dressing room, Cecil placed an arm on Guy's shoulder. Guy felt a rush from the point Cecil touched him into the back of his neck, the sensation erupting in his brain.

Feeling Guy shudder, Cecil released him. "It could not have gone better! I have the power now to work my will—the power to help choose her Majesty's successor." Cecil grinned. "We can turn the English throne into one that welcomes our lords of the underworld."

Guy froze. He wanted to protest, to draw his sword and take out this scourge before his evil roots could bed into the royal party. Every muscle in his body tensed, leaving him trapped in a stilled body.

"You will, of course, have a seat at the table."

Cecil looked upon Guy with disdain. "When you shake off that worthless body."

A bead of sweat trickled from Guy's hair onto his forehead, but still, he couldn't move.

Cecil stared at Guy again. "Though the body could still work for us. Her Majesty is having a celebration on Saturday at Richmond Palace. I shall put this Guy Fawkes on the guest list so you can ride with him there. I shall think of a way to elevate you further." Cecil walked around Guy. The Queen's spymaster grabbed Guy's chin and pulled his mouth open, examining his teeth. "It doesn't look to be the body of a complete commoner." Cecil pushed Guy's chin up, closing his mouth. "If not, you could find another to seed. Such a shame you couldn't finalise the transition with the young girl at Cowdray. She has the status we require."

A young man entered carrying boxes. "Okay if I leave these here?"

Released from his stupor, Guy turned to him. "Of course. Thank you."

"I had best be off," said Cecil.

Guy moved to follow.

"I'll see myself out." Cecil nodded toward a chair in the corner, and Guy sat.

Cecil stood over the desk, took a piece of parchment from within his jacket, grabbed a quill, dipped it in the ink, signed it, and placed it in Guy's lap. It was an invitation to a party at Richmond Palace.

Cecil once more made for the door before turning back and plucking a pouch from his belt. He tossed it toward Guy. "And get yourself some attire fit for a nobleman."

As the familiar weight of coins dropped into Guy's palm, he became alert once more, the conversation lost in the confusing fog of his mind. As he clasped his fingers around the pouch, he realised where he must spend the money.

• • • •

"SO, ROBERT CECIL GAVE you this money?" Percy looked quizzically at Guy from the other side of his counter, where he leant on a roll of royal blue fabric.

"That is what I told you. The life of a London tailor has done little for your memory, my friend."

"He told you to buy something nice to wear for a party at Richmond Palace?"

"Again, aye, that is what he told me to do."

Thomas scratched his head. "I can only assume he has mistaken you for his mistress. Are you his mistress, Guy?"

Guy paused. There was a strange sensation that overcame him when he had been with Cecil. Their conversation had left him feeling as if his head was stuffed with clouds, but there was no kind of affection between them. No, and the stabbing pains in his head he suffered whenever he considered Cecil were not indicative of any kind of pleasant experience.

"Perhaps I shouldn't attend," Guy said.

"And miss an opportunity to speak to the Queen from the status of a noble? Surely this is the best chance you have to warn her of the threats she faces, to inform her of the demons that stand against her."

Another throb of pain grew in Guy's head. He stepped toward Percy's counter, supporting himself with his hand and took several deep breaths.

Thomas grabbed a measuring tape. "I suppose we'd better get you measured. Once you're out of here, I'll work on scoring myself an invitation."

"Whatever do you want to attend for?"

Thomas smirked. "Someone has to act as your chaperone, don't they?"

• • • •

BY THE TIME SATURDAY arrived, Guy had written home to Anne, and to Ghost, and had collected his attire from Thomas Percy's tailor shop. Rather than arrive on horseback, as would have been Guy's preference, he travelled in a carriage with Thomas and some of his tailor friends. Marlowe had been unimpressed to be denied an invitation. Guy's attire comprised of a salmon-coloured doublet under a mustard-coloured jerkin and matching breeches. A stiff and uncomfortable ruff complemented the outfit at the cost of a restricted peripheral view.

Guy remained silent for most of the journey, tuning out the conversation about unfair haberdashery taxes and bold new trends in millinery. Exactly how much was there to say about taffeta? Lost in his own mind, he found himself ransacked by memories of demons past. Guy remembered his final encounter with Sandys, and the demon he had summoned, Master Leonard, who had almost torn him asunder. He remembered his struggles in the days after that battle and how the demon so long occupied a space in his head, ransacking his thoughts. He remembered his home with Maria and that damned cow who carried the seeds of those awful beasts. When he tried to recall Maria's face, he was horrified to discover only the succubus version resided in his mind. Walsingham brought further pain, and the memory of the way he'd disappeared when he sunk his sword into him, the feel of the weight of his clothes on his sword arm niggled at the back of his brain, echoing around the back of his head and rebounding with a peal of laughter.

Richmond Palace came into view, with the sun low in the sky. Guy counted turret after turret after they passed through the gatehouse, and the dozens of carriages awaiting in the courtyard indicated the volume of guests Queen Elizabeth had invited to this gathering.

Once they disembarked from the carriage, impeccably dressed servants ushered Guy and the other guests into the great hall. Elaborate chandeliers hung from the many arches above, hundreds of candles illuminating the room. Along one wall ran a long table stacked with food, a roast pig centre, but all around it were freshly baked loaves of bread, huge pies with thick pastry, bowls of honey-mustard eggs, great wheels of cheese, and a wobbly substance of various colours that Guy later learned was gelatine. Encased within some was shredded meat, in others, fruits. All around the table, peacock feathers displayed in narrow vases added a dash of colour. The room was further decorated with great tapestries along the walls, some containing decorative patterns, others telling stories of great battles won.

Servers wandered the halls, carrying trays with intricately carved wooded goblets filled with wine. Thomas's first port of call was to one of these, grabbing a goblet and draining it, while Guy continued to take in the grandiose hall and its visitors. As overdressed as he felt, he came to realise he was reservedly attired compared to some of the other guests who'd adorned themselves with solid gold rings and had tried to show their wealth and good taste with the rich colours weaved into their attire.

When most of the guests had arrived, a herald sounded his trumpet and announced Her Majesty, Queen Elizabeth. Servants pulled the double doors open, and the Queen entered to a round of applause. She wore an elaborate white dress decorated with red and green gemstones sitting in a nest of gold thread. A string of pearls framed an elaborate necklace of the same colour. With the dress covering her feet, she appeared to glide along the floor. From one end of the room, a harpist played, and conversation filled the room once more.

Guy had not set eyes upon Robert Cecil until he was before him, dressed in a tawny jacket of velvet and a forest green robe. In his previous encounters, Guy had noted Cecil's lack of height, a situation augmented by his stoop. On this day, however, he stood taller, his back a little straighter. Perhaps he wore some kind of girdle to fix his twisted spine. Upon glancing down, Guy noted that Cecil's leather boots had been double, if not triple soled.

The spymaster's large, dark, sunken eyes continued to have that dizzying effect, and as he spoke, Guy found himself fixed on every word. "Mister Fawkes." Cecil grinned. "So glad you could make it. Allow me to introduce you to Her Majesty."

Guy fell into step alongside Cecil, matching his slow pace as he headed for the Queen.

"I have a new persona for you, one which will get you back before the child." Cecil grinned.

Her Majesty smiled as Cecil neared, showing her blackened teeth. "Ah! My little pygmy!" She touched Cecil's cheek with the back of her index finger. "Who is this chap?"

Cecil bowed. "This, Your Majesty, is Guy Fawkes. He helped to discover the plot against you."

The Queen placed a hand on Guy's shoulder and nodded. "Then, I am in your debt. Please, enjoy this feast tonight."

Mimicking Cecil, Guy too bowed before his Queen.

"Fawkes is also a skilled physician." Cecil grinned.

Guy blinked but knew he'd agree to anything asked of him in this role.

Queen Elizabeth nodded. "A worthy profession. Tell me, do you know anything about strange sleeping sicknesses?"

The flickering candlelight from the chandelier highlighted Elizabeth's pale complexion, something aided by the thick layer of make-up. With an Earl beside him and a Queen in front, it was possible for Guy to forget who he was, to feel as if his body was possessed by one quite other than himself. Lavishness lay all around him and he wanted more.

"That... I do." Guy spoke, but the words were not his own.

"Mister Fawkes has studied alongside some of the finest medical minds in the land," Cecil added.

Inside, a voice remained. It sounded like his sister, Anne, calling out to him, telling him to remember his roots and to remember his duty. His primary reason for wanting an audience with the Queen was to warn her of the plague of demons assaulting the country, filling her court and planning to overthrow her to bring one with a heart steeped in devilry to the throne.

Her Majesty's mouth tightened as she stared at Guy. "You look familiar. Have we met before?"

Guy froze. If she recognised him as the one who had served her at the Rose Theatre, any chance of mocking nobility to gain her trust was gone.

The Queen raised a finger as realisation hit her. "Were you not at Cowdray House when I visited?"

Guy smiled and nodded. Perhaps she had seen him with Anthony Browne and assumed he was a friend rather than an employee.

"I believe our stays may have overlapped."

"Perhaps you could put your medical skills to good use."

"How can I be of service?" Again, Guy spoke involuntarily.

"My dear relative, Catherine Stanley, was taken ill while at Cowdray. Still, she remains there in perpetual sleep."

Anguish hit Guy. He'd hoped to hear better news of young Catherine. "That must have come to pass after my departure. I'm most saddened by the news."

Queen Elizabeth clasped Guy's hand. "I look forward to your report from her bedside. I'm sending a party to Cowdray in a few weeks, and I expect you to have made progress by the time they arrive." Queen Elizabeth's look was one of great concern. This was a ruler who wouldn't allow evil to consume the country, not if she knew its true extent. She had to be told.

Shaking the clouds from his head, Guy sunk to one knee. "I must warn you, Your Majesty, there continues to be great danger all around you."

Queen Elizabeth laughed. "Oh, do tell my little man all about it. I trust him to keep me safe."

With that, Elizabeth turned away to face the other nobles desperate to speak to her.

Cecil led Guy away. "Be careful what you say, you fool."

Guy looked at Cecil blankly. It might have been a reflection from the chandeliers, but fire burned in his eyes once more. "Speak not too openly of threat. Let her believe I manage it all." Cecil brushed the front of Guy's doublet. "No, this will not suffice. We'll get you back to the Stanley girl, let you reside there while I work Her Majesty into naming her as heir."

Guy's muscles tensed in rebellion. He knew he should attack. Cecil was every bit his enemy, an enemy of the state and an enemy of the Queen. Why he always fell into this submissive trance, he had no idea. Anger welled inside, but without an outlet: his arms refused to act on the orders of his brain. Was it decorum holding him back? No, he felt there was something more, some kind of poison within. A server walked by carrying more goblets. He grabbed one and drank the wine in one gulp.

"There," Cecil said. "Try to relax a little. Mingle. Make yourself known, Guy Fawkes: Physician Extraordinaire! When you use every ounce of your strength to save the girl, the future queen, your name will be recorded in the history books for your sacrifice!"

The arrogance that dripped from Cecil's lips again made Guy wish to raise his fists against him. How he longed for his whistle, left in Anne's care, so he could reveal the demon inside him to the gathered nobles.

"How much control do you exert over this vessel? Not enough, I'll wager." Cecil pinched the flesh between Guy's shoulder and neck, spiking a pain into his skull, freezing Guy on the spot. In his head came a scream, but neither his lungs nor his mouth reacted to vocalise it.

Only when Cecil moved away could Guy react. He beckoned a server over so he could guzzle another goblet of wine before he headed over to the food. Much of the pig had already been carved. A knife rested by its side. Guy clutched it, taking him back to his days at Clitherow's Butchers. Margaret Clitherow's death by pressing had horrified Queen Elizabeth. Surely that showed her opposition to evil. There was certain to be a shrine or other place of worship on the site. Guy could bless the weapon and charm it with life and behead every witch and demon in the room.

As he contemplated glorious bloodshed, the face of Master Leonard came to his mind once more alongside the sound of thundering feet on the steps of a crypt. Guy put one hand on the table to steady himself, while the other gripped the knife. He eyed another server and waved them over. As the young man closed, he tried to drop the knife, but his fingers had locked around it. With his other hand, he took a drink and drained it.

The thumping in his head gave way to a splintering sound, and a mad cackle resonated within him. He whirled around. Queen Elizabeth was only a few steps from him, facing away. Her hair shifted, and a protrusion push out of the back of her head, a fleshy nodule the whiteness of the Queen's face. As Guy stared, his eyes fixed on the spot, his body frozen in wonder, it pushed out further, the distinct shape of a nose. Cheekbones, the brow, and a jaw followed a fraction of a second before the entire face, Maria's face, became visible. The Queen's ginger hair framed the face, and when its eyes opened the imposter revealed herself, the succubus that had climbed into his bed after Maria's death. The eyes were ringed with purple. She opened her mouth and brushed her lips with her tongue.

His hand, clutching the knife, lifted into the air, acting independently of Guy's brain. He stared at it, unable to believe it was acting of its own will. He grabbed the wrist with his other hand and squeezed, trying to force himself to let go.

Maria's voice, tainted with the slur of the succubus, entered Guy's head. "Come on, Guy. You know you want to stick it into me."

Cheerleading voices egged him on inside his mind. He forced all of his strength into his left arm, trying to pull his rogue right hand away.

Instead, his feet shuffled forward, edging him closer to Her Majesty.

Two voices competed inside his mind for attention, and neither was his own. The grandmaster of nocturnal orgies himself, long imprisoned in Guy's mind, roamed free, forcing Guy's body to do its dark bidding. The other voice, encouraging Leonard, promising dominion upon the earth, was that of Walsingham. Surely Guy only imagined that voice. Walsingham was dead, slaughtered in Durham. A mocking laugh responded to his thought as Guy shuffled forward again.

Queen Elizabeth was but a couple of steps away, still engaged in conversation with nobles while a crude, demonic facsimile of Guy's wife tempted him to do unspeakable evil. Guy scanned the crowd. Why was no one looking at him? Did no one see the knife he wielded so close to the Queen? Why was no one racing to stop him? Was the face sticking out of the back of the queen's head invisible to everyone else? Could they not hear its obscenities? The only eyes upon him were Cecil's. The Queen's spymaster stroked his beard as he feasted upon Guy's trauma, a mere appetiser for the main course of delicious regicide that was to follow.

"Throw me to the ground, Guy. Force your body on top of me!" The succubus made her mouth an O and groaned.

Guy concentrated his efforts on his legs, refusing to allow them to move forward. While the will of those that controlled his body was stronger, the stiffening of his muscled reduced his step to mere inches. As long as the Queen didn't make a sudden movement toward Guy, he had time to ward off the dark influence. The lure of the succubus was strong. Last time, it was only his sister's intervention that saved him. She was far away now. He cast his mind back... how had he stopped the agonising nightmares of Master Leonard? The image of the ash tree on the crypt door had held him back. As he took another micro-step forward, he scanned the room. Still, all parties were engaged in conversation. Only the servers moved through the room, carrying the wooden goblets of wine.

"Come on, Guy!" cried the succubus. "Don't leave me so unsatisfied!" Her canines elongated, and she polished one with her tongue. Oblivion's appeal beckoned. While the voices in his head insisted this demonic version of his wife was better than being alone a competing voice urged him to fight back.

He eyed a server. While it meant releasing his possessed knife-wielding hand, he beckoned a server over. There were four goblets on his tray. While not an expert on trees, one he knew was ash. There was another voice competing inside his mind, pointing him in the right direction. The hand that clutched the knife shook, resisting the temptation to stab the server in the throat. As much as it wanted carnage, the chaos of slaughtering the queen would be oh so much more satisfying! The intoxicating mixture of malevolence and the joy at the thought of causing misery stirred the bile in Guy's stomach. He took the goblet and splashed it over his face, the shock giving him full control over his body. He turned back to the table and flung the knife. With force, he brought the bowl of the goblet on the table, separating it from the stem, leaving a jagged point. It was the hand that he'd lost most control of, the hand that needed intervention. He ran the sharp point against his palm, drawing blood, and held the stem against it. While blood gushed from the wound, the wood had a cooling effect against his hand. Inside his mind came a duel of screams.

"What are you doing?" Thomas rushed over to Guy, his face white.

Guy glanced at the knife, then at the blood pooling on the floor. He caught the tip of a nose disappearing inside Queen Elizabeth's ginger hair. "We need to get out of here."

Thomas glanced over his shoulder then manoeuvred himself to a spot immediately between Guy and Queen Elizabeth. "You don't say, Guy. What were you thinking?"

"I don't think *I* was."

Percy turned Guy toward the exit and hurried him along.

"There's something wrong." Guy glanced back across the room.

Cecil stared at him.

"He seeded me."

Thomas spoke quietly between clenched teeth. "Seeded? What the devil are you talking about?"

"Exactly that. It's Walsingham. He lives on inside me."

Chapter 42—In Which Guy Fawkes Returns to Cowdray House

Could Thomas Percy have sped Guy Fawkes out of Richmond Palace any faster? Not without raising greater suspicion of their actions. Once he'd deposited Guy in the carriage, giving the driver strict instructions not to let him leave, Thomas returned to the gathering to make his excuses.

While alone, Guy considered his situation. Some sort of parasitic entity controlled his actions, something much like the blood imp he'd encountered when isolated at Brimham Rocks, but much stronger and further embedded in his mind. How Guy longed for the knowledge of his former mentors, but agents of evil had taken Pulleyn, Clitherow and Ingleby from the world. Gretchen would no doubt have had a potion or some sort of ritual to exorcise the demon from his mind, but the noose had taken her wisdom too. He'd write to Ghost once more and hope he had some kind of insight into possession. If he could let him know he was about to return to Cowdray House, perhaps he'd discover a solution before Guy arrived. And therein lay another problem. Viscount Montagu would not have him back in the house. He could arrive in disguise or go by another name, but Queen Elizabeth would contact Cowdray House, asking about the progress of the physician, Guy Fawkes. His addled brain was in no condition to seek a solution to the conundrum.

When Thomas returned, the carriage departed. He stated that the gathering continued in typical fashion, with not so much as a whisper about Guy's antics.

"And Cecil?"

Percy shook his head. "Absent."

"I'm going to need a favour."

Thomas touched the tips of his fingertips together. "You only need to ask."

"Watch over me until I leave London. Keep Cecil away from me, and for the Lord's sake, don't let me anywhere near the Queen."

Thomas raised his eyebrows. "Do you know how hard it is to get this close to Her Majesty?"

Guy peered out of the window, back toward Richmond Palace. "Aye, but it's Cecil. He's trying to orchestrate something. I don't know if he wanted me to slaughter the Queen tonight or not, but something inside me did."

"What's going on inside that head of yours? Is it Maria? Has her death left you discombobulated?"

Guy's head throbbed and his chest ached, for he could not remember his wife's face. But that was not the cause. "No, it's Walsingham... was I different, after?"

"After Durham? Of course. You were grieving your wife and avenging her death. That would affect anyone."

Guy placed his fingers against his temple. "There's more. Walsingham... he infected me."

"With?"

"Himself."

Thomas's brow furrowed. "What do you mean, infected with himself?"

"I feel like his spirit is inside me. Tonight, I didn't have control of my body. Not entirely. He did. Does that sound possible?"

Thomas shook his head. "Until I met you, I wouldn't have thought so, but given your track record, anything's possible?"

"That's why I need you to monitor me, to give me time to find help."

Conversation faded. Outside was only darkness, and to keep it at bay inside, Guy concentrated on the rhythm of the horses' hooves and the clatter of the wheels on the ground.

• • • •

GUY DID NOT RETURN to Marlowe's dwelling, but to Thomas's. The tailoring business, and his familial wealth, had allowed him to purchase a property with sufficient space to accommodate Guy: a room with a lockable door. That was Thomas's method of keeping Guy safe from negative influences. Guy insisted on being kept away from Thomas's wife, Martha, too. He didn't want anything he did to bring harm to her.

The following morning, Thomas called from behind the wooden door. "Give me Marlowe's address and I shall collect your things."

Guy gave Thomas the name of the theatre, for that's where Marlowe was most likely to be found. Left once more with his thoughts, Guy tried to formulate a plan. Reasoning with himself was difficult. Irrational thoughts batted away every rational one. Every calm approach was superseded by one which caused pain, bloodshed, and anguish. This was not Guy's planned approach, but that of the entities residing inside him. Without question, they were growing in strength. Not only had they control over his thoughts, but they also had the power to bring visions before his eyes, and control his limbs at times of weakness. What was to stop them from causing him to harm himself? No, they needed him. Walsingham had clung on to life by entering his mind, and Master Leonard too continued to hold ground on earth by occupying Guy's mind.

The desk in the room had paper, a quill, and a half-full pot of ink. Guy sat ready to compose a letter to Ghost. He took hold of the quill, which spiked pain in his hand. He examined the wound he'd made with the stem of the goblet. A black gash ran along his palm, thin, branchlike tendrils running toward his forefinger, index finger and thumb. Guy touched the wound, expecting to feel heat, but it was cold. He gritted his teeth and clenched the quill between finger and thumb once more. His fingers had other ideas when he tried to write the name of his dear friend, continuing to scratch at the paper long after the ink had run out.

Guy stared at the page. *Rat bastard! Roaring fustilugs! I'll be jiggered in a vaulting house afore you place your poxy fingers on me! Cur!*

So, writing to Ghost was out. He'd dictate to Thomas later. Meanwhile, he grasped the quill, hoping to gain knowledge from the page. He dipped the quill in the ink again.

"Who are you?" He placed the quill on the page.

His hand quivered and scratched at the page.

Your doom.

Guy sighed. "What do you want?"

Your doom.

Guy's hand went back to the page again, marking it until the quill ran dry once more.

Your doom. Your doom your doom yourdoom yourdoom yourdoomyourdoomyourdoo

No, this too was futile. As he pondered what else to do and the contents of his letter to Ghost, he heard the opening and closing of a door, and seconds later, the rattle of the key in his lock.

Thomas smiled as he placed the bundle of possessions on Guy's bed. "There was this, too, delivered late yesterday." Thomas handed Guy a letter.

Guy broke the seal, and opened the letter, scanning for the signature at the bottom: Anthony Browne. It was from Cowdray House.

Guy read the letter. Viscount Montagu had passed away following a short illness (the symptoms similar to those suffered by Catherine, but in this case fatal). As such, Anthony Browne was now in possession of the house and the title. There was no one left to dictate which guests were allowed at Cowdray House.

So, it was decided. Guy would travel back to Cowdray immediately, without sending a letter in advance. There he would seek Ghost's help. There he would put an end to the curse, no matter what it took. The life of Catherine Stanley was in his hands, the Queen ready to hold him accountable for her return to health. The solution to all of his troubles was before him: rid himself of possession, save the girl, and Queen Elizabeth would trust him. From that position, he could warn her of the demon threat and aid her in cleansing the country. Simple.

• • • •

GUY DIDN'T TRUST HIMSELF to return to Cowdray House alone. Even on horseback, the journey was impossible in one day. Would those that controlled his mind drive him to cause mayhem on his travels? Thomas, alas, could not leave his shop, and Marlowe could not leave his theatre. Thomas hired a gentleman named Oliver to accompany Guy. Oliver had the unfortunate fate of having had his tongue cut out at a young age, and became adept at communication with gesture. When that didn't work, his fists did. If the malevolent forces controlling Guy tried to corrupt Oliver too, they'd have a hard time doing so, and after a two-day journey, Guy found himself at Cowdray House once more.

Anthony Browne was not there to greet him, and Ghost neither, but up-on knocking at the door he found that Catesby's responsibilities had been upgraded. He was dressed now in the clothes of a noble rather than a servant.

"Guy!" he cried and ran over to embrace him. "We had not expected your return." Catesby beckoned Guy inside.

Guy looked around the large reception room. He was much more used to entering via the servant's quarters. "I am in dire need, friend. Where is your master?"

"They will return before sunrise. Now he's Viscount, our young noble's in demand. What's so urgent to cause you to speed from the capital?"

And when Guy recounted the events in London, Catesby understood the urgency.

• • • •

BEFORE THE RETURN OF Anthony and Ghost, Guy needed to become reacquainted with another member of the staff at Cowdray House. Catesby was more than happy to let him visit the stables alone.

Francis Tresham had a pitchfork in hand to load filthy straw onto a wheelbarrow.

Guy stood with the sun setting behind him, staring into the stables. "So, your dishonourable lies did you no great service."

Tresham leant on the pitchfork. "Well, Guy Fawkes, I'm surprised to see you again. I'm glad you're back." The concern at the corners of his mouth gave away his lie.

Guy stepped forward. "Don't give me that nonsense. You sold me out. And what for?"

Tresham grinned. "The Viscount made me master of horses."

"And yet, you're still knee-deep in shit."

Tresham leant the pitchfork against the wheelbarrow and showed his open hands. "You would have done the same, given a chance."

Would he? No, Guy wasn't the sort to throw someone in front of driving horses, but the part of him he didn't have full control of might do something worse. He felt his hand tighten into a fist and he stepped forward.

Tresham must have read the malice on his face, for his own dropped, and he stepped back. Guy strode forward until Tresham backed against the wall. When beside the wheelbarrow, Guy grabbed the pitchfork.

Tresham held out a pleading hand. "There's no need to do anything rash."

Guy continued to stride forward.

"With Montagu gone, it's a chance for us all to start over."

Guy grabbed the handle of the pitchfork higher with his left hand, not trusting the right not to commit murder. His legs were not his own. He was going for Tresham one way or another. Master Leonard's glee at the idea of plunging a pitchfork into Tresham's belly built inside him. The tension in his right shoulder grew as it tried to take full control of the pitchfork.

Leading with his left hand, he pulled the pitchfork horizontal, pushing it against Tresham's neck and pinning him against the wall.

Tresham grabbed the handle and pushed against the weight, gritting his teeth and muttering, "I'm sorry."

Guy pushed up, forcing Tresham onto his toes. He applied more pressure. The idea of choking Tresham was not unappealing to any part of Guy until a call of his name came.

"Guy, that's enough." It was Catesby's voice.

Guy released the pitchfork and let it clatter to the floor. Tresham scrambled away, his hands rubbing at his neck as he gasped.

"Browne has returned," Catesby said.

Guy turned and headed in the direction of the house.

"You're not going to let him get away with that, are you?" Tresham rasped. "He's an animal."

Catesby turned back. "You reap what you sow, Francis. You reap what you sow."

Chapter 43—In Which Guy Fawkes Leans on the Wisdom of Ghost

Another reunion: by this time, Guy assumed associates were gritting their teeth and cursing under their breath when he returned to them, for more often than not, it meant trouble. Anthony, however, welcomed Guy back to Cowdray House with genuine affection. The young Viscount had aged in the time since Guy had last seen him. The sudden illness and death of his grandfather and the responsibilities that fell onto his young shoulders we no doubt the cause of the lines of concern on his forehead and the loss of the youthful brightness in his eyes.

"I'm so sorry for the way things ended on your last visit," Anthony said.

Guy waved away the apology. "It wasn't you that set the dogs upon me."

Anthony shook his head. "After what you did, they should have heralded you a hero here, not chased you off."

"What *I* did? It was you who plunged your sword into the demon's flesh."

Anthony smiled. "I did, didn't I? It's funny how these things go out of your head."

Ghost intervened. "There are so many low-level demons out there polluting the air; it's what they do. They affect how our brains work."

"That's why I'm here." Guy puffed his cheeks and wiped his sweating palms on his hose. "The demons: they're doing more than affecting how my brain works."

Ghost invited Guy to explain further, and Guy told them of the end of Dudley, the encounters with Cecil, and the events at Richmond Palace.

"Tell me more about what happened with Walsingham," Ghost said.

Guy recounted the battle and what happened when he plunged his sword into Walsingham's gut.

Ghost hummed as he cycled ideas in his head. "Remember Cynocephalus? You hesitated rather than slaying the creature."

Guy froze.

"Have you killed any demons since that moment?" Ghost asked.

Guy thought back to the encounters he'd had. Opportunities had come, but he had not killed a demon with his own hands–unless pulling a chapel upon one counted... "Not as such."

"Guy, you might not be the only one affected here."

Guy glanced at his companions. "What do you mean?"

"When you were here last, did you come face to face with the child that was taken ill, Catherine Stanley?"

Guy remembered her falling into his arms at the stables. "Yes... why? Is her illness related?"

Ghost shrugged. "Every physician has found nothing physically wrong with her. Some suggested it was an ailment of the mind keeping her from waking, and the last... she suggested it could be an act of devilry."

Guy sighed. "Cecil spoke of the girl. I believe they want Walsingham's spirit to take over her body."

"You say Walsingham has been growing bolder in recent days? Taking control of your limbs, yes?"

Guy flexed the fingers of his right hand. "Yes, this arm in particular." He held out his hand.

"What's that?" Ghost nodded at the wound on his hand.

"I cut myself with the wood of an ash tree. It helped me regain control."

"Come with me."

Ghost led Guy and Anthony up the grand central staircase. It was the first time Guy had visited any of the upper floors of the house. They passed several doors before Ghost stopped and knocked upon one.

Catherine's guardian, Jane, answered the door. Her weeks sitting at the girl's bedside left her looking drained. A window was open to let in the fresh air; nevertheless, a stink hung in the room, a bitter, mustardy odour that Guy associated with the creatures from the depths of Hell.

"Has it always smelled this bad?" Guy asked.

Ghost approached the bed and pulled back the covers. "No, only the last couple of days. Since this happened to her arm."

Little flesh remained on the bones of Catherine's right arm, the shape of meagre muscle and tendons showing through almost translucent skin. Ghost turned over her arm to show the palm. It was bandaged, but a blossoming flower of blood stained the fabric.

"The wound appeared on Saturday night." Ghost turned to Jane. "Could you tell Guy more?"

Jane swallowed hard. "It was an hour after sundown. By candlelight, I was working with my needle when I heard a crack of bone. I put my sewing on the table. Catherine's head moved from side to side. She's done that a time or two, and I called her name, hoping she was close to waking. The bedsheets twitched, so I pulled them back. Her hand was in a fist and pulsing, but then her fingers spread wide and that gash opened up, right in the centre."

"That's when the stink came."

Ghost put a thankful hand on Jane's shoulder before addressing Guy once more. "That's when we called in the last physician who said it could be some kind of devilry. Now you return with a matching wound."

Guy glanced at his hand. "So, what do we do?"

"The demon's in her, Guy, and it's in you. When Walsingham focuses his mind on controlling you, she grows weaker."

Guy gazed at Catherine Stanley's fragile frame, her pale face, and her dry and cracked lips. "What can we do to save her?"

Ghost put a hand on Guy's shoulder. "Find the strength inside you to call it out. Draw him into you and free her of the curse. You must defeat him from within."

Guy looked into Ghost's eyes. "And if I can't?"

"If he takes over your mind, there may be no way back. If Walsingham takes control of your body..."

Guy brushed off Ghost's hand. "You'll have to kill me."

Ghost stared at the floor.

"There's more," Anthony said, stepping forward.

Guy noted the quizzical way Ghost looked at the young viscount and understood this would be news to him, too.

"Let's leave the child and discuss this downstairs." Anthony turned and left.

Guy and Ghost followed Anthony into the library, where Anthony lit the candle on the low table and sat in the armchairs.

"One reason I needed to venture out today was a send a messenger to you Guy, so imagine my surprise when I returned to find you here."

"I did not mean to arrive unannounced," Guy said.

"No need to apologise. I am glad you are here. The request for your presence was urgent, but I fear what I tell you next will make you both believe I have gone quite mad."

Guy smirked. "I can assure you, there's little left out there that could shock me."

Anthony wet his lips. "How would you react if I said the name Thomas Percy to you?"

Guy shrugged. "I was with Thomas in London only yesterday."

Anthony looked at the floor. "Not that Thomas Percy."

Guy's eyes grew large. "You've seen the floating skull!"

Ghost, too, knew of Thomas Percy and his disciples, those that had visions beckoning them to a life of demon hunting. He had held the skull that resided in Saint Robert's Cave.

Anthony sat forward. "You know of what I speak?"

"I have been seeing the blasted skull in my dreams since my earliest days. Did he tell you why he has forsaken me?"

"Quite the opposite. He came to me to tell you he *hasn't* forsaken you. He spoke to me first when Grandfather passed. Yesterday, he spoke of you. He said he can no longer reach you and that you are in great danger."

Ghost rubbed his chin. "These discordant spirits block your mind. That's why Percy can no longer communicate with you."

Guy's head throbbed with the sound of a thousand strangled voices. "What did he ask of you, Browne?"

"He only asked that I bring you here and told me it was a matter of great importance."

Ghost slapped his knee. "We are no closer to a solution at all!"

Anthony jerked and leaned back in his chair.

"What is it?" asked Ghost.

But Guy knew by the way Anthony fixed his eyes on the corner of the room. While Guy could see nothing, he knew his young friend looked upon the skull of Thomas Percy. "He's here, isn't he?"

Anthony gulped. "He says he's been trying hard to communicate with you."

Guy listened to the discordant voices in his head. Was it possible that the rationality was not his own, but the guidance of Thomas Percy?

"Ask him," Guy said. "Is it Walsingham in my head?"

Anthony stared into the corner. "It is. But he has opened another door."

Guy felt the pain of whips. "Master Leonard."

"That's right."

"What does Walsingham want?"

Anthony stared into the corner, taking in Thomas Percy's message. "A body. He wants to live again, and he can do so in an appropriate human vessel."

"That's what Cecil alluded to. He wants my body to do this?"

"Yours or the girls." Anthony paused, listening again. "The girl gives him a path to the throne."

"No!" Guy thumped the table, causing the candle to quiver and send shadows dancing around the room.

"The only way to stop him," Anthony continued to stare into the corner, "is to draw him into a body, and kill it before he can leap out once more."

Guy stood and shook his head. "It cannot be her. We cannot let evil ruin another young life."

Ghost stood and put a hand on Guy's shoulder. "But Guy..."

"I'm ready to die. Draw him into me and end our lives."

In his chair, Anthony slumped. He sighed. "Thomas Percy says there may be another way."

Chapter 44—In Which Guy Fawkes Battles with Creatures in his Mind

It was deep into the night by the time they were ready for the ritual. Ghost had sent Catesby to secure a goat, and Tresham had joined him, claiming to be eager to make up for his past offences. While Guy didn't want such a weasel involved, Ghost convinced him that the more hands they had on deck, the more likely they were to secure the most desired outcome. When they returned with the beast, the last aspect required was in place and they gathered in Catherine Stanley's room.

The need to keep the window open to combat the stench meant the chill of a December night seeped into the room, drawing a creeping frost over the window panes and turning every breath into a cloud of vapour. The fire burning in the fireplace did little to warm the room. Anthony had ordered extra blankets to keep Catherine warm, and Jane had one wrapped over her shoulders. Incense burned on the hearth, bringing a hint of spice to the room. Its purpose was not to combat the smell but to create an atmosphere seasoned to discomfort malevolent spirits. Ghost had concocted the fragrance and alongside it, he had drawn powerful runes on the wooden floorboards, and around the makeshift bed upon which Guy was to sleep.

The plan was simple: force the essence of Walsingham into Guy, drawing the residual parts from Catherine's mind. There, Guy would take Walsingham on, and drive him out, with the only refuge, the goat. At that point, they would slaughter the goat, and the ordeal would be over.

Through Anthony, Percy had directed Ghost to a passage in one book he always kept with him, the *Clavicula Salomonis*, a text that combined knowledge of Greco-Roman Late Antiquity magic with that of the grand Jewish kabbalists and Arab diviners. From the extensive herb gardens of Cowdray House, Ghost has sourced much of what he needed for the concoction that would put Guy under.

Ghost approached Jane. "It would be for the best if you stepped outside while we conduct the exorcism."

"I'm not leaving Catherine's side."

Anthony placed a hand on her shoulder and gave a supportive smile.

Ghost handed Guy the draught. "When you drink this, you will be susceptible to spirits. We will have about one minute before it knocks you out."

Guy looked at the swirling concoction, his nostrils twitching at its overpowering scent. He knew what he had to do: he would enter a sleep-like state and navigate his mind to locate Walsingham. Of course, the memory of Master Leonard existed in there too, and the echoes of every conversation, the residual pain of every wound, and the tears of every heartbreak were all inside there to contend with. While he expected to be occupied within his mind for hours, in reality, the process would take only minutes. Catesby held the reins of the black goat while Anthony and Tresham stood by with swords drawn.

Ghost turned to them now. "Wait for my signal. If you act too soon, if you strike before he's in the goat, he'll have nowhere else to go. If he's trapped, he could destroy Guy's mind."

Guy took in several long, deep breaths as he gazed around the room at his companions.

Ghost placed his hand in the bowl of holy water and drew a cross on the heads of Catesby, Tresham, Anthony, and Jane. "This will stop him from entering you."

Ghost turned back to Guy. "Remember, Percy said you'll find him locked in there somewhere, too. Free him, and you'll have his guidance."

Guy gazed into the mug. "Aye, in a crypt, I'd expect."

Ghost looked round to check on the others. All was in place. "Okay, go for it."

Guy drank the concoction, tasting bitter tones but most of all a density. The liquid dropped through his body, bringing an intense heaviness.

Ghost leant over Catherine, rubbing a substance under her nose. He grabbed a stick, brought it to the flame, and then wafted it in front of the child.

A rush of air hit Guy, and as he gasped, Anthony guided him toward the rudimentary bed. The heaviness grew and his vision closed in as he lay down.

· · · ·

GUY STOOD SURROUNDED by blackness. There was no ground beneath his feet, no ceiling or sun, moon, or stars to indicate if he was inside or out, if it was night or day. He walked. Beneath his feet was solid, but not the solid of pavement or of the earth. The sound below changed to wooden floorboards, and instead of his foot finding the ground, it fell, hitting something a foot lower. He was on steps. He touched the wall of a place he'd touched a thousand times in his youngest days: the stairs of his home in Stonegate, York. With the realisation came vision. He saw it all before him, the property in the days before it burned.

A knock came at the door, and Guy knew not only where he was, but when. He raced down the stairs as his father opened a letter. Guy's younger self and Francis Ingleby looked on. Demonic transformation came over his father, the corruption visible in the darkness of the veins that rose to the surface and in the sickly yellow around his eyes. Guy watched as his father and Francis Ingleby fought. Mid-battle they froze. The demonic Edward Fawkes turned his head ninety degrees to stare into Guy's eyes. "And you stood there and did nothing. Coward."

Guy looked at his younger self, backed against the dresser.

"Useless boy," the demon version of Guy's father hissed.

Edward turned his attention back to Francis, once more gaining dominance and knocking his sword from his opponent's hand. Guy watched the brawl, powerless to intervene in the memory: his younger self raced forward, grabbed the sword, and behead this demonic incarnation of his father.

The head crashed to the floor, and the room darkened, Ingleby and the younger version of Guy Fawkes disappearing from view.

Even the body of Edward Fawkes disappeared. Only the head remained on a black canvas. "Cutting your own father's head off. You were always such a disappointment as a son."

Guy covered his ears, but the voice penetrated them.

"We all had such high hopes, but you're a failure."

The door appeared once more and crept open. With his broken neck causing his head to slump to one side, Guy's former headmaster, Pulleyn, entered.

"Time for your school report," Edward said.

Pulleyn opened his mouth and waggled what remained of his tongue.

"That's right! You cut your headmaster's tongue out. Not the academic success we were hoping for, my boy."

Pulleyn faded away, and the door crept open again.

Edward grinned, showing his pointed demon teeth. "Maybe someone else can help? Oh, look, Ingleby's back."

With his neck similarly broken, and vitality drained from his face, Francis groaned at Guy.

Edward cackled. "Another teacher with nothing good to say about this student."

With a crack, twisted branches burst from the floor, imprisoning Guy.

"What's this?" Guy's father said as the first demon Guy encountered swirled as smoke between the branches before materialising in the flesh before him.

A new door burst open, and in his robe, sword in hand, Oswald Tesimond dashed through.

"You didn't even have the judgement to see the good in one so pure and holy!" Edward Fawkes laughed as Oswald lunged for the demon. The creature disappeared, and Oswald turned around, gazing into each corner in confusion.

"I'm here!" Guy called.

Oswald ignored Guy as his face thinned, the eyes become more deep-set and filled with anguish. A cut opened on his cheek, then healed, leaving a deep scar. Oswald turned back to the door and left.

"And those you didn't destroy abandoned you! Pathetic child!"

Guy grabbed the branches restraining him. They crumbled to ash as he touched them. Suddenly free, he broke for the door, only for it to fade to blackness, leaving him trapped in the void.

"Looks like no one has a positive word to say. What a terrible disappointment you are!" Edward laughed as all around him turned dark, and he, too, disappeared.

Bright orange light flared as the room returned, flames spread on every wall. His childhood home was burning once more. He fled for the door and stood in the darkness of the street.

As he looked back at the house, first Kit emerged through the window, followed by himself, with Jack struggling out a moment later. The trio fled, with buildings materialising on either side of them as they ran. Guy followed to The Shambles, where a figure in silhouette ushered the trio into a low pig door. The light shifted, revealing the horror of Margaret Clitherow, naked, tortured, and crushed. With half of her hair torn out, and a rib poking out of her side, she stumbled toward Guy. "You couldn't save me, either, could you?" She grinned, showing blood-stained teeth.

Guy skidded to a stop. He was heading in the opposite direction of where he needed to go, his memories leading him astray. He needed to go to York Minster, to the crypt, to free Thomas Percy. But when he turned, all the buildings fell away.

Knavesmire sprung up around him, the twisted trees appearing behind him as the ground grew soft underfoot and a hundred corpses swung from the extended scaffold. Every execution he'd ever witnessed occurred again. In unity, the ropes snapped, and the dead collapsed to the earth, only for them to rise and march toward Guy. "You killed us," they murmured as they traipsed ever closer. In every direction, they marched toward him. He tried to run, but Knavesmire lived up to its name, gripping his feet in its clutches and refusing to let him go. The dead were upon him, coming together, falling on top of him, smothering him. The considerable weight of York's dead was a burden too heavy to carry, and Guy sunk further into the mire, through the mire, until the earth disappeared altogether and he was falling. He rushed through the air, wave after wave splashing at him, and ice daggering the exposed flesh on his face, hands, and neck. The combined aerial powers of Hastings and the Dudley brothers battered Guy as he sailed through clouds, through storms, through blizzards. He twisted in mid-air and a familiar building appeared on the horizon. He'd recognise the towers of York Minster anywhere, and he was falling toward them at pace. The pull of the wind altered his trajectory at the last minute, directing him through the window and leaving him to plummet to the ground in the centre of the nave.

He stood. By rights, every bone in his body should have shattered, but he remembered he was not in his body but in his mind. Here, he could take such punishment. The only danger was losing his mind and never finding his way out, and that was what Walsingham wanted. If he could drive Guy out of his mind, it was free for Walsingham's reign.

The crypt at York Minster was the mental prison he'd created to imprison Master Leonard. It stood to reason he would find Percy trapped inside. He approached the door. The seal of the blackened ash tree was gone, replaced instead with a pattern resembling hellfire. Guy reached for the door, but its incredible heat sent him reeling back. He'd burned himself on this door before when bursting through from the other side. The pain wasn't so bad. He could take it again. He prepared to shoulder-barge the door when the crack of a whip drew his attention to Master Leonard, grinning his terrible grin. As before, two of his arms carried weapons, the vicious cat-o'-nine-tails, and a flaming sword, while his other two hands formed fists, blackened, and ready to do damage. This vision of the demon had grown ghastlier while in Guy's mind, its three horns mammoth, twisted, and split. Cruel barbs sprung from its shoulders and elbows.

"You only beat me before because your sister untethered the link. Well, guess what, pizzle-chin? Your sister isn't here now!" Master Leonard grinned. He stepped forward, and the walls of York Minster shook. Squeal after squeal came as rats fell from the ceiling.

Guy reached for his sword, but his scabbard was empty. Of course! He'd lost his sword when the chapel collapsed on London Bridge. Walsingham had kept that thought from his mind, rendering him unarmed when he most needed protection. Guy batted one rat away, but another landed on his shoulder and nipped the back of his neck.

Master Leonard lashed with his whip, wrapping it around Guy's leg. He yanked it forward and pulled Guy from his feet. He crashed onto his back.

Master Leonard leapt into the air. Guy rolled, and the demon landed beside him. "You know you can't defeat me. I destroyed you night after night in your dreams."

Guy struggled to his feet.

Master Leonard lunged forward with his sword, and Guy leant back, the edge of the blade passing within an inch of his neck. Again, Master Leonard lashed the whip, catching Guy's other leg. Guy crashed to the stone floor on his back. The demon dragged Guy toward him. He flicked the whip to release Guy and kicked him. Guy sailed through the air, crashing into the crypt door. Searing heat passed through his body as he clambered back to his feet.

"Guy!" came a shout from below. He recognised the voice, Percy, calling from the crypt, his voice travelling through the vents. "Guy, fight back."

Master Leonard leapt into the air once more and crashed down beside Guy before lifting him into the air with an uppercut to the stomach.

Guy collapsed to the floor beside the crypt vents.

"Fight back," called Percy again.

Master Leonard loomed over Guy.

"How can I? I lost my sword."

Master Leonard swung his sword, and Guy barely rolled away in time, the vibrations resonating through the stone floor and quivering along his spinal cord.

"It's your imagination, Guy. You can have any sword you wish."

Master Leonard slashed again, and Guy raised his arm in defence, now carrying his faithful scimitar. Master Leonard's sword bounced off it with such force, he had to take a step back to regain balance.

Guy whispered the words to the sword, and it grew to proportions never seen before. He slashed at Master Leonard, who deflected the blow. The demon stamped on the floor, causing it to quake once more. Guy focused on his balance, and when the whip came, he jumped. Again and again, man and demon clashed blades, with Guy ducking under the flailing whip and dodging smashing fists. They circled the nave, the cathedral a theatre for their glorious show, and when the doors to the main entrance burst open, Master Leonard looked around with glee. The hanged masses poured through the door, heads slumped to one side, arms stretching before them.

"Prepare to be drowned in woes, Guy Fawkes!" Master Leonard hissed.

Guy flew at Leonard once more, slashing with all the strength he could muster from his mind.

"They're not here for me!" Guy cried as the masses closed.

Master Leonard faced the crowd and shrunk within himself.

"This is my mind, and I summoned them to take you back where you belong."

Master Leonard flicked his whip as the nearest dead man approached. As he recoiled, Guy slashed at the demon's arm, severing it, sending it cascading to the ground, whip and all.

The first of the hands grabbed at Master Leonard's charred flesh, and he cried out. More grabbed him, dragging him to his knees. Two grabbed at his horns and pulled his head back.

"You have no dominion here in my mind!" Guy dragged his sword across the demon's throat. First, a slew of blood and fleshly lumps slopped out, but then the wrongfully hanged fell on top of him, driving him into an ever-deepening black pit. Once Master Leonard had descended beyond sight, the pit closed and the stone floor repaired itself, leaving Guy alone in York Minster.

He hurried to the crypt. The sign of hellfire on the door had disappeared. He kicked the wood, and the door flew open.

"Percy!" Guy called as he headed into the gloom.

From around the corner came the light of the lantern, and a figure Guy didn't recognise stepped out. His hair was dark but cropped short, and his facial hair thin and framed his face. Perhaps it was the way the lantern lit him, but his cheeks were overly pink, and his ears large. "Come on!" he called, before heading back around the corner.

Guy remained on the steps.

The man returned. "Don't you recognise me with my flesh on?"

"Percy?" Guy took a few more steps.

"Of course! Now follow. We have to go after Walsingham."

"I can handle it."

"Don't be so sure. What you've dealt with so far has only been the manifestation of your own emotions, your guilt, your fears, turned against you. Walsingham's real. He's been living inside your head. He knows your every secret, and he knows how to turn them against you."

Percy strode further into the crypt, heading toward the subterranean passages that would take them to the King's Manor.

"Why do we have to go this way?" Guy asked, a tightness growing in his chest.

"Boy, the only way you're coming through this is if you face the darkness. Now hurry!"

Chapter 45—In Which Guy Fawkes Goes Mind to Mind with Walsingham

The tunnel in Guy's mind was far shorter than the one he'd traversed in reality back on the night he'd met Maria, and soon they were in the basement of the King's Manor.

"You must face Walsingham with great caution," Percy said.

"But I can use the power of my imagination against him. Whatever I can think of, I can use to my advantage."

"He is not a figment like Master Leonard was. Any tricks you can play, he can too. He will do what he can to drive you out of your mind, and you must do the same to him."

"What will make him depart?"

"Prove your will is stronger than his. He has control over your mind, but remember, all of this has made you who you are. Own it and he can't turn it against you."

Guy and Percy walked into the main chamber of the basement. Two demonic guards circled it, floating in mid-air as they had done so long ago when Guy last visited the basement of King's Manor.

Percy drew his sword.

Guy followed the path the demon's circled with his eyes. "So, we need to battle with these?"

"Show your will is stronger. You're willing to fight for your mind."

Guy drew his sword and nodded toward Percy's blade. "So, I'm going to witness the moves that lost you the rebellion of the Northern Earls?"

"I don't *have* to assist you here."

Guy glared at Percy. "Aye, you do. You're in my mind. You'll do as you're told."

Percy grinned. "Now you're getting the hang of it."

The demon soldiers screeched and flew toward them. Guy and Percy stepped forward and slashed, their blades searing through the creatures' torsos and leaving them in a twitching mess on the ground.

Guy looked back at the carcasses. "Are they all going to be that easy to deal with?"

"I wouldn't place a significant wager on it."

The room shook, and light flickered on the wall of the staircase. Booming footsteps echoed around the chamber as Walsingham stomped down the steps, cracks appearing beneath his feet through which the fires of Hell glowed.

He stood eight feet tall, no longer bound by the frail frame of a human body.

"Walsingham!" Guy cried. "I cast you out. This is my mind, and you have no place here."

Walsingham laughed, a cackle that resonated from every direction.

"Are you sure we're in your mind?" Walsingham said as the filthy walls of his torture chamber rose around Guy. He was back in the depths of Durham castle's tower, the wails of tormented prisoners resounding all around him. There was no exit.

"Come and get me!" Walsingham cried. He stood with his arms outstretched, his sword sheathed by his side.

As Guy touched the hilt of his sword, a cry came from his left. "Help!"

Kit Wright lay stretched out on a torture rack. Another rack appeared beside it, with another version of Kit straining on it. On Guy's right, another pair of racks appeared, Kit gritting his teeth on each as they groaned under the strain of pulling every version of Kit's joints apart.

Guy slashed at the ropes, relieving the first Kit. His friend disappeared as soon as he was free of torment. Guy slashed at the ropes tying the version of Kit behind him.

"I'm right here," Walsingham called.

Guy turned again and freed the third of the tortured Kits.

The original had returned, once more in shackles and again being stretched by the torture device.

"The only way to stop it is to stop me."

Guy slashed at the ropes, even though the cycle continued. Each time he saved one Kit, another appeared in peril.

"Can't you see it's futile?" Walsingham called.

"Help me!" called Guy, glancing over his shoulder at Percy.

Guy continued to slice through the ropes as the fallen rebel joined him.

Walsingham clicked his fingers.

From above, a flock of bats swooped, screeching, and clawing at Guy's bare arms, and at his neck, landing on Percy's face, seeking his eyes.

But every time Kit screamed, Guy's attention switched to where it was required, taking the weight away from the machine and relieving the pressure.

Walsingham sunk to a knee, sapped by conjuring the same image over and again.

"I will always defend my friends before I strike down my enemies," Guy called as he kicked a clasp free from one torture rack and sliced the ropes of another. This time, a replacement didn't materialise.

Walsingham clenched his fists and mimicked dragging something from the ground. Nothing came. Walsingham repeated the action, as Guy smashed through the last of the torture racks.

Walsingham cried out, drawing strength from his wailing, and rose to his feet. He stamped, and a crack opened beneath him, swallowing him up, leaving only his robes behind.

The walls around Guy and Percy changed, leaving them once more in the basement of King's Manor.

"Is that it?" Guy asked. "It is over?" He prodded at Walsingham's robe with his sword.

Percy glared at Guy. "I wouldn't have thought you'd be fool enough to make the same mistake twice."

"Where now?"

From above came the sound of music, clashing tankards, and revelry.

Percy nodded to the steps. "Upstairs. I get the impression we're about to attend a banquet.

Of course, Guy's manifestation of King's Manor was based upon the only time he'd been inside with the *other* Thomas Percy, when they'd posed as servers to gain information on Walsingham. It was his continued interest in the Queen's Spymaster that had cost him so much. He'd gone after Walsingham, made an enemy of Dudley, and it had cost him everything. As Guy clenched his teeth together, King's Manor shook.

"Keep your head, Guy," Percy urged. "This is what you must overcome if you're to drive Walsingham out. Own your memories and draw strength from them! Don't let him turn your past against you."

But how could Guy draw strength from memories which stirred such self-loathing? How could he not hate himself for the mistakes of his past that had cost him so dear?

Unlike in reality, the stairs led into the banqueting hall, emerging before a grand table stacked full of food that had never been there. The sound of chatter and the music ceased, leaving only his echoing footsteps as he approached the table. All revellers had disappeared. In the centre was a three-headed calf, the hide torn off, leaving the flesh glistening in the candlelight. Disembodied sheep heads surrounded the cow's carcass, their eyes alive. One gave a weak bleat. Entrails hung from every edge as visceral bunting.

Further inside, guest tables surrounded the room in a horseshoe. The guests reappeared, sitting at the tables, their faces a constantly shifting carousel, from Walsingham, to Robert Dudley, to Walter Dudley, to Cecil, to every other noble knave he'd had the misfortune to encounter. The door to the left opened and a parade of servers marched out. While the guests continued to shift shape, the servers were all alike. Every one was Maria, her dark hair pulled into a tight ponytail. They carried silver platters with domed covers, but instead of approaching the tables from opposite their guests, they moved behind them, set the platters on the table and sat on their laps. All guests' faces deformed to that of Walsingham.

The army of Marias removed the covers to reveal bunches of red grapes, which they held to drape into the mouths of their Walsinghams who chomped on the fruits, letting them burst, the juice running down their chins, staining them red. The actions were the same wherever Guy looked. The Marias flung the grapes over their shoulders, wrapped their arms around their Walsinghams, and kissed them. When they broke the embrace, their mouths too were stained red. Each stared at Guy with bloodshot eyes. They tipped their heads back and laughed.

"No!" Guy cried. He ran around the feasting table, into the centre of the hall, but Walsinghams and Marias alike disappeared. Candles flared, illuminating the tapestries on the walls. The one at the end rippled, demanding his attention. He approached the tapestry: the castle in its background looked much like that at Knaresborough. In the foreground, three men shepherded sheep. Guy hurried to the next tapestry where a market was depicted. Next came a cow. The house on the next could only be that Guy had built for

Maria. Guy dashed from tapestry to tapestry as the story of the worst time of his life played out. The cow grew fat, pregnant with those beasts of destruction. The next showed it erupting with tentacles. Guy fought them on the next, with one racing toward his house in the background. The penultimate tapestry showed his bedroom window. He didn't want to look at the final tapestry. A moo from the banquet table meant he didn't have to. The three-headed, skinned calf raise two of its heads, while the third remained slumped on the table. One head lowed, and the second imitated it. Cries came from all around. What were once sheep heads had transformed, too. A dozen heads cried together, all bearing the image of Guy's son John.

Guy dropped to his knees.

The cow pushed itself onto its front legs, and clattered off the table, sending some John heads to the floor, where they continued to wail.

"You have to fight it!" Percy called. "He's using your pain against you."

The side of the cow burst open, and a barbed tentacle flew out, showering the hall with viscera.

Guy roared as it flew toward him, welcoming its attack.

Percy slashed at the tentacle, severing it in two. The wet end continued its trajectory, slapping Guy in the face before tumbling to the floor.

Another tentacle burst from the other side of the beast.

"Fight back!" Percy called.

"What's the point?" Guy cried.

Johns continued to cry, their wails no longer a raucous cacophony of discordant bellows, but in harmony, a mournful dirge, a song fit for the end.

"I can't bring him back. I can't bring Maria back."

Percy slashed at the second tentacle as a third erupted from the beast.

"When I tried to avenge them, I only made things worse. The world is better off without me."

The third tentacle avoided Percy's strike, wrapped around his leg, and yanked him away. He fell back, his shoulder first smashing into the floor before his head cracked into it. The creature dragged Percy's body away, leaving the skull behind. It rose into the air, in the form Guy was most familiar with.

"You're not fighting for you, Guy. You cannot get back what you've lost. No one can. But you can't let that suffering spread. Your pain is meat to these monsters."

A pair of tentacles burst from either side of the beast.

Percy continued. "But your joy is their suffering. Don't let them use your memories of those you loved to bring pain to others. Own your emotion, Guy."

Guy gritted his teeth and pulled out his sword, lifting it to slice through the flesh of a darting tentacle. He rose to his feet and leapt over the second, running toward the lowing beast.

But it wasn't that he was after. He took one of his son's heads in his arm. As he did so, the rest of the body appeared, and its duplicates vanished. Guy gazed at his perfect child in his arms. He'd forgotten the joy of the warmth of his child at his chest, close to his heart. The crying eased as John's heartbeat matched the rhythm of his own. The cow calmed too. Guy stroked his son's hair, remembering the softness. He ran the back of one finger across John's smooth cheek, and John gurgled, his lips twisting into a smile. Guy touched the palm of John's hand, and let his tiny fingers curl around one of his. He pulled John closer, cradling him into his shoulder, and as he held him, the child passed into him, became part of him, overwhelming Guy with pure love.

He faced the beast, but it had slumped onto the floor, dragged down by the weight of a second dead head. The eyes on the third closed, and it sunk into the ground, leaving not so much of a trace of its existence.

The skull of Percy rushed to Guy's side. "That's right! Draw strength from what you had."

The lights went out, and all was dark once more. In the distance, if distance was a thing in this dreamworld, a light glowed. Guy raced toward it, and the closer he got, the clearer the light became, a rectangular outline radiating from behind a door. The handle rattled, demanding his attention. He knew this door; he'd built it himself. Within was his bedroom. Groans of pleasure came from beyond.

Guy knew how Walsingham would play him. He had to resist the temptation to rise to the bait. Another groan came from the other side of the door. He gulped, placed his hand on the door handle, and pushed the door open.

The intensity of the groans magnified as he looked upon his marital bed, Maria smirked at him as Walsingham sneered from on top of her. Staring at

Guy, he raised two fingers above his head to symbolise horns. "Ahoy, Cuckold!"

He knew what Walsingham wanted as he leered.

Walsingham wanted Guy's anger, Guy's jealousy. He wanted a moment of fury in which Guy thrust his sword at Walsingham, and through into Maria. He wanted anguish, pain, and suffering, a feast from which he'd draw greater strength.

"I made this bed," Guy said as the headboard clattered against the wall.

"I built this house." Guy touched the wall.

"And I cast thee out." Guy pointed with his sword at Walsingham.

The house quaked. Dust fell from the ceiling and the beams creaked.

The floor shook, and a crack appeared below, taking one of the bed's feet. It tilted and another leg broke, followed by the remaining two, and as it crashed to the ground, Maria disappeared.

Walsingham roared, and he too was gone.

A beam above Guy creaked. He stretched, his arms impossibly long, and held it in place. "This is my home. I won't let you tarnish its memory." The beam cracked again as it righted itself.

Guy lifted the end of the bed. The legs reappeared, and the crack in the ground closed.

In the bed, Maria rematerialized, her head sunk into a pillow, her eyes closed as she slept softly.

"Rest here," Guy whispered. "Whenever I need you, I can close my eyes. I'll be with you soon."

Maria became distant as the bed moved away. He blinked, and he was looking at his home once more from the outside, the only sound, Maria's soft snore and John's gurgling. A smell of apple blossom lingered in the air.

The room faded, leaving Guy in darkness.

"You cannot summon ill from my mind, Walsingham. Your power here is gone!"

Sunrise came swiftly, dispensing the night, revealing a golden field of barley with lush green hills dotted with sheep in the distance.

Walsingham too stood in the barley, shorter now, his arms raised to shield himself from the sun's rays. He fled the field and followed a rough path along a slope toward a barn.

Guy pointed and with a flick of his finger, the door opened.

Walsingham continued running, stumbling toward the building.

A bleat came from within.

Walsingham turned back to Guy. "It doesn't have to end this way. I see your strength. We can rule together."

Guy strode forward as Walsingham took steps back.

"You've had a taste of the high life in the capital. All that and more can be yours." The flesh on the demon spymaster's face grew thin.

"It's time to go, Walsingham. You have no sanctuary here." Guy clicked his fingers and the crypt door at York Minster appeared.

Walsingham leant away from it and turned back to the barn, from where another bleat came.

Guy closed his eyes and focused his mind on forcing Walsingham out as the master of spies voluntarily took the step into the goat's domain.

Chapter 46—In Which Guy Fawkes Leaves the Chaos of England Behind

Indistinguishable voices called from the real world.

"Now! Now!"

"Don't let go."

"Quick! Kill it!"

"It's not dead. Stab it again."

"Sever the head."

Guy's other senses returned soon after: the chill of the frosty December air on every gust that blew through the open window and the stench of spilt blood. His vision cleared slowly to reveal the felled goat's carcass. Tresham stood over it, holding its severed head by one horn. Blood covered the floor, Ghost's symbols washed away.

Guy took a deep breath. "Did you get it in time?"

Ghost looked on with concern.

Anthony nodded. "It slipped its rope, but Catesby got it."

Tresham tossed the head to the floor. "And I made sure the job was done."

Catesby shoved him. "It was your job! You should have killed it when we said."

"The girl?" Guy asked.

Jane, who had sat by Catherine's bed throughout, stood facing the group. She pointed to the bed, her face white, ridden with concern.

Her mouth dropped open and a slew of blood spilt onto the floor. Through her dress, in the centre of her gut, came the claws of a tiny hand.

Jane dropped to the floor as Catherine withdrew her arm. Her eyes had become beady, resembling Walsingham's, and the shape of her head had deformed, her chin thinning to a point, while the top of her head became bulbous.

"You were too late," Ghost yelled at Tresham, but he was already out of the door.

Guy scrambled to his feet. "Force him back into me!"

Catherine leapt from the bed at Catesby, clinging onto his back and clawing at his head. Whether deliberately or by accident, Guy didn't know, Catesby backed into the wall, causing Catherine to squeal and release him.

"Leave her, Walsingham," Guy cried. "Come back into me."

"No!" Ghost stepped between Catherine and Guy. She thrust out her hand, the sharp talons punching through Ghost's chest.

Guy gasped as his friend slumped to the ground.

"Why would I want your body?" Catherine grinned, showing her bloody teeth. "I know all of its fragilities! And young flesh is so malleable!"

Anthony stepped forward, pointing with his sword. "Back! Back I say!"

Catherine pointed at the window and yanked her hand back. It slammed shut and shards of glass flew at Anthony, embedding in his neck and face. He screamed and reached to pluck the glass out, only succeeding in slicing his fingers on the jagged edges.

"In this form, I shall be Queen!" Catherine laughed the deep and booming laugh of an old man, an ancient sinner, a primaeval demon.

Anthony fell to the floor, gasping, not knowing which wound to cover.

While Catherine chuckled at the chaos and destruction she'd reaped, Catesby jumped from one side and flung her on the bed. He drew his sword, but Guy grabbed his arm.

"We can't!" Guy called. "She's an innocent child."

Catherine shuffled back onto the corner of the bed and smiled.

"What else can we do?" Panic wracked Catesby's voice.

"Force Walsingham back into me. Take my life instead."

"Is that what you want?"

Guy slipped back into his mind, to his home, to Maria waiting for him in the bed he'd built. He released his grip on Catesby's arm.

Catesby held Catherine at bay with his sword. "Without Ghost, I don't know how."

Guy glanced again at Ghost's corpse. "We have his books. Percy can guide us through the process."

"What do we do with her in the meantime?"

"Lock her up. Somewhere secure. We'll douse everything in holy water."

Catherine continued to cower at the edge of the bed.

"He doesn't yet have full control over her..."

As if on cue, Catherine reacted. Whatever level of control Walsingham exerted, it was more than she'd revealed. The sheet on her bed, guided by Walsingham's malevolent intent, wrapped around Catesby's sword arm, twisting it around, pulling the blade toward Catesby's neck.

Catherine grinned as she contorted her arms, manipulating the sheet with demonic power, sending Catesby's sword ever closer to his throat.

Guy had no time to think. He had to sever the link. He grabbed a fragment of broken glass and lunged at Catherine, plunging it into her throat.

The sheet became loose, and Catesby dropped his sword.

"No!" Guy cried as Catherine slumped back on the bed, blood squirting out of the wound. He leant toward her, but Catesby pulled him back before grabbing the bowl and splashing his face with holy water.

"Stay away," Catesby cried. "We're not letting that villain get back into you."

Catherine continued to gasp on the bed, spitting out curses and staring with eyes full of hate until she choked her last breath.

"You had no choice," Catesby said.

Guy looked from Catherine's blood-stained body to the floor, at the slumped bodies of Jane, Ghost, and Anthony. "It didn't have to end this way."

"But it did. It could have been worse for me, for all of us, if you'd hesitated."

Sobs racked Guy's body. "I'd have given my life for hers."

From the corner, the skull of Percy chimed in. "And that's why he wouldn't return to your body. Too much good to overcome."

Percy disappeared again before Guy could respond.

Catesby placed a hand on his shoulder. "I know, now, I have a friend I can lean on no matter what, who will do the right thing when life is on the line."

From the ground came a splutter.

"Anthony!" Guy knelt beside his young friend. His front was awash with blood, and glass stuck out of him in five places. "Catesby, we need to act now. I'll take out the glass, and you cover the wounds, stop the flow of blood. "

Catesby tore strips from the bedsheet with which to make wadding and bandages.

Guy plucked the first piece of glass from the wound, and as blood jetted out, Catesby covered it. Four more times they did the same before Catesby made bandages to cover the lot, swaddling Anthony's neck and half his face.

Anthony lacked the strength to speak. They struggled with him into the next room where there was a spare bed, and with the young Viscount resting, Guy and Catesby passed out in the armchairs.

• • • •

WHEN MORNING CAME, Anthony stirred in his bed. As he turned onto one of his wounds he grimaced, and his eyes eased open.

Guy stood over him.

"Is it over?" Anthony asked.

Walsingham had passed away with Catherine. There was nowhere else for him to go. "Aye, it's over."

A cough at the door drew their attention. One of Anthony's servants awaited a response.

"Yes?" Anthony managed.

"We have a messenger from Her Majesty. She demands an update on her niece, Catherine Stanley."

Anthony looked from Guy to Catesby.

Guy stepped forward. "Tell them the child has passed on. Tell them Guy Fawkes could not save her."

Catesby held out a hand to stay the servant. "Don't make yourself the scapegoat. There must be another way."

Guy shook his head. "No. We cannot let her take umbrage at Cowdray House," he gazed at Anthony, "or against the young Viscount."

Catesby nodded at the servant, releasing him to deliver the ill tidings. "You'll be a pariah. She'll sling you in the tower."

"Better I than any of you."

"But what will you do?" Catesby asked.

"I made a promise to catch up with an old friend when the time was right." Guy took a deep breath. "Europe calls. I'll make for Portsmouth..."

Anthony coughed and waved his hand. "Avoid Portsmouth. They will expect you to flee that way."

"Where then?"

Anthony squirmed on the bed. "Make for Gillingham. I have a trade ship docked there, the English Ship Castor. Speak my name and they'll grant you safe passage to France."

Guy leant over to embrace Anthony and left.

Catesby followed Guy along the hall. "Take a horse from the stables. Stick to the old droves and avoid the major roads."

Guy shook Catesby's hand. "And Tresham won't have a problem with me taking a horse?"

"He and I have unfinished business after his performance last night. If he so much as raises an eyebrow, I'll knock lumps out of him."

• • • •

TRAVELLING NO MORE than fifteen miles a day, following rivers and droves, Guy made for east Kent. For the first time in a long time, Guy was alone, no parasite in his mind to stir negativity. Even Thomas Percy didn't appear with any words of wisdom, though Guy could sense his presence, knowing he could lean on his advice if required. Grief would remain, always, but he understood grief only existed because he'd had something special, even if only fleetingly.

Winter meant he couldn't camp in the wild, which drove him to find small settlements. In the taverns in which he stayed, he gave fake names and avoided conversation, choosing always a seat in which he could stare into the fire while he ate. The flickering flames remained strangely comforting.

After seven days, the sea came into view, the salty air inviting him to experience somewhere new. At the docks, Guy asked after the English Ship Castor, but as a drunken sailor pointed toward a ship, Guy noticed movement in the shadows, someone slipping out of sight behind a ramshackle tavern.

Maybe they'd got to someone at Cowdray House. Perhaps Queen Elizabeth had sent an assassin. Well, Guy wasn't about to give her the satisfaction. No, he no longer welcomed the idea of death, though he knew happiness waited in eternal rest, with Maria and John snuggled together in the bed he'd built. He'd return there one day, but not yet.

Guy had still to replace his sword, carrying only a dagger in his boot, but that would suffice. He cast one look back at the ship he was about to sail on: a fine vessel he hoped to board soon. He made for the tavern, ready to fight.

When a figure stepped from the shadows, all idea of attack disappeared and a smile spread across his face.

"I don't believe it," Kit said, wrapping his arms around Guy.

Guy released his old friend. "What are you doing here?"

Kit had let his hair grow longer in the time since Guy had last seen him, so it framed his face, his complexion darker after time abroad. "I could ask you the same thing, but a mutual friend told me you'd be here at some point. I'd almost given up waiting."

Guy raised an eyebrow. "A mutual friend?"

"Aye, Oswald Tesimond. He claims he heard a voice calling from the beyond, stating you were in trouble, and you might need help to find the way."

Guy smiled as the sea breeze rippled his cloak. "So, you made your way back across the sea to guide me? Where to?"

"As Uncle Francis always said–hope lies in Spain."

"Hope lies in Spain," Guy repeated as they made their way for the English Ship Castor.

Aye, Guy had found comfort while alone, but travelling with a friend was much better.

Epilogue

Jamie hears a nurse clear his throat. He turns to face him.

"I'm afraid visiting hours are over." From the look on his face, it appears visiting hours were over some time ago.

"No!" Jamie calls, before realising where he is. He glances at the clock. Hours have passed since his arrival. His legs are asleep, his throat dry and scratchy. "One sec..."

The nurse frowns.

Jamie stands and approaches Sidney's bed. "I don't understand; we're still years from the Gunpowder Plot."

Sidney lifts his shoulders in a weak shrug. "You have to know what he went through."

Jamie looks again at the empty shelf beside Sidney, the place on which other patients have cards and gifts. No one else has been in to visit over the last few hours. Is Sidney Jamie only here to satisfy this lonely, old man's need for company? Jamie's journalistic brain kicks in: there's no sellable story, here. He's worked with plenty of other professionals who'd walk away.

Jamie knows he can't, and the narrative alone isn't the only reason he's listened so long. More than the story is at play. In this lonely old man, he sees a mirror for his future: all relationships failed, all friends and family forgotten. The fear that no one will listen to Jamie's story in the years to come binds him to Sidney. Moreso, he wants to hear more about Guy, and Kit, and Spain. He wants to learn how they became involved in the Gunpowder Plot. How can anyone ever excuse an act like that? Was parliament so full of villainy that he thought there was no other option?

Sidney beckons Jamie to come closer.

Instead, he grabs his phone from his pocket. So engrossed in the tale, he has missed several messages. Michael has sent him details of three other occasions on which Sidney has suffered burns on Guy Fawkes Night.

Jamie steps toward the bed.

Now, Sidney's voice is hoarse. "I need you to do something for me before you return."

Jamie nods. He's expecting another name. Instead, Sidney beckons him closer still and whispers: "Guy Fawkes Arms, Scotton. False panel behind the bar."

Jamie backs away. The old man's hot breath makes his face tingle, the pain of the burns on his cheek and neck flaring once more. "What's there?"

Sidney smiles. "Proof."

He turns and walks away without looking back. He doesn't want to give the old man the satisfaction of knowing he's got him hooked.

Scotton's not far away. Maybe he could take a friend. Any adventure is better with a companion.

Acknowledgements

The period of time which this novel covers is when we know least about Guy Fawkes' life. I remain indebted to Nick Holland whose fabulous biography, *The Real Guy Fawkes* gave me enough touchstones with which to build a plausible narrative. Or semi-plausible. You know, if you forget about all of the implausible stuff for a second.

If the first book was a coming-of-age tale, perhaps this one is a coming-to-terms tale. Maybe it's youth and young manhood. It's a story in which Guy Fawkes falls in love and finds happiness. His is only fleeting. I have been lucky to have my wife by side for significantly longer. I thank Lisa for her belief and support.

I'm repeated myself here, but it needs restating. I've borrowed characters, that really existed, and used them for the purpose of fiction. I take full responsibility for how they appear in this series. My intention is not to present them as they would have been, but for the purpose of my story. If they're evil demon-worshippers in my book, it is not a reflection on their actual lives. Where the history is inaccurate, that's on me, despite my attempts to make it authentic.

Without readers, this would be a lonely process indeed. Thanks to everyone who has taken the time to pick up my books, share posts on social media, and review my work. Jim McLeod at Ginger Nuts of Horror has been incredibly supportive. Kayleigh Marie at Happy Goat Horror continue to be amazing. Check out their websites. Thanks also to Dave Jeffrey who is one of the most supportive people in the horror community and a brilliant writer. This thanks is extended to everyone I've interacted with in person or online that has helped me to get through the wobbles or distracted me with some other kind of relief of nonsense which certainly helped me keep my head together as I was pulling together this novel, which, at just shy of 100 000 words, if the longest thing I've ever written.

My thanks also to all at Shadow Spark Publishing. Thank you for continuing to believe in this project.

About the Author

Benjamin Langley lives, writes, & teaches in Cambridgeshire, UK. He studied at Anglia Ruskin University, completing his MA in Creative Writing in 2015. His first novel, *Dead Branches* was released in 2019. *Is She Dead in Your Dreams?* is his second novel, released march 2020.

Benjamin has had over a dozen pieces of short fiction published, & has written Sherlock Holmes adventures featured in *Adventures in the Realm of H.G. Wells, Adventures Beyond the Canon,* & *Adventures in the Realm of Steampunk.*

He can be found on twitter @B_J_Langley

Printed in Great Britain
by Amazon